Chapter One

"There are witches and there are Witches. I know it sounds silly to say so but it's true. Anyone can learn one of the usual forms of witchcraft, or even a few charms and cantrips, and become a witch.

A Witch is born.

I come from a long line of Witches. Which is why it's so disappointing that I can't do any magick at all."

Mr Ogilvy caught me as I was about to dash across the street between carriages and heavily laden carts in pursuit of my chaperone, Sylvie. I had not seen him until he called my name and I turned to see who it was that had called my name.

Once he had caught my eyes I could not politely extricate myself even though I very much wanted to do so.

It was something of a feat for him to have done so because the street was busy and loud with people moving to and fro, sharing conversation; hawkers selling their wares as they called out to passers-by with offers of oranges or hot chestnuts, with the smell being as much a part of the noise of the city as the people. The clatter of the carriages and the tattoo of the horses hooves on the mud-covered cobbles, these were the sounds of London.

It was the first day of clear weather after four days of icy rain and it seemed everyone in London was making the most of it despite the early December chill. On the corner was a witchfinder, notable by his grey coat, stood on a wooden box and waved pamphlets at the sky. The only words I could make out were *witch*, *babies* and *river* so I assumed the story went that witches were eating babies to prevent the river freezing over, or to cause the river to freeze over. The Witchfinders were everywhere in the city but other than rousing rabble they were not much thought of. They shouted misinformation and lies and tried to convert any passer-by with the misfortune to catch their eye into their policy of hating all Witches, witches and magick.

Still, I would have preferred being accosted by a witchfinder than Mr Ogilvy.

For a whole second I thought I might

approach him and ask him for a pamphlet to avoid the odious vicar. Mr Ogilvy cut off any escape attempt I had even thought of before I could bring it to pass.

"Miss Peake," he said with an oily smile, "I thought it was you."

Mr Ogilvy was the vicar of the village of Mudford near Miss Featherby's School for Young Ladies which I had attended until the age of fourteen and where I had, as the youngest of a flock of twelve girls, marched into the church every Sunday to snicker at the vicar and his overblown and dramatically minded rhetoric.

Mr Ogilvy was the sort of fire and brimstone preacher that for two hundred years had been deported to the Americas with a jolly wave and an exhortation not to return. It was even a common joke that America had revolted to stop them from being sent.

Needless to say, I was not pleased to see him in London on the street that I was trying to cross to get back to my chaperone, who had- again- wandered off without me.

Mr Ogilvy was a man whose looks were shortened by being shaped not unlike a spinning top with a small head and thin legs under a barrel belly and a corseted posture. His cheeks were reddened by a taste for port and his hairline circled the back of his head causing him to thickly grow the hair on the sides to brush across the expanse to try and recreate the look of a fashionable hairstyle. It was obvious even under his topper.

He was an unpleasant man with a temperament as welcome in company as a bad smell. So I pasted on a smile and pretended that I was pleased to see him.

It should be noted that I was not a great actress so it was probably clear that Mr Ogilvy had decided to ignore it because it suited him to do so.

It should also be noted that Mr Ogilvy was the sort of man not even a novelist would lampoon for fear of being accused of exaggeration.

He wiped at his forehead with his handkerchief, despite the winter chill he had a sweat on his brow, and began to wax lyrical about how nice it was to see me after all this time.

It was obvious that his pleasure had less to do with our history and more to do with meeting an heiress abroad without her chaperone upon whom he could press his suit.

Again I lamented Sylvie's excited insistence on the new fashionable poke bonnets where if one of us stopped the other could continue on their way without the other noticing, and in my defence, the boots in the window of the cobblers were exceedingly handsome. And I hadn't noticed Sylvie walking on any more than she had noticed that I had stopped.

"I was on my way to arrange a meeting with your aunt," Mr Ogilvy began, "Miss Peake, dare I say," he paused, "after our long acquaintance, Flora, if I may be so bold?" The morning was cold, even for December and there was talk that with the Thames frozen there might be a winter market, but still, he removed his hat.

At the same time I said "no, you may not."

I had not seen Mr Ogilvy since I had left Miss Featherby's School for Girls at fourteen, which had been four years previous, and even then I had not cared for him. He was an unpleasant man who had taken it upon himself to correct the girls in the school for a litany of imagined crimes and more than once I, myself, had felt his cane across the back of my skirts for sauciness despite Miss Featherby's defence of us. that had been before he had learned that I was not a poor orphan girl taken on the school's charity, as he believed, but instead the heiress who, in fact, owned not only the house where the school was situated -and the reason it existed- but also his patron owning the vicarage which he occupied, and the heir to both Fell Leaf House and one of the most powerful Witches in Europe - advisor to the crown and erstwhile advisor to the Summer Court.

Now, weeks before my official presentation to the crown, Mr Ogilvy had come to London to visit my aunt, one of the most powerful Witches in Europe for permission to court her only living family member.

Surely I was not the only one to find it absurd?

If he wasn't so very odious I might have felt sorry for him.

"Mr Ogilvy," I made sure to be firm, "this meeting is inappropriate, approaching a young woman from good family without first gaining permission from her guardian," it would fall then on Aunt Jemima to put a flea in his ear about his terrible manners because he would not listen to me, "and to address her so intimately when she is yet to have her presentation, it is simply not done and certainly not good *ton*."

I was trying not to look panicked and look around surreptitiously because Sylvie had to have noticed by now that I had been distracted and left behind and this was exactly why I had a chaperone. Damn these new poke bonnets.

"And yet, Miss Peake, we do not need a formal introduction for we are old friends."

"No, sir," I tried to be as firm as I could, "we are acquaintances at best, and it is not an acquaintance that I think back on fondly," Dammit, where was Sylvie. No one would bat an eye if she broke her fan over his head- even on a London street corner. She carried a pewter weight in her reticule in case she was required to defend my honour by using it as a cosh. "When so many of your sermons were about the necessity of gentility and good breeding in the young ladies of England I am well aware that you understand how very inappropriate," I lingered on that word, "it is to accost young ladies about their day." I was carrying the books that I had just collected from the booksellers for my aunt and I wondered if I could swing them like a morningstar to make him leave. I had a reason to be abroad in London that December morning.

My eyes caught upon a familiar figure as he approached. I was not so lucky that it was Sylvie but, instead, Major McConnell striding through the carriages near enough to me that I might suborn him for my purposes.

Major McConnell was, like most of the wolves of the Empire, in military service as a member of his majesty's Dragoons and as such was wearing his uniform. Unlike the brilliant red usually expected of the English army - the navy conveniently wore a dark blue - the Dragoons wore a bright blue- called Adelaide blue after the duchess - spencer style jacket covered in rows of silver soutache embroidery ending in curlicues and flourishes, embossed steel buttons with the wolf's head motif formed a line down his breastbone. His vest was army red and his slim blue pants were tucked into riding boots with a silver line of trim covering the side seam.

In deference to the weather- although it was well known that wolves ran hot like the Ophidiae of India ran cold - he wore a short red broadcloth cape with matching braid at the collar and trim of brown fur that curved around his neck like a series of curls that almost matched his hair.

He was wearing his non-formal uniform - the one for formal events had yet more soutache and braid and the cape was made of velvet - and seeing me he removed his fur cap. Once I had laughed that it looked like a portly tortoiseshell cat that had sat upon his head and he had been offended, although we took to calling the cap George, for surely only the king of felines was suitable to keep the major warm.

Major McConnell was a tall wiry man, standing a whole head taller than Mr Ogilvy, and the term rangy had almost certainly had been coined with him in mind. He was hard-featured with a square jaw, a straight nose and dark brows that were made more prominent by a pair of grey-blue eyes with a gaze like that of an adder. When he smiled, a thing that he did not do often, he looked like one of the sharks in Aunt Jemima's books of the creatures of the South Seas. It was a comparison that I had informed him of but one he took better than the mockery about his hat.

I liked Major McConnell who, because of his work for the Tower, called often upon my aunt and as such was counted as a family friend.

"Major McConnell," I said brightly, "I was just explaining to Mr Ogilvy that I couldn't linger as I was meeting with my chaperone and now you are here," I was not directly saying he was my chaperone - an irony as it turned out because of what happened later that day - because that would have been a lie, but I was certainly letting Mr Ogilvy come to that conclusion on his own.

Major McConnell did what I hoped that he would, he pulled his lips back into what could be mistaken for a snarl but he insisted was a polite smile that would certainly turn Mr Ogilvy's guts to water. There was a strange comfort to Major McConnell's shark smile as it was a weapon in his arsenal that he would use in my defence. "Delighted," he was perfectly brusque, clearly his immediate impression of Mr Ogilvy was one of distaste. "Miss Peake," normally he called me Flora but it was possible that he didn't want Mr Ogilvy to claim the intimacy, unaware that he had already tried and been rebuffed, or because he wanted to maintain a more formal appearance.

People always thought that the people who worked for my aunt were the very models of propriety. It could not have been farther from the truth.

"Are you ready to return home? Your aunt

shall start to worry." He held out his hand to take the books from me, wrapping the strap around his hand.

I slipped my arm through his, a thing that was perfectly proper for a girl with a hired chaperone, and I wouldn't have thought about it with Sylvie but I felt Major McConnell flinch. I had forgotten that he didn't like to be touched. He didn't drop my arm though, "Mr Ogilvy," he said crisply, "it has been a pleasure," it was clear from his tone that it had not been.

Major McConnell had an accent that Aunt Jemima called practised neutrality, with short northern vowels but precise London consonants and he didn't swallow any of his letters, like h or g, it was neither high class of the London ton, nor that of a rough tradesman and it allowed him to mix with both socially, but there was a hint of a Celtic lilt if you listened to him enough. The crown had given the town of Llandudno to the wolves in exchange for their service, giving them space to run in a harbour surrounded by tall rolling hills. It sounded lovely but the wolves did not speak of it fondly.

"I shall call on your aunt, Miss Peake," Mr Ogilvy said as Major McConnell tried to usher me away, "I do hope that you will recommend me to her." He was nothing if not persistent.

"Good day, Mr Ogilvy," Major McConnell said much more firmly and with a flash of fang as he turned me away to end the conversation so that Mr Ogilvy would be forced to talk to our backs if he continued, and would be seen to be ignored. When he hurried his pace to fall in step with us Major McConnell turned his head and snarled at him.

It was finally enough to rid us of the man.

We were across the road and had turned a corner before Major McConnell slipped my arm. "Where is Sylvie?" he asked as we turned towards my aunt's house.

"It's these damn bonnets," I said pulling at the brim of my new sunny coloured bonnet, "I know that they are designed so that I might not catch the eye of potential suitors to avoid such conversations as with Mr Ogilvy, but I stopped to look at a pair of the most handsome boots in the window of a cobbler and Sylvie must not have noticed for she carried on without me. I was trying to catch her up when Mr Ogilvy, who had the raw audacity to suggest that I want to accept his suit because I knew him as a child, called out to me."

Major McConnell was clearly displeased because he growled under his breath. I was not sure if it was at Sylvie, who had walked on without me, or Mr Ogilvy who had seized the opportunity to accost me without her.

"I was too polite to point out that my aunt

would probably turn him into a frog."

"A teapot," Major McConnell said, seemingly apropos of nothing.

"I'm sorry," I had clearly missed a step in the conversation for I did not know how it was that he had arrived there.

"She'd turn him into a teapot, Jemima wouldn't make him something for which she had no use. She is always complaining that when people bring her gifts they never think to give her teapots when they're trying to buy her favour. Or tea. Instead, she is given knick knackery for which she has no use and gives to anyone who will take it. So no, she wouldn't turn him into a frog, but a teapot," he had an impish look like a predator deciding not if he wanted to eat that which he had caught but how to play with it first.

"A teapot, not a spinning top?" I asked for his absurd posture and the line of tan vest made him very much look like one.

"I am too much a gentleman to say so, and besides I thought that we agreed that your lady aunt had no room for useless things." I laughed, I very much enjoyed the major's dry humour and he did not complain of my sauciness. "Even if she still does pay Sylvie."

"Sylvie is not an employee," I said, "you cannot hire a Courtier, least of all a fox, she is my chaperone because she wants to be."

"I suppose then that one cannot not also terminate that employment for gross negligence of duty like losing the person they are meant to accompany."

"Well, I suppose it's possible," I said, "but I do think I might possibly become a teapot if I tried."

"A teapot?" he asked with that devil's grin of his, "not a frog." I laughed so loud that the people on the street turned to look at us askance.

The Haruspex had a fine house on the north riverbank of the Thames which had been hers so long that no one remembered a time where it wasn't. Local memory spoke of other buildings there before the white stone facade on a modern brick house, certainly, a white-faced building with thatch and black beams appeared in the stories but the house had always been the Witch House and it had always been avoided.

It was a desperate woman who knocked on her door for a solution to their woes when the local midwife would welcome them into a room behind the tavern with a smile for a copper penny.

There were witches and Witches.

A witch held a licence to perform herb craft or sell minor charms or hexes.

A Witch was something other and powerful and often too busy with the business of Kings and Countries to bother with common witchery or magick.

The Haruspex was the image that the witchfinder pamphlets used to talk about the godless corruption of the supernormal that they claimed infested Britain and was responsible for the loss of the Americas; the war in France; and the madness of the king. For surely the abdication of Princess Charlotte upon being made a vampire had driven him insane, but to me, she was Aunt Jemima.

Tall, stentorian, in sleek black wool and a high necked black chemisette she wore her ink-black hair in a crown around her handsome face. She was blunt featured with observant black eyes and a thin mouth under a Roman nose. From the waistline of her dress, she wore a chatelaine, the tools of which included - amongst scissors and pencil and thimble, a velvet pouch that rattled as she walked and three silver keys that I did not know the use of.

She was waiting for me at the foot of the stairs that led up to the sitting rooms of the house. The persistent damp from the river and the mud made it unpleasant on the ground floor so it was been turned into the kitchen and storage. For her to wait in the chill damp of the December morning air in the vestibule did not bode well even as the major offered his cloak, hat and gloves to the butler, Jenner.

I turned the ring on my smallest finger. I wore three rings: my mother's engagement ring on my right ring finger, an iron band for protection on my right pinkie and on my right index finger I wore my cluster ring. When I was nervous, with nothing in my hands, I turned the iron ring that protected me from Courtly magick. Everyone in London who could afford to do so wore iron jewellery, which had become very fashionable, although those who wore a glamour to improve their appearance would wear a facsimile.

Everyone knew iron dispelled Courtly magick.

If I had have had something in my hands I would have tapped my cluster ring against it so it made a clinking sound against the gold.

Facing my aunt I was turning my ring furiously enough to form a blister. I had lost Sylvie and walked abroad in London when I was unpresented and anyone could have compromised me to claim my fortune for their own.

In all the screeds and warnings about

unscrupulous fortune-hunting rakes, I had convinced myself that they would be more attractive than Mr Ogilvy.

"Major," my aunt said acknowledging my companion, "you found her." It was bad if she was addressing the major instead of her.

The major tapped his nose. "It was no effort, Jemima."

"Nevertheless," my aunt said turning in a swish of black wool and the clatter of her chatelaine, "your assistance is always appreciated. We do not care to keep Dr Dee waiting."

There were many things that I could have expected but a visit from the Sorcerer Royal wasn't one of them.

With my head bowed, my accursed yellow bonnet handed to Jenner, and unbuttoning my pelisse I climbed the stairs.

Dr Dee was the Witch who worked directly for the government as The Astrologist. Political cartoons showed him as a hunchbacked old man with a knee-length beard and skull cap in a Tudor robe doubled over a spread of arcane looking symbols. perched on the couch warming his hands at the fire was a figure that was the perfect image of middle-aged virility with ash blonde hair loose about his shoulders in loose curls with a waxed moustache and a pointed beard in a grey superfine and cream wool pants. He had a tankard of hot red wine and a platter of cheese and crackers, complete with a blob of chutney, almost completely demolished on the table beside him.

"Uncle Jack," I said moving across to kiss him on the cheek as he gave me a tight embrace, filling my world with the smells of old tobacco and books and horse, scents I had come to associate with safety and reassurance.

Dr Johannes Dee was many things to many people but he had always been my champion since I had met him.

My aunt glared at me until I took a seat, placing myself beside the fire but behind the fire-screen with my hands in my lap and at least maintaining the image of being a demure society maiden even if I wanted nothing more than to pepper our guest with questions.

My aunt had a way of sitting in her velvet armchair exactly as if she was sitting on a throne in a flounce of black skirts and petticoats. She often appeared stern and authoritarian when it could not be further from the truth. She just understood how appearances and people's snap judgements could be used to her advantage.

If Uncle Jack was here it was for a reason and that reason included me, and I wanted to know, but my aunt waited until Major McConnell was given a tankard of hot wine before she encouraged Uncle Jack to speak.

"I am here on official business as Sorcerer Royal," he said looking at me, "because I need your help, Flora."

"Mine?" I asked. I had once served as a secretary for my aunt for she thought that my penmanship was finer than hers, but Uncle Jack had a secretary called Owen whose hand was neater than copper plate printing. He would not need me to take a letter for him - even if Owen suddenly could not write he had the entire staff of the Tower to choose from, so I could not imagine why he might want my aid- let alone need it.

"Flora," he started, "do you know Lady Davenport?"

"I do not," I told him, Lady Emma Davenport was a member of the *Haute Ton* and I was unpresented and so could not attend the balls, routs, card parties and Venetian Breakfasts that made up the season where I might be introduced to people outside of my aunt's small social circle. I knew of her, but I did not know her.

"Lady Davenport was married three years ago to a man much older than her and the summer before last she was delivered of a son," I nodded and wondered if I should be taking notes. "Her husband is currently serving on the peninsula and left his young bride alone. She is staying in London at the moment." I could not imagine why this mattered. It was unconventional- a lady who had just had her confinement usually would spend time in the country where life was slower, especially in the winter, but it was hardly noteworthy.

"We want you, Flora," Uncle Jack said, "with Major McConnell acting as chaperone," the major blinked to show that he understood, "to call on your dear friend, Emma, who has kindly offered to help you with your presentation."

It was so obvious, in retrospect, why I had been chosen for this role, and why they were so desperate to create the charade. It was not because I was witchborn - as I had thought - but because a young woman visiting a friend would cause no gossip or scandal, and could grand Major McConnell access to the house without anyone ever questioning it.

There was only one thing that I could say, "what do you need me to do?"

Chapter Two

The Davenport town-house was in a much more fashionable part of London than my aunt's, and also lacked the familiar modesty. The hall into which Major McConnell and I were ushered by the butler was so unlike my aunt's stolid and dark entryway that I spoke of it to the major. Although both shared a staircase the granite stairs that curved around the duck egg blue walls of my aunt's house were two wide stairs that met halfway down and were richly carpeted in a plush blue pooling down to cover a strip of the black and white diamond tiles that reached towards the door. There were benches for callers to wait, and even a fireplace that crackled warmly to welcome callers who got through the stone-faced butler without being driven off leaving only a calling card in their wake.

As I walked to the steps of the house I saw the iron horseshoe that was cemented into the path. A second one was at the top of the basement stairs that led to the kitchen, underneath the iron gate that blocked the way. A rowan tree grew in the small front garden but was not large enough to hold an adult or even a large child. The branches were still full of berries and Major McConnell pointed out the iron spikes set in the stone sills and lintels of the windows. Those on the ground floor were also barred despite the fashionable address.

I had barely gotten the warmth back into my fingers before the major and I were led up the stairs and into the heat of Lady Davenport's sitting room where two young women were huddled together on the couch, clearly Lady Emma and the nurse, Button, and were both distraught.

Lady Emma wore a heavy banyan which she had pulled her knees up under so the tips of her stockings were visibly curled over at the edge of the couch. She looked very young and like a girl my age reacting to an illness or minor upset. It was not a minor upset. Her nurse, a woman who seemed prematurely aged in a drab wool dress had her arms around her employer but looked no less distraught.

The housekeeper put me in mind of my aunt, tall and slim, in a dark dress and chemisette, but with a cap over her hair and pristine black apron over her skirts. "You are sent by the Sorcerer Royal?" she asked in a voice that was used to commanding calm.

"My lady," Major McConnell said with a bow of the head, and his hand on the hilt of his sabre, "the Sorcerer Royal insisted there was a need for discretion so Miss Peake is here so that if questions were to be asked the answer is that you are serving as a mentor to a friend on the cusp of her presentation. I am here as a chaperone as a favour to her guardian, the Haruspex."

The housekeeper was the one managing the conversation because it was clear that neither

Lady Davenport nor the nurse could. "If word of this gets out Lady Cordelia will see the mistress ruined."

"Lady Cordelia Atwood?" I wasn't sure if Major McConnell was asking for clarification for himself or for me.

"The master's daughter from his first marriage," the housekeeper explained, "how rude of me," her eyes flitted around the room as if looking for unseen eavesdroppers who would judge her for her lack of manners, "guests, and I have not gotten you refreshments, I should fetch some tea."

The entire house was clearly out of sorts with the housekeeper trying to fall back to the old rituals of *politesse* to find a measure of peace in the face of what she considered to be a calamity. I did not know then what had happened to so completely overthrow the social roles in London, especially in the *Haute ton*, everyone had their role to perform and everyone in this room was out of place, and without those roles, they did not know what to do, and I found that more terrifying than the stories of the Courts that my aunt had told me.

The only one who knew what to do was Major McConnell, who looked as out of place as a rapacious wolf. "There is no need for that, Mrs Montrose," he said, "although Miss Peake is here to provide discretion Dr Dee has entrusted this to me because I have advantages many of the other investigators do not," he tapped the side of his nose, "I have the information given to me by the Sorcerer Royal but I would like you to tell me what happened in your own words."

Lady Davenport was a lovely woman- the sort that was considered a diamond of the first water with lustrous blonde curls neatly pinned, wide-set pale blue eyes under a clear forehead, strong jaw softened by a plush straight mouth. I couldn't help but feel intimidated by her loveliness. I was about to have my first season and Lady Davenport had been engaged only three months into hers.

She was the perfect paragon of the marriage mart and it was only the promise of a comfortable inheritance that might prevent me from being a spinster.

She snuffled and wiped at her face with the velvet cuff of her banyan before hiccuping out, "someone took my baby."

Mrs Montrose, the housekeeper, wrung her apron between her fists looking as if the fabric might give way under the strain. "Button," her eyes found the nurse who was trying to soothe her mistress who had collapsed into another bout of weeping, "put the young master down just after two in the morning,"

"Can you be sure?" Major McConnell said, "of the time." He had taken a small leather-bound book from his jacket and had started to take notes.

"I," the nurse said with her eyes on the floor, "Bunny, I mean the young master," she corrected herself from the intimacy that escaped her. She was not like Mrs Montrose who was used to speaking to members of the *Haute ton* and the calamity had left her even more bereft and unsure, "he's been colicky, and with the bells, he cries through half the night. I picked him up and let him suckle, it was just past two, I could see the clock clear, sir, I could." The major nodded, scribbling it down, "I put him in the bed, he's fussy, I made a nest of blankets and pillows though Mrs Montrose scolds me for it, she says he should sleep in his special basket, it's so fine that it's almost a shame to put it to use and Bunny's such a fussy babe, so I put him down in the bed and I sat in my chair till he fell asleep, but I did, and when I woke, the bells woke me, and" she let out a terrible noise not unlike a wounded animal, "when I woke," with a sniff she snorted up the following torrent of mucus before she could finish, "he was gone."

"And you searched the house?" Major McConnell asked and had already braced himself for the inevitable upset that his question would cause.

"Major," Mrs Montrose said in a way that would have been a rebuke to one of the servants in the house but just stayed short of being inappropriate, "what kind of household is it that you think I run here?"

To his credit, the major did not react with anything other than an equanimity that made me feel even more extraneous. "I understand in smaller households like this children are a treasure," as he said this I watched Mrs Montrose's tight shoulders soften, "and I'm removing every possibility such as a maid with multiple younger siblings knowing steam can ease a colicky babe if he's been ill and might take them to the laundry without thinking to wake the nurse asleep by the fire," he waited before continuing. "I'm ruling out all of the mundane possibilities. I'm not dismissing any concerns."

As calm as he sounded, as calm as he

presented, it was hard to reconcile it with the rapacious beast that was his default presentation to the world. If I had been casting a play on the stage then I would have had him play the beast who gobbled the baby down in a single bite, not the hero searching for it. His Majesty's dragoons were on the frontline of the peninsula because of their savagery. I did not know why Uncle Jack, Dr Johannes Dee, the Sorcerer Royal himself, had decided to appoint the major to a case that so clearly needed delicacy and discretion.

"I can assure you," Mrs Montrose started but stopped when the major raised his head.

"I am not here to judge," he said, "as I said, my intent is to cross out all of the simple solutions."

"If it was that would we have gone to the Sorcerer Royal?" Lady Davenport snapped in between her tears.

"Just ruling things out, as I said," Major McConnell spread his hands.

"I locked the door," Button blurted out, "and the windows were latched," once she had started to talk she couldn't dam the torrent of words that flowed from her almost as if she was enchanted. "The floors in the nursery, they creak something fierce and if someone opened the door the draft from the hall would come in and it gets so cold at night. It would have woken me, it would have."

Major McConnell attempted a conciliatory tone as he tapped the side of his nose with his fingertip, "I believe you," he said, "we of his Majesty's Dragoons can smell lies, you know."

I had not known of that and neither had the others in the room. If it was untrue certainly we accepted it as truth.

"Before we go upstairs to the nursery," he said, "I want to make sure that we have all of the information correct." He paused turning his gaze to Button, "you were in the nursery with the young master," she nodded, "and you locked the door because the baby is colicky and you didn't want anyone disturbing him," wet faced from crying she nodded, "at two you fed him to help him settle," he spaced out the information and pauses so that they could correct him, "sat by the fire you fell asleep," there was no hint of an accusation in his voice, just a dry recitation of events, "when you woke up an hour later to the bells ringing he was gone."

"And the door was still locked from the inside," Mrs Montrose said. "Button screamed so that we went to get one of the footmen to batter the door down, she struggled to unlock the door so," he added that to his journal, "the lock will have to be replaced."

"I'm sure that she did this," Lady Davenport managed to say through her tears, "she hates Bunny, she'd kill him."

"Who, my lady?" The major asked her.

"Cordelia," Lady Davenport said it with such anger it contorted her pretty face, "she wants the money, his lordship married me and she thought she was his heir, and then I had Bunny and he cut her off proper and her awful husband," that was as much as she managed before the tears overtook her again, collapsing into incoherent and violent sobs. I was surprised that she had managed as much as she had she was so distraught. It was not a thing that I could accuse her of being false.

"Lady Atwood?" the major clarified.

"Until my lady's marriage, Lady Cordelia was my Lord's only child."

"She wouldn't have got anything," Lady Davenport said with a lace handkerchief pressed to her mouth, "it's entailed, and there was no money, he married me for my parent's money, but," she blew her nose and Mrs Montrose couldn't share this information, at least not in front of her employer, so she couldn't finish. Housekeepers were prized for their discretion. If she was heard speaking out against any of her so-called betters she could be let go without a reference so she couldn't find work elsewhere. "Cousin Eustace would have gotten everything, and before he married me there was nothing." She blew her nose, "it was a perfect match, an heiress and a penniless peer."

No one could miss the bitterness in her voice.

"Does she know that?" Major McConnell asked without looking up from his note-taking

"Her husband writes to him asking him for money, they're broke again, he doesn't want me to know, for so long there was just her and so she's the golden one, and Lord Atwood has debts and he's on the hook with some bad people, I've heard, and it is bad enough that he came begging, but, but," at that she dissolved back into sobs and it took a moment to collect herself, "he's on the

peninsula. I know it, she took my baby, she's,"
that said she buried her face back into the nurse's
shoulder.

"We'll look into everything," Major
McConnell said, "and leave no stone unturned
and get your baby back as soon as we can."

I knew that I was only sitting here as a
way to provide a reason for Major McConnell to
be here without stirring gossip or revealing that
the baby was gone, but I believed him so surely at
that moment that I would have followed him into
Lord Atwood's club, a place barred to women -
even powerful Witches like Aunt Jemima -
carrying spare pistols like a bizarre, frocked
second.

I knew that His Majesty's Dragoons earned
their rank because supernormal people couldn't
hold peerages and buy their commissions like the
rest of the army. Until that moment I had thought
that the major had climbed the ranks for martial
prowess and ferocity but I could see why - at that
moment - people would follow him. Even if he
did look like a hungry fox come upon an
unguarded hen house.

"Lady Davenport," he said in a calm but
firm tone, "I will do my best to find your son."
That same eerie feeling that I would follow Major
McConnell into Hell settled over Lady Davenport
and I could see it put her at ease, and when he
smiled it was not his shark's grin, but something
softer, something almost seductive even though I
knew that it was completely fake. I had known
the major for two years and never seen that smile,
"Now, I need to see the nursery."

Mrs Montrose let her hands finally let go

of her apron and went to the door, glad of something she knew how to do. "If you could follow me," she said and, looking at Lady Davenport, I scrambled to follow almost tripping on my petticoats as I got to my feet.

The nursery was a sparse, small room on the third floor of the town-house with a bed pressed into the corner between the wall with the door and facing the fireplace with the windows to the rear. The walls were freshly whitewashed plaster but the wall which linked the town-house to its neighbour, the one with the fireplace, was covered in old wainscoting whitewashed to match its fellows. A faded pink velvet nursing chair was between the door and the fireplace with a blanket draped over it, and the key, with a silvery chain holding its tag, was in the lock, but the door frame was split around the knob where it had been forced open. A few pieces of furniture were in the room, there was an ottoman with a blanket folded several times to form a cushion was under the window, which formed a bed for changing the baby's napkin.

At the bottom of the bed was an elegant wicker basket with a hood and festooned with brilliant white silk and lace trimming on a stand clearly made to hold it.

It was both much newer and more extravagant than anything else in the room, excepting the velvet and silk trimmed blanket hanging from one of the hooks which held the nurse's two clean dresses and several aprons. It was a room that would not have looked out of place in Miss Featherby's School for Young

Ladies.

Every room in my aunt's house was neat and decorated with sturdy furniture built to last, and when the straps loosened in the seat of a chair or the upholstery wore thin it was fixed or replaced with equally sturdy fabric. Lady Davenport's sitting room was elegant and lovely with Persian rugs and Chinese vases with silk fabric on the walls, but the house was tired and I began to realise that she had used her own money that was given to her by her parents. Lady Davenport had been honest when she said that her husband had no money - she did and her parents might have protected that ownership. Even if that was not the case she was spending what money she had on her baby, Bunny.

The irony of getting a werewolf to hunt a Bunny was not lost on me.

The first thing I noticed upon entering the room was a faint smell, something cold and quiet, damp and green, that caused an almost chill to run through me although, even with no fire- the remnants of the previous night's blaze remained in the grate - it was pleasant despite the early December chill. It had felt like walking unawares through a spiders web studded with dew. The room was south facing and as such caught the warm sun all day long. With the fire lit and the heavy wool curtains pulled tight over the shutters on the only window the room was probably quite cosy.

"Do you smell that?" I asked, raising my face to see if I could catch any more of the scent to find out what it was. But it had been faint and now I could not detect it at all, but the major had a much keener nose than I.

Major McConnell took an obvious deep breath through his nose, and then a second in his mouth making it clear that he was trying to catch a scent in case it had anything to do with the baby's disappearance. He didn't say anything when he shook his head, he looked at me as if he had never truly seen me until that moment and had redefined his image of me. He did ask me what it was that I had thought that I smelled though.

"I didn't recognise it," I admitted a little ruefully, "it was like walking across a lawn so deep in frost it crunches underfoot, and you crush something and it releases oils and for a second you smell it, it was like that."

He nodded, although I found it patronising that he did because I was sure that he was humouring me. "Let me know if you smell it again."

I told him that I would as he began to search the room, tidying up as he went. He lifted every blanket, then his search of the fabric and what was underneath it complete, he neatly folded them and placed them on the deep windowsill with its stuffed snake of a draught excluder.

The bed remained unmade, the nest that the nurse had described was against the wall and covered with a knit shawl that was finer than anything else and must have been one of Lady Davenport's wrappers. Every detail of the nursery showed that Lady Davenport was an active part of her baby's life and care.

Most ladies of the *Haute ton* had nothing more than a passing interaction because their

children belonged to their husbands and they
might not have any control of what happened in
the nursery or schoolroom, so they simply didn't
care.

Lady Davenport clearly loved her baby.

If Major McConnell noticed these things
he didn't mention it as he dropped to his knees to
look under the bed. I moved out of the way to the
cabinet on which the unused and clean napkins
were folded.

I was incredibly out of place and didn't
know where to stand or what to do. I would have
liked to help but I didn't know how. I was moved
by Lady Davenport but I was too awkward to act
because I didn't know her, and certainly not as
intimately as I was being advertised as being. Part
of me wanted to just flop on the pink nursing
chair, ask Mrs Montrose, who hovered in the hall
with no more idea of what to do than I did, for
chocolate to rid myself of the last of the winter's
chill.

But if I did I would have interfered with
the investigation so I remained in the way instead.

Finished looking under the bed, where he
was unlikely to find anything but dust - the bed
was very close to the floor- he checked the
curtains and then the back wall, running his
fingertips over the wood panels. "Why, hello
there," he said, "what do we have here?" his tone
was flirty and I asked him if he had found
something, but he didn't answer me just pulled his
hand away and when he put it back his nails were
sharp and long, and he wedged one of those nails
under the panelling before managing to work it
loose with a loud creak of long-unused hinges it

swung upon.

I moved to look around the small door and saw an alcove. It was clear, now that I considered it, that the panelling hid the chimney breast and made the wall look flush with the fireplace. The alcove was built perhaps halfway up the wall, sandwiched between two heavy oak beams, with a shallow storage space that didn't look to be much larger than a lock box and almost certainly predated the room's use as a nursery. He ran his hand, claws and all, around the outside of the alcove and found nothing. It abutted the property next door and could have explained - even with the very loud hinges - a way that the baby had been taken from the locked room - but it proved fruitless.

That avenue exhausted he moved to the sash window, cracking it open to check its stringing and tapping each of the nails in the window frame before pointing out "another horseshoe," it was set into the lintel, too small for anything but a toy, but it was pointed towards the room and not away, so if one of the courts had entered the room, despite the iron nails, it could not escape that way. It must have been turned, I reasoned when the shoe had been painted over.

After the window the door received the same detailed inspection, the panels tested and the key removed from the lock, "this chain," the major said holding up the key to reveal the loop hanging from its shank made of a metal chain with a thin wooden fob labelling it as belonging to the nursery, "silver, and this," he held the fob carefully between two claws, "rowan, whoever built this house didn't want anyone even vaguely magickal living here."

Then the bells started to ring.

It was the second time they had rang since we had entered the house, and it was only then I paid attention to them. Despite the bells being beside the kitchen in the basement as if someone in every room had all at once found every bell pull and tugged it viciously like a small dog swinging upon them as a game, and they went on for at least a minute. From the hall outside the nursery, I heard Mrs Montrose curse those "infernal bells". Bells that were much louder than they should have been.

I joined her in the hall to ask if this happened often and she said "every hour at quarter past the hour, the entire house rings as if in sympathy with London's bells. It is like the great bells of Bow in the kitchen. Half the staff are threatening to leave if we cannot find the cause. We have had a builder here this week past and he thought it might be the rivers. London is riddled with underground rivers, he said. I have heard that there might be as many as seven and if that is so, then why is it on the quarter past the hour every hour without fail, and why only this sen'night past."

"That can't be right," I said without thinking, "the clock on the mantle says it's only five past." I could see the clock from where I stood and it said five past but now I looked at it I got that eerie spiderweb feeling again, the hour was wrong and the second hand laboured twice before moving on.

"The clock's wrong," I said, "Major McConnell," I added speaking a little louder, "the clock's wrong."

He had his hand down the cushion of the chair but got up, wiping his hands down on his trouser legs and checked the clock against his own watch for what felt like long minutes. "When was this last wound?"

"Two days since," Mrs Montrose answered, "the butler winds it once every week. He is very good about it, he checks every clock in the house."

"This is wrong," he said, "it seems to be running fine but it's an hour and ten minutes slow. That is curious indeed." He pulled out his journal and jotted down something quickly before sticking his pencil back in the spine of the book and putting it back in the inner pocket of his jacket, before attempting to open the glass face of the clock, but it was locked. That done he dropped to the floor to check the fireplace, "and another horseshoe," he said before standing up.

"I don't know anything about that," Mrs Montrose said, "Lord Davenport got this house when he married- from her ladyship's family. They own many houses like this across London."

Major McConnell sighed as he straightened, "I'm going to need to talk to the staff."

Chapter Three

I felt almost nostalgic in the kitchens of the Davenport House in Golden Square. As a child I had spent as much time in the kitchen of Miss Featherby's School for Young Ladies as I had in the classroom. Miss Featherby was an austere woman, slim to the point of being skeletal despite her healthy appetite and she had ideas regarding the girls in her care. She was raising them to marry gentleman, or men of comfortable trades, but understood marriage could not be the only goal. So we learned how to write a menu along with the recipes to make the food we put on it; how to find the best produce; how to manage a household's finances along with our French; the hierarchy of the courts of both Europe and the Fae and how to haggle for the best prices.

She created lower society wives who could be governesses or housekeepers, who spoke languages but knew how to make gripe water and lavender oil and stuffed grayling. Not one of us could play an instrument because there was no one to teach one on the staff, but we learned the simplest charms and cantrips - the sort every woman in England knew - and they were taught by Mrs Cauthen, the cook.

I had spent more time in the kitchens than any of the other girls, both because I had, when I left, always been the youngest, and because I had been unable to perform even the simplest magic like heating a cup of tea. Some girls had accidents with water surging or the glass exploding when they tried, but I was left waving my hands over a decidedly cold glass of water and a feeling that all I was achieving was looking ridiculous.

Many of my memories of the kitchens of Fell Leaf House- where the school was based - were confused: of stolen honey cakes and frustration at both my status as the youngest - being little more than a baby when Miss Featherby took in her second student who was twelve - confused loneliness in a house that bustled with people - and frustration at failing a lesson most girls learned in the nursery.

I came from a long line of Witches and couldn't even manage the simplest magicks.

My aunt's kitchen was a forbidden place because my aunt wanted me to understand that the kitchens were not a place for society ladies of the *haute ton*, so the kitchen in Lady Davenport's stirred an old well of memories associated with scent and sound. The bustling of bodies; the boiling of pots; clanging pans; kettles shrieking and the smell of meat sizzling on the fire for the evening meal; cinnamon; flour for the next day's bread; hanging herbs that scratched at my uncovered hair, plates clanking together - all of those things together were, in many ways, home to me.

I had secretly once harboured dreams of being a cook in a kitchen like this, but had to quash it down because who would hire a cook that couldn't even use a cantrip that prevented the souring of milk.

The cook of the Davenport House was a woman called Mrs Florizel who called me Miss Flora and was clearly irked by the major suborning her staff. She paused from her work long enough to tell the scullion to fetch me a chair from the staff hall, and then another of the girls in her domain, there was at least four, to make me up a cup of spiced milk and a slice of cheese on toast.

I was sat on a wooden bench with a cushion out of the way and given food that was hot and good without comment about why a Miss was in their domain as Major McConnell took them out one at a time, occasionally giving them odd commands like making a posset as if it was for Lady Davenport- which he didn't drink himself but left to go cold - and then one for the nurse, Button.

In comparison I was a problem but my place allowed me to listen to gossip which ended with the bells clattering on the quarter hour. When it happened everyone stopped often with white knuckles over whatever it was that they held.

Mrs Montrose had said that the bells had been doing it at quarter past the house for the last week.

"It must be the Kindly Ones," one of the scullery maids said, "who else could take the young master from his bed without waking Button? Everyone here knows she sleeps like a cat and wakes easily." At the door to the laundry I thought I saw a little girl looking into the kitchen almost hungrily. She was dressed in a drab black dress, but it was her blonde curls that caught my attention, but when I blinked she was gone. She was probably the laundress' daughter, peeking where she was not allowed, drawn by the noise and chatter with a child's curiosity before going back to her mama's side.

Had she lingered a moment longer I would have offered her some of my hot milk.

"Shush," Mrs Florizel said firmly, "it is poor luck to speak of them."

I had never heard of the Kindly Ones and thought, wrongly it turned out, that they were talking of the Courts.

"Who else could it be?" she asked. "If a pooka took him they'd leave a cuckoo in his place, and now the High Witch General has his dogs in the house." The maid was older than me by ten or so years and work in the kitchens had taken a toll on her face and hands, both of which were red from the heat.

"It aint no tick," one of the footmen said as he put an empty tea-tray to the side to be washed by the pot boy. Tick was an unpleasant slang word for vampires. For the most part the vampires were solitary, sticking to their coteries and paying for donations to places like church hospitals for London's poor. Even if a vampire shunned the coteries they were wealthy.

Vampires that shunned, or were excluded from, the coteries and fed where they wished were Ticks but the word was used as a slur against all vampires.

"A tick would have slaughtered you all and gorged himself for days," I was surprised that I spoke up, "they lose themselves in the bloodlust and feed and feed and feed till their belly is as swollen and stretched as that of a tick found on a dog's ear." I was surprised that I was so outspoken because I was usually only so among people I knew well.

London was stained by the memory of the last Tick, although it had been over sixty years since Varney had been burned for his crimes. I suppose that it was because the footman had called the Major a dog that I had been so outspoken.

The footman, I think, hadn't know that I was there because he jumped when I spoke up. "What do you think it is then?" he said and it was almost a snarl. He was plainly handsome, with dark hair neatly oiled but he had a terrible angry scar that stretched from his temple to the corner of his mouth. It rippled when he talked and his eyes were bright coals under heavy brows.

I was cut off by the bells jangling in the corridor and Mrs Florizel muttered a curse about the damn bells as she slapped her dough down on the worktable. I saw a flash of movement beside the hearth but no one else reacted to it so I assumed it must have been a cat disturbed from a quiet warm nook where it was sleeping by the staff reacting from the bells.

The bells rang solidly for at least a minute, "Miss Peake," the Major said popping his head around the doorway, "can you give me a hand with this?" I put my cup and plate by the sink for the pot boy before leaving the warmth of the kitchen to the chill of the corridor outside it that led to the stairs. By then the major was stood upon the wooden chair left out for the night footman, fussing with the now quiet bells.

"What are you about?" I asked him.

"The bells are fixed by wires, see," he pointed to the springs to show me the mechanism, "tug the wire and the bell rings, it's very simple and you can look at the bell to see which room that you have to go to. It means a servant doesn't have to linger to see if they're needed." Neither my aunt or Fell Leaf House had the bells so I wasn't patronised by him explaining the mechanism. "For the bells to go off as they do someone would have to be at every bell pull and the front door. I think we can agree that is not happening here, so I'm checking for either sabotage or a separate wire fixed to a watch that uses the bells as an alarm. I need you to verify that I have checked for this for my report, is that well?"

"I understand," I said, "what do you need me to do?"

"Just hold the chair steady," the major never deferred to my delicacy as a woman but instead treated me as one of his recruits, not ready for heavy or unfavourable labour but with the expectation that I would be.

He ran his hands along the visible wires and then against the wall leading to the window. "There's nothing that I can feel, can you see anything, Flora?" He was asking if I could see a magical trace but I never could and I said so. "I still had to ask,I want to be as thorough as I can in my report. The more thorough I am now the less chance I'll have to come back and upset Lady Davenport more." He hopped down from the chair as elegant as a fallow deer. "One more look around the nursery to see if we missed anything and then I think we're done."

"The staff think it might be something they call The Kindly Ones."

The major's gaze was coolly assessing, "they could have, certainly, but there doesn't seem to be a reason. The answer's in the nursery, I just haven't found it yet."

As we climbed back up the steps, bare stone giving way to carpet then to rough floorboards I heard the tell tale slap slap slap of a child running and smelt that cold herbaceous smell and shivered, making a noise. It caused the major to turn back to look at me. I told him it was a momentary chill, like someone walking across my grave, and his answering smile was odd, and made me feel both uneasy and uncomfortably seen.

The nursery window was open wide and the major made the noise again, and I knew that he had a lot of very different questions for the household. He had said specifically that the nursery was to be left alone whilst he investigated.

He went straight to the alcove that he had found in the wainscoting and fussed with the shallow shelf there that formed a floor to the alcove. Then he lifted that shelf up and out, with a muttered, "I thought so."

He put his arm into the opening he had created and with a wrench began to pull out fabric, and it went on and on until he was able to shake it out, dust, spiders and all on the bed.

It was a gown, but it was old, perhaps as old as the reign of William of Orange, with a reeded bodice and wide ballooning sleeves. It have been beautiful, a masterpiece of heavy white silk satin and tatted Valenciennes lace around the neck and shoulders.

But the dress was ruined by more than just the way it had been stored. The silk satin had shattered in place revealing the reeds and buckram underneath of the body and the linen in the sleeves. When the gown had been made it had been of a high enough quality to be worn at the royal court.

An old and rotten blood stain ran the length of the skirt front, the fabric panel thinner than the heavy pleating of the back, from the gathered waist to the hem it was stained red as if someone had tipped a bucket down the front.

Whatever had happened to the woman wearing the fabulous dress the evidence of it, the expensive gown, had been shoved down in the scant inches between the panelling and the brickwork that backed the alcove, beside a fireplace with a hidden horseshoe in a nursery so protected from the magickal world that it might as well have been made of iron.

Lady Davenport was more put together when we returned to her sitting room, even though I could not, or would not, begrudge her her distrust. She had her hair neatly combed and pinned although she still wore banyan and bed socks.

We had been in her house for several hours and I mistook the glassy look in her eyes for exhaustion.

"Have you discovered who took my baby?" she asked, her tone was imperious - a spoilt queen commanding her kingdom and if I had not seen her before I would have thought it the truth of her, certainly I had met many women like her in the *ton* who swept into my aunt's house in a cloud of perfume and commanded, then cajoled and finally begged.

"No, my lady," the major told her.

"Then what use are you?" the venom in her tone was so thick that it should have dripped to the carpet. "I should engage a witchfinder in your stead to track down the fairy responsible." The term fairy was an insult to any member of the Three Courts and spoken in the presence resulted in retaliation. One did not lightly draw the ire of the Three Courts.

"It was not one of the Courtiers," Major McConnell said, ignoring the fact that when the Courts take a child they leave one in it's place, there were hundreds of tales and anecdotes about babies replaced with cuckoos, "no courtier," he used the formal term, "could enter the room, the protections on this house are frankly absurd and I doubt the Witchfinder's headquarters in Lambeth are as well protected." He was a military man and a werewolf besides. He was not easily given to temper because he knew how people saw it when he did.

No one really took the Witchfinders

seriously, not really, until the magickal world did not work in their favour then someone was sent for, even if all they did was stir trouble and pass out pamphlets.

"It remains a mystery, but I was hoping that you could answer some questions about the house," Lady Davenport sniffed in disdain as him, "it is unusual that you have your child in London instead of the country."

"My husband," she said, and her head's movement seemed exaggerated to me but I said nothing, "has let out the country house, this town-house was a gift from my father when Bunny was born," she took another sip of the glass of water beside her, "I don't know how he came by it, but until Bunny," there was a hitch in her voice every time she said the baby's name but she was trying to conceal it from us. Judging by how devastated she had been when we first arrived I suspected someone was going to call who put store in appearances.

She was happy for the two of us to see her at her worst but not her guest.

"We found a gown in the nursery, stuffed into the wall beside the chimney breast." Major McConnell was being much more cautious with her since its discovery. "I'd like to take it with me. It might not be related but I'd still like the royal alchemists to go over it, just in case."

"A gown?" she asked.

"A white one, it's quite old," I said and Major McConnell looked at me askance and I swallowed down the words about the horrific bloodstain on the skirts. "It was probably just to block a draft, but I know more about styles than the major," I hoped that she realised how little that I knew about what was going on and would leave me from the conversation.

"I believe," the major said, "that you have a haunting and your ghost is a poltergeist ringing the bells, I can ask the Tower to send someone to evict the spectre but in the short term I have had the butler stuff oakum into the bells." It was, I knew, a sop to her. No one believed in hauntings and everyone knew ghosts weren't real. There would be an explanation for the bells, perhaps some type of fae or creature from the Undercity that was manipulating them.

"Could a haunting take the baby?" a woman, a newcomer asked as she opened the door. For a moment I thought her to be Lady Cordelia Atwood, Lady Davenport's daughter by marriage, but as I looked I could see how the woman shared facial features with Lady Davenport, sharing the shape of the jaw and eyes but this woman - a sister I guessed - lacked Lady Davenport's striking beauty and her hair was a mousy brown instead of ash blonde. She was attractive but not a diamond of the first water like her sister.

She wore a wool dress not unlike mine, although it was black and an Adelaide blue broadcloth pelisse but a dour untrimmed black bonnet that made her look sallow. She had a tight lipped sternness that made me think of the school room.

"Janet," Lady Davenport said, "you didn't have to come."

"Nonsense," the newcomer - Janet - said as

she unbuttoned and slipped off her pelisse. She was taking charge and I supposed that this was the person that Lady Davenport was making the effort for, and that she was not as welcome as they pretended that she was. "I came as soon as I heard."

"How?" Lady Davenport asked, "I did not send word, I dared not speak of this."

"You are my sister," Janet said, pulling at the bow under her chin to reveal that her hair was tightly bound apart from the pin curls at each temple. "Or course I know."

"With your leave, my lady," Major McConnell said with a formal bow, "we'll go."

"Yes," Janet said in a tone full of disdain, "you are clearly of no use, you and your little jade." I could not say that I cared for this Janet.

"Mrs Haye," the major said, "I do not care if you cast aspersions towards my character. I am a grown man with a gentleman's manners who thinks little of others opinions of me." He spoke much more formally than I was used to from him, "But your accusations against my companion cannot go unanswered. Miss Peake's attitude and composure are beyond complaint and she has accompanied me today only to provide respite to your sister's reputation and if you have something to say,"

"If I have something to say," Janet, Mrs Haye, said leaving it open as a threat. She was clearly very used to getting her own way and bullying those that she considered beneath her into getting her own way. I knew far too many people like her.

"It is well, Major McConnell," I said smoothing my hands down my skirt, brushing off the insult with imaginary wrinkles. "I am sure that my aunt will worry, she will want a full recounting of the day if she is to aid you in this matter." I gave Mrs Haye my sweetest smile.

"Run back to your aunt, little girl," Mrs Haye said, "I am sure that a woman of trade will be of great," she put distinct emphasis on the word, "help."

"I'm sure she will," Major McConnell said, "as her aunt is the Haruspex."

We took the opportunity to leave her behind as the colour ran from her face.

Rather than summon a hansom Dr Dee had allowed us the use of his trap which the major helped me into. The driver was an employee of the Tower called Betterwerth whom I had known since my arrival in London. He had been the one to fetch me from school to bring me to my aunt, letting me ride next to him on the driver's seat rather than being locked inside the carriage. He was a barn of a man with a grim expression and a long coat that had made me feel intimidated when he had draped it over my shoulders but now he just made me feel safe.

When we were settled in the trap, facing each other on the bench seats with only a swinging lantern between us, our knees almost touching most scandalously Major McConnell spoke. "What a horrid woman." He had said it before I could, "if she were my sister I also would take laudanum before her arrival." That knowledge explained a lot about how Lady Davenport had been when we had returned to her sitting room.

"I agree," I said, "she's very used to getting her own way, for a widow in her married sister's house. It's usually the one who married well that pushes it in the other's face."

Major McConnell looked thoughtful for a moment, "that is odd, but I want to know how did she know? As soon as the Tower was informed," the Tower was the colloquial name for the Royal Alchemical Society that oversaw the magickal events of all of the Empire because they were based in the Tower of London. "W had a guard on the house protecting the flow of information. No one outside the house knew about what happened and nor did anyone leave."

"Lady Davenport probably sent word to her family when she sent word to Dr Dee, her father could have told her sister." It seemed perfectly obvious to me.

"Yes, you're probably right, the simplest answer is usually the correct one." I got the impression that he was chewing over all of the information that he had - much that I had not been made privy to.

"Where should we begin to look, if it is not one of the Three Courts, a Tick, could it be The Kindly Ones?"

"It could," the major said, "but could and even would do not mean did. Your aunt could, for sure, does that make her a suspect?"

"No," I protested. Aunt Jemima certainly would not. I could not imagine that she would. It was entirely out of character. Even if she had I would have noticed a baby in the house.

"There are many witches who have certainly heard of such nonsense about how the rendered fat of a high-born babe can be used to create a potion that enables flight," he was determined to show me how ridiculous my question was. "And as many Witchfinders who would tell you that witches would offer stolen babies to the dark lord for their power. The Witchfinders recruit with such misinformation and fear spreading. It doesn't make these things true."

"If the potion exists," I said, "the one that allows you to fly, then you have to use some to get to the window on the third floor and babies are small you would not get much fat from one, then there is the potion or charm to make them invisible so that they could drug the nurse without being detected."

"You might make an investigator yet," he said with his shark's grin, but I took the compliment that I was offered.

"Whoever it was," I continued, "did something to the clock and the Courts couldn't get in, and even the Fine Gentlemen of the Hills who are most like to snatch babies if the stories are to be believed, could apply for one from the foundling hospitals with much less effort, and no cuckoo was left behind. Someone took the baby and the how should reveal the who. If someone intended to destroy Lady Davenport it would certainly work," I licked my lips, lost in thought and unaware of how the major stared at me, "to take the baby through the window they would need a very tall ladder or to have already been in the house."

"All the staff were accounted for," Major McConnell confirmed.

"So it has to be magickal," I said, "or we're missing something, some part of the puzzle that would unlock the riddle and reveal the perpetrator."

"I'm beginning to see why Jack is so adamant that you are a Witch." I could hear the emphasis in how he said it.

"I can't even do the simplest magic, no charms or cantrips and my potions are just herbs in water," I shrugged off the compliment, "I can't be a Witch." Rather than answer me the major just fussed with his cape. I often suspected that the people around me knew more about me than even I did.

Chapter Four

After returning me to my Aunt's the major thanked me for my help with the promise to inform me when the baby was found. Neither of us spoke of the state we expected the child to be found in. The fear that the baby was dead was something that we didn't want to speak aloud in case it was true. He denied the invitation to dinner and left with a bow of the head and apologies for being too busy to catch up.

I was questioned through dinner. My aunt and I had always been frank with each other but as soon as I mentioned the name that I had heard in the Davenport House - that the baby had been taken by the Kindly Ones - my aunt heavily dropped her cutlery against her plate. "You will not speak that name in this house." Very little affected my aunt, or roused her to anger, but that did and closed the conversation firmly.

When I went to bed Sylvie decided that she was not talking to me because it was apparently my fault that she had wandered off and left me behind so the major had to rescue me. She was brushing out my hair and punctuated each complaint with a bob of the brush in my direction. I adored Sylvie. When Betterwerth had fetched me from school the person who met me at the door of this house, pushing the rest of the staff out of the way to give me a hug, was Sylvie.

She had been, officially, an apology to me from the Summer Court but it was easy to forget she was a fox. With her hair pinned up she just had rust coloured red hair and the white ends were tucked away, and the black tips of her ears and her fingers weren't' always obvious in the lamplight. The only thing she could not hide were her bright gold fox eyes.

I knew that I couldn't ask her about the Kindly Ones. She was my chaperone and my companion but we lived in my aunt's house and Courtiers, even ones like Sylvie, firmly believed in not offending the person whose hospitality that they took part of. A guest could be killed in the Three Courts for that kind of rudeness.

All of the rules of society were simple in comparison to the rules of the Three Courts, but just as dangerous. I had privileges others didn't because of the nebulous position that my aunt held in society, so I could be chaperoned by a major in an investigation that otherwise would have ruined Lady Davenport, not just socially but if her husband believed that she had hurt the baby- a baby that by law she had no rights to - she would hang, rich parents or not.

I couldn't leave the investigation alone; even if I should have.

As Sylvie brushed out my hair she reminded me that I had a lunch arranged with those viperish Lowell sisters, as she called them, at their house and I had to be up early to prepare.

As we lay in bed together I made the decision that I would ask the Lowell twins about the mysterious Kindly Ones for they were much more aware of the gossip and rumours of the city than I.

The Lowell sisters were the twin daughters of the Baronet Sir Charles Lowell. Their older brother, the right honourable Ambrose Lowell, was currently on tour - last heard of in Saint Petersburg with the Upiri, and had already arranged for them their vouchers for Almacks, even from the far east of the continent.

It was accepted that both would be married by the end of their first season. They would be the ones who set fashion and that the other girls would emulate.

The Misses Phyllida and Cressida Lowell were pale lovelies with dark black eyes and neat black hair with a mouche under one eye. They had, they had once admitted to me, cultivated a way of moving in tandem and finishing each others sentences because it made everyone uneasy. They were sat in the parlour with a silver tea-set on the table between them.

Phyllida sat on the left wearing a wool wrapper and silk turban, her nose was red and agitated and I wondered if she had climbed out of her sickbed to see me and it was that kindness that made them so dear to me.

"Dearest Flora," Cressida said standing up to kiss me on both cheeks. "It's so lovely to see you, you must tell us all of your news, we have been kept cooped up in the house this past week, seeing none but the modiste and the family's hearth witch, and no real correspondence other than the latest fashion magazines, we are starved for the outside world."

"Phyllida," I said sitting, "are you unwell? If you feel ill you must return to your bed with honey and lemon tea. An ounce of prevention can make all of the difference in speeding up your recovery."

"Nonsense," Phyllida said with a head full of mucus and a distinct scratch to her throat, "nurse has fetched me some tonic from her most trusted Cunning Woman with mallow root and I am sick of being sick. You must entertain us. Mama is convinced that the chill air will drive me to my grave and it is just a sniffle." She wiped at her nose with a lace edged kerchief which she kept in her lap, "come, Flora, surely you have some gossip."

The sisters had to know that I was little given to gossip. I had neither access to the gossips of the ton or interest in what they said and if I was somewhere with gossip - like a modiste's store - people would fall quiet as if my overhearing some news or scandal would cause them to burst into flame. I was left to the gossip sheets, which my aunt usually removed from her daily collection of papers after a cursory glance to check for anything that might affect the supernatural community and then used as kindling.

It made the rare access feel wicked and naughty. like how biscuits stolen from the kitchen's crock tasted sweeter. I wasn't given to gossip because I didn't see the point when I wasn't even allowed access.

After some thought I decided to go with the truth. "I was accosted yesterday on the street by a suitor."

"Flora, how awful," Cressida said.

"You must have been so scared," Phyllida finished.

"You would think you'd be the last person it would happen to." Cressida added before I realised that it might be offensive.

"I was wearing my new poke bonnet," I said and both sisters looked as if that answered their questions as to why, "and Sylvie carried on without me after I saw the most delightful pair of boots in a shop window." I paused for Phyllida to loudly blow her nose on a scrap of lace edged linen and when she was done her sister urged me to finish. "Oh, they were most delightful, oxblood leather with an Adelaide blue nankeen upper, so it looked like a stocking, and there were false buckles with red tassels. Had Sylvie not continued without me I would have gone into the store to order a pair there and then."

"They do sound delightful," Phyllida said waving her hand, "and normally we would want to hear all about them, certainly the store that they were in."

"They do sound like they would be worth investigating although the blue might be a bit brash and hard to pair with a pelisse or spencer."

"And I am unsure of the tassels, were they

silk or leather?"

"But you spoke of a suitor?"

"Was he handsome?"

"Was he rich?"

"Would we know him?"

The questions bounced back and forth, the sisters each seeming to know what the other would say so neither asked the same question. Phyllida had once told me that their brother thought that they should take their act to the stage but such ideas were ridiculous for ladies of good breeding- and their father was a baronet.

"I do not think so," I told them, "he was the vicar at Mudport, the village near Fell Leaf House."

Hearing that the sisters turned to each other and said "ah," as if that was enough for them to completely understand.

"It was perfectly horrid," I told them, warming to my topic in front of an appreciative audience. "He used to harangue me constantly for my tart tongue before he found out that I was his patron and then he became oily and despite only being in his thirties, I think, his hair would better suit a man in his sixties and," I laid my hand over my head to simulate his distinctive choices and the twins laughed in horrified glee.

"I had to call on Major McConnell to rid myself of him. He was fixed on me like a lamprey."

"The major?" Cressida asked in an arch tone.

"You speak of him so often," Phyllida continued.

"It makes us wonder,"

"If you hold a *tendre* for him,"

"He must be handsome,"

"He does occupy your thoughts so,"

"We do wonder,"

"In what direction,"

"Those thoughts lie."

"Are they?"

"Unladylike," Phyllida said as Cressida chimed in "salacious."

I went as red as the sash on my dress. "Major McConnell is,"

"Handsome,"

"Dangerous,"

"An animal,"

"In all the best ways."

"I suppose you want him,"

"To gobble you up." they then shared a bout of giggles behind their hands.

"You must introduce us, Flora."

"We shall send him an invitation."

"To our coming out ball."

"It would be inappropriate for him to court *us*," Cressida emphasised the last word.

"But the rules are different for you,"

"It's good that you are an heiress,"

"Being witchborn,"

"It will certainly make you less attractive,"

"To eligible suitors,"

"Many won't consider,"

"Marrying someone magickal,"

"Even as barely magickal,"

"As you,"

"It would be so inappropriate,"

"If we even danced with a wolf,"

"Why London could be rocked by the scandal,"

"But if you danced with him,"

"No one would mind."

I thought of dancing with Major McConnell, not a waltz for that was far too scandalous to dance with someone that was not your husband, but the idea of him willingly taking my hand, even for only a country dance, made me blush.

The twins were putting ideas into my head, of the major in his formal uniform giving me his shark's grin like we were the only two people in London.

In my imagination he danced wonderfully.

"There are so many things that you can do," Phyllida started that volley of conversation.

"Things that we,"

"As good daughters of the *ton*,"

"Cannot."

"We are quite green with envy."

"You could have your coming out ball,"

"Wearing scarlet with those delightful sounding walking boots,"

"And no one would speak of it in the gossip sheets."

"It would be unremarkable."

"But if we did it,"

There was a moment of pause when Phyllida coughed into her kerchief and took a sip of her tea before they continued, "word of it would even reach Ambrose in St Petersburg."

"I doubt he would come back," I said, "you say his letters have nothing but love for the city and that he was so fascinated by the Upiri that he was going to write a book. He would probably just write a disappointed letter saying "you wore what? good show," and by the time it reached you the scandal would have been forgotten and you would have married gentlemen of good families and were enjoying a scandal free married life."

Something dark crossed Cressida's face before she continued as brightly as before, "the rules, my dear, are so different for you," she said it as if it absolutely did not matter what I did and because of that I could not possibly understand.

"You must marry your major," Phyllida said and poured more tea into her cup. The twins had their own tea-set for guests, complete with lace circles to protect the linen tablecloths. She said it so matter of factly that I could not answer.

"We have questions," Cressida said as she lifted a biscuit, biting into it with a loud snap.

"And you know that we cannot find out for ourselves."

"So we need you to find out,"

"Is he hairy?"

"Does he have a pelt over his shoulders?"

"And down his back?"

"Is there a tail?"

"Does he keep it tucked down his pants?"

"Or tie it about his waist?"

"Those questions are really offensive," I told them.

"Then it is good that he is not here to be offended by them, it's just us." Cressida had a sweet smile as she said it with a mouth full of crumbs, but her smile didn't quite reach her eyes. She had turned cruel when I had spoken of their marriages.

"And they are just questions," Phyllida continued.

"There are no offensive questions," Cressida drew out the word.

"You all but called him a dog."

They looked horrified that I had said such a thing. It was not done to call out someone who was your social superior and not even my nebulous social standing could protect me. I was both part of and outside society. I could mingle with both the *haute ton* and the magickal societies but truly I was part of neither, and just pointing out that the twins were being awful could see me banished from both.

Perhaps the life of a governess would suit me much better.

If not for my fine estate in Somerset, less than a day's travel from Bath and worth twelve thousand a year- most of which was rents and other charges from Miss Featherby's School for Young Ladies and the rest from investments made on my behalf by my aunt's brokers - I would not have been welcomed.

I had a security net to protect me despite being witchborn. It allowed me freedoms that the Lowell twins could not share, despite that their baronet father was active in politics and very well thought of. They would be a good match for any of the younger sons of the aristocracy, but could not really hope for better, but it was likely that they would marry a gentleman, perhaps a solicitor of good prospects, or a military officer.

I could have married a pickpocket fresh from Newgate; a vampire from the Limehouse coterie; or an imperial prince from Austria and society would act if they had known it to be so all along.

"Apologies," Phyllida said with a rub of

her nose, "we went too far."

"We think of you like a sister,"

"And between sisters it's easy to forget"

"What is too much."

"Sorry that we offended you,"

"It was not our intention,"

"You are like a sister to us,"

"And we would certainly each ask the other."

I accepted the apology but I was still annoyed. The major was a good man and it was unfair that they thought of him so, but I had no other real intimates so perhaps I allowed them liberties I would not give another, but the major was not my suitor. He was a dear acquaintance, and sometimes it was necessary to remind them of that.

However they had planted the idea into my head; that the major might be a suitor - that I could dance with him. I had never thought about him like that. Now I could picture an assembly room that might as well be empty, flooded with candlelight and wall mirrors and the two of us dancing - perhaps even the waltz.

"We must change the subject," Cressida said with a sunny smile, the one the twins used to get their own way.

"Have you heard?" Phyllida began.

"Lady Lamb has cut off all of her hair,"

"She says it is *a'la Titus,*"

"It is the very talk of the town,"

"We wish that we had the courage,"

"She called on mama,"

"We were sick with envy,"

"It looks so well upon her,"

"If we did it,"

"If mama would let us,"

"How easy it would be to curl,"

"And those riding caps we like so much,"

"That currently suit us so ill,"

"They look so well with the new style,"

"You have one, don't you, Flora?"

"Don't you think they go ill with long hair?"

"What did they do?" Aunt Jemima asked as I removed my bonnet and revealed to her my now short hair.

"It is all the style," I told her. As the conversation with the twins moved on I had found myself agreeing more and more. My hair had a natural wave that did not get shown to best advantage and was certainly too loose to form ringlets and it would not be much of a scandal, and before I had time to second guess myself the pins came out of my hair and shears came out of the drawer. "The style is a'la Titus."

"That is not the new style," Aunt Jemima corrected. She was aghast and could not, or chose not to, keep the horror from her face. "That is what happens when spoiled children talk gullible girls into bad decisions."

I did not like it when Aunt Jemima spoke so poorly of my friends. They had been welcoming when I had first come to London when no one else had. "It is only hair, and it shall grow back." I protested in their defence.

"It shall not grow back in time for your presentation," Aunt Jemima had a terrible point to her argument that I had not considered, and was certain that the Lowell twins had not either - that it was less than two months until I went before the queen and now my hair was cur short.

"Even if I were to brew you a tonic it would be still summer before it was long enough to pin," Aunt Jemima wasn't angry. Worse. She was disappointed. "Jenner," she called for the butler, "send for Major McConnell."

"Why?" I was more aghast at that than the hair that the twins had left on the floor, "he doesn't need to be distracted, I'm sure that he is much too busy, he is looking for a missing baby."

"And if I send him word he will come when he can," she answered, "and he will be able to arrange for you to tidy that up so it is at least presentable," she made a gesture to my head with a wave of her hand, "Sylvie certainly can't use the shears," had she been angrier it might have been easier, "I should have those girls dragged into the street for this."

"Aunt Jemima," I protested, "they are my friends."

"With such friends France would be easily defeated." My aunt had a cutting way of speech that would have been the envy of any playwright. "It is not as if I can send for Dr Dee, the peacock could only show you how to curl it, it is not as if he knows a barber, we have reached the point where we will have to do what we can to make this," she waved her hand again, "neat."

"What is the point of being a Witch then," I argued, "if you have to reduce yourself to such mundanities." I was angry at her. I was angry at myself for forgetting about my presentation and I was angry at the entire ridiculous system of expectations and unwritten rules. I liked being a girl, I liked the gowns and the jewels, which again I could not yet wear in public. I liked the perfumes and the bonnets but not for the first time I wished that I was a boy so that all these rules did not matter.

"My magick can not, certainly, there is Bonifaccia, she might be able to, but she lives in

Bastia and it would be weeks before we got there. Normally it would not matter, we Witches have nothing but time, but we would still be on the boat at the time of your presentation, possibly not even around the peninsula on our journey. The Columbine, he might be able, but he was last seen in the far north of the Americas, and it would be late summer before we made landfall, but I agree, what use is my divination if I could not foresee what you have done to your hair?"

"We could take the opportunity to dye it," Sylvie offered from the doorway, "perhaps a pink, like the lip of a rose petal, or the purple-black of a pansy's heart."

"Enough," my aunt said at the same time that I said "Sylvie!"

Sylvie harrumphed and crossed her arms across her chest, "I think it would look well is all," she muttered, "in the Summer Court of Alfhame the Graces often change their hair to be the colour of flowers and wear it at all lengths."

"This is not your majesty's court," my aunt said, "Flora is watched most closely because she is my niece, my only family. Until she is wed every foible will be magnified by the gossips to promote their own daughters on the marriage mart by comparison."

"Oh, like farmers pouring walnut stained water on their neighbour's sheep before the fair?" Sylvie knew that example because it was one of those things that country farmers often blamed on mischievous courtiers, like laying a curse on someone's cow and blaming Pucca for souring the milk.

Sylvie was very dear to me but she wasn't a great chaperone. She was a fox who chose to look human and centuries in the Summer Lands of Alfhame had given her the Summer Court's view of things with a fox's skew.

My aunt and I were still bickering when Jenner led in the major and his batman, Thorne. Thorne was a barrel of a man with short stout legs and arms and the face of a lady's pug dog wearing a jacket that matched the major's only in colour for it was drab and well mended and lacked the flourishes of soutache and braid.

"Oh dear," Thorne said looking at my hair, "oh dear, dear, dear," that was clarified for me that my hair was poorly cut. I could see his fingers twitching for the shears as he frowned. "What happened, duck?" Thorne was the sort of man who called everyone duck. He had previously told me it was common in the area in which he had grown up before he had been bitten, and probably would have called Queen Charlotte duck as he served her perfect tea on a silver platter with perfect etiquette and not a moment's mockery. He just called everyone that.

Nicholson, one of the other Dragoons, had unironically called Thorne the unit's mother.

"The Lowell twins," Aunt Jemima said in a flat tone.

"Were they not allowed dolls as girls?" Thorne asked, then made a harrumphing sound, not unlike the one Sylvie had made earlier. "I can fix this but," he shook his head, "I'll need water, a bar of soap, a chair, obviously, and a sheet," he let out a breath from his nose as he thought, "next time you need a haircut, duck, ask for me."

Chapter Five

In order to prevent what Aunt Jemima called further mischief she asked if Major McConnell could find a task for me with the Dragoons, "military units always need needlework," she said, "her needle is fine enough for basic mending and shirt making." He agreed that he would find me something to do but that I needed to be ready for nine in the morning which was when he started his working day.

I went to my room and took my supper on a tray, knowing that my aunt and I would continue to bicker and spoil our digestion. I had a bath and sat at my vanity to appraise my hair before I went to an early bed.

"We can still change the colour," Sylvie said as she fetched the comb.

Thorne had done an excellent job of turning it from a mop of loose curls that were obvious as having been cut at lots of different lengths and angles to something neat and flattering. He had had to cut the sides very short leaving me with a pile of short curls that swept forward over my brow and ears in a style more like that of Lord Byron, or any other poet, and not a half sheared sheep as Thorne had put it.

I was never going to be lovely like Lady Davenport or the Lowell twins but the style suited me better than the Grecian style with its pin curls that was currently fashionable.

Looking at myself in the mirror I lamented my lot. I had an oval face with a pointed chin and hard jawline, a wide mouth with thin lips and my eyes were wide set and heavy lidded, which combined with arching eyebrows gave me the look of a smirk. Sylvie had once said that my expression was perfectly vulpine even if my features were not.

From my mother I had inherited a complexion that although clear of blemish - apart from a single beauty mark on my wrist that could be hidden by the sleeve of my chemise - and looked best my lamplight, and from my father I had inherited the tendency that - with only the slightest hint of sun - a stripe of freckles appeared across my nose and a second along my upper lip that looked not unlike a narrow moustache drawn with a kohl wand.

I knew very little of my parents. They had died when I was still in the nursery and left me with my governess, Miss Featherby, whilst I waited for my aunt to collect me. At the time Aunt Jemima served as the English Ambassador to the Summer Court of Alfhame, and the solicitor who sent the message did not know that when asking a courtier to perform a task it was necessary to include specific instruction as to how, and particularly in that case, when. The message had been passed on, and my aunt retired her position to raise me, and it had only been a decade that had passed when I lived under the ingenuity of Miss Featherby.

When word of my parent's death reached England the banks put their accounts on hold so that no money could be drawn, including wages for the staff left in Fell Leaf House to watch over me in their absence. Most of the staff had been forced to leave in those early months, which again I was too young to remember, and eventually Miss Featherby, the head gardener, Murphy, and the cook, Mrs Cauthen, had decided to take village girls in during the day as a paid school teaching important things like book keeping and managing a kitchen garden in addition to reading and needlework.

By the end of that first year girls came from all over the country, never more than twelve were in attendance including myself.

When my aunt came for me I was fourteen- the age that most girls started their education - and Miss Featherby's school was one of the best regarded in the kingdom, and there were so many applicants that they had to refuse boarders and offered day classes in exchange.

I wondered what would have happened if the Courtier had never delivered the message and I had grown up as a student. At eighteen would I still have been presented to the queen or would Miss Featherby have worried over the future of her school if I came out in Somerset society, with a presentation in Bath and married someone like Mr Ogilvy to come into my inheritance. Would she have encouraged me to become a teacher in the school and never known that the building and lands were my own?

It was a moment's reverie as Sylvie

chattered and tied strips of linen into my hair to
fix curls for the morning.

Had Aunt Jemima not come I would never
have met Sylvie and my life would have been
worse for that. Even when she opened a new pot
of cold cream and after exclaiming "it smells so
good" and dipped in her finger and scooped some
of it putting it in her mouth and her facing
running the gamut of emotions from anticipation
to absolute disgust until I laughed out loud.

It was not the first time that she had done
it; it happened every time a new herb or oil was
added to the recipe.

I didn't want a world without Sylvie.

So I cleaned my face with the cold cream
and drank my valerian tea before I got into bed,
tapping the empty space for Sylvie, in a matching
nightgown, her white tipped red hair in a braid
tied with a curling rag, stretched out, her
fingertips and toes black against the warmed
sheet and more fox in that moment than she
usually allowed herself.

Major McConnell fetched me at exactly
nine in the morning - the clock on the mantle was
still chiming - just as he had promised. Jenner,
pressed a basket with breakfast into my hands, as
Sylvie fussed with my bonnet ribbons. It said so
much of Major McConnell that my aunt trusted
us without a chaperone, just the admonition to be
good before she released me into his care with a
pair of kisses upon my cheeks. I had the idea that

I would have been in one of the Tower's cottages - where the Dragoons lived - beside a small fire darning stockings but I was wrong.

We did go to the Tower, briefly, and I smiled at the young boy running amok among the ravens as they fluttered about around him in what was clearly a shared and favoured game. Neither Betterwerth or the major paid him any mind as I appreciated the icy green scent that I would later recognise as strange but thought at the time was just the smell of an early December morning lawn in the Tower.

In Thorne's cottage, pin neat and each surface gleaming bright and even the hearth scrubbed clean, I was given a set of page's clothing from Dr Dee's service and told to wear it.

It was a sturdy brown wool with knee breeches and a short jacket with a pale yellow waist to match the brown buttons. I was even given a pair of hard leather soled shoes that pinched a bit at the toes but otherwise were a good fit.

When I was dressed I looked at myself in Thorne's small vanity mirror, which he used for shaving. I looked like nothing more than one of the many pages that ran back and forth through the Tower corridors and staircases carrying messages between departments and offices.

The Tower had been, when the magickal world was first confirmed, a palace used primarily for imprisoning high nobles before their inevitable execution. Even before then it had had an unsavoury reputation of murder and violence

It was quite possibly the most famous

building in London.

With the then Queen, Elizabeth, never in residence she had established it to be the place visiting magickal royalty could stay and from there it had been easy to ask her only magickal courtier, Dr Dee, to establish an embassy there. It had, over time, become the heart of the magickal in the British Empire. When people spoke of the magickal infrastructure they called it, informally, the Tower.

Instead of being a dreary place the Tower sparked with life and crackled with magic - sometimes literally.

I didn't know why I was dressed like that, wondering if I was to serve as one of the pages running to and fro with sewing kits and coffee pots to keep both the bureaucrats and researchers happy in their work. I was not but I considered it as I pulled on the knee breeches.

Instead I was folded into a greatcoat that almost dwarfed me and put back into the carriage where the major was working his way through the breakfast Jenner had given me. He had half of the crust of buttered bread hanging out of his mouth as he tried to peel one of the boiled eggs.

Instead of stopping, and possibly apologising, he crammed the leftover piece of bread and the egg into his mouth so it bulged out his cheeks like a squirrel and covered his mouth to awkwardly chew. Seeing a lost cause I gave him the corked jug of raspberry vinegar that he used to wash it down. "Sorry, I haven't had a chance to eat since lunch yesterday."

"If you told me where we were going," I

said as the carriage lurched forward, "I could have recommended a place to eat."

He wiped his mouth with the back of his hand, "I was going to visit a pie shop, but there was a basket of bread and boiled eggs," he admitted, "I left you the ham."

"Because you've only just found it."

In addition to his shark's grin he had a smile that was not unlike that of a naughty boy hiding frogs in his pockets. It was charming.

"You can have it," I added, "I have no real appetite in the morning, and I had a honey cake when I was dressing and I'll be fine until lunch."

"I'm not sure that we'll be able to stop once we start," he banged on the carriage with instructions to Betterwerth to call at a pie shop on the way. "We have a lot to do today and I need you to be unobtrusive and take notes for me."

"I'm pretty sure that this isn't what my aunt had in mind when she came up with this punishment," I felt it best to be honest.

"Thorne was irate last night at the idea that he can't keep up with the sewing and the mending," the major told me, "since he returned from the peninsula." He had been invalided home and had a mechanised leg that the upkeep of which preventing him joining the main force of the Dragoons on the peninsula and kept him with the small group who worked for the Tower, officially on defence, but more to police and investigate magickal incidents- from Witches unknowing finding their affinities to ticks slaughtering their way through London. "Thorne has made sure we don't even have thin spots on our socks and we can use our cook pots as mirrors he scrubbed them to such a shine."

"He worked wonders on my hair," I admitted touching my new short curls, "but the back of my head is freezing without all that hair to keep it warm."

"You'll be less visible as a page taking notes," he said, "if I'm to use you than you can be of help to my investigation."

"About Bunny Davenport," I asked, "I tried to ask the Lowell twins if they knew anything but their gossip was a few years old."

"What did you tell them?" I suppose that he thought me a silly girl sharing every detail of my life with other equally silly girls but I had been circumspect.

"That with my season fast approaching Lady Davenport had offered, as a favour to my aunt to act the role of matron in presenting me in the January events if we got on well."

The major visibly relaxed, "so what gossip did they have?"

"Only that she left London just before her first season to spend months with her sister during her confinement. The twins remembered it because their father had had an eye on her fortune for Ambrose but thought that if she wasn't going to take her coming out," - without a link to the peerage Emma Davenport wouldn't have been presented to the queen and court so it all relied on

how she acted during her season proper -
"seriously her family had no serious hope of
seeing her wed."

"I saw her sister yesterday," the major
said, "she is recently bereaved, lost her husband
three summers past to a shooting accident and her
daughter this last autumn. She came to London to
get away from the memories and spent the night
that the baby disappeared at the gaming tables of
the Comptesse de Verre, which I have verified.
She's a deeply unpleasant woman but I don't think
she's responsible."

"Again this is gossip so treat it with a grain
of salt," I said, "Mrs Jane Haye was married in
haste. The late Mr Haye was said to be free with
his hands, and his fists."

"I heard that too," the major confirmed,
"and he was not a well received solicitor, but
certainly his wife's fortune was welcomed
because he left his practise, bought a pile in the
country and spent his days shooting. She put the
house up for sale this October, and took rooms in
town."

"Dying in a shooting accident, how
ironic," I drawled it out.

"The magistrate investigated at the time.
I've got Bruxby riding out to get the details just in
case they're pertinent, but it's crossing the t's and
dotting the i's, with deaths in the family it's worth
looking into but there is always sickness in
London and children are susceptible."

"They didn't tell me about the Kindly Ones
though." I didn't mention that I had forgotten to
ask them.

"The Kindly Ones are a goblin tale for the poorest children of London, to go to sleep or the Kindly Ones will take them from their beds for their cook pots, like not to lie or the Rawhead and Bloody Bones will come from under the stairs to gobble them up."

"You know that Rawhead and Bloody Bones is real." Like most of the worst ghouls and goblins of Alfhame a treaty kept them in Alfhame under the courts of Summer, Winter and the Erl King's Hunting Lands.

"Not all Witches are like your aunt," he said and then determinedly changed the subject. "Today, we're calling on Lady Atwood."

"So there is no hint where the baby is yet?"

"None," he told me, "and the more time passes the more chance that we will never find him or find him dead and then the entire investigation goes to the magistrate and all of London considers Lady Davenport a woman who killed her baby and fabricated the abduction to look innocent, regardless of what actually happened. And with what always happens with such a public outcry, and there will be one," he wanted me to understand that because he leaned forward as he said it, "the magistrate and court will most likely see her hang, so we need to find out what happened as soon as possible."

"It had to be magickal," I said, the carriage was slowing on the cobbles so I guessed that we had reached one of the pie shops that were as numerous in London as streetlamps.

"Or," he countered, "the household lied to

protect the mistress."

I was mostly dozing as the carriage rocked and swayed along the cobbled and rough roads of London. The swaying and jolting in the velvet seat with the velvet curtains drawn was warm and comfortable in my borrowed greatcoat and muffler I had pulled my legs up to the side of the bench and just let myself drift, so when the noise of the crowd yelling and shouting distracted me as we drew nearer. I heard shouts of witch and filth and England's sacred shores so I recognised it as a witchfinder rally even before the crowd forced the carriage to a stop.

On the whole the Witchfinders were more of a pest or nuisance than a threat to any of the witches of London. They had powerful backers, nobles who could not benefit from the magickal landscape and wanted to remove it, so they were allowed a measure of liberty but very few people took them seriously when witches saved them coal for their fires, prevented milk from souring too soon and tended their ailments cheaper than a surgeon and often better.

I could only make out that a man was shouting when the major knocked on the wall of the carriage to tell Betterwerth to stop.

"Is something the matter?" I asked him, I had expected that we would stay in the carriage and Betterwerth would encourage the crowd to part to let us through.

"They're talking about the children in the

Thames, I'm going to go and ask."

I held up my hand to cut him off. "I can do it," I told him, "they'll take me for a boy and won't cause the fuss they would if you show up in full uniform looking like a threat."

"I don't like it," he said with a deep harrumphing breath through his nose, "but you are right, if you need me," I swung my legs down to the carriage floor in order to get to my feet, "for any reason, your aunt would have my hide as a parlour rug if I let them even muss a hair on your head."

"I'm flattered," I told him with a smile as I climbed down from the carriage.

The crowd was about thirty people, certainly no more than fifty and all tradesmen and women in broadcloth and wearing linen and leather aprons. There were two Witchfinders, a sergeant at arms, recognisable by the tabard he wore over his work clothes, and a young man of about my age handing out fliers and when he paused by me I took one and asked him "what's happening?"

"They found another babe in the Thames," he said, there was no additional rhetoric about filthy witches or monsters. "That makes four now since the beginning of November."

"What are the river police doing about it?" If bodies were found washed up it was the business of the river police, who were, usually, good at their jobs. Comprised mostly of selkie and other river folk they were fastidious about keeping the river clean for their young so people who disturbed it were dealt with. They used the law for it because, as they said, they knew about the river not about the rules of land-folk.

"What they can," the young man said. He was brightly earnest with a head of brick red hair peeking under his cap and grey green eyes. He had a tabard, much plainer than that of his sergeant which was decorated with flames, over a much more basic suit that looked like it had been around for centuries. "But word gets around, the big houses," he was appraising the uniform I was wearing, "they don't care if don't affect them, the Tower only serves the Tower," that had the sound of rote recitation as he said it, "but it's been four babes now," he was genuinely disgusted and I must admit I shared that opinion. "Found all slashed up with magic symbols all over them like some disgusting spell-book."

"That's horrid," I genuinely felt that. It was horrible that someone would do anything like that, especially as I knew enough about magic, about real magic, to know that such sacrifices and rituals had nothing to do with magic but instead mummery   .

"It's been over a month and the Sorcerer Royal has done nothing. The bigwigs in the Tower never do and people ask why we need Witchfinders?"

"Someone has to do something," I agreed because if the Tower wasn't acting then even the Witchfinders were better than nothing. The Witchfinders were a rabble of men, usually younger men and sons who were more easily swayed because they had more time and money without a family to support. They gathered to blame their grievances blaming every sorrow in their life on the magickal communities. Groups better suited to defence, like the Uflbar, werewolves or Leonmensch - of which there were two in London - did their best to discourage violence against the magickal communities so the rallies never got truly violent.

I imagine that it was hard to intimidate a community with ridiculous strength, claws, and fangs that could tear you to ribbons with no real effort. It took the power from throwing bricks, when they could determine who threw it by scent and chase you down in revenge.

Yet the Witchfinders still thought themselves important, "I'm Penreith, by the way," the young man said offering his hand to shake. "If you wanted to attend one of our meetings. Even if you didn't want to join we could do with more bodies on the street making people aware. We might not have the powers to stop the killer because we can't storm the Witches' houses to find evidence for the magistrate but the more of London that knows the closer they watch the children and a child closely watched doesn't end up in the river." I thought about Bunny Davenport, taken from his bed with his nurse right there and bit my lip.

"Peake," I introduced myself. I didn't want to lie to him but I was happy to let him continue his misassumption. "How long has this been going on? Specifically."

"It's been," he paused to count off the days, "twenty seven nights now, we've been patrolling for ten, and there has been four bodies. The selkies are at a loss, they think the babies were dropped in the river from the bridges but so many people put so much in the river. We caught a man throwing in a live chicken in a sack," I nodded, hoping that he would elaborate. "There are people who worship the Rivers of London like gods and give them offerings, if you can believe it, live chickens."

I had heard of that although it was ridiculous, I doubted the ancient gods of London's rivers cared for *coque a'la sacque.*

"Is someone sacrificing the babies?" I asked him.

I expected another screed of rhetoric but Penreith surprised me, "I doubt it," he said, "whoever carved up these children," he sounded genuinely upset and his caring moved me. He was a handsome young man with a shock of dark red hair despite an olive complexion and gray green eyes with lips so soft and pillowy that would have made him the envy of any ballroom. He was tall and slim but his shoulders were broad enough to make his jacket hang on him strangely and his hands were callused from work, but it looked to be pen calluses. I made the assumption that he was a notary or clerk. "Whoever did it," he repeated, "they were doing a spell, alchemical symbols and arrays."

"Do you have any ideas who did it?" I wanted to hear this whilst being terrified that they would name someone I knew. My aunt's house was literally on the riverbank as was the Tower which could implicate my uncle Jack.

The Witchfinders were mostly harmless but if some random witch or magician was killing babies it would be easy to build a mob to attack those places full of righteous indignation and fear for their own children and grandchildren.

It was easy in the bubble of high society to forget that the rest of London was there and their woes were distant and meant nothing to the people in the whirls of galas and gaiety.

Thinking of it like I could understand his frustration.

"Our office's address is on the pamphlet," he said giving me a welcoming grin, "if you hear anything," he paused, "anything, at all that might help come there and we would be ever so grateful." He had an earnestness that was infectious, if all the Witchfinders had his charisma even parliament would have had to take them seriously instead of considering them a nuisance.

I promised him that I would and beaming from the force of his smile I returned to the carriage and the major handing him the flyer before I say down again. "You heard that then," I asked him. His advanced hearing meant that I didn't have to repeat the conversation.

"They must have found the new body today," he said with a sigh, "if Jackson didn't mention it over muster at the mews." He looked at me hard. "The Tower knows," he continued, "Jackson is looking into it with the River Police. He's not stopped since the first body was found nearly a month ago. If Thorne didn't threaten him with bloody violence, I doubt he'd stop for a meal and a rest more than he gained waiting for someone."

I hadn't met Lieutenant Jackson, but I knew that he was thorough, I felt the weight of the ring on my finger as a reminder I knew personally that Jackson was very thorough. If any investigator in the Tower could get to the bottom of the case it was Lieutenant Jackson.

Lady Cordelia Atwood was a portly woman with a piggish face in an unflattering white cambric morning dress with lace ruffles and fastened with cotton ball tassels. It was matched with an equally ruffled cap she had decorated with a pink silk rose pinned above her left ear. Instead of a wrapper or banyan she wore a Kashmir shawl was draped over her shoulders but the entire outfit made her look, instead of wealthy, short and stout and much older than she was.

It must have offended her when her father had chosen to marry a woman young enough to be her daughter, especially when there was no real male heir and her father immediately returning to the peninsula. She had to know that the estate was entailed but perhaps for a better settlement from her cousin than her father's new wife. Especially if the rumours about her husband's finances were true.

The woman at the breakfast table sipping watered honey and apple cider vinegar, for her weight she explained, didn't seem to be as much a villain as tired.

The major introduced us as investigating a threat to Lord Davenport reported to the Tower and that we were interviewing her to be thorough.

It was a simple fiction but one that was easily accepted.

I was given the major's freshly sharpened

pencil and notepad and looking through it I could see the notes were in a dense shorthand filled with small hieroglyphic doodles.

Being a page allowed me both unique allowances and restrictions. I was not expected to maintain a conversation but nor was I offered refreshments. The only consideration that I was given was a stool by the fire, close enough to the interview to take notes.

The calmly efficient major who had interviewed Lady Davenport was servile and oily with Lady Atwood, a functionary that was ticking off boxes that he thought unnecessary but orders came from above, he was sure that Lady Atwood understood. I had not realised that he could even be unctuous let alone to the extent that he was.

"We'll do our best to make this as quick and painless as we can, my lady. The boy will just take notes if you don't mind." Whether she minded or not I was under the direction to take notes. "Lady Atwood," he began, "tell me about your father."

She seemed surprised at first and then began to reel off the sort of exhortations that made him seem unreal, a paragon among men who had adored his only daughter until his head was turned by that young jade. She used that word specifically and it was a deathly insult equating her to a dockside whore in nicer language.

"He is a military hero," she said, "bravely serving king and country. I'm sure that you understand how difficult that is," I wondered if she was attempting to make love to him. I didn't know if it was in her nature. "Have you served, major?"

"In the far East, yes," he said in a clipped tone. I remembered Murphy, the gardener at Fell Leaf House, saying that soldiers didn't like to talk about their time under the Flag and anyone who did was a liar. The major never spoke of his time in the wilds of British Columbia but he always had a few shillings to give to the veteran beggars that he passed.

"He serves beside Lord Wellington himself," Lady Atwood continued, "and eats at his table most nights. He has many men under his command and is very well respected by his peers and he was devoted to my mother. I never thought that he would marry again." I had no idea if that was true.

"Do you have any idea why he did, surely as his only child, perhaps a distaste for his heir?" the major left it open for her to fill in the blanks.

"My cousin is perfectly bland, fair in his accounts, and married to a good woman who has been well for him, he has a bushel of well behaved children that my father likes to dandle on his knee," I couldn't help but notice the rancour in her voice when she spoke of children.

"If you had a son," the major had not missed it either - the resentment, "it would mean that your father's estate would go to your husband in trust for your son."

"We have not been blessed with children," Lady Atwood said and I found it hard to read her tone, "at first that seemed a curse but with my husband's predilections I wonder if it was not a blessing." There was obvious sadness in her voice as she said it.

"In case it matters into the investigation to protect my dear father my husband is a gambler with poor luck and a taste for the light-skirts of London, if it were not so well known I would wonder if it would be used to leverage my father, but he has long since cut my husband off, even before Father married the chit."

"Could he have worried for his estates in the hands of your husband in case you did have a child?" Major McConnell asked her, and I knew him well enough to know that he had a suspicion. He had a thread and with it he hoped to unravel the entire scheme. If Mr Atwood thought that by removing the baby he could take control of the estate would he do it? Could Mr Atwood, not his wife, have hired someone to take the baby? I scribbled that down.

"You assume my husband capable of thinking that far ahead." Her entire tone and posture spoke of malice. Lady Atwood despised her husband. "My husband is weak and cowardly, afraid that every shadow is one of his creditors. If I had been blessed with children," she paused to add sugar to her tea, "my father would have made promises that my husband could not touch a penny of his inheritance."

"Does he know that?" I blurted it out.

"After twenty years of marriage I should think so." Lady Atwood said curtly. "As it stands any child that I had would only inherit debts."

"Lord Davenport lost fortunes in bad investments," Major McConnell said checking a second notebook, "there is speculation that he only married her for her fortune."

"Slanderous lies," Lady Atwood snapped it out, still defending the ideal of her father in her head, "that doxy has something over him, or more likely under him. Her parents arranged the marriage and my father would never stoop so low as to marry someone like her in exchange for something as base as money. Especially with the rumours about her."

"Rumours," the major had broken down any reticence that she might have had and had Lady Atwood eating out of his hand like a docile mare.

"I'm not one to gossip," I was not worldly but even I knew that "I'm not one to gossip" always preceded a lot of gossiping, and usually something salacious. "A diamond of the first water does not abandon her first season to share her sister's confinement unless she has something to hide," she nodded as she patted her stomach as if there was only one inevitable conclusion, "I heard from a reliable source," that was a gossip's code for someone I know well who heard it from another source, "that it wasn't her sister that was increasing, but my father's lady wife, and that the babe, a daughter, was passed off to the sister."

"Not two week past I received this," she stood up in a ruffle of Indian cotton ruffles and clip clop of wooden heels on the bare floors. It was then that I realised that there were no rugs or carpets, even the window shutters were bare of curtains. I was so used to these soft furnishings that until I heard their absence I had not even noticed. From a drawer that squeaked loose from the escritoire she took a small paper box which had not ribbon or address. "It was left on my doorstep," I didn't know it then but the package had been left on her doorstep on the day that the bells began to jangle in the Davenport Town-house

She removed the lid from the box and handed it to the major who from it took a milky green stone about the size and shape of his thumb hung from a leather thong. "I think we can all agree what it means," Lady Atwood said passing over the piece of jade.

Chapter Six

I asked if I could excuse myself to get some water whilst the major took coffee with Lady Atwood and they excused me even as the lady complained of my impertinent manners I was not, in fact, thirsty, and I still had some of the raspberry vinegar in the carriage, thickly watered as it was, but I hoped to listen to the staff as I had in the Davenport Town-house

It was a mark of honour to have a discreet staff that were not carrying tales about town but it didn't stop them from gossiping among themselves. It was unlikely that I would learn anything but I wanted to be useful and it was unlikely that Lady Atwood would confess that either she or her husband had arranged for the baby to be snatched, even more unlikely that they would have the funds to pay for such detailed magic because those that could do it wouldn't accept credit, but I might learn something.

The corridor leading to the kitchen was almost icy, especially after the cosy warmth of the sitting room and it had a soft green smell, like frosty grass crushed underfoot on a winter morning. A shiver ran down my spine and I jerked with it and seeing the maid on her knees scrubbing at the stone steps I apologised for startling her.

The maid turned with the scrubbing brush still in her hand but when she turned the side of her head was open and bloody, pulsing wetly in the light that fell on the kitchen stair from the upper windows. I gasped and stepped backwards colliding with the dish cabinet behind me with a clatter so I turned around to make sure I had not broken anything but when I turned back the maid, the wet brush, the bucket and even the water on the stairs was gone.

It took me a long few seconds before I convinced myself that I had been mistaken. "Are you well, dear?" a woman asked from behind me, "you look as if you saw the devil himself."

"I don't know," I answered because I didn't. Had it been a creation of a few overwhelming days and with the poor lighting but I had been sure, to the point that I had spoken to her, that there had been a maid scrubbing a dark stain on the kitchen steps.

"A cup of tea will set all to rights," she said and the tone was so maternal I was sure she could make everything well. "You go on down to the kitchen and I'll be right behind you."

The kitchen was hot and sweetly spiced by the glazed meat on the spit and the biscuits cooling on the side in a messy pile. The cook was folding dried fruit into a dough with a tankard of ginger beer beside her that she occasionally took lusty swigs from. She was a tall, meaty woman with hands like slabs of beef and a brown apron over a blue wool dress with long sleeves shoved up to the elbow. Grey hair wisped from under a

white cap and there was a sweep of flour on her
brick-red cheek.

"Can I help you?" she asked wiping her
hands on her apron. She was alone in the kitchen
without even a scullery-maid to help her. Now
that I thought about it I had only seen a butler and
the old housekeeper at the top of the stairs. There
was very little staff which was unusual for a
house that was inhabited by a member of the
peerage. Mr Atwood might have only been a
gentlemen but he had married a Lord's daughter
who was entitled to the title lady. There should
have been at least ten staff for a house of this
size.

"I am working with Major McConnell," I
said, "I was hoping to get a cup of water."

She looked me up and down with a critical
eye, "there's ginger beer in the cask," she said,
"you can make yourself useful and put some
water on the fire to boil."

I unhooked the cauldron that she indicated
and carried it over to the pump, "how much do
you need?" I asked her and she told me to fill it to
the brim. Instead of boiling the water in a closed
kettle for tea or coffee, a cauldron like that was
used for hot water, for scrubbing pots, floors or
laundry. It was common that a cauldron like that
would just be topped up during the day. It would
be a scullery maid's duty and with it being mid-
morning it was an indictment of the staffing that I
was doing it for her now.

It took longer than I thought it would to
carry the cauldron the five or so steps to the hook
and swing it over the fire, for it seemed to have
grown exponentially in weight with just a

bucketful of water.

"It must be hard," I said taking one of the clay cups from the shelf to fetch myself some of the ginger beer and offering to refill the cook's tankard, "with so few staff."

"Just the two of us," she admitted, "makes it easy to cook, just Lady Cordelia, Butcher and me."

"I spoke to the housekeeper," I said.

The cook cut me off by bursting out laughing, "Old Madam Price," she said, "you'd have a hard job, she's been dead this ten years past."

In the carriage, we settled down with slices of cold pork pie and a jug of ale each as the carriage rattled along the road. "I don't think," the major started wiping his fingers clean after polishing off the first of his three wedges of pie, "Lady Atwood knew what this is," he took the piece of jade from the neck of his jacket where he had tucked it for safety and offered it to me. It felt warm to the touch. I thought it was his body heat that I was feeling.

The jade was carved with a bird a very long tail, but not a peacock, on its face. It was a deep even green, more like agate but it was strangely translucent despite that. "Jade is rare, isn't it?" I didn't want to let go of the pendant. I was overcome with the urge to hang it around my neck and let it sit against my skin and never remove it, and I had to fight with myself to offer it back.

"It's rare in England," he confirmed, "and its trade is highly regulated, meaning it is often faked or, more likely in this case, smuggled."

"Then why give a large piece of it, a carved piece of it, to Lady Atwood?"

"I can tell you that everything about this case just gives me more questions, so we're going to Islington." There was only one thing in Islington that we might be visiting, one of the largest coteries in London, the one located under Bunhill Field Cemetery

Vampires liked to surround themselves with death and so created their coteries near, or even under, cemeteries. The more ornate the cemetery the more the vampires worked to keep it, to an extent, wild. Because of that, the cemeteries of London were like parks, but the paths were interrupted by overgrown headstones, with walkways and walls covered with ivy and mistletoe and lawns of herbs that gave off sweet oils to the air when it rained.

Benches, ornate twists of wrought black iron or poured stone, as lovely as the clematis that grew over them circled the graveyard giving a place for the vampires to just appreciate the beauty that they managed. Many moved in society enjoying the nights of balls and routs and card parties: one was even a famed actor in the theatre and another an opera singer but they were from the Limehouse Coterie, I knew very little about the vampires in Islington.

Being November it grew dark early and we arrived there in the late afternoon as the sun was getting ready to set in the west through the houses of London. I could see the smoke from the Angel Islington public house that gave the area its name.

The vampire was sat cross-legged on one of the raised tombs amidst the unpruned branches of a dog rose, still heavy with bright red hips. He looked to be no older than me, with a sharp, pointed face and a boyish expression of mischief that made him look young. He could have passed for any age between fifteen and thirty. He dressed like a dandy with floppy black hair that curled on his nape and fell across his collar.

"A boy and his dog," he said with a French accent, "how delightful."

I had the strangest feeling in the graveyard and I put it down as nervousness. The only times I had ever met a vampire I had been with my aunt and without that shield, I felt somewhat naked, even in my oversized greatcoat. It was like I usually wore armour and I was suddenly without, or that I had been caught without the tight embrace of my stays. I did not know how to process it. After the ghosts and the jade and now a vampire I felt positively unravelled.

"I sent word ahead," the major said, "you know why we're here."

"A jewellery appraisal, how diverting." The vampire was mocking us but he was sat cross-legged on the tomb and made no move to move towards us. If not for the graveyard smell of him he could have been any dandy in London. Outside of the boneyard, I might not have known him for what he was.

"Beausant," the major said drily, "it must be so boring to be you, with nothing to fret over but your clothes, it is wreaking havoc on your complexion, why you look almost pink." The vampire, Beausant, hissed at the insult, baring his fangs and the major just raised an eyebrow in comment.

"Beausant," a man's voice emerged before he did stepping out from between the trees, "our lady is asking for you." Beausant moved like a string fixed between his shoulders pulled him to standing, bonelessly, mocked out a bow at me, and a dark look to the major before jumping down back off the tomb and walking like a pierrot on the stage back into the trees.

This vampire was not the boyish-looking fiend who gave off a threatening air but instead most resembled an office clerk or secretary, if one had been brought back from distant China in order to serve the office. He was handsome, thin and pale with neatly cropped black hair and a pair of wire-rimmed spectacles. "Major," he said, "Miss Peake," he said that with a polite bow of the head. It was then I realised none of the vampires were wearing hats.

Before we left the carriage the major had bundled me up in the giant greatcoat, a wool cap and a knitted scarf and I understood why Beausant mistook me for a boy at first glance, but I didn't understand how this one knew me by name.

"Miss Peake," he said, "I imagine this conversation will take some time, perhaps you would be more comfortable in the carriage. Our Lady Below has guaranteed your safety but the wind can whip through the trees that you will find most uncomfortable if it picks up."

"Your garden is beautiful," I didn't know why I said it, they were not the words I had planned to say, certainly.

He had a faint smile in the corner of his lips as he thanked me. I might not have meant to say it but it was true. Hidden under thickly wooded canopies and almost embroidered with flowers and ferns and moss and that defied the cultured wildernesses of the country parks, and even the statuary was almost swallowed by the creeping green giving the image of figures dancing and twirling in the twilight glow.

But even as we waited lanterns bloomed to life amongst the branches and paths, throwing puddles of light here and there to make the cemetery seem more welcoming.

To most of London, this was just a boneyard, a place where they buried their dead in the neat field to the north, but given time the vampires would extend their influence as the ivy and herbs and climbing flowers slowly covered the grass. This was the vampire's home and they had a love of the funerary arts and the wild and created these pockets in the city to suit themselves.

"Thank you," he said, "it is best about now, with the carpet of golden-red leaves that crunch underfoot. The bench by the fountain has the best views of the sunset. I can't imagine that our conversation will be interesting." The vampire was giving me a polite dismissal, "we will be able to see you and Our Lady Below guarantees you will be safe." They spoke of the leader of their coterie with such reverence as if she was a goddess and her word could shift mountains.

I looked to the major who nodded and touched his eyes telling me to stay in sight even if I did wander. The vampires had guaranteed that nothing would happen to me but the major still wanted me to stay where he could protect me. There might be other things in the cemetery, connected as it was to the Undercity.

I walked over to the bench by the dead fountain, which had been turned off for the winter, and found I was nicely out of earshot. I sat there and watched the sunset, taking deep sucking breaths of the forest and flowers, the wood dampened by melting frost and the sweet-sharp and threatening. I felt like I was being watched by hundreds of unseen eyes. It felt like I was in a ballroom full of dancing couples and I was sitting outside looking in and bristling every time they glided past talking about me.

"What are you doing?" the little girl surprised me. She was so small that she needed to clamber up to the seat of the bench. She wore a black wool mourning dress and pelisse with a rabbit fur muff that had been inherited for it was almost as big as she was. She had blonde curls falling out from under a hand-knit cap and her shoes were a little too small to her - even to my eye. I concluded that she had escaped her mother or governess who had come to mourn in the newest part of the cemetery. As a child of her age, I was guessing four or five, I would have escaped too. I had loved the gardens of Fell Leaf House and escaped my studies as often as I could to run through them.

"I'm enjoying the quiet," I told her, "I've had a long few days."

"My name is Sophia," the girl said proudly, the way kids often were about any information about themselves. "It means wisdom, what does your name mean?"

"I am named after Flora, the goddess of spring in ancient Rome, in Greece she was called Persephone." Sophia seemed interested. I had been desperate for adult attention as a child and had right then I had nothing else to do but talk to her. I also knew that if she was with me then the vampires wouldn't be tempted by her. "My father was a botanist so he named me after the goddess of flowers."

"I like the name Flora," Sophia said brightly, "it's pretty," it was unpopular because the fashion was for Greek names, not Latin. "I like flowers, this place is so pretty."

"It is, have you been here in the summer when everything is blooming?"

"No," she said, "I've only just come here," Sophia said kicking her feet back and forth. "Did your father like flowers too?"

"My father loved flowers," I told her, "he liked flowers so much that he was asked by a Rajah of India to grow roses in his palace."

Sophia was reasonably impressed, mostly by the exoticism of distant worlds that might have been new ideas to her, just because she was so young.

"Roses?" she asked, "is it hard to grow roses in India?"

"It must be," I answered, "he asked people from all over England to do so. The flowers in India are very different to our flowers, even the birds are different. The peacock comes from India."

"Peacocks are very pretty," Sophia said, then lowered her voice to add, "but they're very loud. Does that mean all the flowers in India are pretty, are there Indian flowers in England?"

"Yes," I told her, "in Kew Gardens, in the greenhouse, there are flowers from all over the world."

"Did your father bring them back?"

"Some of them, yes," I answered, "but my father didn't make it to India that time, there was a shipwreck and he died."

"Are you here to visit him? I'm here to visit my papa but I saw you and you talk more than my papa."

"I'm here with my friend Damien," I looked across to the where the major was talking to the vampire about Lady Atwood's piece of jade.

"I like you," Sophia said with her cloak splitting to reveal that her skirt was pulled up to her knees. It revealed that she wasn't wearing stockings and her legs were blue with bruises. "Do you have brothers and sisters?"

"I don't," I was honest with her, "I always wanted some though, I went to a school and girls with sisters had friends who came with them and I wanted that. Even now my best friends are twins, and I don't have that closeness that I find enviable." It was easy to be frank because I would never see Sophia again.

"I have a baby brother," she said, "but all he does is cry. It makes my head hurt. You can have my brother." She looked like a little doll and was delighted to have someone to talk to, someone who listened. With a new brother, it was possible that her nurse was overwhelmed with the baby and didn't have the same amount of time to let the girl chatter.

"Babies cry," I told her.

"Who are you talking to?" the voice came from behind me. I turned around and saw the young-looking vampire from before, the one that McConnell called Beausant.

"I," but as I turned backing thinking that he had missed her because she was small and not visible over the back of the bench which had a dense hedge behind it, to introduce Sophia I found that she was gone. "Oh," I said, "you must have missed her. She was with the mourners but she's gone now."

"I heard you were witchblood," he licked his lips like I was supper and he wished to lick the plate. He was sharp in feature and in the now almost dark- although lanterns had been strung through the trees they were not yet lit so the twilight gave him hard shadows and prominent lines. He was beautiful like the edge of a piece of broken glass. He had flat black eyes like chips of Whitby Jet, everything about him was hard-edged like he was carved from marble. It made him appear like he belonged in this garden cemetery like he might pause and be mistaken for one of the angels covered in moss, ivy and climbing flowers sat between the trees.

"The term is witchborn," I corrected him.

"Oh but, *Berushka*," I had never heard the pet name before, "I am a creature of this place and we are all fascinated by blood." He clicked his teeth after the final syllable. He was trying to unnerve me and it was working - but I didn't want to let him see that.

"Oh, but *Berushka*," I answered, "I thought that you were fascinated by pretension." As soon as I said it I realised that I had insulted someone very dangerous. Vampires paid for their meals at the poor hospitals and Hotel Dieu but it was never a good idea to poke a beast.

To my surprise he burst out laughing, his head thrown back to show a long line of marble pale throat through the open collar of his shirt and contrasted against the dark fabric of his patterned vest. "I like you," his smile was a predator's, if Major McConnell had a shark's grin this was something older, darker, glimmering in the black. This wasn't a rapacious wolf come upon an unguarded hen house, this was the winter wind whipping across moorland to consume all it touched with frost and ice. He was a beautiful cold.

My skin prickled around him.

"It's better to be liked," I said unsure how I should speak to him. We had not been introduced and it was desperately improper and with it being so dangerous I was clinging to propriety to protect me.

Yet I still felt like a mouse in the claws of one of the lions in London Zoo, played with but not as food, but as a brief amused in an otherwise indolent life before snuffed out by a heavy paw.

"To be liked," he said, "is all that you can wish for, *Berushka*?" He put his hand on my shoulder, the bench and the thin hedge remaining between us and I was overwhelmed with a sudden blast of desert heat, of sunburned air and old sweat, of iron and copper, like hands that have held pennies, and yelling, harsh and guttural in a language that I had never heard before and then he jerked away like I had burned him.

"Not Witchborn," he said, "a witchling," he had a dark chucked that scared me more than his posturing had, "what an understatement," he licked his lips again, trying to regain his apparent insouciance, "you are more dangerous than even you know," he bowed to me.

It was such an abrupt change, from the bored predator to a reliable servant that I was shocked.

"Beausant," even from the twenty or so paces that separated us I could feel the air rumble with the major's growl.

"Appreciating an uncut gem," Beausant said with a glib smile. "A witchborn is a rare dish indeed."

"And to think I thought that we were going to discuss lace merchants for your cuffs," I said. I was unsure where I had found my tongue but Beausant seemed to enjoy my sauciness which only encouraged me, unfortunately.

"Silks for your presentation," he corrected, "we can talk about the queen's ridiculous insistence on panniers with *robe a'la Athenienne*. She must be aware that she makes those girls look like simples."

The major didn't seem any more at ease than he had before Beausant and I began to discuss fashion. "*Come now, meine Liebe Hund*," Beausant's boyish grin was an attempt to soften with the diminutive he used both to insult the major and make himself seem less dangerous, "the *mädchen* and I were getting to know each other. She is to be presented and who knows more about silk and velvet than a vampire?"

"To dress your coffin." the major drawled, and his voice was low and rumbled like coal falling into a chute. He put his hand on my arm to pull me towards him.

"On my hunger," Beausant said suddenly shedding the mask of the dangerous elite and was replaced by something noble and regal, like a hero in a fairy tale. The rake that lingered in the dark alleyway replaced with a chessboard knight, "no harm shall come to her by my hand."

Chapter Seven

"Vincent Beausant is not a person that a young debutante should be making acquaintances with," the major said as the carriage rocked its way back to my aunt's house. It was a long journey made longer by his disapproval.

"I can't say that I made the decision to go to Bunhill Fields entirely to make his acquaintance," I told him, "like a good society girl I've gone where I was taken to do what I was told."

The major let out a deep sigh as he pinched the bridge of his nose, "my apologies, Flora, I'm the one putting you in harm's way and then blaming you that one of the most dangerous vampires in England, not just London, thought that you were *interesting*." It didn't sound like much of an apology and I said so. "I'm sorry," he finally said, "this case has me at sixes and sevens. I am faced with dead ends and mysteries at every step and failure to solve this and solve this quickly will mean the death of a child if he's not already dead and the idea of it, that if I had been quicker, or asked a different question, or followed the trail in another order that I might have already found who is responsible with the clock stopped."

I offered him a wan smile in comfort, and anyone else I might have patted their knee to offer them solace but he didn't like to be touched so I stayed my hand. "We will be in the carriage for some time," I said, "even before accounting for London traffic. I know about the case and I can listen. Use me to go over the information out loud so you can narrow down the information and ask the important questions."

The look he gave me was dismissive but he decided to humour me, undoing the collar of his jacket and stretching out his cravatte to the side. He was tall and lean with broad shoulders and although he might not have had a shaped waist his uniform gave him the illusion of one, and simply undoing the top hook of his jacket and tugging at his neck tie to reveal his neck created a different image of him and the long expanse of throat on display was almost scandalous. I blamed the twins that I was even having the thought that he looked attractive and not half-strangled by his uniform.

"He was taken from a room in a house that was protected against almost every magickal creature in England to the extent that the crown would be envious," he counted the detail off on his finger.

"So the usual child stealers like Jenny Greenteeth and Rawhead and Bloody Bones are ruled out."

"No baby was found in its place."

"So it wasn't a pooka or other courtier making a changeling swap."

"There was no blood or signs of violence and nothing hurt the nurse."

"So it wasn't a tick."

"The nurse wasn't drugged but fell asleep on the chair waiting for the baby to fall asleep."

"With the bells ringing randomly she would have been woken up every hour so falling asleep out of plan could easily happen, the entire house was exhausted."

"But it couldn't be predicted so a human thief is unlikely, unless they had the means of ringing the bells."

"And the key, with a silver shank, was in the lock on the inside, and the door was locked, the footman had to kick it open."

"The bells have rung on the quarter-hour every hour with nothing to cause them to ring, equally loud throughout the house despite being in the kitchens."

"Wrapping the clappers in oakum did not stop them ringing I had to take the clappers out."

"Which is the second question. Why do the bells ring and why didn't they wake a colicky baby between being put down and the nurse waking when they rang a second time?"

I could see him chewing it over, I didn't think that he had considered that. "We can't be sure of the nurse's timekeeping because the clock was broken."

"I took the clock to The Horologist," The Horologist was one of the London Witches whose affinity was clocks and clockwork. I didn't understand his ability but if he spoke about clocks it could be taken as absolutely true, "and that was a mystery in and of itself. The case was locked, the back was locked and so the glass face was fixed in place, but the clockwork broke when the hands were held in place when it was running. Some force held the hands in place long enough that the mechanism stretched the spring, despite the glass being shut."

I agreed that was very strange.

"So we have a baby taken from a locked room, we have bells that ring every hour, we have a clock broken through the case, we have a *fang shi* token sent to the baby's adult sister."

"What's a *fang shi*?" I asked, struggling to repeat the word that he'd said.

When he looked at me he was exhausted. It was not the question that tired him but the entire mystery. "A *fang shi* is a type of Witch," he said, "from the far east, they can turn the newly dead into a *Nu Gui*," he was uncomfortable with the terms as I was, and it was clear he had just learned them from the vampire he talked with. "The vampire I checked with, Louis Cho, came from Beijing originally, he said it was a token used to send the ghosts to attack the holder of the token, but the token is old and doesn't work."

"Mr Atwood is broke," I offered, "if he owes money they might be using it to scare him."

"In that case, it missed the mark," he

pointed out, "Lady Atwood thought it was casting Lady Davenport's virtue in doubt and had her husband received it he probably would have tried to pawn it."

I couldn't help but agree with that. "The Atwood's cook had said that Lord Davenport was paying the staff's wages because Mr Atwood was a terrible gambler and his creditors had given him beatings before now."

"Which gives Mr Atwood's creditors reasons to steal the baby."

"But there has been no ransom request," he said spreading his hands.

"Could the *nu gui* ghost have taken the baby?"

"That's the first idea that could work, but the Atwood's would need both the token and a *fang shi* to use it. It works like a cantrip so unless one of them learned the specific death spells and had an affinity to use them they couldn't have summoned it and then where is the baby?" He let his hands fall into his lap and his head fall.

"Then let's look at the other side." I told him, "Lady Atwood clearly has an issue with his father's new wife."

"Mr Atwood can't have children," Major McConnell said, "he was kicked by a horse as a boy and his family kept it secret. Lord Davenport won't allow his daughter to petition for a divorce because it will threaten his position at court with the scandal. She is desperate for a baby but if she takes a lover her husband will have proof of infidelity and can cast her aside and still keep access to her bank account."

"How delightfully fair," I drawled.

"She's jealous and if she took the baby she'd have the baby."

"Then what about this supposed scandal?" I wanted to make sure that everything was questioned no matter how trivial it turned out to be.

"It was all rumour, Lady Davenport, then being courted by Lord Davenport, left her season early because her sister was in confinement and was ill. The timing caused people, Lady Atwood especially, to say her niece was her child and the rumour stuck as gossip, you know what salacious gossip is like. I've checked the parish records, well I had Bruxby check them, and the midwife confirmed that Mrs Haye was the mother, but she was unwell for months after so Lady Davenport didn't marry until late that year. She had the same nurse that gave suck to Mrs Haye's daughter, and fed her until the baby was born to keep her milk." He answered a question I didn't have. "Button, the nurse that was with Lady Davenport."

"I asked Louis Cho, who directly serves their Lady Below, Ysabeau, if he had heard of any vampire that might have taken the baby and was powerful enough to do it without a staff member carrying the baby into the gardens, and the only vampire in London, if not England, that could have done it is Beausant and I already checked his alibi, he was at the cholera hospital all night and the doctor is willing to sign an affidavit to vouch for him." The London vampires, under the treaty with the Tower,

worked with the poor much in the way of a
farmer tending cattle. They paid in labour for the
blood that they took so it was not unusual to see
an elegant, perfectly groomed vampire wearing
an apron as they worked as nurses and porters,
especially if there was a virulent contagion as
they couldn't sicken.

This meant that vampires were generally
associated with charity and kindness, they were
accepted in society in ways that shapeshifters and
Witches weren't. Every vampire registered in the
coteries worked in one or more of the hospitals or
Hotel Dieu that tended to the city. The only ones
exempt were the mysterious Ladies Below.
Female vampires were never seen abroad,
keeping to their coteries and cemeteries

"So we have a false scandal, a Courtier
proof room, a vampire who could have but didn't,
a token to summon a ghost that could but no one
able to use it, a clock held in place despite a
locked case, a nurse who fell asleep despite loud
bells, and a historic gown covered in fresh blood
shoved into a cavity in the wall." I ticked it off on
my fingers.

"And the bells," he added.

"There's a question," I said, "when we
were in the nursery we heard the bells like we
were directly underneath them," he nodded, "but
they didn't wake Button and she said that Bunny
was colicky, not that the bells kept waking him."
I could see the thoughts in his head moving, "why
didn't they wake the baby?"

"I gave her into your care," Aunt Jemima shouted at the major. She was so angry that even her neatly pinned hair seemed about to fly out of its braid with rage and there were loose strands around her face and her chatelaine was jingling with the very force of her will not to lose her temper even more than she already had. "You took her to Bunhill Fields?! At twilight?!

"Lady Ysabeau guaranteed her protection," the major responded trying to calm her but she was only just warming to her topic.

"This was a punishment not a gallivanting jaunt around London," she took in a deep breath, "she was supposed to be darning socks and mending shirts, not introducing herself to the Islington Undead."

"Aunt Jemima," I tried to interject, she needed to listen.

"And Beausant took a liking to her?!"

"I needed to know about the jade pendant."

"She's a child!"

"Aunt Jemima!" I repeated, trying to be more firm but she didn't even look at me.

"Which turned out not to be important to the missing child, it was another dead end." She looked fit to explode with rage which was not something I wanted to see, "so you took her to a vampire's boneyard as the sun set."

"You can't talk to a nightwalker when the sun is up, it's in the name." The argument was such that the major himself was about to start shouting and I could see his fangs when he spoke.

"Aunt Jemima," I tried again.

"Enough," both of them turned to look at me which was what I had wanted because I did need their attention at that moment, and it silenced both of them because I had the missing baby settled on my hip.

They were quiet after that, Aunt Jemima sitting on the couch like the legs had been swept out from under her and the major leaning against the mantle and not looking much better.

On my return to my aunt's town-house, I was immediately sent to my room to change into something more appropriate to my station and gender, and I had desperately wanted to get out of the pants. I felt cold and and restrained in ways that I never did in my stays and petticoats. It seemed odd but my cotton dresses were warmer than this wool suit so I had been more than ready to dash up the stairs and get back into my skirts.

I could see the advantages of pants, and certainly for being mistaken for being a boy - being outside the restrictions society put upon me as a girl was a delight, but I liked wearing dresses and Thorne's cut of my hair and the way Sylvie fixed my hair meant I didn't quite recognise the girl in the mirror looking back at me, so I had taken a moment to look at my reflection because I thought a stranger to be in my room.

That was why it took me so long to recognise the pile of blankets on my usually neatly made bed. In the centre of the nest, trying to fit a pudgy foot complete with stocking, into his gummy mouth was a baby. He looked like he didn't have a care in the world, warm, well-fed and in a clean napkin.

His contentment didn't answer how it was he had gotten into my bed, in a Witch's House beside the river.

Aunt Jemima kept looking at me, then the baby and back to me, then at Major McConnell, silenced by a pudgy baby with his fist in his mouth and a simple in the other hand, opened her mouth once, twice and then a third time like she was one of the ornamental carp the Lowell's kept in their garden pond. It was not often that anything shocked the Haruspex, whose magic had its affinity in Divination, but this had shocked her silent.

"I thought that we could eat it," Sylvie said carrying in a tea tray, "all that fat to sweeten the meat," leaning over the baby she snapped her teeth at him. Bunny was delighted, slapping at her face with a saliva soaked hand.

There was very little that could make a person look ridiculous like a baby.

The major crossed the parlour to me, leaning into the side of Sylvie and took a few deep breaths before shaking his head. "I've learned nothing from that about where you were, your lordship," then he looked at me, "May I?" He took the baby from me and certainly seemed more comfortable holding him than I had, tucking him into the crook of his elbow so that he was supported and could see everyone without interrupting his switching from fist to biscuit being shoved into his mouth.

The Lowell twins had unleashed a demon in my head in suggesting that I might find the major attractive, or least have me seriously entertain the idea.

Certainly, I had recognised that other people might find him attractive, and objectively that he was a good match for someone, but until the sisters had said it I had not considered that he might be a good match for me.

Now I realised that I had been remiss in that because he was stood before me, gloriously dishevelled and holding a baby with such ease that I couldn't not think of him as a father and wondered how he would be if the baby was his own, and if the baby was mine, more than that, - if the baby was ours.

I was sure I blushed redder than Sylvie's hair.

I was very lucky that at that moment no one was looking at me, but instead Bunny, and it said so much that I didn't know his actual name and only what his mother called him so fondly.

Honestly, I did not think that the image of a handsome, virile man in command of his circumstances and holding a fat, happy and healthy baby - who was doing his best to grab things with his free hand to shove them into his mouth - left even Aunt Jemima unaffected.

"Madam Haruspex," the major said, unusually using her formal title. "Will you send a message to the Tower on my behalf?" The Tower had ways of communicating the magic was limited and by sending word to Bunhill Fields it was likely he had used what he had access to up, and so it made sense that Aunt Jemima sent the message.

"And not Lady Davenport?" She asked with an arched eyebrow.

"A baby was taken from a house with a level of protection that the Witchfinder General would consider excessive, and then returned to the house of one of the Magnificent Seven Witches of London, do you not want a second Witch to see if there is something amiss before returning him to his mother?"

"I'm sure you are over-estimating those protections," Aunt Jemima dismissed him, "you are known for hyperbole after all."

"Buckingham Palace does not have those protections," it seemed that baby or not, the argument between them was not finished.

"Flora, Sylvie," Aunt Jemima said, "if you would take the young lord to the kitchens, I am sure that Cook will be able to find something to do with him."

Sylvie clapped her hands together in delight, "we *are* going to cook him," she enthused and then wilted under the combined glares of both my aunt and the major. She grumbled under her breath as she took the baby who immediately grabbed the meat of her braid and tugged it hard with both fists. She gave me a look as she walked past me that made me laugh out loud.

      Uncle Jack arrived sloughing off his greatcoat and draping it over the chair, ignoring Jenner waiting to take it, and revealed only his shirt which was open at the collar and a pair of double-fronted doeskin pants with knee-high riding boots looking like every pamphlet's portrayal of the wicked French *emigre* come to seduce virtuous English maidens for their inheritance and the frontispieces of books those English maidens weren't supposed to read but traded amongst themselves like contraband. The girls at school had loved those pamphlets because certainly those men didn't exist and then in flounced Dr Johannes Dee looking like he had spent the day posing for the engravers.

      He looked even less impressed by the baby than Sylvie was, actually taking a step back from the couch where the baby was wedged between Sylvie and myself as we tried to keep things out of his mouth that he was not supposed to have and instead of letting him gum at an ivory bracelet that had been scrounged up for him from one of the crates in the basement.

      Bunny, used to being fawned on by everyone, saw a new person and immediately had both arms out shouting buh buh and expecting to be lifted.

      Of course, Uncle Jack made it look not that he was disturbed by a baby but that he wanted to stand leaning against the mantle and he must have heard Aunt Jemima call him a peacock

under her breath, "well, that's definitely a baby,"
he said, "why do we think it's the Davenport
baby?"

"Who else would it be?" Sylvie asked, "do
you think that I went to the Foundling Hospital to
see if they had one spare," she yelped as he
grabbed her braid again, seeing that she was
distracted, and pulled it hard so that a twist of it
came free. She took her hair back and snapped
her teeth at him before she tapped him on the
nose with a black-tipped fingertip. "Will you stop
that?" She rolled her golden eyes, looking every
inch a fox, "at least kits stop when you yelp."

"Pin your hair up," I told her, "keep it up
out of your reach," of course that was when he
tugged on my pendant and nearly strangled me.

Uncle Jack looked vindicated as he skirted
the room as though if he broke eye contact with
Bunny he might be mauled to get himself a drink
from the decanter. "I am going to get a Tantalus,
just for you, Jack, no one else comes here just to
sup my brandy."

"But, it's well known, my dove," he said
with a grin, "that you have the best brandy in
London." Uncle Jack had a pet name for everyone
and never mistook one for another.

"No one else upon whose household you
call leaves their brandy without a lock on," she
replied. It was easy to think of my aunt as mean
but she enjoyed the verbal sparring she shared
with uncle Jack. She was also protective of me in
the way that someone who had never wanted or
expected, children and thus made no provision for
them suddenly found themselves in possession of
one.

I was shy, though given to sauciness when I felt comfortable, so she felt vindicated in her decisions to protect me and she was afraid for me that made her snippy with those who she felt had endangered me.

The wit she had once been celebrated for was now most at use in this sparring with uncle Jack, whom she respected as a peer even if she did consider him a vain and useless peacock who called upon her to raid her kitchens and drink her spirits.

It looked like Uncle Jack was using the brandy as an excuse to completely avoid the baby on the couch between Sylvie and I.

"The baby," Major McConnell said, "is wearing a silver bracelet with his name, and date of birth there on his ankle," it was accompanied by a string of amber beads the point of which was to ease the pain of teething, "he was wearing a gown of linen finer than I've handled but got stewed apple all over it when we fed him and it's now soaking in a bucket in the kitchen. He's in perfect health, he doesn't smell like the Davenport Town-house, but he's been elsewhere for the past few days so that isn't a surprise to me."

"And you sent for me specifically," Uncle Jack left it open, "because although I accept the invitation I doubt that it was to offer me dinner."

"Idiot peacock," Aunt Jemima said pouring herself a brandy and draining the glass in a single swallow. "They called in the Tower because he was taken by something from a room warded against pucca and then he appeared in *my* house," she emphasised the word my, "without tripping any of my wards or protections and you wonder why we might need a second Witch."

"I prefer the term sorcerer," he said primping himself up, and with a final swirl emptied his brandy glass, before giving a quiet cough as it burned his throat on the way down. "Now let's have a look at the sprat."

He came over to the couch and squatted before it which caused Bunny to bounce excitedly, and make happy buh buh noises but I suspected that he was less interested in a new person to dote on him than the drop pendant of shining black stone hanging from the new person's ear that was almost in reach.

I was sure that Sylvie saw it the same as I because we looked at each other over Bunny's head and smiled. Like Aunt Jemima Uncle Jack's primary affinity was divination, but he didn't see it coming the way that both Sylvie and I did, when, with Uncle Jack leaned in and holding a coloured lens in front of him to look for residual spells, Bunny grabbed the stone hanging from his ear in his fist and pulled.

Uncle Jack yelped like a cat whose tail had been stood on whilst leaping backwards and landing hard on his ass clutching at his ear expecting fountains of blood not the sordid little chuckle from his miniature assailant.

The second time he brought out his lenses, holding them in front of his face, he remained safely out of reach.

"That is peculiar," he said as Sylvie raised the makeshift chemise the baby wore - it was made from a dishcloth pinned with brooches and buttons - to show a little pot-belly and napkin held in place by a ring of rubies. Every woman in the house had offered up her jewellery for pins to keep the baby dressed. It was not safe to have him dressed in the long-shanked pins that held shut my own dress, for he would have pricked himself with every wriggle.

"Apart from a charm against colic that I myself have used on a horse, there are no spells or magic on him. I'm not sure that I would use the charm, because it's designed for a much larger animal, but it seems to be working. If he develops stomach problems I'd remove it but no magic. There's a strange residue, like a cloud of shimmering dust in his hair, if you look at him reflected in the obsidian lens," that one was like a slice of shining night, black and clear as a mirror, "But I've never seen it before. It's the only hint of where he's been. We can certainly safely return him to his mother."

"Will this close the investigation?" the major asked him. I couldn't see his face as I was trying to remove Uncle Jack's jet earring from Bunny who was trying to eat it, whilst clutching Sylvie's white-tipped braid with the other hand.

I wondered idly why nurses didn't, to a person, have short hair.

"As was pointed out," Uncle Jack said, trying to regain some composure so he did not look quite so ridiculous as the baby had made him, "something took a lord of the peerage from his locked nursery without waking his nurse and was not stopped by myriad protections against pucca,"

"The protections seemed to be in place to

prevent a Courtier from leaving, not gaining entry." The major was sure to correct him so that the details could not become muddled.

Uncle Jack continued as if he had not been interrupted. "and delivered him to a house that's protected against forceful entry by one of the Magnificent Seven Witches of London until we found out what did this and why we can't stop looking into it but we certainly do not have the pressure that we did before."

"The jade token will certainly," my aunt said, I suspected that it was because the magic was appealing to her because it was different and unknown. As much of the magic of the world was innate it could be studied, and in some cases learned.

"It's chipped," Uncle Jack told her, thrusting out his hand to take the token from the major who handed it over without complaint. "The Islington Coterie might know more about the Chinese art but the Limehouse Coterie are more aware of what is brought into London, and they certainly don't like people interfering with their," he paused to give the words emphasis, "perfectly legitimate trade." It was a delightful way to say smuggling. "Their Lady Below has agreed to share the results of her investigation with me."

If the Coterie of Bunhill Fields were the effete noblemen in the overgrown grandeur of a graveyard the Limehouse Coterie were rough tradesmen inhabiting the tunnels of the Undercity and maintaining, through intimidation and the promise of protection, the warehouses and shipping that was Limehouse's very lifeblood.

He threw the jade token to me. "It'll make a lovely pendant, Flora, jade is supposed to be good for inspiring honesty in others and even the remnants of old magic can be a protection."

I caught the stone and felt that overwhelming desire for it again, it was as if it was a piece of me that I had never known was missing. This was not an intellectual knowledge of how the pendant completed me but instead a visceral reaction. I could not even consider the idea that it not be touching my skin and I had no idea why.

From one of her pockets, for she had fixed pockets even into her sprigged muslin gowns tucking the ties into her petticoats to hide cinching at her waist, Sylvie pulled a few hair ribbons and yard of loose lacing which she offered me to thread the jade on and I took a ribbon and hung the pendant around my neck, tucking it into the collar of my house dress so it hung against my skin.

Chapter Eight

I was with Major McConnell the morning after Bunny had arrived in the Witch House so mysteriously, and Uncle Jack's staff had returned him to his mother visiting with Lady Davenport to make sure that all was well.

We were let into a fine sitting room with the duck egg blue wall silk and the previously devastated young woman was replaced by a perfectly primped and polished Lady of the realm. She wore a warm pink house dress under a Kashmir shawl and her hair was elegantly pinned to the height of fashion. Her face had been powdered and rouged with neat swipes of kohl at the outer corners of her eyes. I hoped that I might look nearly as elegant when I was allowed to wear cosmetics.

I knew from the older girls at Miss Featherby's school for young ladies that some girls enjoyed the rituals of dressing up and others felt it formed a necessary armour to get them through the day and would never be seen than be seen without their cosmetics.

I didn't know which applied to Lady

Davenport but she looked every inch the society Lady from her Indian muslin and Kashmir shawl to the rings on her fingers and brooch on her breast.

She was the sort of beautiful that caused people to stop and stare.

I felt very inadequate in her presence, just a funny-looking girl who had been talked into cutting off her hair.

The weeping woman had been replaced by the perfect society maven who everyone wanted to be.

"Major McConnell, Miss Peake," she said standing up from where she shared a tea service on a side table with her sister. Janet Haye was in full mourning, even wearing a ruffled linen cap on her ash blonde hair. Her features were harder-edged than those of her sister with looks too wide for conventional beauty but with an eerie symmetry. Something about Mrs Haye made me wary. I could not have said why.

"It is so lovely to see you both, I cannot thank the pair of you enough, both for what you did and your discretion." She delivered powdery kisses on both of my cheeks. She smelled divine. "Come, have some tea, we have some delightful simples here, you must tell me everything."

It was overwhelming to be in her presence because it filled the room. The major was wearing a superfine instead of his uniform and styled his hair so he looked more like a Corinthian than a major in His Majesties Dragoons. He sat furthest from the fire. "I'm glad to hear all is well," he said, "and I hate to be a stickler for propriety but can you introduce us to your guest?"

A glut of emotions crossed her face quickly, surprise, horror, embarrassment and then settled on resignation that was poorly papered over with a society smile that gave nothing away. Her sister had a flintiness that seemed at odds with Lady Davenport's soft welcome. "Major McConnell, this is my sister, Mrs Jane Haye. Janet, may I introduce Major McConnell and Miss Flora Peake, I am going to be serving as a chaperone for her at a few outings this season." Lady Davenport hadn't told her sister of our true purpose there.

Mrs Haye made a disapproving noise. "Miss Peake, do you not have a female relative that could introduce you? my sister has just come out of her confinement after all."

"My only living relative," I said with what I hoped faked the appropriate deference of an unpresented society daughter to a married woman, "is uncomfortable in society. I am grateful for Lady Davenport's kindness in offering to help me." I was usually shy amongst new people but I did not care for Mrs Haye at all. "My aunt finds that when she attends even at a dinner it is because people ask so much of her as the Madame Haruspex."

If anything Mrs Haye seemed pleased by this information and not off-put, "how convenient that Emma has a magical problem and Madame Haruspex needs someone in society."

If I had been a cat it would have been possible to see me bristle. Even though I was arguing with my aunt I still loved her dearly and would not hear anyone speak ill of her and this accusation was also baseless.

"Mrs Haye," I said in a tone that I had taken entirely from a very unimpressed Miss Featherby and I hoped it had the same effect on Mrs Haye as it had on me, "I must correct you on your misconception, my aunt did not ask Lady Davenport but Dr Dee asked Lady Davenport on my behalf."

"Madame Haruspex," Major McConnell added, "received offers from both Duchess Medway and Lady Lowell, it works out in Miss Peake's favour for it means that she can choose which events to attend without having to fear her chaperone has another invitation or has cancelled something just to gain favour with her aunt." He said it with a loucheness that promised violence. He was doing it entirely on my behalf.

"Lady Lowell," Lady Davenport said with a clap of her hands, "I know her well, is she hoping that if you come out with her twin daughters she might save the money on the assembly rooms. She doesn't lack for blunt but she spends like she must save every penny." I laughed at the deliberate joke and it was only a little fake, it seemed Lady Davenport did know Lady Lowell quite well. I had not known until the Major said it that the offer had been made. I also imagined that my aunt laughed in her face at the presumption if she did not say something unflattering about her daughters as well.

"Mrs Haye remained stony-faced, "you should be pleased, Emma, to have triumphed against such fierce competition," everything she said was snide and full of vitriol. I did not believe a nice word could pass her lips.

Before I could say something in retaliation, and it was likely that it would be something that would have made me look very unlike a lady, the major silenced me with a snap of a biscuit between his teeth. "Oh don't mind me," he said with his shark's grin, "I'm just enjoying the show. I'm not sure that I've seen such bloodshed outside the peninsula."

"Janet," Lady Davenport said with a firmness I had not seen in her or thought her capable of, "if you continue to behave like a child I shall send for Button to put you in a napkin, give you a cup of warm milk and put you down for a nap for it might sweeten your mood."

Judging by the shock on Mrs Haye's face her sister never spoke so to her and it was likely that she'd bring Lady Davenport to task for it, and my presence wasn't the impediment that the major's was.

When Button brought in the young lord in a fabulous linen and lace gown that hung over her arm like an apron Mrs Haye had an expression to chill the room. I expected upon seeing her that the baby would start wailing but he just held his arms out for his mother who took him with not even a receiving cloth to protect her dress and let him shake his slobbery rattle against her face. Lady Davenport was at ease and devoted to her baby, long past the protection of her dress. She'd rather her baby be happy than appear perfect to any callers.

That seemed to sour Mrs Haye even more than our appearance did. "Will you stand to see me so abused in your home, sister?" Mrs Haye asked when Lady Davenport returned to her seat with the baby in her arms, "by a trifling witchling."

I knew myself to be cosseted and kept away from things, the knowledge that I had been introduced to would upset my aunt but I had never heard the term witchling, where witchborn was the correct adjective so I took it as an insult even if I didn't know what it meant.

"I see no insult," Lady Davenport said and looked at the major as she said it, using his strength to bolster her own. I had done the same and similar in the past using someone else to make myself brave. I did not know the relationship between the sisters but there was none of the convivial warmth which I expected - even knowing that the Lowell twins were an extreme example who completed each other.

"I do not have to stay to be so abused," Mrs Haye snapped it out, there was a threat there even if I did not know what the threat was for. She clutched her lambskin gloves so tight in her fist her knuckles whitened as she stood.

"No," Lady Davenport said and her voice cracked a little in the saying of it, "you do not, you arrived in a foul temper with no invitation and have created your own discomfort by your inclemency to guests who did announce their arrival. I am loathe to see you in such spirits and have no true desire to see your return to your empty rooms, but Major McConnell and Miss Peake have done me and my lord a great service and I will not let your petty upset,"

"Petty?" Mrs Haye snarled, sounding much like a rabid dog as she cut her sister off, "you consider my mourning petty?"

Lady Davenport stood up and looked

around for the nurse because she was sure that her upset would spoil the baby's good humour, but Major McConnell reached out his arms to take her from him instead. I would later learn that the major would never miss an opportunity to take a baby from their mother in the short term. Werewolves might have been excellent soldiers for the empire, known for their ferocity and fearlessness, but they loved children - even unpleasant ones.

"I do not envy you your mourning," Lady Davenport said to her sister, "nor do I wish you to return to your empty rooms. I know how much love and joy that Bunny has brought to my household, knowing it all the more keenly because of how close I came to losing him. Yet your mood today is black, you seem determined to find insult where there was none," she paused to take a breath running her hands along the front of her dress, as if wiping her hands clean on her apron, "I repeat my invitation, come, live here, I would not have you wallow in that quiet cold home."

"How kind of you, sister," Mrs Haye said, pulling on her gloves, "to think of me wallowing in my grief whilst you bask in your good fortune." Her tone which had been viscerally acidic now actually seemed threatening and I flicked my eyes to the major to see if he had felt it too. His posture had changed and his arms, and shoulders made a frame around the baby sitting blithely in his lap.

"Janet," Lady Davenport began but Mrs Haye had warmed to her topic, and had no intention of stopping and she landed each word like a blow and the way that Lady Davenport began to cower -this was not new behaviour. Mrs Haye, as the elder sibling had not offered her sister kindness but instead scorn. I did not know if this was new, a gift delivered by her grief or if it was jealous of a sister who seemed to have been given all the blessings that she herself had been denied.

"Shall I return to my cold rented rooms by the river to think upon my loss, what was the word, wallow, in my grief like my own child does not lie cold in the ground this past month?" The words were baleful and full of hate. It was not jealously I realised that moved her. She hated her sister. I had known that she was widowed and that she had chosen not to leave mourning, although it had been three years since the death of her husband, and Lord Davenport had not, even on the peninsula, complained or tried to pressure her father into finding a new husband for her. If her rooms were rented, as she said, instead of living with her sister, she had a patron, but I thought it was odd, because it would be usual for her to live on the kindness of family. Combined with that was the new knowledge of how soon it had been since her child had died.

I had the uncharitable thought that I would not wish to give her houseroom either. She was a viper. She lived alone because she chose to but I'm sure that her family were happy that she did because she was so desperately unpleasant. Every word she said was loaded with venom like she had drunk poison and by spewing hate hoped everyone else would die.

"Mrs Haye," I said, I didn't know why I spoke up but I did not care for acrimony, it unsettled my stomach, "the cold weather makes us all harsh, and new grief can make demons out of angels," I had watched my aunt perform the role of conciliator, and before her Miss Featherby with girls ready to fight like gladiators over missing ribbons or combs, "things can be thrown out of proportion. Come, sit, we shall drink tea and talk of other things." I kept my tone quiet like I was talking to a spooked animal that might, if I made the slightest error, bolt.

"You see that," Mrs Haye said, "Emma, you see that, she seeks to bewitch me."

Around my neck the jade pendant suddenly pulled downwards, caught in my stays as I moved - or so I thought. I couldn't help but reach for it, hoping to rearrange it, a gesture of comfort like twisting my iron ring or tapping it on a cup and as thought-free, but Mrs Haye shrieked like I had splashed her with boiling water. "See, she tries to hex me." I could only blink at the accusation, "she's reaching for an amulet."

Even if I tried to speak reason she had warmed to her topic and she wouldn't stop. "Is this how she reacts, the Witchfinders are right, they can't be trusted. She seeks your fortune, Emma, and to kill Bunny, witches render babies down for their fat," I tried to speak but a look from the major cut me off, "she tries to silence me, sister, so that she can continue her plot."

I was angry. Of course, I was angry. This awful woman was having histrionics and spewing lies about my aunt, about uncle Jack, and i had less magic than the flint and steel in a housewife's apron pocket. The accusations didn't stop and her dramatics, I was sure it was all false, were starting to upset the baby.

"The oil of babies," I said with a coldness that surprised me, like there was a film of frost over my words, "what is it for, or more specifically, Mrs Haye, what do you think it's for?" I felt as cold as the jade had been when I had first hung it around my neck, as cold as the cluster ring I wore, as cold as a late December frost. I felt strong in the cold. "There are so many testimonies, aren't they? but I wonder which you think I would want." I paused, as aware as she of the dramatics of this and that - this entire thing was intended for an audience. "I mean there are so many grimoires available at book stores, all over London, the Malleus Maleficarum, the Lesser Seal of Solomon," I waved my hand to dismiss them, my cluster ring catching the light. "But magic," I paused again, "true magic, not household charms or light automation - true magic," I repeated it for emphasis, "in innate. It can't be learned or taught, only commanded. So which of these rituals in those false grimoires speaks of rendering down a baby," I maintained a look of ennui and condescension as I said it, pretending that I was one of the Lowell twins so that she couldn't see that she bothered me at all.

"Never mind it is a scandal in London how easy it can be to buy a baby, never mind take one from a foundling hospital, when the child was found, he was in my care until he was returned to his mother. Could I not have taken him then? And what of the children found in the Thames," I watched her flinch, "am I also responsible for those? Perhaps in between dress fittings and chaperoned visits I crept quiet as a frost into those houses and take babies,"

"She admits it," Mrs Haye said.

"She admits nothing," I answered. My entire body felt chilled and I felt much stronger for it. I was powerful in the cold, as dangerous as falling drifts of snow. "The books are nonsense and the spells useless, nothing more than people writing down nonsense to make themselves feel relevant by tricking nobodies who hope to feel powerful."

If looks could kill Mrs Haye's gaze should have struck me down.

"You called me a witchling, someone born of a Witch's family, and by my own admission my aunt is the Haruspex, so why would I need a ritual from a book of lies, and which recipe should I use, pray tell," I had warmed to my topic but the cold was in my bones like I was made of stone standing proud in a winter garden. In that moment I was a goddess spreading a chill with every word. Like an actress at the theatre, I commanded the room. "Perhaps I would spread it on a besom to take flight, or mix it with ambergris and perfumed oils to make a cold cream to maintain an illusion of beauty. I gave her my most condescending smile - a smile I knew from the Lowell twins. "I could stuff his mouth with an apple and serve him to Dr Dee like a suckling pig, he does like stewed apples. Of course, a piglet would be cheaper and easier but it's not as spectacular when dished up for the right company. " In that cold, holding the jade pendant in my fist, I diminished her and I did it deliberately and knowingly.

In front of her sister, the quiet nurse in the corner and major McConnell, sat with the young lord on his lap brandishing the ivory bracelet he had been given to amuse him in the witch house I insulted her so there was no room for an answer. Of us all only Bunny didn't react to what was happening in the room.

"Of course, it breaks my heart to do this," this was a blatant untruth - at that moment- in that cold, I truly didn't care for her feelings, "but it is well known that I have no magic. I have no

magic, no talismans or amulets to activate. I can't
even reheat a cup of tea," I lifted one from the
tray and took a sip, "and know too much of magic
to even attempt to fake it," over the rim of the cup
I smiled at her and like everything else my smile
was ice cold. "So no, dear one, I'm not trying to
bewitch you, but the histrionics should work on
someone."

She was furious with words trapped
behind a locked jaw and caught in white-
knuckled fists. Her features, blunter than her
sister's, now seemed craggy like something inside
her had cracked and the ice-cold that had come
over me had crept into a wedge that cracked open
wider. She turned and left the room, closing the
door behind her with a certain finality.

In that moment she stopped being the
horrid woman who had accused me and become a
grieving wife and mother. Of course, it hurt her to
see her sisters baby returned to her when her own
had sickened and died. Of course, she wanted to
vent that anger on someone, anyone, and in
reaction to that anger, I had made a fool of her.

I realised then that I had made a terrible
mistake.

"You've made an enemy today," the major
said but his eyes were on the baby he was
bouncing on his knee by lifting his leg up and
down but the baby was unimpressed by the game,
happier gumming on the bracelet in his fat fist
and drooling all over his expensive lace and linen
dress. Now that he was in motion, waving one
hand with the other pulling the bracelet from his
mouth I could see a muslin tied around his neck
like a scarf to try and sop up all the slobber. He
was much like a large dog with the amount of
saliva he produced but without the benefit of

lying on your feet on icy nights.

"Was I meant to sit there and take such slander?" I asked, again sipping my tea. "I only worry that I forgot myself and that she was in mourning."

"My sister," Lady Davenport said, "she has never been kind." It was clear she was choosing her words carefully.

"A bully," the major said, "needs neither kindness nor cruelty, they just seek the satisfaction of power over another." He had a beatific look on his face, one better suited to a portrait of Madonna and Child than a feared soldier. "I have encountered more than enough of them over the years. You have an enemy now, Flora, and she'll do what she can to make you small again to make herself feel bigger."

"She's in full mourning," I tried to brush it off, "she cannot join society for another six months by then I'm certain that she will have forgotten. She can't embarrass me in front of people if she can't encounter me in public." I was trying to convince myself that I had been right to put her down the way that I had. "I only regret that I did it so close to her bereavement."

"If you want to be cruel, Flora," the major said and his disappointment made me feel small in a way that Mrs Haye had been unable, "be cruel, but do not hold your tongue because you think that you should be kind. Circumstances will always get in the way."

I wanted to leave, to find a quiet place to think about what I had done; what I had said. How I had clutched the jade pendant tight and the cold that had settled over me and how at the last I had felt what could have been cold arms draped over my shoulders.

"We're here for two reasons," the major said changing the subject, "to make sure that this little rabbit," he bounced the baby who had a dirty chuckle that filled the room, "has no lasting ill effects from his journey." The baby smacked both sticky hands against the major's freshly shaved face and the major snapped his teeth at him to make him laugh some more.

"Do you have children, major?" the nurse, Button, asked from the doorway where she had been standing, as unobtrusive as she could be - she was so successful that I had forgotten that she was there. "You're so good with him."

The major took a moment before he answered her, "my kind loves children, we are rarely blessed with them and so they grow in the Packlands in Wales, my work keeps me in London so even if I were married, which I am not, I could not do what I do and see any child that I had."

Even if it was the stereotype that werewolves loved children it was an unalterable truth that Major Damien McConnell adored babies.

"Are you searching for a wife?" Button asked him.

"Are you offering?" He asked her with a saucy wink that was designed to change the focus of the conversation to her and she blushed clear to the roots of her hair.

The other topic that we asked Lady Davenport about was the white gown that we had found in the nursery wall. "The dress is old," the major told her, "as old as Charles the Second according to the witches in the Tower who went over it, it's not a modern dress that rotted in a cool damp but," he paused, "the bloodstain is less than a month old, they can't be more specific than that. That means someone in your household, or with access to it, went into the nursery, knew about the alcove and hid the dress there."

"Why would someone do that?" Lady Davenport beat me to the question.

"I'm waiting on word from a specialist, the gown is with her now."

"There are specialists in this?" Lady Davenport asked, but I couldn't but think "he's taken the dress to a vampire." Vampires were often old, Beausant was certainly old enough to know about the dress, and no one knew more about blood than a vampire. But the Coteries and the Tower maintained a distance - they only helped the other where they themselves benefited.

"A Witch in Glasgow," the major qualified, "her affinity is blood and blood rituals."

"You said," Lady Davenport wanted more information, "that magic was innate, and that there's no power in rituals."

"No," I corrected, "I said that the rituals in the books were nonsense, but there are orders that things need to be done, different sacrifices that should be made, different consequences for actions. Different cultures thank gods or demons for their magic and give offerings, fetishes can be used to draw ghouls or other necrophages and anyone with the knowledge could make them, just like how most people can do household magic. Even entering a Courtly Hill is done by following a specific order of things."

"And false rituals, things that people think will work," the major said, "you'd be surprised what people think will get them what they want. I supposed you would call this black magic and it has nothing," he paused to emphasise the word, "to do with witchcraft."

"How would you even learn such a thing?" Button asked.

"The Kindly Ones," Lady Davenport flinched as if struck as I said the name.

"Don't be so quick to apportion blame, Flora," the major corrected me, "if you were paying them for such a ritual they might as well perform it themselves. They wouldn't need to use trinkets or fetishes to target their spells. You seem determined to make enemies today, will you be best served by returning to the carriage with a pot of chocolate to keep you company?" It was a threat, an admonishment to behave or I would be excluded. It was cold in the carriage so I bit my tongue.

"The only Witch who would likely do it this way in the Empire lives in Glasgow where she serves at the University Hospital treating diseases of the blood. We have evidence of her whereabouts. The Kindly Ones would not have returned this little goblin," he bounced his knee again, "and the Tower watches them closely, so it's very unlikely to have been them. It's likely a witch and it's very likely," he didn't want to commit, "with whatever took this little goblin from the nursery," he sopped at the baby's chin with the linen that was pooled around his pudgy legs on the major's knee.

"It's not an attempt to supplant him with a cuckoo," I said, "because the nursery is Courtier proof," I couldn't have brought Sylvie into this house because she wouldn't have ever been able to leave.

"And none of the Coteries would, and we know where the vampires who could were that night," he was listing the suspects off to rule them out for Lady Davenport.

"No shapeshifter could have done it, breaking the clock and not waking you," he looked at Button, "Necrophages don't leave the Undercity," London was riddled with tunnels as old as the city itself. Over time modern buildings tended to be built on top of what was there creating the Undercity - it was mostly inhabited by creatures that despised or could not bear the light, and the lowest levels of necrophages like ghouls, "and would have killed you outright," Button took a deep breath, "and a tick would have killed everyone inside."

"I didn't live in this house a month ago," Lady Davenport said suddenly, "my father, when I said I wanted to take rooms in the city, bought this house for me, and had some rooms prepared for my arrival, you know my father, yes?" she asked.

"That he left for Venice a month since," he said, "and that he made his fortune buying up debts and bringing them to court to make them pay. We are looking into who owned this place before, just in case that's why Bunny was taken, to force your father or revenge themselves on him."

"As far as we know," he continued, "the dress was a lure, it could have been put in before the house was even sold. Your father has enemies. Your husband has enemies. The more that we exclude the more questions we find."

"A lure for what?" I asked.

"Whatever took him," he answered, but what I heard was "I don't know."

Chapter Nine

When we returned to the carriage it was obvious that the major was unhappy with me. He sat with his back to the driver's seat and crossed his legs to close himself off. "I shan't be needing your help from now on," he said firmly. He had damp spots on his superfine under his greatcoat and mashed biscuit on his cravatte, but with his firm mien and closed off posture he was the perfect image of the Regency gentleman, even down to the hat sat next to him on the bench.

"I spoke out of turn," I admitted it, "but,"

"Flora," he leaned forward. For all that we were familiar he made a point always to call me Miss Peake so it said so much of his anger that he used my name. I cursed the twins for the frisson that it gave me. "You are not a servant of the Tower. It is not your place to worry about these things. It is not your place to reveal things to people to interrogate them. You were asked there to give Lady Davenport a reason for me to be there. We don't know if the two cases are even connected and you ran the very real risk of offending Lady Davenport and barring us access even though we returned her son."

He took a deep breath to calm himself before he continued on, "you told a new mother about taking her baby and stuffing and apple in his mouth when you served him up as a roast. That isn't speaking out of turn, Flora, it's," he went quiet and pinched the bridge of his nose as if staving off a headache. "I'm taking you back to your aunt, and she'll at least be happy with this turn of events even if she doesn't blister your ears for what you said."

There was not a lot that I could say to that. I had been so angry at Mrs Haye, and I had been so cold, that I had to diminish her. I had to make her feel small.

Since I had been asked to help I had felt myself changing - the need to make myself small and invisible was becoming frozen over and the new version of myself had nothing in common with who I had been.

"I've included you too much," the Major told me, "relying on you being quiet and listening to challenge my own thoughts so that I knew what to say when Jackson brought me what he knew about the children in the river."

"You knew about that before visiting Lady Davenport," it was almost an accusation. I don't know why I thought that he had not.

"Flora," he said with a deep sigh, "I'm a Major in His Majesties Dragoons, do you think that the Tower would send me just for a baby taken from a town-house?"

"I," I had thought it. When one moved in the circles of the *Haute ton*, even as peripherally as I, it was easy to believe that the institutions of the king would bend double to prostrate themselves to the gentry.

"The Tower sends its best to the cases that are most likely to break the public's faith in the magickal." He said it calmly as if it was an ineffable truth. "I was already looking into the bodies in the river when young Lord Davenport went missing. I was expecting to find a servant who took the baby to get a payout or revenge on Lord Davenport, whose reputation certainly suggests that he deserves it, or Lady Davenport's father who has made enemies of most of the aristocracy. I thought that I could quickly rule it out and get back to the more important case or I never would have included you at all."

"I don't want to give it up," I said, "I want to know what's happening."

"And I want ten thousand pounds and a house in the south of Italy," he snapped at me, "but we don't always get what we want." His anger at me was not undeserved. I had lashed out. I had gone too far but it didn't make it easier to hear.

Suitably scolded and afraid that if I spoke up the Major would have more to add I sat in silence and he pulled out his journal and began to make notes.

He didn't walk me up the stairs to my aunt's house, just left me at the gate to go in by myself. I reassured myself that I would not cry but my feelings were ravaged.

My anger at Mrs Haye followed by the intense contrition had left me more exhausted than I had thought possible which meant that as soon as I saw my aunt - who exclaimed you're back early - all my hard-fought control was lost and I burst into sobs running into her arms.

The best thing about my aunt was that she understood that sometimes it was best not to have to answer questions until the storm of tears was long past, and a tray of spiced tea and sugar-laced fancies had been delivered before she had sent word to the kitchens.

She listened and offered no promises of vengeance or accusation, she just asked if I wanted to have a lie down before supper and as much as I wanted to sleep, I did not want to be sent to bed like a baby. I knew that I would have a terrible headache if I did not so I retired, kissing her on the cheek with a promise to come back down for supper.

In my room I stripped down to my stockings and chemise, pulling on my banyan before getting into bed. With no fire lit the room had a latent chill but the blankets quickly formed a warm nest around me. I felt like I had been wrung out and slopped across the kitchen floor like an old rag. I had not thought that I had done enough to warrant it but it was true. I fell asleep before I truly had a chance to relive my day in gruesome detail and torment myself about it.

I did not wake for supper and my aunt must have thought that I needed the sleep because she didn't send Sylvie to wake me. What did wake me was what sounded like gravel hitting my window despite there not being a storm to do it.

My room overlooked the river.

The house was built into the river bank so that the front of the house was twelve feet or so above the waterline where at times the basement flooded if we were not careful. There was talk that this winter was cold enough for the river to freeze but it was still flowing freely and my room was four stories above the surface of the water and someone was lightly throwing stones against my window to catch my attention.

Whilst I slept someone, probably Sylvie, had set a fire in the grate and set a lit oil lamp beside the bed which I picked up after pulling a blanket around my shoulders and stuffed my feet into my slippers. Suitably covered I went to the window. Due to the vagaries of the house my room had a pair of double doors that had an attempt at a wooden balcony, it was only a step or so wide and that space was crowded with potted plants that looked like empty terracotta pots or sticks this deep into winter, and a small railing preventing them from falling into the river below.

Sitting cross-legged in the air, about level with my waist so that we were face to face was the vampire Beausant.

He was dressed uniquely in a brightly coloured robe belted at his waist that was patterned with clouds and cranes which he wore over his shirt and vest. Strange silver filigree nail caps were on his fingers held in place with chains that vanished into the cuffs of his shirt.

In those colours, caught in the river lights of boats and moonlight reflected off the water he looked like a ghost. If I had not known him for a vampire I might have made that assumption.

"Hello, witchling," he said with a grin. He had lost none of his boyish looks in the few days since I had seen him but his mischief seemed less hard edged now, and much more genuine. He had none of his previous malevolence.

"Is this where I'm supposed to invite you in?" I asked him, unimpressed by his display. I was sure a good deal of what he was doing was to shock me.

"Certainly not," he said with a bark of laughter, "you must think me a fool to want to set foot in the Witch House. I am sure that there are protections enough in place that I would turn to dust leaving only my new robe. I like this," he pulled out the lapels to show me the fabric, I guessed that it was silk. "I just got it. I would like to appreciate it." Had he been sat on the floor it would have pooled out around him but in the air as he was it hung down behind him like a curtain.

"It is nice," I said, "but I doubt you've come just to show it to me."

I felt safe in being saucy with him. He couldn't enter the house without permission and as a witchborn, I was supposed to be immune to a vampire's hypnotic gaze. I'd never put it to the test but when I had met him he had not even tried to charm me - but that might have been because I was with the Major.

He barked out another short stab of laughter, "*Berushka,*" he said with delight, "I do come bearing gifts."

"I know better than to accept gifts from strange men," I said, "and they don't get stranger than the one floating over the river outside my window."

He grinned showing the glint of his teeth, sharp little canines resting on his lip. I wondered if they had been like that when he had been human. "I am making an entrance. What is the fun in having these abilities if I can't get young girls out of their beds in the middle of the night by floating over the river?"

"You could terrorise pigeons, I suppose."

He was enjoying the conversation and I felt safe teasing him in ways that I didn't with the Major despite that I had known him much longer.

When I had touched Beausant at Bunhill Fields something had changed between us. I had, for a moment, felt the heat of the burning sands, smelled scorched air and iron and known the clash of blood and sweat but I did not know what it was. I did not know if he had seen something in me although I could not imagine that there was anything to see.

Except for the cluster ring on my finger I was not very interesting at all.

"You're going to be a delight to watch grow," he said, "now, as I said," he was trying to bring the conversation back on track, "I bring gifts and when you're as old as I time can certainly fly."

"Don't you mean *haemophagus fugit*?"

He clapped his hands together in glee so that the devices on his fingers clinked together. "Oh I could just eat you up," he licked his lips and seemed happy when I didn't even raise an eyebrow in reaction, "you are much more of a delight than your Lady Aunt, but I do bring information for you, about your new pendant." My hand nearly dropped the tails of my blanket as I reached for the stone hung around my neck. "Do you know what it is?"

"Some kind of token, I thought," I said, "made by the sorcerers of the far east to summon a ghost or a facsimile of it."

"Not a token," he said, "a marker," he was correcting me, "the name of a murdered woman but that's unimportant, in the now it was sent to Lady Atwood."

"How did you know that?" I asked.

He tapped his hears, "shifters aren't the only one with enhanced senses, *Berushka*. I heard everything Louis told the wolf. This token is," he stopped. "In the East End there are many Chinese Immigrants, and some of them are prone to illegality - they are people after all. One of these gentleman runs a rather profitable trade selling opium and renting beds to rest upon during the resulting fugue." He paused, "for every legal ounce brought in for the manufacture of laudanum and other medicines at least another one makes its way into the opium dens. Mr Atwood is a frequent visitor to one of these and with that and gambling at an associated hell he has amassed a rather considerable debt - with no intent to pay citing *noblesse oblige*, arrogance about the superiority of the English, the usual nonsense," he waved his hand, "of course our entrepreneur does not agree and made it clear that payment in full would be made and so sent Lady Atwood the marker."

"If it's a warning why send it to Lady Atwood and not her husband?"

"Because they're not death threats, but instead a marker for protection - a protection in place of her husband. Markers like that had ghosts, spirits more than ghosts that you would get in the penny dreadfuls, forces that exist in the space between. In the hands of a Witch whose affinity is one of the funerary arts, blood, bone, ash or cold flesh, to awaken the spirits but the knowledge of how to use the markers is lost. Yet the markers remain, so that the men who work for the entrepreneur," he was careful not to use the man's name - not that I would have known him if he had introduced himself to me, "will leave Lady Atwood alone."

"She gave the major the token thinking it was an insult to her daughter in law."

"The message was a warning to get her husband's affairs in order. They won't go after her, killing a debtor, even one of the gentry, is a hazard of business. They'll sacrifice a peon to hang usually in exchange for protection to their family, and word of their ruthlessness and power spreads - that can pay off Mr Atwood's debt and Lady Atwood gets to move in with Lady Davenport. Everyone gets what they paid, or did not - in this case - for."

"Why tell me and not the Tower who might make use of this information - that the jade has nothing to do with the baby or the bodies in the river?"

"Because I like you," he said, "I don't like the Tower but I appreciate why they exist and why they're necessary. The Tower only ever serves the Tower. I don't like people who kill children any more than the Major. You can tell them what I told you tomorrow when you see the Major."

"He doesn't want my help any more," I was still bitter over it and the scolding that he had given me, even if I had deserved it.

"His loss," he shrugged, "would you like to go to Vauxhall Gardens with me?"

I thought of him in flight like this, of him holding me above the winter night of London whilst people slept below, or prepared their morning bread or soothed colicky babies to sleep. I thought of the romance of it - the dreamlike dance of flight in the frost laden winter night.

"I'm hardly dressed for it," I said finally.

"The invitation wasn't for now," he said with another of those sharp-toothed smile on his boyishly handsome face. "The gardens open with the season. I would love to escort you through the trees. I am of the impression that walking with you under the lights talking about what people are wearing will be a delight."

"I dare say that my aunt will not allow it." I had to be honest about it, "but it does sound like jolly great fun."

He stood up, still floating four stories above the sludgy river as it twisted its way to the sea, and gave me a strange, almost archaic bow, "your growth shall be a joy to watch, Miss Flora Peake, and the most interesting thing that I have seen in decades." That said he took a step back and in the space between one blink and the next he was gone. He did not vanish or speed off. He was there and then after I blinked, unaware that I had even done so, he was not.

I closed the windows and went over to the fire, putting the lamp on the mantle as I sat in the chair beside it. After a short while letting the heat prickle against my skin I rang for Sylvie that she might bring me a hot posset and a fresh hot brick for my bed.

Sylvie came in with her usual aplomb, the sort that best resembled an invader kicking down doors in their search for gold. If Sylvie had thought that she could kick down a door in the Witch House she would, even if she lacked that conqueror's aura, that sense of presence and largeness that was a trait of all the Courts but the part of her that was a fox could vanish into an empty room like she was not there.

I loved Sylvie. She was the closest that I had to a sister and my dearest friend in the world. It was why I lied to her.

"You had the window open," she said giving it a dark glance with a flick of her golden eyes, black fingertips fussed at the handles as if she might at any moment throw open the doors and see what it was that I was hiding.

"Bad dream," I told her, "like I was trapped in a box," it was a dream that I had once had that haunted me, "I woke up desperate for fresh air. I stood for a few minutes looking over the river."

"You'll catch a chill," she said. Sylvie, like most of the members of the Courts, couldn't lie, but she could knot the truth so well that people called her kind double-tongued. Lying to a courtier was easy because they took absolute statements as truth, shifters and vampires could smell a lie but the courts didn't have that benefit. She would say things like that because she was fishing for information.

"The cold never really bothered me," I said, "I imagine that's why the Queen gave me her token."

Sylvie didn't need words to say volumes. She started to fuss with the curtains, making sure that they were pulled tight over the windows even as she took advantage of the small gap to look out over the river before finally closing them to block out any draughts. "I'll get you a posset, it's too late for supper, if you eat now you'll be awake the rest of the night with indigestion," she fussed with her braid, throwing it over her shoulder with a flash of white at the tip.

I don't know why I didn't tell Sylvie about the charming vampire at my window. I don't know why I didn't tell her about the jade pendant and that it was a promise to Lady Atwood of protection by some criminal syndicate who were going to kill her husband. Some women were happier as widows and maybe Lady Atwood would have been one of them. She could remarry. She was not past the age of having children and a murdered gentleman would not lose everything the same way that one who had committed suicide would. Lady Davenport would open her home to her even if she particularly disliked her and Lady Atwood would dote on her new brother. Her envy of her father's young new wife would be mitigated by access to the baby. Babies had that effect on people.

I could have told Sylvie.

I could have passed on the warning to the Major. In retrospect I probably should have - but I didn't.

Having contented herself Sylvie left the room, pulling the door closed behind her and I was pretty sure that she knew that I was hiding something - or someone.

The firelight caught the facets of the cluster ring I wore - my gift from the Winter Queen when I was a child, given to me in a walnut shell rimed with frost that felt like her kiss when I picked it up. The Winter Queen had been beautiful wearing a cap and pelisse in in golden spider silk and white fur, and her skin was the colour of cracked mud and her hair the brown green grey of tree bark. She was beautiful as a snow storm and as dangerous. At her side was Tam, the Winter Knight, hand on the hilt of his sword, offering me a smile that felt genuine and warm as the Winter Queen kissed me on the forehead and pressed the walnut shell into my palm.

I had hidden that ring until I showed it to my aunt, not even a year past, as we discussed my coming out, and I had watched the colour run from her face, the olive going ashen before Sylvie insisted that I wear the ring and never take it off.

It was beautiful and had clearly been made in Alfhame, it was as if someone who had never seen a ring but had read the description of many rings and tried to cram all of the details that they thought were necessary into the smallest possible space.

Gold bugle beads were shoved between garnet tears, long fingers of rubies, enamelled golden scrolls staying *Amor Fati* were twisted under an enamelled cross and the whole thing was smaller than a shilling.

It was beautiful but it was obviously not a human design. I wasn't sure that a human could even make it.

I tried to remember if I had always loved winter or it came with the Winter Queen's ring. I loved winter. I love the sound of frost crunching under my boots. I loved the way that the cold seemed to settle on my shoulders and around my neck like a shawl. I loved the crispness of a cold moonlit night where the very air felt lighter. I loved ice skating and I had loved my single jaunt in a sleigh. I loved catching snowflakes on my tongue. I loved watching the snowfall from the windows of cosy sitting rooms. I loved when the wind caught my hair tugging it loose from its pins and bonnet. I loved winter. I couldn't remember when I hadn't.

Frost kissed, that was what the Witches called someone who loved winter.

Maybe there was a reason for it that I'd learn later, or maybe some people just liked winter more than any other season. Nevertheless, I sat by the fire with my posset cup cradled in my hands as Sylvie held a toasting fork at the flames and cursed the capriciousness of bread that refused to toast.

Chapter Ten

I did my best to stay abreast of the news even though my aunt did her best to have the newspapers shredded and turned into tinder before I had finished my breakfast - especially the gossip sheets. I had to go to the kitchen to read the London Times, looking for news about the children found in the river, but found nothing.

Aunt Jemima read the papers in bed, sipping strong black coffee and eating quarters of sugared oranges. It was expected in society to not rise before noon but Aunt Jemima was up with the sun. She had a second breakfast of a poached egg upon a slice of toasted white bread with a pot of tea in the dining room with me. I often had oatmeal with spices, honey and a large dollop of cherry jam.

At school, we were given a bowl of oatmeal made with milk and honey, but the spices had been saved for special occasions. When the other girls returned home for Christmas, especially the ones who held events or had families either visiting, or were visiting, and wanted their daughters to be seen, I would be allowed hot chocolate and candied fruits and when I was the only girl left in the school I could spend the whole day eating treats and running amok through the corridors and pathways of the gardens.

This meant I loved oatmeal even though my aunt was sure that it was food for pigs.

It meant that I enjoyed breakfast. My aunt talked about fashion plates that she had seen; fabric samples that had come from the drapers and which modistes had openings- because it was apparent that the six gowns that I already had were not going to be enough for a whole season, as having cut my hair and having to maintain it I would need new hairpins and curling papers and then I would need new dresses and shoes to match.

I was perfectly aware that this was meant to be a distraction, especially when she suggested that I go shopping with the Lowell twins. I adored Phyllida and Cressida but I was sure that my aunt was in her study most days trying to find out how to exorcise them as demons.

The day was crisp, with the sort of blistering freshness that usually preceded snow. I had put on a shawl with my pelisse and a cap under my poke bonnet before I was driven to the Lowell house before all three of us, the Lowell twins and myself because Sylvie detested the cold as much as I loved it and had declared the opportunity to spend the day drowsing in front of the fire, were taken to Mayfair shopping. It allowed that we each served to chaperone the others or the Lowell twins chaperoned me, and their mother trusted me to keep them from mischief.

Other debutantes were milling about on

Rotten Row visiting the same milliners and drapers that we were, accompanied by mothers, aunts or governesses and many of which Phyllida and Cressida knew by name, and took the opportunity to introduce me to as we talked about lace and the pile of velvet for making pelisses or gown for older women who could wear fabulous colours and fabrics and the suitability of silk flowers to decorate our hair.

We went to Gunters for ices and discussed which gentlemen were expected to be bride hunting and who were known rakes. We tittered politely behind our hands at lewd jokes that we weren't meant to know. We chattered about novels and Major McConnell though I didn't mention the vampire who had called at my window those few nights before.

I showed them the jade pendant with the edited truth that it was a gift from Dr Dee for my coming out and shared appreciative murmurs about its deep green colour and its strangeness and how jade was smuggled and wasn't that scandalous and how someone had been attacked on the South Bank of the river and her father was pressing for marriage but the scandal was how her father couldn't afford a season, not really, and the man who attacked her had applied for marriage but that the girl's mother had forbidden it but it was going to happen anyway and how that it was disgusting and that it shouldn't be allowed and how Ambrose had told his sisters that in ancient Rome men who ravished young women had their genitals crushed between flagstones and how it should be so in London not that those terrible men be rewarded with marriage.

Of Lord Atwood's murder, which was the talk of London, we did not speak at all.

We talked about Lady Davenport and how she was as beautiful as people said and surely that was why such rumours remained.

Unaware of them I asked, "What rumours?"

"Scurrilous ones," Phyllida said.

"Ridiculous ones," Cressida added.

"You know what rumours are like,"

"Half fairy dust,"

"Half nonsense."

"Oh certainly," I said, "she's a good woman and I know that it must be false but it is so easy to be starved of gossip in my aunt's house. Did you know that she takes the gossip pages from the papers and has them torn up for kindling without even looking at them?"

"How awful," Phyllida gasped.

"Truly monstrous," Cressida agreed.

"She puts no stock in gossip, not even as entertainment where nothing comes of it and it's just us girls."

The twins recognised it as manipulation, but they were savvy enough to know that I was an audience starved for rumour and gossip and they liked the way that it made them powerful and needed. It was harmless and we both benefited from it.

"These are just rumours," Phyllida started.

"Made entirely out of whole cloth,"

"We got the story from Ambrose,"

"Dear Ambrose,"

"He was new to society at the same time as Lady Davenport,"

"Before she was married."

"Her sister was three seasons deep."

"And the story goes,"

"She was engaged to Lord Davenport."

"But she eloped with a rake."

"And her sister married old Lord Davenport in her place."

"But the marriage was rushed."

"By special licence."

"And her sister had a new babe before the year was out."

"But before Lady Davenport's wedding."

"They waited,"

"In the country,"

"The story goes."

"The sister's confinement,"

"Was truly Lady Davenport's,"

"And it was all hushed up,"

"So she could marry a peer."

"But this is just a rumour,"

"With no truth to it."

"None at all."

I thought about it, chewing over the idea, Lady Atwood had said that Lady Davenport was a jade, and if she had heard that rumour would she have thought that Mrs Hayes poor dead child was in truth her sister's bastard passed off as her own legitimate daughter. I thought about it, about how unreasonable it was, and how hateful. Even the Lowell twins called it outright falsehood and they loved gossip - the more scandalous the better.

London kept rumours better than its history. The Undercity was a testament to London papering over the cracks and building over its stories - but its gossip might as well have been written across the night sky in starlight so it might never be forgotten.

"There are plenty of cut wives in the city," I said, "a marriage is only forced if the girl's ruination is known."

"And yet," Phyllida offered.

"Both daughters married in haste."

"Rumours linger for less."

"Mrs Haye is not a nice woman," I said offhand, "and I suppose that it doesn't matter now, not with both married and the poor child in the ground."

"We didn't hear that," Cressida said leaning across the table, having finished her lick of ice.

"It wasn't in the papers,"

"How curious,"

"If it was outside the city,"

"It might have been announced in a country rag,"

"No one in London gets a," Phyllida paused and I expected Cressida to fill in the blank but she continued, "provincial paper."

"We get the paper from New York," Cressida said.

"For papa's investments."

"They are always months old."

"But so delightful."

"It's all slander, name-calling and cotton prices."

"I wish our papers were so,"

"They'd be so much more fun,"

"Can you imagine,"

"Between theatre reviews,"

"And marriage announcements,"

"The prime minister joining a member's only club,"

"And was seen sharing dinner,"

"With the aide of the opposition,"

"To bribe him with news of their plans." The two of them burst out laughing at the very silliness of the ideas.

"Who knows,"

"The Tower might be found."

"To be working with the Witchfinders."

"The Witchfinder General found,"

"Wearing women's clothing."

"Sacrificing goats to Baphomet,"

"And in the very next issue,"

"In tiny print,"

"The tiniest print,"

"Witchfinder General does not nor has been seen,"

"To wear women's clothing,"

"Whilst sacrificing goats to Baphomet,"

"With the retraction not clarifying,"

"That he wasn't sacrificing goats."

"Or wearing women's clothes,"

"In the first place."

"It's a delight."

"Much more fun than the London papers,"

"When you get a rumour like that in the London papers,"

"It's Are Kindly Witches responsible for newest child murder?"

I couldn't help but interrupt, "Kindly Witches or Kindly Ones?"

Both sisters thought about it before Cressida answered, "Witches," she nodded, "It wouldn't be the Kindly Ones, they're a myth."

"I heard they went to France after the revolution," Phyllida said.

"You never told me that," and just like that, the conversation was derailed by them bickering.

Yet as I was driven home before I got into the carriage I found a paperboy and gave him two farthings for his last paper with the intent of reading it on the way.

The article was mostly complaints about the state of London's poor: their licentious nature how they had more babies than they could feed; filth, gin, the usual gripes but that Witches who lived in the Isle of Dogs under the benevolent gaze of the Tower were being accused by locals of stealing their children and using some of them in terrible rituals. The Witchfinders were desperate to find out the truth of it, but couldn't act against the Witches even to search their house because of Tower interference and that it was apparent that the Tower turned a blind eye to the magickal citizens of London whilst blocking the honest investigation of the Witchfinders then in the next paragraph calling the Witchfinders a mob and the Tower civilised members of the gentry.

No wonder Aunt Jemima tore up the papers as kindling - this was incendiary nonsense and worse yet it wasn't clear which group it was intending to rile up.

The predicament that I found myself in was that was no longer required as camouflage for Lady Davenport so there was no reason to tell me what was going on with the children found in the river or it that was even linked to Bunny Davenport's disappearance at all.

I was no longer in the investigation so I was no longer privy to the information, and that, I was finding, was the absolute worst place to be.

As I arrived home Jenner was at the door talking to a lady and as I climbed the steps, allowing the carriage that we had hired for the year, to go around to the mews further down the street where we had bought stabling. As I climbed the stairs I heard that Jenner was driving the woman away. She was trying to gain access to my aunt, and kept bouncing a baby on her hip, as she tried different approaches.

"What is happening, Jenner?" I asked our butler.

"Miss Flora," he said lowering his eyes and taking a deep breath, "this lady is trying to call on your aunt but she has no appointment and Madame Haruspex has asked that none disturb her."

"The Lady Witch," the woman said, she had a smear of flour across her face and although her clothes were worn they were in good order. The same could not be said of her shoes, it looked like she had walked across the city and the baby on her hip, which was perhaps eighteen months to two years old was mewling and the shawl around it kept slipping, "I was hoping she might help protect him."

The only difference between this woman and Lady Davenport, I thought, was that Lady Davenport was rich. This woman worked for her living, possibly as a baker, and she did as much as she could with her baby in a sling on her hip and even so she had walked here to ask for something, anything, that could help protect the child who, now I looked at him, appeared unwell, he had a crust of mucus at his nose and his face was perhaps a little puffier than the rest of his body. He was wearing a knit sweater but his legs were only kept warm by the shawl that his mother had draped around the both of them.

"My aunt is indisposed," I said, "but Jenner, the least that we can do is invite her into the hall to share our fire, and perhaps a bite to eat."

"Miss Peake," Jenner protested but I glared him down.

"I understand, Jenner," I said, "that my aunt cannot help, I have no intent to make promises in her name, but a moment's charity and warmth at our fire is surely the least of what we can offer."

With Jenner being forced to demur I invited the woman into the Witch House.

I must admit that my intentions were not entirely altruistic.

For the most part, we did not live on the ground floor of the house because of the rising cold from the river, the family sitting rooms were up the first flight of stairs and although the kitchen dominated the ground floor there was a small waiting room for guests that had a pair of wooden benches, a circular table no larger than a tea tray and a fireplace that had never been lit in all the time that I had lived in the house. The heat from the kitchen kept the waiting room from being overwhelmingly cold, in the way that the basements were, but it remained cool and this deep into winter there was an edge of chill that gave the brick floor a frosty feeling that none of the rest of the house shared.

I led the woman into the room, gesturing that she sit, and told Jenner to lay a fire and bring us some tea, and perhaps some sandwiches if there was still cold tongue and cheese in the pantry. She looked desperately uncomfortable as if I was the wicked witch in the old stories luring her in so that I could gobble up her baby. She did untie the baby from her hip and set him on the bench on one of the tapestry cushions but he clutched unto the ties of his mother's cotton dress. He had a little knit cap in a mismatching yarn to his sweater that looked like it had been fashioned from cut pieces of knitwear as opposed to knit just for him. He had dark brown hair that looked just long enough to wrap around a finger and he was sniffling and looked too tired to openly cry but Cook, Mrs Merryweather, came in with a tray of sandwiches and hard biscuits which she put down on the table with the instruction to ask for more if it pleased me, she said that with a little curtsey and a wink. There was very little ceremony in the town-house and I was surprised that Sylvie, who in the winter tried to stay in the kitchen as much as possible because it was warm and full of delicious smells, had not been the one to bring it in.

The fire was quickly taking the damp coolness from the room and the woman, who introduced herself as Miss Donner, was effusive in her thanks.

"It's nothing," I said, "no more than a bite to eat and some time off your feet to get the warmth back in. It's so cold this winter, there is talk that the river might freeze over so sharing our fire is hardly an imposition." From my reticule I pulled a clean kerchief and offered it to her for the trail of mucus that was making its way down the baby's lip, even as he gummed at the biscuit that Cook had put in his hand, it was gingerbread pressed into a design of a playing card - such baked goods were called simples, where those with layers of cake and fondant which were covered in icing were called fancies. There was a pot of honey on the tray and a small cup of hot water so Jenner had almost certainly told her about the baby clearly having a head full of cold. So I put a dropper of honey into the cup and stirred it because the drink would soothe the child's throat and ease his cold.

"I," Miss Donner said, "the baby, I." She let out a deep breath to calm herself.

"I understand, word of what is happening has reached even here," I told her. No one called unexpected to the Witch House unless they were desperate and if she already had a babe in arms it was unlikely she wanted a cut wife so it had to be the fear that was spreading across the city about the babies found in the river.

"I hoped that she might be able to offer me some help." She said. She was a tired-looking woman, with her face scrubbed clean under its streak of flour, and her hair neatly caught under a linen cap which peeked out from under a wool hat. As well as the shawl draped over her shoulders and around her baby a smaller one was crossed over her breasts and tied under her apron, and she had used a third to tie her baby to her hip. Wool gauntlets, made of the same knit as the baby's sweater, covered her to the elbows but the fingers had been cut away.

What surprised me was that she was no older than I was but she acted much older.

"This is my brother," she said, wiping at his face with the kerchief that I had offered her, "he's all I have in this world, my parents died, and we ain't got anything but the other. I have money, it's not much, but if you could, anything."

This young woman, left literally carrying the baby, had crossed the city to visit a woman she was half sure would demand the life of that child to try and save him from the panic that was filtering through the city like a plague in regards to the babies in the river. This sort of fear wasn't stoked by the Witchfinders, but instead couldn't be appeased by them. The small amount of money that she had, and had to be small because there wouldn't be much left after she had paid for food, lodging and other necessities, she was willing to sacrifice. The difference between her brother's knit dress that almost covered his napkin and the lace dress that Bunny Davenport had worn was striking.

"I shall be as honest as I can," I told her, "the Tower is doing all that it can."

"The Tower only serves the Tower," she said firmly. I kept hearing that phrase.

"Have you not considered," I said pouring her tea and offering it to her, "that solving this plague that is terrifying the city would serve the Tower." I gestured to the sandwiches, they were cold beef tongue and cheese cut into little fingers and there was a waxed cloth on the plate so that they could be taken with her. "If someone, even a witch or Witch, is doing this they are sowing dissatisfaction with the Tower, so it is in the best interest of the Tower to end it. They are investigating it, that I do know."

I wondered if I was right. I wondered if they were investigating because it would be so detrimental to the Tower.

I would ask someone else what it meant, why the term kept reappearing because it said more than I believed it did. It struck me that it was about more than simple public perception but certainly it was a bad thing if the people believed that the Tower was allowing its witches to kill children. I was also certain that if it did allow such murders the bodies wouldn't be dumped in the river.

"How am I supposed to protect my brother?" Miss Donner asked, she was overwhelmed, "he cries and cries and I don't dare take him to a herb witch in case they're the one doing it," there were sobs in her voice, "I can't take him to the Tower," she said, wiping her face with her apron, "I have to do something."

I put my hand on her knee, "let me arrange a meeting with a good cunning woman, one I know and trust, the one who tends to me when I sicken," that I could do, it wasn't very much but it was a start. "He's just a little snotty, I'm sure it's not much more than a cold," I looked at the cup of hot water and honey, "and that will help if his throat is sore. I can't give him a fetish or amulet to protect him, because such things don't exist." I didn't want to lie to her, I got the impression that far too many people had lied to her if she had gotten so desperate. "I'm sure we can also have something more substantial than gingerbread for him to eat whilst we wait for the cunning woman." She wiped at her face again.

"You are too kind," she said through a thick throat.

"None of this is kindness, just simple human goodness," I told her, and rang for Cook to come in so I could tell her what I had said. Cook was a fat woman - my aunt said never to trust a skinny baker - in a cambric dress with an apron and cap where her light brown hair, peppered with silver, and a reddened face was happy to arrange what I asked and invite Miss Donner and the young Mr Donner into her kitchen.

Evicted from her cushioned chair by the fire for another baby Sylvie groused and took one of the gingerbread biscuits for herself, muttering about roast suckling pigs. By the time I left the kitchen Cook was rubbing butter into the baby's lips to help with the vicious chapping even as the child, tucked into Sylvie's chair, was griping in a way that would precede a good wail.

Chapter Eleven

My aunt had opinions about the Donners and more specifically about me letting her into the house. She was adamant that instead of simply allowing the two of them to come into the house long enough to take the blue from their lips that I had accepted them into the household and that I would have to find employment for Miss Donner and arrange a wage.

I should take a moment to explain about my aunt's house. I had heard it said that houses took on the personality of their owner and it was true of the Witch House. It is not unfair to say that magic is contagious, no more that it sheds like a beloved pet. One of the girls at Miss Featherby's gave an excellent allusion, her father had a ratter, a dog trained to protect the house and farm from vermin and as such was a very valued member of the household, but it left hair everywhere. She would return from the holidays and spend at least an hour brushing her dresses in the garden to rid them of the gouts of white hairs. The dog lost so much hair in a day that it was a wonder that it was not bald.

Magic was the same.

Every spell that worked, and those that didn't, left parts of itself on the surfaces and buildings where it touched. This was doubly true of the Witch House so the house had its own peculiarities. It was not fair to say that it had a personality, for it had nothing of the sort, but it was helpful. It had once when I had woken in the middle of the night and unable to fall asleep, lit every sconce with green and cold bale fire in the library.

It did it again when a plain wall certainly had been suddenly having a door that opened to a small staircase, and a room that was perfect for a young housemaid who was raising her brother with a small bed, a stove fireplace and a window that overlooked what passed as a garden to the house. It even had cheery yellow window curtains and a day bed that would be perfect for a young child. The small dresser that sat under the window had a small glass vase with a flower and drawers full of practical clothes for a housemaid.

As my aunt complained about how she had no control left in her own house and as if in response the house gave a little shudder.

After learning her brother had nothing more serious than a mild head cold and it could be treated Miss Donner eased into the household as if she had always been there, with a roped off play area for her brother to smash wooden blocks - found in a drawer that Jenner swore had been full of old sheets needing darning - and a wooden horse - a gift from Sylvie of all people - together in glee slipped sweet treats and cups of hot milk by the entire household - my aunt included.

The following Wednesday the river below my window was syrupy, the winter cold creating pockets of sludge that slowed its progress to the sea and the talk all over London was that it looked like the river would freeze. Aunt Jemima took to sighing in an overly dramatic fashion and changed her silk shawl, which she hardly ever wore, to a wool one and thicker slippers although the temperature in her sitting room and the library had not changed one whit.

Aunt Jemima had told me once that she was born in a hot country, but I had only ever experienced English weather, quixotic as it might be, so my idea of hot was that of a late summer day in Somerset and I suspected it was much cooler than she preferred.

I accompanied her on her errands which allowed me to spend some time in the lending library where a novel that I had been waiting on was available, Aunt Jemima went into the reserved section that was for Witches that worked for the Tower where the books were not as oft used as those that were stored in the Tower library, or that those who owned the library refused to pass over. Hearing that the lending library had an occult section that was closed to the public sounded very much like a shadowy room with heavy doors and chains holding the books to the shelves when in truth it was a small room behind the staff desk with about fifteen books, most of which were in languages that the common witch in London could not read.

Had the perpetrator of the crimes which were rocking London taken one of these texts unless they spoke something like Han Chinese or High Babylonian it would have meant nothing to them. The Tower library contained the translations where they could be easily accessed in the never-ending room that the Tower created for them in the basement that led into the Undercity.

Just as the Witch House had its own quirks due to centuries of my aunt living there doing magic as a matter of course so did the Tower, even if it was less a home welcoming people into its shelter as a trickster that liked to move the outhouses.

Until the Tower had become the centre of magick in England it had been both a palace and a prison for highly ranked members of the British court and as such there were parts of it soaked in violent death, if it had been a person I would not question it being treated in Bedlam for such things were scarring and the Tower was not a person, it was not even something that could be defined as a consciousness, but it had suffered as if it was one.

The talk that day in London was of the almost certainty of a Frost Fair and the hawkers and barkers whose stands covered the squares of the rougher parts of London - for such squares in the more exclusive parts of the city would not tolerate such - were talking about moving their stoves to the river for the imminent demands for chestnuts and hot wine, and one admitted to me with a smile and an extra roll of bread to eat on the way, that his wife was making buttered ale that could be heated in her largest pot and sold to people enjoying the fair. Everyone seemed excited by it, except Aunt Jemima who had lived through several and hated the cold.

I asked most fervently if I could attend and eventually, after a hot supper of rabbit fricassee and onions, she relented on the condition that I attend with the Lowell sisters and their chaperone and that I was to be on my best behaviour for such fairs were full of mountebanks and murderers. Sylvie could not attend, she said holding a kerchief to her nose, for she had caught a cold from the baby and mustn't leave her bed.

As I shared a bed with her I knew that this was a lie - it was too cold for Sylvie and she worried that she might be caught in snow which she hated. I sent a letter to the Lowell sisters suggesting that if the river did freeze and the Frost Fair did happen that they attend with me with their chaperon for my own was ill.

For a simple visit to the modistes or library then we could serve as chaperones for each other - for a Frost Fair to appease our guardians we might have been better served with Major McConnell, for Aunt Jemima made sure to inform me of every crime, real or imagined, that happened at such things as Frost Fairs, or midsummer fairs in the country, a Samhain festival or some revelry in Russia for midwinter that I had forgotten the name of which apparently was some kind of gluttonous licentiousness that saw maidens ruined.

When my Aunt was like that- everything saw maidens ruined, even a roll of fresh warm bread from the baker as a thank you for the large amounts of bread we ordered and paid for on time.

It took three days for the river to freeze solid, and another two before the frost fair was to open, allowing the vendors to source large flat stones to rest their braziers and stoves, on top of several thick straw mats, so that they wouldn't melt the ice and the passage of time just served to make me more excited, even if, on the morning of the day I was to attend, with the Misses Lowell and their chaperone, my aunt received a visit from the odious Mr Ogilvy.

With him, as Sylvie so eloquently put it from her place on the club fender in the breakfast room, unable to take a hint, it fell to my aunt to meet with him and make sure that I was corralled out of the way so I might not say something which he might wilfully misinterpret as flirtatious. This might include, my aunt said, words like Hello.

Mr Ogilvy had certainly not intended it when he had called to see if my aunt was available - and she was only to tell him to leave and not return - to give me access to the daily news.

I had been every part the good girl, and had asked no questions about the case, or the children in the river. I had been quiescent and not resentful when my aunt sent the papers to the kitchen to be turned into tinder so I could not read them. Girls shouldn't fill their head with such things, she said, it makes them less likely to attract a good husband. I didn't believe, even for an instant, that my aunt believed such things but there were many in London who did, Lady Lowell for one. The Lowell twins were uninterested in such topics and Miss Donner. Lizzy, who would happily sit with her mending whilst I was at some task or the other, including what might pass for embroidery to someone who had never seen embroidery but was the sort of thing a girl should be able to do, or practise the pianoforte - again poorly as I struggled to read sheet music, was only aware that the killer was still at large and her fear and lack of education meant she only knew the rumours and even I knew that they were untrue.

I was not aware of the politics that govern the newspapers and how they might encouraged to reduce panic in comparison to the sort of news that would sell papers. It was a constant battle between notoriety and being respectable enough that people didn't kick down their doors and set the place ablaze to silence them.

The article that I was searching for was on page eight and explained about the dead children, how they had been found by the river police and how the river police, the parish constabulary and the King's Dragoons were all investigating the case, and if anyone had any information in regards to it that it should be forwarded to a certain address. There was no mention of Bunny Davenport but another child had been found back when the river was just syrupy and I had been fascinated with the idea of a Frost Fair. It made me feel selfish and I scowled into my tea.

An article about the wolves in London zoo having successfully delivered a litter of eight puppies caught my attention for a few minutes and another about a small outbreak of choleric fever in Cheapside and that the hospital had appealed to the nearest coven of vampires in order to stand as nurses. It made me think of Beausant, who had a cheeky boyishness and smiled in a way that showed the points of his teeth. He struck me as being like a medieval troubadour but was more a figure of romantic debauchery. He did not strike me as the sort of person who had ever denied himself a single moment of pleasure.

That of course made me think of Major McConnell who had a sort of strict leanness and where Beausant laughed at the petty humanity of those around him with a manic glee McConnell took it all in with a quiet disdain. I thought about the young witchfinder whom I had spoken to when I had travelled to Bunhill Fields, with his red hair and grey green eyes. He was younger than the others, charming and earnest and eager to see the world and believed that he was doing the right thing. Where Beausant's cheeks were round under high cheekbones and were an obvious source of his boyish beauty, McConnell's face was long and sleek, with a clear forehead that seemed to project his mood even when he kept all of his face still, and Penreith, the witchfinder boy, expressed himself with all of his being without the years teaching him the detachment the others had.

The three of them were investigating the murders, Beausant because it amused him, McConnell because it was his duty and Penreith because he believed it was the right thing to do.

I considered then, Mr Ogilvy, who looked like a spinning top, with a round belly over thin spindly legs and his hair swept across his head to hide the growing bald patch - he probably didn't even care about the children found in the river with an heiress in mind - the one who ideally held the land upon which he had his living.

I found an article about a stolen pair of ear fobs with emeralds that were family heirlooms and were half an inch baguette cut stones surrounded by French cut diamonds and set in platinum, the ear fobs had been so well regarded that their absence, taken from a locked room in the house, were of interest to the parish constabulary and Lady W--- had hired several guards to help them on their way. She was adamant that none of her staff had taken the earrings and the reporter wondered if it was related to the loss of a brooch from an amethyst purrure several weeks before where the jewel had been taken from a locked box. There had been no mention of this kind of theft before the start of November.

It was, the reporter noted, a strange winter.

I was distracted from my reading by Jenner who carried a parcel that was addressed to me. Having put ideas into my head by reading the paper I was apprehensive but Sylvie loved parcels. Even as I fussed with the address worried that someone might have sent me something that was either stolen or murdered, she willingly extracted herself from the club fender to come over to see what it was, fussing at the string that wrapped it, and bobbing excitedly beside me so she could see what was inside. For all of her excitement she never opened a parcel that was not addressed to her.

It was a pair of boots, that I had not ordered, nor mentioned to my aunt that she might order them from me from the cobbler who had the lasts that all my shoes were made from, Osborne and Benevente, who had a shop in Mayfair. They were beautiful, a vivid Adelaide blue with a pointed toe with a faux wrap feature that went around the ankle like a shawl and buckled on the outside. They had a small heel, no more than half an inch, and the leather was trimmed, as if with tape, with a scarlet edge to highlight the unusual design. They were not the beautiful boots that I had seen the day that Mr Ogilvy had introduced himself to me on the street but they were highly fashionable and were exactly my size as if I had ordered them myself from lasts.

It was a puzzle that someone was sending me boots, and certainly to send me boots that fit me so perfectly it was as if my foot had been used as a last, and were exactly to my taste and entirely leather and so would not lose colour as the nankeen of my existing boots did when they got wet - or allow long access to water to soak into my stockings.

I was not as wary as perhaps I should have been, as I sat down, took off my tan nankeens and pulled on the new boots in their place.

Chapter Twelve

When the Lowell twins arrived in their Berlin carriage with their nurse between them, my aunt was still trying to work herself free from the company of Mr Ogilvy. I took the opportunity to leave quickly to avoid her protestations of being unsure if I should go, her fears that I would be snatched by Barbary pirates or some similar excess. I should have paid more mind, my aunt is the Haruspex, her affinity was in warm flesh, bright stars and the murmuration of birds. These were things her magic was strongest in and as such she served as an oracle. Sometimes her divinations were clear and present dangers, often to England or the monarchy, who used her services through the Tower, but sometimes they were senses of unease.

Yet I was a girl on the cusp of her presentation who was, for the first time in her life, given a small amount of freedom to do things that were inappropriate for girls still in the school room when they were to be presented to the court. I was old enough to want to do things, sure enough in how grown I was that I knew all of the things that could happen and convinced that her worry for me was based on familial affection and not a premonition.

Lady Lowell, I told myself, would have the same worries, and she trusted the girl's nurse enough to make sure they would be returned home in the same state in which they left - even somewhere as licentious and debauched -- I could say this in the arch tone of someone who knew that these were hyperbole even in my own mind - as a Frost Fair.

My conversations in the carriage were almost entirely about my new boots and I can not say that I disregarded any questions about their provenance and let the twins tease me about them being from one of my suitors, teasing me that my affection was being bought, and that it was good that they looked so comfortable for they were sure that the Major liked to walk, the same could not be said of Monsieur Beausant for most long walks in the country took place in the sunlight and they were not known for their sunlight escapades.

I bristled at the intended slight towards the major, that like a pet dog that he needed to be walked but it had been said in such a way that I could not be sure that they were even aware of the comment. So I brought the conversation back to the boots and how it was so convenient that they had arrived when they had for I had expected that my feet would have been cold after a day on the frozen river in a pair of nankeen boots which, although excellent for walking through London's streets and thoroughfares, were not the best at keeping the wet from my feet.

The twins had a very simple pair of black boots with no heel, as was the more common fashion, but it gave me the advantage of being of a height with them, rather than the difference between us being noticeable. Ambrose, the twin's brother, had said that it was like the edge of a castle wall, up, down and then up again, and I mentioned that as the carriage trundled along to the main gate to the Frost Fair.

A Frost Fair could not be gated off in the same way that perhaps a market fair could be, because it was spread along the frozen river, but someone had the thought to throw up a quick cross-braced beam and drape it in fabric announcing it as the entrance to the fair. This meant that the vendors had put together thoroughfares leading from the gate towards things that would attract spending customers like roasted meat or chestnuts, huge cauldrons of hot buttered ale - sweetly spiced - merchants from across the world taking the opportunity to appeal to a richer crowd than would frequent their shops with bolts of exotic cloth, baskets of foreign spices and dried fruits, and even, in one stall, fine ceramics. A coarse jeweller with a thick moustache, the ends of which drooped almost to his chest, hard black eyes under thick browns and yellowed teeth offered chips of green and white aventurine he passed jade polished into tiny beads and strung on thin chains of silver which made my hand immediately go to the jade pendant that Uncle Jack had given me, the one that had been given as a notice of protection to Lady Atwood, that I found in my hand every morning when I woke - having clutched it in my sleep.

Nurse, a woman I had known for several years now and had never learned the name of- or if I had I had long since forgotten it with protestations that I call her Nurse- tucked us in like ducklings with warnings for our purses, hidden in the pockets on the inside of our muffs, when we stopped to admire a tiny monkey in a tiny pink silk waistcoat covered in embroidery as it gambolled and leaped about for the crowd to laugh.

A young lady in a dress that appeared to be *robe a'la turque* if such could be made of clothes that had clearly been purchased from the rag merchant - played a fiddle so sweetly it brought tears to my eyes as the coins that hung over her brow tingled together with the force she restrained in herself and let out through the music. I liked the *robe a'la turque* style but my aunt was adamant that I was too young to make so definite a decision with my styling and could I please go through my presentation before I made myself the talk of London. It was made by layering robes over a fine cotton chemise, and instead of fastening them normally, they were pinned in place and belted to create a unique style that could be altered simply by choosing different layers.

The lady in question wore a black coat, trimmed in wool fringing - like the bedraggled coat of a sheep before shearing - over a linen red gown that showed the tie of her stays through a sheer blue sash, and her skirt was bright yellow trimmed with red flowers. She had a Kashmir-style shawl tied into a turban around her head through which the string of coins was arranged. Other than the coins the only jewellery she had was a pair of iron ear fobs that looked to be bells, but if they chimed the fiddle drowned out the sound.

Her song, strange and lovely as I found it, and the way that she stood, away from the braziers, with only the music to warm her, made me want to stop and listen. I urged Nurse to fetch some cups of buttered beer, and one for the musician, and went to put two bright new shillings into her bowl when Nurse tried to stop me citing that she was a Rom and that they were all witches out to curse us. I did not answer her in words, for I did not have to, my upraised eyebrow said it for me, and again I sent her to fetch some cups of beer and that the twins and I would stay here. I added a third shilling to the girl's prize and smiled at her when she looked at me curiously. "You play magnificently, madam," I told her, "certainly the finest musician at the fair today, please, play on."

"I do not know," Phyllida started.

"She is not like us," Cressida continued.

"I worry what Mother shall say,"

"When Nurse brings word of what happened here,"

"Back to her, she shall be incensed,"

"And like as to lock us away until the start of the season."

"She thinks that you are a bad influence, Flora."

I could not help but laugh for my aunt thought the same of the twins and my hair was a testament to that, tucked up under a neat fur toque the lack of curls would have marked me as unusual if I wore a bonnet but the shorter hair allowed me a little more freedom when it came to keeping my head warm. The twins had the very modish jockey style where the silk was pleated into a spiral and with their high collared, trimmed in black fur, pelisses they looked every inch the society maidens, where my pelisse was scarlet and trimmed in squirrel. I had a large wool muff trimmed in matching fur and I knew it made me stand out just a little more with the flash of my new Adelaide blue boots under my grey wool skirts. My dress might have been staid but my pelisse and muff were not. "I am a terrible influence," I said with a jut of my jaw, to show just how terrible I was, "why I spend my days with the king's dragoons and my nights with the wicked Monsieur of Bunhill Fields." It was a jest but Nurse did not take it kindly for she hissed at me to be quiet as I would be judged and murdered for such things.

"I am hungry," Phyllida said seeing a brightly coloured tent, striped in brilliant yellows and gold with tassels hanging over the opening. Inside, a wooden floor had been laid on the ice and three ceramic stoves were about the tables to keep the customers warm as they served slices of hot cake and tea spiced and sweetened with dried orange peel and spices in the Russian fashion.

"I think we should stop to eat," Cressida said. It was unclear if they were changing the conversation or just distracted by the fine ladies who were sitting in that little pocket of warmth against the frozen river's chill or that they wished for cake. Perhaps their own sheltered upbringing, being less surrounded by magickal London as I had been, had made them uncomfortable. As the season neared I found that more and more the twins were quietly discomfited by things which had never bothered them before.

"The fair shall run late into the night," Phyllida said walking to one of the tables, pulling out the chair and sitting down with a flick of her pelisse and resting her muff, with its coin purse on her knee.

"Mama has said we do not have to be home until supper," Cressida took one of the other chairs. The table had settings for four and both Nurse and I were quickly seated. It was a pleasant seat next to the tiled stoves which gave off a delicious heat. I was not unaware that my own seat was the one furthest from the stove but the cold did not bother me muchly.

"She expects that we shall gorge ourselves on treats,"

"And hot wine," that was said with a saucy wink and a roll of the eyes from Nurse.

From the palanquin that was set up as an impromptu tea room, we could see some of the more magickal vendors, selling flowers that were in bright bloom and in colours that could never be seen in nature, bright blue roses and pale orange orchids amidst bunches of scarlet heliotropes and star coloured geraniums where even the simplest flower, grown in the land of the three Courts, became strange and other. A pair of tree nymphs, hair the colour of new foliage and skin that was the brown grey of the bark of oaks in deep midwinter danced for coins and winked shyly at the promises of lusty young men who seemed insensible to how dangerous the beauty of the magickal world could be. There was even a pair of bridge trolls, some redcaps and other things I could not recognise, usually denizens of London Below, were acting as porters, carrying heavy boxes and grunting at people who made comments at them. Even after two hundred years the magickal was not so common in London that people did not gawk and spit hate at those that were different.

London was different in the frost, even rude ostlers had a polite word for others as they gathered around public firepits or merchants with stoves selling hot foods, from baked potatoes wrapped in paper, or chestnuts in waxed bags. It seemed that every inn and public house had a stand outside selling hot buttered beer, which was made from their usual beer at the end of when they could sell it by law, heated and mixed with butter and spices, usually beside a large cauldron of red wine with cheap spices that they had next to a pot of soapy water so the glass could be washed between customers. Long fingers of ice formed under the auspices of the bridges and eaves of the larger houses, threatening to fall on the well-wrapped children that whooped and hollered outside of them, or were even now skating under the bridges between ropes and making the same noises. Somewhere on the ice a child was wailing, probably having slipped and fallen on the ice and looking for its parent to soothe it. The air was thick with the aroma of hot tea, toasted tea cakes, hot wine and beer, fresh roasted pork and chestnuts and body odour, sour wine burped breath and the cold fingers of frost underneath it.

I could not say why but I felt more at peace sitting there drinking that rather indifferent cup of tea than I had in a very long time.

I would say that the cold never really bothered me, and that was true, it certainly did not affect me as it did my aunt or Sylvie, I was never chastened or worn down by it. Instead, it gave me a sense of ease and well-being. I understood the cold and that understanding was almost empowering. More than once I had been called frost kissed.

I hadn't been listening to what the twins said and so was a little surprised when they asked my opinion directly for what was clearly the second time. "I'm sorry," I said with a smile, "I do believe I was quite away with the fairies," those words meant different things when I had been a child at school. There was a fairy road and a fairy hill on the Fell Leaf estate so the London aphorism was not used in case someone thought you had truly been abducted. Almost without thinking about it I was tapping the little iron ring that I wore on my smallest finger against the cup.

"It was nothing important," Phyllida told me.

"We were discussing jams," Cressida said.

"Nurse said that the best jam for putting in tea,"

"Is strawberry," Cressida said that- even as she was pulling a face.

"And Mother believes it is plum," Phyllida was no more impressed by that.

"But we think,"

"And we're sure that you'll agree, Flora,"

"For we're so often of a mind of such things,"

"That the best flavour of jam"

"To add to a cup of tea,"

"Rose," I said, "Rose jam, if you can't get locum from Fortnum and Masons,"

Both girls looked at Nurse as if I had presented her with a burning bush or something equally divine. Rose was the best jam to add to tea, if you liked your tea sweet, I preferred the rose petals dried and added to the caddy, it was how Uncle Jack drank his and I had, in a fit of surly girlhood temper, insisted that I be treated like an adult and have tea the way that adults did for I was not in the school room right then. Uncle Jack had tried to hide his smile and told me "you are very forthright, Flora, and you have a will of iron, two things that would stand you in good stead if you had been born a man, unfortunately, it just means that now you get to be upset that no one will share with you the good tea."

To continue that tantrum I had taken his teacup from its saucer- ignoring the heat, and I scalded my tongue, drank it down in a few swallows.

Uncle Jack was both the Royal Sorcerer and a vain peacock who liked fine things, so he had always drank his black tea served with rose petals gathered from his own roses in his own house in Mortlake because he liked the very idea of such things. Whether he had been the one to think of such things - the act of adding jam to tea was directly practical, jam kept fruit fresh but used sugar, sugar was expensive and so wasting an entire spoonful in tea was just not good *ton*, as the twin's brother would have put it, a spoonful of jam sweetened the tea and saved the sugar. Adding rose petals to your tea was just a touch pretentious.

It tasted excellent though.

I could not have said why I found it so hard to concentrate.

When we had walked through the bustle of

the fair, between the boats frozen into the river and used as bridges - where the ferrymen had not thought to bring them up unto the banks before the Thames had frozen solid - I had been fascinated by the things around me but very much in the moment, but now it felt like my hair was full of dandelion fluff that might at any moment carry me away on the whimsy of something like the taste of locum melting on my tongue, sharp with mint the way that Aunt Jemima liked it. I knew that it wasn't Courtly glamour because I was wearing my iron ring but it was, it was like drifting to sleep on the most comfortable bed in the world, safe and warm with a heavy down comforter and a fire in the grate and every now and again you remembered you needed to be awake, to get out of the bed, to do things, but the sleep just pulled you back into that warm, safe, comfortable space. My thoughts were like that, dragging me into this warm, soft almost unconsciousness, where I made agreeing noises to the twins as they discussed the price of Indian muslins in the drapers that they had attended only a week past and how they were supposed to be buying satins to take to the modistes but they had been such a bargain and then their mother had been furious at them wasting their allowance - which was meant to be preparing for their season - on utterly unsuitable fabrics that could not be made into something that would snag them a good match.

It was almost like, as I looked at Phyllida, with her black hair and pale skin, that I could see into her mind and think that their mother would only be happy if they used the muslin to snag themselves a husband by tying it around him like a rope.

Cressida's resentment made the air around her sour.

They didn't want to marry, not really. Oh they did, they wanted the glamour of it, the season and all the men paying court to them to gain access to their father or their brother and wanted connections, or perhaps some young buck might fall in love with them, and they might like to be loved, it sounded delightfully amusing, but at the core of it was something that they could not share with people that were not them. They did not wish to be married, not because neither wished to never find a spouse and live alone in some country house they opened to the paying public like the ladies of Llangollen, it was not that they did not want children, for they had never thought about that, not really, but more simply that those things came after the truth of being married and what it meant to them - it meant that they would be parted.

They were twins, they had shared a womb, a crib, a nursery, gowns, toys, and even a pony. Everything about them was in the plural in a way that I, as an only child let alone a twin, could not truly comprehend. Since they had been aware of themselves they had been a "we", not "I" and being married meant separating them. There was the option, whispered between them in their bed late at night whilst nurse snored, wedging them in between the wall and her body pressed against the edge of the bed, that one marry and the other could come to live with them, then they wouldn't have to be parted - but that introduced a second divide - which would be the one to marry and who would be forbidden it. Such could only cause rancour between them where they had never been before.

They resented their season, they resented their mother, and even to an extent they resented me - because their season meant marriage, and marriage meant that the Lowell twins would become Miss Lowell and Miss Cressida Lowell, and twins became sisters, and from there it was only a matter of time before they were no longer the most important thing in each other's lives.

In that tent, with the frozen river under my feet, I could articulate the thought I had had but did not want to face about them and why they were often so vicious, and why I knew that there was no harm in it.

It was no different from me demanding to be served tea like Uncle Jack, an argument that wasn't an argument that was always going to be a loss.

My thoughts felt like, no, I felt like I was just like the river, moving sluggishly under the thick ice.

I ate my food without tasting it. I chewed without considering and made all the right noises to the twins, who gasped and gawked at a pair of redcaps ferrying large boxes across the ice. Small and squat, they had short stumpy legs and huge brawny arms, like they had been designed by someone who did not quite understand proportion, and carried boxes as large as they were on their shoulders, their faces gnarled like old wood and their hats glistening wetly. Such things as redcaps were not often seen and then in circuses and carnivals where they performed feats of prodigious strength like pulling apart rings of wood with their thick, leathery brown fingertips. They were twisted and dark, like oak stumps pulled from a field, containing multitudes in it, on its side on the mud and its roots, which had once been endlessly strong, reaching futilely at the sky.

The Courtiers were as different from each other as they were from the average citizens of

London. The Court of the Erl King was made from those members of Alfhame that would mostly live in the Undercity, the catacombs and tunnels that ran beneath the city and predated even its most ancient wonders. They were the twisted folk of bark and stone and the quiet of the dark. The Winter Court was the wisps of wind, of frost, the figures in the blizzard calling people out into the bitter endless cold. It was deep depression, ennui and malaise. The Summer Court was the beauty of flowers and frenzy, Summer was dry, relentless and madness. Only a fool thought that any Courtier, or whichever name they chose to use, was not to be feared.

And at their hearts were the Queens and the Erl King, forces of nature, the void, madness and the quiet creeping dark given flesh and will.

They were not human, and would never be human and it was very much a mistake to think them as such.

If the redcaps were carrying boxes it was because a Courtier more powerful than they were had told them to, and if some human stopped to jeer then they would learn why their caps were always wet to the touch.

It was in that mechanical reverie that I saw her, out of the corner of my eye, a child in a black winter coat and hand-knit hat from which perfect blond sausage curls fell. With a polite excuse that I needed to visit the privy, I excused myself to follow her. I did not know why Sophia was at the Frost Fair but the press was dangerous and it was getting dark. I didn't want her to come to harm. I might have been struggling to think, wondering perhaps if something had been slipped into my tea that morning, perhaps a few drops of laudanum, to make my thoughts so syrupy- like

cold molasses. I called to her and she didn't
answer so I sped up my steps, pushing through
the crowds to find her, and I should have
reckoned of the strangeness of it when she turned
back to see me following her and smiled.

Chapter Thirteen

I woke to voices and the security of being warm and in my bed where it was safe and comfortable and I did not yet have to climb out of my safe, warm, comfortable bed and into the cold room with its floors icy against my bed warmed toes even though thick socks. In the back of my head, someone was softly singing "London Bridge is falling down." Every part of me wanted to just drift back into that safe comfortable place where I had been before but people were calling out and shouting and I couldn't quite catch what they were saying and what I could made no sense to me. "Get back, he's frenzying," or "God's wounds, man, this can't go on," and then a quieter Welsh voice saying, "he's keeping her safe," as if it was a miracle and I had no idea what was happening outside of my window but I did wish that they would be quiet because I was trying to sleep.

It would only be a moment, I thought, that Sylvie would get out of the bed and go to the window to give them a piece of her mind, or several pieces, and possibly something thrown from the balcony.

London Bridge is falling down,

Falling down, falling down.

London Bridge is falling down,

My fair lady

The rhythm was soporific and soft and it was like fingers stroking my hair.

But the men outside my window kept shouting.

That couldn't be right, I thought, aware that I was thinking in a more reasonable way, and that I was starting to make chains of thoughts where before it had not much exceeded that my bed was warm and lovely and I wanted to stay in it and the voices were getting in the way of that. There couldn't be men stood outside of my window - my window overlooked the river. How could they stand there? The water was deep enough for boats to pass.

Off to prison you must go,

You must go, you must go;

Off to prison you must go,

My fair lady

But the river had frozen, yes, the winter was hard and the river had frozen thick enough to skate on. There was a Frost Fair. I had gone to the Frost Fair. How had I gotten home?

I couldn't remember and as I had these questions it was like another blanket lifted from my perfectly warm and comfortable bed. I started to fight against the lassitude and lethargy and forced my eyes open.

"Don't get up!" Lieutenant Jackson said holding out his hand, "stay exactly as you are."

Across the bridge of his nose and cheek were four perfect slashes, still bleeding sluggishly. I felt nauseous and like I might cast my accounts across the ice I was laying on. There was a figure between me and a few gentlemen that included Lieutenant Jackson, he was the only one I recognised but the figure with his back to me had silver claws on the very tips of his fingers that glinted in the half-light from the lantern that one of the men was holding aloft.

I was on the riverbank, the reeds and trash of the river pushed back by the encroaching ice and we were under a bridge, London Bridge? I wondered, was that why the song was in my head?

My hands hurt, the very tips of my fingers burning, and when I brought them around to look at them I couldn't help but cry out. The fingernails were gone and blood was splattered in furrows carved into the ice, some of them with my nails caught there. I had torn my nails out clawing at the ice, trying to dig something free with my very hands.

I didn't know why I would.

I didn't know what was happening.

I didn't know how I had gotten here. The twins would be beside themselves. How long had I been gone? How dark was it outside the tunnel? Who was the man who kept Lieutenant Jackson away; who had cut those four perfect slashes across his face with the sort of claws vampires wore to open veins in the hospitals, perfect little flechettes on their fingers - like the man in the tunnel was wearing? I wanted to scream but I couldn't. The scream caught in my throat like there was something there to catch it.

The vampire, and I did not recognise any part of him from his scruffy wool jacket to his blonde hair, was keeping me away from the people who were trying to rescue me, and had, judging by the slashes Lieutenant Jackson's face, used violence to do so. I remembered the word that I had heard as I started to come around, frenzying.

Even though I was still splayed out across the ice, with my fingers pressed to my chest, with no gloves or muff to protect them, I was doing my best to fold them into the opening of my pelisse and didn't care that I might be staining my coat, chemisette and gown doing so. I didn't even know if I was holding the blood away from a vampire who had lost its mind. He was frenzying. He had lost his mind the way that vampires had done on battlefields or in a place where the bloodlust was too much for them and they needed to be restrained.

But why would a vampire be wearing claws - the idea of a vampire biting someone was nonsense, it made a terrible mess where most of the blood went nowhere near where they wanted it so they wore claws- sharp as razorblades where they could, in hospitals or with doctors, bleed a patient and feed be frenzying as if he had not fed in months. They couldn't sicken so they worked in the poor hospitals tending plague or cholera or typhoid. They would slice open the arm of the patient and take just enough of the bad blood, and go to another patient, and another - so they didn't hunger. This vampire would have come from one of the hospitals, with a belly full of blood willingly given and consumed, and came across me on the river and stood between me and the river police, I assumed the two men in shapeless wool benjamin coats with Lieutenant Jackson were river police, they had the brown salt and pepper hair and immense black eyes, as far as I could tell in the terrible light that was failing more and more as the moments went on. Was he guarding a potential meal? I wondered, or had he decided to save me and didn't know that they could be trusted, that he was waiting for someone he recognised to unleash his duty so that the girl on the ice would not be sold into a brothel or murdered further down the river.

I looked at the furrows in the ice, deep as an inch in places, streaked with blood and ice I had scraped into a fine powder, dirt from the riverbank and broken reeds, and under the ice a shadow. It was small, wrapped in hessian, a little thing, an unremarkable piece of rubbish but I had wanted so desperately to dig it free. I had not had mind or wit but I wanted to free it from its icy prison and even now I wanted to dig, to break the ice and present that small jute parcel to the men, the selkie holding aloft the lantern and Lieutenant Jackson using the back of his hand, insensible to his white gloves and Thorne would have such a problem removing the blood, I wanted to give them it. I wanted to break the ice, to reach into the water and lift that small parcel. I had wanted to do it so badly when I was insensate that I had dug into the ice with my very nails until I had torn them free.

I was surprised to find that I was crying. I could only tell because the wind that whipped through the tunnel was sharper on the skin of my cheeks where it was wet. My mink toque,of which I was so proud, was askew and my ears must have been bright red from the cold and it was such a silly thing to think of but my hands were too sore to adjust it, so the selkies with Lieutenant Jackson were seeing me for the first time with my fingers torn to shreds and my nails ripped free and my ears bright as lanterns on my head.

"Flora," Lieutenant Jackson called out, "we've sent for your aunt, you're going to be fine, we're going to get you through this." He was using a sort of mollifying tone such as Lizzy used with her brother, or Mrs Lowell used for her awful dog if she had to doctor it for some reason. It was patronising and it irrationally made me angry. I didn't need petted and pampered, I needed plasters and bandages and a cup of hot tea. I wanted a chair and to let the Lowell twins and Nurse know that I was fine, and arrange to return back to my aunt's house so she didn't have to worry and let her know that everything was resolved. It was almost true. If not for the vampire who had come to my defence and now wouldn't let me be rescued from him, who snarled every time it looked like one of them would take a step towards me.

I did not know him.

I could not say to know many vampires. I knew Beausant who was a wicked mischief of an imp and so old the very earth ached at his steps. I had briefly been introduced to Louis Cho, a Chinese vampire who had known about the jade pendant that the opium sellers had sent to Lady Atwood and she had given to Major McConnell thinking it was useless, and he had given it to his superior, the Royal Sorcerer, who had given it to me because he saw no harm in it.

I did not know when I had taken that stone into my tattered hand, but I had.

There was a lot that day that I did not know. I was not expected to know such things. I did not know how I had come from seeing Sophie in the crowd, with her blonde curls against a black coat to kneeling on the ice trying to dig out the parcel there. I did not know what it was that I was trying so hard to extricate from the riverbank under the bridge. I did not know the vampire that was frenzying in my defence. I did not know the selkie who worked for the river police who was holding aloft the lantern. I did not know how Lieutenant Jackson ended up with those scratches across his face. I did not know why I kept grabbing the jade pendant, why it gave me such comfort and even with my fingers numb from cold but still so very sore that I pulled it so hard that the chain it was on tugged on the skin of my neck.

I did not know, not then, what the drumming was, until Lieutenant Jackson swore, a word that I should not have known but did, and asked rhetorically "Who informed them?"

The Witchfinders had made a procession of it. They wore heavy grey benjamin coats and black hats, looking interchangeable under their pennant which they held aloft like they were going into battle, their pace set by a familiar face under a shock of red hair playing a drum. Of them all I only recognised Penreith, the boy I had spoken to when I had been with Major McConnell on the road to Lady Atwood's house. He was the one who had informed me about the children found in the river and not the one taken from Lady Davenport's nursery. It didn't soothe me to see a familiar face under the banner of a red cartwheel on white surrounded by golden tassels meant to represent fire.

What attempts that Lieutenant Jackson and the river police were making to resolve this peacefully were collapsing under the steel grey gaze of what appeared to be a Witchfinder General.

He was a tall thin man with sharp features and a beard that was neatly trimmed around his mouth and chin in a style that was years out of fashion, and looked to be more the style of the restoration portraits that I had seen at the museum tours I had taken. There was a sour twist to his mouth and his eyes took in everything. He had a strong nose and wrinkles came down from the bridge under his eyes highlighting low cheekbones but a square jaw. He had been, in his youth, a beautiful man, but years and lack of care gave him a haggard appearance despite how well groomed he was. The men beside him looked to be carved from granite, such was the softness in their features, one had a Roman nose but all of them looked with such disdain that their gaze should have scorched the very earth beneath them.

Many Witchfinders, or those who supported them, wanted to defend the public from what they considered the weaknesses of the law where the magickal was concerned, they generally cared and worked with groups like the river police to make sure that the law was done, and that the guilty were punished but there would always be men like this who believed that they were doing God's work in burning out the magickal I knew how I must have looked to them, a girl brutalised by a vampire whilst the Tower did its best to protect the terrible beast.

From beneath the folds of his grey wool benjamin one of the Witchfinders, a lieutenant I presumed, pulled a metal device that looked not unlike the sort used to smoke bees out of the hive for the collection of honey and wax, a metal cylinder with a waxed leather spout, an affixed bellows and a small opening for a portable oil burner or a cake of burning spirit.

"Don't hurt him," I shouted, surprising myself.

Everyone turned to look at me.

The Witchfinders started shouting, barking commands amongst themselves like they were a military unit whilst Lieutenant Jackson and the river police lurched forward trying to put themselves between the vampire and the Witchfinders My shout had almost paralysed them into inaction but it only lasted seconds as the vampire leapt backwards so that he could better cover me. "See how the beast defends its meal," one of the Witchfinders said to Penreith whose steady beat on the drum had wavered.

The smoker was thrown at the vampire's feet where it released a cloud of sweet-smelling vapour that made me want to retch. For long moments the vampire wavered, hand to his face struggling to stand as he wobbled back and forth, before he landed hard on the ice in a heap with his claws underneath him and as the Witchfinders moved in, sword in hand, even as Lieutenant Jackson pulled out his pistol and shouted for them to stop, I couldn't quite comprehend what was happening. It was all happening so fast I could not think. But I was suddenly leaning over the vampire, putting my own body between their steel and the prone figure. It all happened so fast and I could not say that there was thought, I just did it. When I looked at the vampire it was like sometimes, not always, that out of the corner of my eye i could see red and black and white that were not there.

"The girl is witched," the witchfinder said with disdain, "she knows not what she says."

There were few things in the world that truly angered me. I did my best to be sweet and appealing and behave like the other girls, I liked dresses and jewels and shoes and how my hair was dressed but the witchfinder in that moment tried every part of my resolve and found it lacking. Without removing myself from being draped over the vampire to protect him I raised up my head, "I am not witched, sir," I said and I hoped my tone was one of iron, "or if I was, and am now no longer, it was not this citizen," I chose the word to remind the Witchfinders that this was a person subject to the law so that they might, for a moment, pause, "who did so, look at him, he is pinker in the cheek than even I with my rouge, he wears a leather apron and has clearly just come from Saint Thomas' hospital, defend your actions with the Rosmarinus, sir," I said, there was only one compound that could form a vapour that could paralyse a vampire, even one as pink and well fed as this one was. "Something happened here and whatever it was he frenzied to protect me, he has hurt none and certainly not I."

"Your hands, madam, tell a different story," the witchfinder general said, his voice was one of sneering contempt.

"Look at the ice, sir," I said, "something

happened and I was alone on the ice digging with my nails, those nails which seem to be in the ice even now. He came across me and he frenzied, look at Lieutenant Jackson, here to represent the Tower, he was bloodied only because it looked like he was threatening me. There is something here that needs investigating, something that caused a vampire to frenzy, that took me from the market to digging into the ice, to free that shadow in the ice," I looked across at it. "And the matter was in hand, sir, until you interrupted with your bully boy tactics, and now what was a simple task for the Tower has become one of assault for the courts." I glared at him.

"Move, girl," the witchfinder that spoke was not the general, this one was a wiry fellow with a rough voice and eyes like water that made my blood chill in my bones, "and I shall save you from this witching now." He had a sword in his hand. It looked to be an old army sabre with the surface pitted with age.

"You shall not," I said doing my best to sound like Lady Lowell, indignant and doing my best not to burst into tears. My hands hurt. My skirts were damp and the chill was bleeding through the fabric and my legs, despite the heavy stockings and layers of petticoats, were getting heavier with cold. I wanted to go back to my aunt's house, I wanted my aunt so I could cling to her skirts and let her take the strain of this. "I shall not let you kill someone who has worked so hard to protect me. If you must use that oversized letter opener for something you can use it to break the ice and find out what it is that whatever witching overtook me seemed so adamant that I find."

"Miss Peake," Lieutenant Jackson said in a quiet voice, one that was best suited to mollification and I knew him well enough, "I won't let them hurt him," he stepped forward, a brown greatcoat held open in his hands. I didn't know when he had gotten it, was it his own and offered to me now, or had some page or low level member of His Majesty's Dragoon been sent to fetch it for me? "you have my word on that.

Stepping close to me he coughed a little at the residual stench of the rosmarinus smoke, and draped the coat over my shoulders, "let's get you somewhere where you can get some medical attention. I promise I won't let them hurt him." He had put himself, with quiet, careful small steps between the Witchfinders and both the vampire and myself, "go with Mr Schaeffernacker," that must have been the river police officer with the lantern, I thought, "let's get you somewhere warm whilst we wait for your aunt and the axes to open the ice for you."

Chapter Fourteen

Mr Schaeffernacker had decided that there was no point in having this ongoing concern on the ice where I might lose a toe, those were his words, and moved us, Witchfinders and all, to a private room in a nearby public house. He ordered brandy for himself and Lieutenant Jackson, a hot posset for me, a bowl of hot water with a cloth for the vampire who had been protecting me, and left the Witchfinders to their own devices, except one of them, by the name of Watts, who he had arrested for assault chaining to a bench set against the wall.

My aunt was bustled in, complete with Mr Ogilvy, whom she had not managed to extricate herself from, which said much to his odious civility, and Lizzy who had fresh clothes for me, which were greatly appreciated, but I was not allowed to leave the room, even to change until everything was documented.

So my aunt was trying to stroke my hair and calm me/ Mr Ogilvy was doing his best to get in the way by insisting that he was an English gentleman and that all of this could be easily resolved - this was probably true but would be more so if he would leave - and me, with my hands in a pair of leather mittens trying my best to drink a hot posset from a porcelain cup.

It was all very much out of a farce.

Or it would have been if the Witchfinder gentlemen were not shouting about murderers and fair maidens, by which I assumed they meant me, and Mr Penreith, seeing me struggle, with my aunt doing her best to pull my head unto her shoulder - much more upset about the whole encounter than I - to drink my hot posset so I might get some warmth into my body, found for me a foot warmer that he got Lizzy to place under my skirts that I might rest my feet above the burning embers and asked the innkeeper if there was something else that I might find it easier to drink out of.

I didn't know if he recognised me as the page who had spoken to him only a few days before but he struck me as being the only Witchfinder who - to quote Sylvie in her description of a parcel of London gentleman trying to get back to their rooms after a night's carousing - knew his arse from his elbow.

The Witchfinders were arguing with Mr Ogilvy, Lieutenant Jackson representing the Tower, and Mr Schaeffernacker who represented the river police, and it was exhausting. It was not that the Witchfinders were in the wrong - they were - but that the whole situation was complicated and clearly magickal and they were convinced that the Tower would suppress the information of what was happening.

With the child murders that were the talk and worry of London with no answers forthcoming they felt more and more powerless and so saving a girl - me - from a vampire, who was not threatening me at all- allowed them to recover some face - even if no one blamed them for their powerlessness but themselves.

It was loud in that room, and my clothes were full of the cold, and my hands hurt and it turned out I had a nasty graze on my cheek and there was a vampire bound with Lizzy, as the only one in the room who could volunteer, doing her best to wipe the rest of the rosmarinus solution from his face and taking clumps of skin with it.

Rosmarinus was one of the more powerful weapons in the Witchfinder arsenal and they were protective of its creation and formula, but it not only overwhelmed a vampires senses, rendering them inert, it burned them like acid but did nothing to human skin. She went through a large pile of linen cloths before she was content that it was done. Then she was still wiping away the aftermath dumping used linens into a second bowl.

Then to add insult to injury, because clearly it was not enough of a pandemonium, Beausant opened the door and sauntered in like he was the King of England, with Mr Cho behind him.

In a room where everyone was properly dressed in quiet colours and neat tailoring, Beausant was wearing a Russian style great coat, made of scarlet velvet, with thick black sheepskin down the front, and collar and cuffs, cinched at the waist with a belt as wide as my hand. His boots, with a neat heel painted scarlet, were a brightly polished leather that came up to mid thigh showing a thin stripe of matching red pants. He had a black fur toque on his head and when he saw me he winked. Mr Cho looked like he had stepped out of a fashion plate in perfect superfine wool and yellow satin.

I heard my aunt curse under her breath.

"We come as representatives of the Collective of Our Ladies Below." Mr Cho said with a neat bob of the head. He looked like he was about to attend Almacks, with his wire framed spectacles the only part of his outfit that was not pin perfect, even his topper was freshly brushed beaver with a yellow satin ribbon that perfectly matched his waistcoat.

If Beausant was the dandy who made sure that everyone looked at him but was deliberately unfashionable to create comment, Mr Cho was the perfect gentleman and the illusion was only undone by his nationality - which I considered desperately unfair.

I believed that Mr Cho might be the mouthpiece of the Ladies Below but Beausant was a power move. He was old, older than Mr Cho, and he was feared. It could be that if the Witchfinders had not gotten involved that they would not have included Beausant and Mr Cho would have attended to this on his own, but Beausant was there and the Witchfinders went from open animosity to a quiet preparedness that was much more unsettling.

Beausant was the one who squatted on the floor next to the prone vampire and Lizzy who - to her credit- did not flinch when he touched her, telling her that salt would be kinder on the prone vampire's skin and she was to ask the inn keeper for some. The kinder he was the more the Witchfinders bristled and even Penreith, the only

one with any sense, put himself between
Beausant and me.

"By the order of Our Ladies Below," Mr
Cho said in the sort of diction that I imagined was
used for talking to the king, "I am to take custody
of the young unfortunate," his gaze flicked to the
vampire on the floor, "to see if we can determine
what it was that caused him to frenzy."

"He's a fucking vampire, that's what,"
Watts said, he was sat on a bench by the wall
with his grey greatcoat open to show a facsimile
of a military uniform, in the same drab grey with
an old leather belt crossing his chest from corner
to corner, he looked more like he belonged in a
portrait of Oliver Cromwell's chief officers than
in that tavern private room with a cup of tea in a
chipped china cup beside him on the bench. He
had agreed to a thin iron chain fixing his ankle to
the bench because he had been arrested for
attacking the vampire, but it didn't seem to make
him want to reconsider what he had done at all. If
he wanted to he would have taken the bench with
him when he attacked, but I knew, in the way
such things are deep in the bones, that before he
was standing that the two vampires in the room,
urbane and polished as they appeared, would
have pulled on their silver claws and turned
themselves from men of fashion to dangerous
creatures of the night.

"Young Master Martin here," Mr Cho said
in a quiet polite voice that managed a veneer of
such disdain that I could do nothing but look at
him in awe, "had just come from Saint Thomas'
hospital, in fact he was using the frozen river to
cut through under the bridge back to the part of
the city that is owned by his Lady Below, Dido,"
I didn't know the name, "and he is as plump as a
leech right now, if you would care to look you

can see the blood that is coming away with his skin. I trust the Tower has taken action against the one who assaulted him," he looked at Jackson in a way that had I been the one under his gaze I would have done my best to try and vanish into the floorboards. Lieutenant Jackson nodded and indicated the chain at Watts' ankle.

"I think it was my doing," Beausant said, "when I met Miss Peake several days ago I placed an obligation on her," Lieutenant Jackson nodded and I could see my aunt furrow her brows.

Mr Cho looked at the vampire, truly looked at him, in a way that I could see the inhumanity of him cross his eyes. "Yes, I see," he said, "Beausant's promise of protection would cause any vampire nearby to act in her defence whether they wished to or not, such an obligation is not unheard of, Martin is young, that could be the cause of his frenzy." He said it utterly matter of factly, "With such resolved I would like to undertake the second part of my instructions from Our Lady Below." He turned towards me, "Miss Peake, might I see your hands?"

I frowned and carefully with my teeth I pulled away the leather mittens to show the rough bandages that had been done. Large honey poultices wrapped each finger except my smallest which had managed to escape with only a broken nail. My fingers were ruined but it was nothing that would not heal, albeit with some scarring. He took my wrist and felt my pulse, checked my eyes and asked me to open my mouth. I did not know what he gained from this but he nodded. "Might I have some paper and a pen," he said, and Mr Ogilvy surprised us by being useful, having a small packet tucked into an inner pocket of his great coat below where it fell from his waist to his knee. It was not much more than the size of his hand but it was still more utility than I had given him credit for. I had a small packet of notecards in my muff but I had not seen it since I had been in the tea room. Penreith, again proving himself to be smarter than most of the so-called adults that surrounded us, pulled a pencil from the fob pocket of his ill-fitting waistcoat which was clearly inherited and did not suit him any more than it fit.

Mr Cho wrote something out quickly and folded two pieces of paper together to form a functional envelope then, pulling a pair of guineas from his pocket, he looked at Penreith, "here, boy," he said, ignoring the fact that he was with the Witchfinders, "take this prescription to this address and bring back what he gives you," he put the letter and the guineas into the young man's hand, "keep the change. It should be a quick run across the river to the address." Penreith flicked his eyes to the Witchfinder General, whose name was Hopkins, who nodded and he left quickly.

Mr Cho settled down with a cup of tea as Beausant helped Miss Donner peel the skin from the prone vampire, explaining it would be easier for him to heal it when it was gone than still poisoned, and the word poison he ladened with enough venom as he looked at Hopkins that the man should have turned to ooze where he sat. The room was surprisingly crowded. There was a small couch, upon which I sat with my aunt, in front of that was the prone vampire with Beausant and Lizzy and their two bowls of hot water, one clean and one not, on the wall with the door which led into the common room was the bench that Watts was chained to, the wall that stood kitty-corner to it had a fireplace where Jackson had taken over the one chair, Schaeffernacker had brought in a wooden chair from the common room, against the window on the last wall stood

Mr Hopkins, and in the middle of it, unsure what to do and definitely both out of his depth and unwanted, was Mr Ogilvy. I actually felt sorry for him.

Mr Cho had walked into the room and taken complete control as if he were royalty, but Beausant was older and should have been ranked higher in the politics of the vampire underworld where age measured power only behind that of the mysterious Ladies Below. Mr Cho did not take a seat, even when he had checked my hands and my health, or so I presumed, he had just bent before me, like a butler that would serve only Queen Charlotte. Mr Cho, I was learning, was the Islington cemeteries mouthpiece for the Lady Below.

"I have ruined my dress," I said to my aunt under my breath, "but at least I have not ruined my new boots." My aunt chuffed a laugh, my hands hurt and I wanted nothing more than a hot bath, but until everything was at least a little resolved I was stuck here. I did care that my dress was ruined; that I had lost my muff, and that I was sure my new boots could be polished up so it would be as if nothing had happened.

Unfortunately, that was when the two river policemen, axes and other tools still strung across their back, their faces ruddy with cold, came in and whispered to Schaeffernacker who passed the message on to Jackson. "Miss Peake," he said in a quiet voice, "I hate to ask again, do you know why you were so adamant in trying to dig up the ice?"

I repeated what I had said several times now. I had seen someone I knew in the crowd and the next I knew I was on the ice, fingers in the furrows with the vampire preventing the two officers coming to my rescue. I knew there was something under the ice but I could not say what it was, I only knew it was there because I could see it through the ice.

Lieutenant Jackson scrubbed his hand over his face, careless of the scratches that covered it from the vampire's one violent act which had been more to dissuade him than to hurt him.

"Miss Peake, Lady Haruspex, I am afraid we shall have to keep you inconvenienced a little longer."

"What was in the ice, Lieutenant?" My aunt asked as Mr Ogilvy erupted with complaints. Had Lieutenant Jackson not been one of his Majesty's dragoons I doubted he would have heard my aunt over the harrumphing and vocal slurry that Mr Ogilvy was intent in making heard that we should not be so inconvenienced.

"Lady Haruspex," Jackson was suddenly firm in his tone, sure that he was saying the words that they might be recorded correctly, "Miss Peake found a body," I thought of the size of the package in the ice and, in horror, I dropped the posset which fell to the wooden boards with a clatter, spilling liquor and custard over the rug that Lizzy was knelt on. There were only two options of what it could be and I wished hard it was neither - it was either a body part, necessary to life enough that they were set that the victim was dead, such as a head or a heart, or it was a baby.

How fervently right then I wished for the former.

Chapter Fifteen

After the revelation of what had been found in the frozen river it was decided that this would be best managed in the Tower where they had resources. This of course caused the Witch Hunters to complain, and the vampires, whose purpose there I still didn't understand, to bristle but the course was set and once Mr Cho had finished treating my hands, which he clucked over like an old hen, I was put into a carriage with my aunt to visit the Tower, and Mr Ogilvy excused himself.

I had been to the Tower many times since I had moved to London, both with my aunt and with appropriate chaperones, and once with just Sylvie. The Tower of London had a reputation even before it had become the centre of the magical world in England and, from there, a hub of power in Europe and the Americas. It had been a royal palace that became a prison with a grisly history of executions and the ravens which circled it, which had once been used to carry messages, were considered a bad omen.

For the most part the populace of England carried on as if it did not exist unless they absolutely had no choice to the contrary. Yet it

was a place of employment, those members of
His Majesty's Dragoons stationed in London lived
in the mews around the vast internal open spaces
that were used for drills, for carriages to come
and go, and as the favoured play space of the two
little boys I often saw frolicking on the grass.

Many of the Witches in England, who
often had houses apart from London - like how
Uncle Jack apparently lived in Mortlake near
Manchester - had rooms in the Tower, some
squeezed in between offices and work rooms and
more than one had a cot put down in his
workroom so he didn't have to leave his work for
something as simple and necessary as sleep.

The cellars of the Tower, some of which
had served as dungeons, had been changed into
libraries where magickal books were stored, but
also contained the workrooms of some of the less
well-accepted of the Witches, such as the Speaker
who could raise the dead - for about five minutes
or so - or the Bonesetter who could take bones
and turn them into works of beauty, statues of
bone that looked more real than those carved
from marble, but could also tell what a bone came
from just by touching it.

The vast majority of the Tower had been
converted into offices and workrooms where each
Witch had a small battalion of petty functionaries
who were all incredibly useful and were paid
well, and even more brown-clothed pages who
ran to and fro carrying messages - and yet, if they
were asked, none of the Witches who ran the
Tower could say what they did except when they
were absent that their lack was completely felt.
There were kitchen staff on each floor whose task
was to supplement their Witch's coffee diet with
something substantial and keep endless pots of
thick black coffee like tar on the stovetops or

hanging from trivets. There was even a department that managed the laundry of the uniformed functionaries and pages.

In the two centuries, give or take, since the world had learned about the Supernatural, the Tower had become a bloated mess of people who seemed absolutely necessary but had ill-defined positions and as such resembled the civil service of every existing government so perfectly it was assumed that they were one and thus they received a stipend from the privy purse for their needs.

My hands hurt and I had them tucked into a muff, not the one I had started the day with, and with my head on the wool-covered shoulder of my aunt I dozed through the journey. I was exhausted and I could not say why. Normally after something like the fair I was full of energy but I was exhausted and the slow rocking of the carriage on London's streets was enough to push me into a heavy drowse. My aunt wrapped her arm about me and let me sleep. My aunt and I were often at odds because I was coming into the age where I craved independence and to be able to make my own decisions and my aunt knew that the world was not the coddled place that she had made it for me and that acting without her put me at danger.

There were those my aunt trusted with my care, which was a very small number, and my ability to find myself in situations beyond my control that threatened that care scared her, which made her more strict which meant I pushed against her more. But in that carriage, I was the child that I had never been in her care, with my head resting against her shoulder and her arm around me.

Mr Cho had done a fine job with my hands, using his Chinese medicine to treat the torn-away fingernails and set the broken finger joints with glued-together strips of bamboo that he fixed to my fingers to prevent me from hurting them further, and then he pulled on a pair of thick woollen mittens, probably purchased or taken, from the innkeeper upon whom we had imposed so much in the aftermath. My hands hurt but in a sort of distant way that told me that he had used some kind of painkiller on them, and my aunt had tucked my head under her chin so that I could hear her heartbeat, strong and steady, as I drowsed.

I always felt safe like that, like nothing in the world could harm me, and that even if the carriage exploded into flame that she would protect me. Her love made me even more resentful towards whoever it was that was murdering the children and dropping them into the river, because they were taking them from that love, from that protection, and thrown them into the cold river to be buffeted about like trash. I didn't know what had happened that led me to try and dig that body out of the frozen river with my fingers but I was sure that had I been in my right mind I would have done it again.

When we reached the inner courtyard leading to the stairs my aunt roused me from my sleep and gave me a kerchief to wipe my face so that I looked more alert. "Flora?" she asked, "do you have something in your eye?"

"No," I said, blinking furiously in case I had a stray lash that looked set to get in my eye to irritate it.

My aunt frowned and made a disgruntled disapproving noise, "your eye is all bloodshot, I shall get the Astrologaster to look at it when he checks over your hands."

I had hoped that I might escape an appointment with the Astrologaster. The Astrologaster was a Witch of about the same age as Uncle Jack, who had the ability to correctly diagnose and treat ailments with the use of star charts as such he was the official Doctor of the Royal family but he was an odious man who had suffered during the plague years of the seventeenth century when non-magical doctors had done their best to drive him from the country. Those who had known him before his cure for plague said that he had been odious before then, he was a rat of a man with a small chin and a pointed nose that he managed to peer down everyone at. His name was Simon Formin but everyone called him The Astrologaster because he could not claim many friends among those who worked at the Tower and even his staff thought themselves superior to all of the other staff that served in the Tower because they served the great Astrologaster.

He was not the sort of man who ogled me or even had made any crass comments about my youth and my potential, he had always looked at me as a mystery that he was being prevented from solving because he wanted to know why I was a magical dud, his words, when I came from a family that had produced a Witch of the first water. He was sure that given total access to me that he could eventually solve it, it was just a matter of finding the exact star chart from the library that allowed him to explain and correct my lack of magickal ability.

So being taken up the stairs, led by a page, although both I and my aunt knew the way, it was not eagerness that I could claim. Disturbing him from his research without even an appointment made him even more sour. His secretary led me into the treatment room, sat me in a chair in front of the fire and told me to wait, that the Astrologaster would be with me soon, and then left us to wait - long enough that Lieutenant Jackson came to check that we had not returned home without being debriefed about the scene on the frozen river.

It took my aunt, following Lieutenant Jackson's appearance, storming into his office and slamming the door behind her. It was nice seeing someone else bear the brunt of her anger for once, and following it the Astrologaster came out to check my eyes and hands with his head hanging low like a scolded child. He looked like he had slept in the clothes that he was wearing and a gravy stain was on his lapel. I knew better than to ask what he was working on, even conversationally, not because he could not tell me but instead because he would berate me for daring to think that I could understand. This would have been true of anyone that he spoke to. I was too polite to use the words for him that I thought in private or only shared with Sylvie.

He checked over my hands, exclaiming that I had the sense to see a Chinese doctor for their blood clotting powders were the best that there were and he himself used several in his work, and he could not argue with the way my hands were strapped and then left me without the mittens so that everyone could see the ruin of my fingers. He called me a fool for thinking I could dig into river ice, which was in places two inches thick, with just my fingers and I really should have found a tool for there were many workmen who would have picks and even saws for harvesting the ice.

When he checked my eye he exclaimed it
was remarkable and sent his man, Smith, to fetch
his kit - that was the kind of man that the
Astrologaster was, he came to evaluate a patient
with none of the things that he needed to treat a
problem. From the kit he pulled a small dark blue
bottle with a glass stopper, "I am going to wash
your eye out with this," he said, "it will be
uncomfortable."

It did not hurt, which I had thought that it
would, but it was like I had suddenly produced
far too many tears and they all wished to escape
me on just one side in a torrent. He checked my
sight and exclaimed that it was even more
remarkable. He checked my eye with a loupe and
then opened his almanack to cross reference
something. He was more excited by the fact that
my eye was bloodshot than anything else since
we had come into his office. "There is no reason
for this," he said happily, "how remarkable."

How remarkable indeed, I had become a
second unsolvable mystery for him to fuss with.

I was rescued by Thorne who popped his
head around the door, "they're asking for you,
m'um" and that allowed me to escape. I
unthinkingly used my hands on the arms of the
chair to come to standing which caused pain so I
hissed as I stood.

"Please excuse me, Master Astrologaster,"
I bowed my head, "I am unable to stay, perhaps
you might find the reason in your books." I had
become excellent at excusing myself from

uncomfortable situations, I had learned it from Lady Lowell.

As I went down the stairs Thorne commented upon my appearance, "lass, you look like you've gone a round or two with a pug," he said, "I'll get you something cold to put on it, I am sure I can find a piece of beef to prevent it swelling."

"It was fine when she got into the carriage," my aunt said stiffly.

"I probably slept with a loose thread or an eyelash in there," I shrugged it off.

"You are meant to be presented to the queen in almost no time at all, if you did not wish to be presented this year, Flora, you could have said."

I shouldn't have laughed but I couldn't help it. I was exhausted, I had had people fussing over me since I had come around on the ice and it was all too much of a piece, it felt like madness and there was nothing I could do but laugh. It wasn't a hysterical laugh, it was just calm and easy laughter as if what she had said was the funniest thing.

"Come now, m'um," Thorne said, "I'm sure she wouldn't do things like cut off her hair, break her fingers, rip off her fingernails and black her eye just for that, it would be much easier for her to break an arm or a leg instead, much less work."

Even my aunt laughed at what he said. Thorne was a stout man with a face that looked like he had spent his youth as a pugilist and he had large shoulders that he had rolled up so that his head seemed lower, he kept his hair military short and had no facial hair, not even the large sideburns that were currently fashionable. He was the batman for the Dragoons and I got the impression he would be a fierce fighter in a brawl and, knowing that he was a werewolf, I had never felt threatened in his presence if anything I felt safe.

There were pages pelting up and down the stairs, carrying heavy books, scraps of paper and in one case a fresh coffee pot. "I'm always surprised that half of these boys are not in the infirmary with broken legs from having fallen," my aunt said.

"Oh, there's at least one a week that comes a cropper., They keep Madame Madrigal busy, she sets the bone, splits it, and then strips the skin off them with her tongue for wasting her bloody time - her words, ma'am, not mine - and not taking the care to see where they're going."

"Can't she heal the broken bone?" I asked.

"No," Aunt Jemima said, "she can set it, she can manipulate it, but she can't speed up the healing, and I'm sure that would be incredibly painful if she could."

"Just last month," Thorne said, "she untwisted the back of a young woman. Came here from Spain she did, and the Tower shook with her screams. She came in gnarled like an old tree stump and stood straight when she left. I had to hold the major back, he was going to break in and save the girl, and none of her bones were broken, she scared the ravens from their loft." He said this conspiratorially like he was sharing gossip, "wee slip of a thing, she was here for a few days. Funny name she had, Finch or Linnet or some other bird."

"Robin," I offered.

He shook his head, "it'll come to me, but it'll be after you've gone home and I'm up to my elbows in soapy water and I'll say it and the entire Dragoons here in London will turn and look at me like I was shot in the neck and saying things inspired by the drink."

"Do you often talk nonsense when you're in your cups?" Aunt Jemima asked with a smile in her voice.

"I talk nonsense all the time," he said proudly, "my cups just make me louder, I say strange and silly things and then fall asleep in my chair by the fire with my boots on."

"You need a batman," Aunt Jemima said with a laugh.

"Aye, that'd be the ticket." He answered with a wink as he opened the door to the sitting room which had been put aside for this meeting. It was on the main corridor and had its own stairway that led to the courtyard, possibly for the witch hunters to storm out of in a temper when they were thwarted in what they considered their rights in regard to the young vampire.

The room was dominated by a large and

heavy oak table with five sides, high backed chairs, and a fireplace large enough to roast a whole ox in. A comfortable-looking fire had been set in the grate but the room itself was a little chill because the fire was not large enough to burn the cold from a large stone room with old mullioned windows and doors that kept getting opened and closed. Any tapestries or fabrics that had once decorated the room had been removed and with it any insulation they provided. The table was close to the fire so the most heat from the fire could warm those gathered around it, but it was clear people had sat in camps, with the exception of Beausant who had found a leather chesterfield couch which he sprawled over like an odalisque in a painting. I wasn't really sure why he was there but he had found a leather ball and was tossing it up in the air and catching it as if he would much rather be anywhere but someone, probably his Lady Below, thought it important that he be there even if he was to be chaperoned by Cho.

The young vampire, next to Mr Cho and whose name I had not learned, was sat with their backs to the door, the young vampire, whose name I had not learned, and was wearing rough spun work clothes in comparison to the perfect superfine of Mr Cho. I had learned that they were not from the same coterie, Cho was from Bunhill Fields and the young one was from Limehouse. This raised questions but being a good girl of good standing it would have been incredibly inappropriate for me to ask them. As I understood it, I was only there to answer questions so that people who had the standing could solve the issue, even if it had happened to me and I desperately wanted to be included.

Directly opposite the vampires were the witch hunters, with Penreith sitting behind them in the armchair that had matched Beausant's couch, taking notes. He looked the most like he should be there, and on a wooden stool beside the fire was one of the brown clothed pages with his ankle in a split doing the same. They looked like peas in a pod and it made me want to giggle a little. The stern-faced witch hunters with this boy behind them with bright red hair, and his tongue peeking out of his mouth to the side like the stem of a pumpkin.

At the other two sides of the table were the River Police with their rain slickers draped over the back of their chairs and Lieutenant Jackson with a second Dragoon I couldn't remember the name of. "Miss Peake, Madame Haruspex," Lieutenant Jackson said standing up and guiding us to the table, pulling out the chair for me, and pushing it in when I had taken a seat. "What the hell happened to your eye?" Beausant asked, sitting up at a speed that was clearly inhuman.

"I think I got something in it in the carriage, probably rubbing at it with these," I said holding up the wool mittens, "It's been checked, and Master Astrologaster gave me something to wash it out, I'm told it looks quite nasty."

"Nasty, girl?" one of the witch hunters, the one who had attacked the young vampire, "it looks like someone tried to gouge out your eye."

"As I was told," I agreed, "but it does not feel irritated or angry at all, if I had not been told I probably would not have noticed." There was a cup of tea put out in front of the chair where I sat but I just folded my hands in my lap, I would probably scald myself if I tried to drink tea with my hands in mittens, that was something I could try at home with cold water until I got the hang of it. "I am glad that you all arrived with less drama than I did, I appear to be having a day for it I'm afraid."

"Nonsense, girl," the witch hunter said, "I think of us all you are the one who we can least hold accountable for what has happened today, unlike others," he glared at the young vampire, "bewitched as you were."

"Ahem," a young man said coming in, opening the door with his shoulder "sorry I'm late," he had his arms full of bits of paper and at least one pen, "it took longer than I thought to get away." He was tall and slim with a pair of wire-framed spectacles perched on a nose that turned up at the end, and a mouth I could admit that I envied, with dark hair and a few speckled mouche across his cheek, but most notably was a pair of brown eyes that caught the light in remarkable ways. "Nicholas Reid," he introduced himself and as he walked towards the chair, tripped over what appeared to be his own feet and had to catch himself on the table with his papers going everywhere.

"Oh, Colin," my aunt muttered under her breath. I had not met this Witch before but I knew that he was one with a surety, he was too young to hold any other position and neither in uniform like the Dragoons and Witch Hunters, or dressed as finely to suggest he held a position in court or the government. He wore a splattered leather coat that buttoned up the back with a linen cape over the front, so it looked like an Ulster Coat worn backwards, but was clearly a work coat. He had workman's trousers that came all the way to the ankle, and a pair of scuffed and battered black shoes so it seemed that tripping over his own feet was nothing new for him.

"Sorry," he said and pushed his glasses up his nose and, before he could say anything else, let loose a violent hiccup that actually rocked his shoulders.

"This is Nicholas Reid," My aunt said, introducing the hiccuping young man, "he is the Speaker and has been working with the Dragoons since the investigation began," he went to speak but instead just hiccuped "I should have seen this coming," my aunt muttered as Lieutenant Jackson, with a laugh explained.

"Master Reid has a nervous condition."

"He hiccups when he has to address young women," Beausant said tossing his leather ball up in the air, "I've seen it before, it's always hilarious. Why Miss Peake if you were to touch him his head might pop clear off." Beausant was boyishly handsome, his expression struck me as what a boy would have if he was trying to sneak frogs into your pocket or reticule but when he spoke or smiled there was always a flash of his fangs making sure that everyone knew that he was dangerous and he would always be the cat playing with the mouse.

Mr Reid gave him a truly nasty look across the table, "Beausant," he said with the sound of someone who knew exactly who he was dealing with and that the two had a long acquaintance. "Perhaps you would be hap, hic, pier with your ball, hic, if you took it to the, hic, yard."

"Or, hic," Beausant made the noise, "I could stay, hic, here, and see how, hic, long it takes, hic, for you to, hic, give."

"Vincent," Mr Cho barked the word out. "Enough." Like Mr Reid, he pushed his glasses up his nose but with thumb and forefinger at the arms which I had never seen before, "we are all here to discover the truth of the matter, not for territorial pissing or old grudges." I was glad that someone, at least, was taking this as seriously as I thought it should be.

"Dear gods, hic," Mr Reid said, finally looking at me, "what happened to your, hic, eye?"

Chapter Sixteen

I had thought, mistakenly it turned out, that getting all of the interested parties in one room that they would actually achieve something in the investigation, even with Lieutenant Jackson standing in for the major, but it was just several hours of uncomfortable posturing. The only thing that helped was that Thorne came in with an enchanted sachet for my eye and a patch to hold it in place so I made a joke about sailing the seven seas but the glare I received made it clear that my attempt to even slightly lighten the mood had fallen flat.

The vampires bristled at the witch hunters who in turn sniped at the Witches, and they blamed their uselessness on the Dragoons who had no one to blame but the River police, and the selkies were aware that they were only there because it had been Mr Schaeffernacker who had found me.

I repeated my story several times whilst they asked me the same questions which had the same answers, that I did not know what had happened between leaving the tent that served tea and talking to Lieutenant Jackson under the bridge. I did not even know how long it was that I was missing and had to be told that it was nearly two hours during which time Mrs Lowell had sent the river police to find me. I asked to make sure that they had been informed that I was well for they must have been out of their minds with worry.

I saw the charts that had been copied from the bodies, some random collection of magical sigils which everyone agreed were unlikely to achieve anything but Mr Reid, when he could speak for his violent hiccuping, said that whoever had done it had fully intended something to happen for the sigils were the same every time and the ink was made with a rare and expensive magical material used for inscribing household items so that they could be quickly activated. This included things like candlesticks so that they would light quickly and chamber pots that kept their surfaces clean.

The sigils looked like they should be some dark and terrible magic, like perhaps a demon summoning, but it was done with household magic.

I made comment about the demon summoning and everyone assured me that it was not possible and, when Penreith asked if infant sacrifice might not be, he was silenced before he could finish his sentence. This caused Beausant to guffaw and say, with his legs over the back of the couch he was lying on tossing the ball up and down, "There are enough things in heaven and earth, Horatio, than are dreamt of in your philosophy, so lets not go borrowing trouble against a future hurt." Then with a saucy wink at the young man he added, "from your lips to the devil's ears and all."

At the same time as Mr Cho barked out

"Vincent" Penreith said confusedly "but my name isn't Horatio."

	I wanted to say it was a misquote of a play but my aunt placed her hand on my arm and shook her head. I understood what she was trying to tell me, there were things worth getting involved in and male posturing wasn't one of them.

	They argued back and forth, made suggestions, gave fragments of information that the others might not have known, traded titbits and through it all Mr Reid rocked in his chair whilst trying to keep his hiccups under control. He was the one who had investigated the bodies and he was clearly very knowledgable in his area but he had an anxious response to my presence which he couldn't help no matter how many cups of water or frustrated suggestions were made to him.

	A supper was brought in, lamb chops with mint sauce and potatoes, but instead I was brought a thick potage of the same ingredients that had been cooked down to make it soft enough that I could eat it from a large tankard which I could lift with my palms if it was ungainly, with a brandy posset to follow. The vampires were brought a corked bottle each and a glass that they could drink. "I don't drink" Beausant said watching the page to see if he flinched, "wine."

	"It's port and brandy, sir," the page said without missing a beat, "enjoy." That amused me for it seemed the pages of the Tower were not easily spooked even by the creatures of the night. It made Beausant look a little silly for trying.

I could not say when I was excused, with my aunt as guardian, but I do know I had drowsed at the table for a short time for I woke with a blanket over my knee when my aunt told me it was time to go home. She made a joke about even the vampires finding it late and guided me with her hand in the small of my back to the carriage.

Leaving was a bit of a blur for me because I was so sleepy, and I slept in the carriage as well. I wondered if something had been put in the posset that I had been given or if it was just the strong alcohol that I could taste in it when I drank it.

I was still mostly asleep, my face cracking with yawns, as Sylvie prepared me for bed, taking off my dress and my petticoat before unlacing my stays and changing my stockings for thicker woollen socks and guiding me into the bed which was pre-warmed, either by a hot brick or Sylvie waiting for me with a book and a cup of spiced wine.

I slept until early the next afternoon and decided that I would be out to callers and spent the day in the house trying to find things with which I could occupy myself without the use of my hands, which proved to be more difficult than I had imagined that it would be. It ended with Sylvie sat with me on the piano bench turning the pages of a large book about the creatures of South America because it was the only one which would stay open upon the music stand.

I wanted more than anything to complain that the main thing that was preventing them from solving that most terrible crime was the fact that they all despised each other too much to actually work together. The only people who had reacted with any decorum was Mr Schaeffernacker who needed a card thanking him for rescuing me, perhaps with a small gift of tobacco or tea, and Mr Ogilvy because he had at least had the sense to excuse himself as soon as he could but still made sure that I was well to be left among such ruffians to use his word.

It made me wonder if I had misjudged him but then my eyes fell on the poise he had left for me when he had tried to call on me without warning and my good opinion of him soon vanished. In a crisis he hadn't felt that his manhood was threatened, unlike some of the others, but was still determined to court me in the hope of gaining access to Fell Leaf House. Perhaps a card was necessary, certainly nothing more.

"Sylvie," I asked, seemingly - at least to her - out of nowhere as she turned the page to a large and rather lovely illustration of a parakeet, "do you think I should send Mr Ogilvy a card after yesterday?"

Sylvie often looked most vulpine when she was planning mischief, "I could send it on your behalf," she said, "with your hands as they are." It occurred to me as I looked at her golden fox eyes that they were the same colour Mr Reid's had turned when the lamp light caught them the previous night which I had not thought that I noticed, tired as I was.

"Explain that you are grateful for him throwing himself at a frenzied vampire for you but at the same time it was such a reckless act that you certainly could not even consider his suit." I laughed, I couldn't even remember why Mr Ogilvy had done that, or if he'd just gotten too close. "Perhaps include a pressed flower, something as cheap as his posie." She turned her head to indicate the small nosegay in the glass bottle that my aunt had set on the coffee table in front of the couch. It was a motley assortment of flowers, the sort that could be bought from any flower-seller in London, even in November for no more than a shilling, and that was if they didn't haggle. I was sure that Mr Ogilvy had haggled. He seemed the type to see a forlorn waif in rags selling the most pathetic and bruised flowers and try to reduce the price. He had said something about that when I was in his church, that thriftiness was next to godliness or something, which I felt to be quite ironic considering his interest in me was entirely pecuniary.

I wondered for a moment if I was being entirely unfair to him but then I thought about his intent to try and court me before I was presented or to have my first season, and he had come to London to do it, and actively sought me out without calling upon my aunt, which was proper, and then made a point to speak to me when I was without my chaperone. Those reminders made my mind for me, he was certainly not worth my kindness, at least not then.

With boredom and the ache of broken fingers and the sharper pain of missing nails I quickly became irritable and nothing would ease my mood, not reading on my own sat on the piano stool with Sylvie, not Sylvie reading to me from the newest Porter sisters novel which she had just gotten from the lending library, not attempting to play cards which infuriated me more because with the mittens on I could not turn the cards and so Sylvie had to do it for me which meant we could not play games such as *vingt et un* or Boston.

My only respite was the bath where I could at least do something, with my hands kept out of the water but without the accursed mittens or eyepatch, and it made Sylvie make that disappointed noise when she saw my eye, "at least it hasn't puffed shut," she said, "even if these doctors are all nonsense peddlers if they can't even say what it is that caused the irritation."

Sylvie had helped with my bath since I had come to stay with my aunt and it made bathing possible in this state as she scrubbed a piece of linen with soap and used it to wash my legs and back. "You do realise," she said as she let one leg drop back into the water, having been cleaned to her satisfaction, "that every time I have let you out of my sight something strange has happened to you., I am not making that mistake again. You are not even going to the relieving room without me from now on," she tossed her braid with its curious white tip over her shoulder. "Between meeting Mr Odiously and now this I will stand by your side from now until Rapture if that's what it takes."

"Sylvie," I protested, "you can't stay by my side constantly."

She laughed at that with the invocation "just watch me."

My aunt had been out most of the day, probably dealing with the aftermath of the previous day, so Sylvie and I were left to our own devices which had not been something that had been in our favour. Disconsolate and bored I did my best to invent amusements for myself that I could perform with the mittens, which included making young Mr Donner laugh by pretending my mittens were animals who put on a show behind a free-standing credenza as if it were a puppet show. That had lasted a good hour until his sister, Lizzy, took him to be bathed and then to bed. Bobby was a bonny thing now that his cough had been cleared by the herb-witch and was happy with cheese on toast and cups of warm milk and nutmeg. Sylvie liked to stalk the baby, making sure he could see her as she darted between gaps in the furniture so that when she caught him she could blow noises on his stomach and caused him to erupt in peals of laughter.

It meant that after he had been put abed, with a door open in case he cried out in the night, and the house dark Sylvie and I had nothing to do but conversation. Having spent the day mostly reading we were not eager to crack open another volume and having already bathed between tea and supper there was a long period where it was too early to go to bed and too late to have other plans. So with more ease than I thought that it would take I told Sylvie about what had happened on the ice, or at least what I knew of it. I told her how I had been enjoying the frost fair but my moods were all muddled and my thoughts were strange and how, when I left the tent where we had been taking tea, I had the feeling that I had walked through a frozen cobweb when I saw Sophia and how I had wanted to return her to her mother.

"Was she the little girl you saw in Islington?" Sylvie asked.

"Yes, I recognised her quite at once," I answered her and queried further at Sylvie's quizzical look. "Is something the matter?"

"You've seen her twice," Sylvie said, and

pursed her lips, "once in a vampire cemetery and once at a frost fair and both times on her own; doesn't that strike you as odd?"

"As a child, I was often running from my teachers, I would complete my lessons and ditch my chores by running about in the woods belonging to the house," I told her. I had thought nothing of it, children escaped their guardians to play, I had done it so it had not struck me as odd.

"In the safe grounds around the house where you lived where no one was about, and what would Miss Featherby have done if she found you at twilight in a vampire cemetery?" I thought about it, she would be sure and determined in her punishment in an attempt to keep me safe. Even if you absolutely trusted the vampires, there was always the possibility of one frenzying or defying their Lady Below. Vampires were safest when you remembered how dangerous they were and kept that in mind. I would have been made an example to protect everyone.

Sylvie knew me well enough to recognise my expression and how I agreed with her on the matter.

"And what about a frost fair, where half of the Undercity was enjoying the freedom of opening stalls and walking with the rest of the city, you said you saw redcaps acting as porters, would you let a child wander free there?"

I agreed that I would not.

"So twice you saw her and twice she was unattended in places where she absolutely should not be." Sylvie was on the verge of a thought, "and you said when you saw the little girl in Islington Beausant interrupted you and she left," I nodded because that was true, "I," she said, "Flora, I think you might be haunted."

"Don't be silly," I told her, "ghosts aren't real."

Sylvie pouted and went to the kitchen to fetch us something to drink, muttering under her breath as she went.

Major McConnell called just before I was about to retire for the evening. He was looking for my aunt but Sylvie ushered him regardless, calling down the stairs that he was to be let in and to take his coat for he was to settle a disagreement between herself and me. So he came up the stairs to the sitting room, accepted a cup of spiced wine, and sat. He looked exhausted, like someone had drained all the energy from him and the simple task of solving a disagreement would give his mind five minutes rest and that was worth the effort. He had been absent yesterday and had probably spent the day trying to resolve the cacophony I had left behind me, although I had certainly not intended it.

Once he had drained his cup, and Sylvie poured him a second from the pitcher by the fireplace, he asked me how I was doing, having heard of my injuries, and I assured him that I was healing and there was not much I could do at the moment to hurry it along so I could not take notes for him for a while. I said that with a smile. I didn't want him to worry over me but it did make my heart do a little flutter that he had asked me and the image of him in his ruffled uniform, sprawled out, languid and leonine on the couch by firelight was almost scandalous. "Now, ladies," he said, "what is this disagreement?"

"Sylvie thinks that I am haunted," I told him.

"Ghosts aren't real," he answered without much thought.

"Says the werewolf to the fox," Sylvie said drily. Her entire posture was one of casual defiance, as if given the right provocation that there would be violence.

"That is different," he said, "if there were ghosts there would be proof, documentation."

"But there is," Sylvie exclaimed, slapping her fists on her knees in her excitement. "There are volumes of books,"

"Mrs Radcliffe's novels don't count," he answered.

"Ghost stories have existed much longer than Mrs Radcliffe has been publishing, there are even ghosts in the bible and that is certainly older than The Mysteries of Rudolpho."

"Enough," that was said with a growl which caused Sylvie to back down with a low whine that she clearly hated herself for. "There are no such things as ghosts or spirits, there are just people scaring themselves with shadows."

I wanted to be angry with him, even though he was taking my side because I did not like to see Sylvie in such a state - she was a fox and the image of a wolf trying to coerce her into behaving with violence made me want to throw the metal beaker I was using for the spiced wine at him and shout at how he should get out of the house if he could not behave like a guest - but before I could act he apologised and lowered his head with a sigh.

"I know you want to help," he said, "and it is not your fault that I am tired, I should excuse myself and have Jenner ring for a hansom for me. I do not trust myself to even walk home when I am this fagged, it makes my wolf come closer to the surface than would be considered good *ton* and I am easier to anger than I should be, so I apologise, Sylvie, I shouldn't have shouted at you like that."

She accepted his apology with good grace.

"Major," I said, "if," I paused, "and only if," I took a mouthful of my wine, with my hands as they were I couldn't take dainty sips, "ghosts were real would they explain the bells in the Davenport house?"

"If ghosts were real then yes it would explain it, but ghosts aren't real," he repeated.

"For centuries neither were werewolves nor fae like me," Sylvie muttered, "until they were, they'd always been there but hiding."

"You think ghosts might be hiding?" he asked.

"The Speaker," I offered, "Aunt Jemima said he could speak for the dead, am I right?" He agreed that I was, "but you or I cannot hear the voices of the dead the way that he can. Could it be that some people can see ghosts and others cannot?"

"You think that you are seeing ghosts?" he asked.

"There is an answer to that," Sylvie said clapping her hands, "we send for Beausant, if he saw her then she wasn't a ghost and if he didn't then she is and you have to agree."

With a sigh and the promise of a short rest in the warmth of the house whilst waiting for the vampire, the major agreed.

Chapter Seventeen

It was nearly dawn when Beausant finally called on us in reaction to his invitation. Unable to approach the house to even knock on the door, he was relegated to throwing gravel at the window of the lit sitting room where I was drowsing with my head on Sylvie's shoulder and my feet tucked under a blanket draped over the pair of us by Lizzy. The rest of the staff had gone to bed hours before. The major had moved down into the kitchens with the promise of making some lemon tea and had not returned so he wasn't present in the room when Beausant started throwing gravel at the glass.

He was dressed more suitably but had silver claws on his fingertips which I could see reflecting the light despite his black gloves. "You called," he said, floating above the street.

"There is a doorbell," I told him "and a butler."

"There are such protections on this house, my dearest *Berushka,* I couldn't open the gate to climb the steps to the front door." He answered with a bow, "It is flattering indeed when even the architecture thinks you're too dangerous to use the knocker. Is the Major not with you? I received word that he wanted to see me here." The Tower had means of communicating with almost all of the magical compounds in the city, I was not sure how they did it but it worked much better than sending a messenger, even had one arrived in Islington in time, by the time that word was sent back it might be too late in the day for a vampire to be abroad. They were creatures of the night after all.

He looked like he had been at the opera, in a black superfine and excellently tied cravatte, and like he had when he had called at my window before, had crossed his legs so the back of his overcoat hung behind him in the air. It was like he sat on a floating invisible cushion, level with the second story of the house.

"I'll get him," Sylvie muttered, rubbing at her eyes with the heel of her hand, and moving to the kitchen, "I think we lost him to the making of tea." She wasn't awake enough to make a lot of sense yet. The Major had excused himself to use the necessary and bring back tea, but I wasn't sure how long ago that was. It was possible he had put the kettle on the fire, sat down to wait for it, and drifted off just as we had. There was a cantrip on the kettle that prevented it from boiling dry so it could be kept there all day. Still, a comfortable chair, a place to rest his head - on his hand with his elbow resting on the worktable - and the heat of the fire with the security of knowing nothing could happen here, the house would not allow it, and sleep had almost certainly claimed him.

"I'd invite you in," I told Beausant, yawning into my hand, "but the house doesn't seem to like you much."

"I always liked this house," he told me with a boyish grin that flashed just enough fang to remind me he was dangerous and playing with me as a cat might play with a mouse. He treated everyone with that same casual malice so I didn't take it personally. "It has such stellar views."

I laughed, I couldn't help it. I knew I shouldn't but I found him delightful. I knew he was very dangerous, perhaps the most dangerous vampire in London, but he understood my sense of humour so very particularly that he made me laugh and understood my own rather saucy wit which often got me into trouble. My aunt had warned Lady Lowell when I was introduced to the twins that I was forthright and determined, which I later learned was polite speak for speaks her mind and as stubborn as a mule. Lady Lowell could silence me with a look and my aunt just sighed but, for the most part, I had learned to speak in the polite circles of the *haute ton*, I often skirted the line even if I didn't speak in cant like the majority of the city and young men who wished to be seen as separate from their fathers.

With Beausant I could be arch in a way that I could not with the Major, for he enjoyed it when I was saucy with him and it would not reflect poorly on my aunt that I spoke to him in such a manner. She was more afraid that he would devour me than that he would ruin my reputation. It allowed me a freedom with him that was different from anyone other than Sylvie.

"There's a pie and ale shop two streets over," he said, "I'll meet you all there. It's been a long night, *Berushka*, and I want to be in a public space to deal with the major, just in case." He winked at me. I was unsure if he meant that he might attack the Major or that the Major might attack him, or if both were convinced that the other would attack them and being in public meant that they couldn't, at least not without all of London hearing of it.

Sylvie bundled me up in so many layers one could be excused for thinking I was joining an expedition to discover the fabled North West Passage and not going a few streets over to a shop that was open all hours. Every time I thought she was done, something else was added to the layers until I felt more like the back of a rag merchant's cart than a person.

The fact that I barely felt the cold didn't seem to bother her as she unhooked a muff from the coat rack and thrust it at me, "cover those ugly mittens," and with that and the Major walking along behind us, half dozing and half ambulatory. He did not wake easily when his body was convinced that he should be abed, and Sylvie had to grab him by the arm to guide him muttering about him walking into the damn river otherwise.

Old Bailey's Pie Shop was an institution that opened at the same time as the bakery across the road and closed just after the local inns did. It managed a roaring trade by catering both to the early morning traffic of people on their way to work in the city, offering them coffee and a place to sit with their freshly bought Paris bun and a place to eat and soak up the liquor for people on their way home from the taverns. During the afternoon and evening, people returning home from work would call in, have a slice of pie and either coffee, kept hot in the kitchens all day long, or a nip of gin.

More than once my aunt had brought in half a cold pie from Old Bailey's for our supper when we were left to fend for ourselves by the staff. Yet I had never darkened its doors because I had never really had the reason to.

It wasn't full, but it was busy enough to keep the staff running back and forth with coffee pots, holding the handle through a folded cloth to prevent it from burning their hands, and topping up cups for the surly men who sat at the tables staring at the wood grain like it might, in lieu of the coffee which they drank sweet, wake them up enough for the day's labour.

Beausant had already gotten a table which he waved us over to. It was in the window and as such had a bit of a draft which caused the other customers to avoid it. Four cups of coffee were already waiting and a greasy bag of the Paris buns that the bakery sold as it prepared the rest of the breads for the day. The buns were still hot.

In the pie shop, surrounded by workers and the last of the night's drunks he looked even more out of place. I had a simple bonnet over my hair and, over that, a scarf which was tied around my neck and fell over the bonnet crown like an old French hood, and a thick wool pelisse over a functional wool day dress that I had been coaxed into by Sylvie. She had tucked her braid up under a wool cap and put on a blue pea coat and wool trousers with fingerless gloves and shoes so she looked like a young man on his way to the day's labour. Had anyone looked at her closely they might have realised that she was female but she affected the mannerisms of a man and as such I expected most of them to presume that she was my brother. The major was dishevelled but still in a recognisable uniform that caused people to take an extra step to avoid our table.

"So, *Berushka*, you sent for me," Beausant said. He was sat on the only chair at the table, there was a high-backed wooden bench into the centre of which I was squeezed and the major looked like if he put his head in his hand he'd fall asleep again - even as I thought it his face split with an almighty yawn.

"Are ghosts real?" Sylvie asked, "you're old, you'll know."

Beausant laughed. It was the sort of sad patronising laugh of someone much older dealing with what he had thought to be a serious business and finding himself inconvenienced for something that would only matter to someone much younger. The sort of laugh that could easily turn to violence.

"Sylvie thinks I'm haunted," I told him, "but everyone keeps telling her ghosts aren't real."

He sighed, "of all the nights to avoid the drunk cells," he muttered. "Ghosts are," he started, "you can't be haunted by a ghost, but a spirit can mark you."

"What's the difference?" the major asked. He was so tired his speech was more drawling than it normally was.

"A ghost is," he paused, looking for words to explain something that most of the supernatural world ignored, "it's like a memory a place holds of a person, so it might be a lady who lived in the house walking down the stairs."

"Or a maid scrubbing the kitchen steps," I said remembering what I had seen in Lady Atwood's that day.

"Yes," he said frankly, "I never cared enough to learn what the difference was or why, a spirit is," again Beausant paused, "lots of mythologies have spirits and many a vampire has benefited from manipulating those myths," he licked his lips in a way that showed the points of his little white teeth. He enjoyed being a vampire and very much enjoyed making others uncomfortable with the realisation that they were in the company of one. "A Rusalka, for example, can provide cover for missing people near a pond or lake in central Europe." He said, "but Rusalki are spirits that haunt lakes and drag people in, they are entities of rage and pain that are incapable of being other than angry and hurting of someone who drowned there in that lake or pond, often by murder. Spirits are the memory of the rage and pain of someone's violent death."

"Then you can answer if it's a spirit haunting Flora," Sylvie said leaning forward with both elbows on the table. I had taken one of the buns and Sylvie was breaking it into small parts for me to eat even if, now I had smelled food, I wanted nothing more than to put as much of it into my mouth as I could because I was suddenly ravenous. "When you met her in Islington where was she?"

"Alone on the bench," both the major and Beausant said and then looked at each other.

"I had a conversation with a little girl," I protested, I had.

"I saw you talking and wondered who you were talking to, if it was the trees or the flowers, people do that," Beausant said, "that's why I came across to you." There was a beat of a pause, "and to annoy him." He gestured to the Major who was quietly drowsing in his chair.

"I met Sophia on that bench, she was about five and she had blonde curls, she was there, and she was there at the Frost Fair, I saw her without her parents so I left the Lowells to make sure she was safe until she met them." I couldn't help but protest, I had a piece of the bun in my hand, "she was there."

"There was no one on the bench, *Berushka*, and no one would let a child wander off in a vampire cemetery," Beausant leaned forward, "and if the spirit is able to converse and make decisions it means they're new, you say she's about five years old," he left it open and the major spoke as I nodded my head.

"She might be one of the victims of the murderer we just haven't found yet." The major said it and I felt a chill go down my spine, it was like someone had dropped an icicle down the back of my stays. My stays had a comfortable tightness that made me feel safe and supported. I preferred long stays to short ones because the busk worked for my posture. It was the safe tightness of a close embrace and that information made it feel unsafe as if it was suddenly wet and cold against my skin. It was such a strange sensation I was not surprised when both the Major and Beausant recognised it on my face.

"She's got blonde curls," I said, "and a pair of boots that don't fit as well as they should. She asks questions, she wanted to know about my father and the roses. She told me she had a brother," I found myself in shock, telling them about her, the things she had told me that day in Islington. "She had so many questions."

Beausant picked up his coffee and drained it in a single swallow. "Spirits lose their personality the longer they are active," he told the table, "and that's when they become dangerous."

"She's already dangerous," Sylvie was irate at the idea that my haunting wasn't considered dangerous, but Sylvie had only to protect me, the Major had to protect London.

"Could a spirit go into a room warded against the fey and both vampires and were?" he asked and I could see the terrible logic of what he was asking. I could not help it, the answer was apparent and I could not help but see its terrible conclusion.

"Yes," Beausant said, "I know someone," he said it with an offhand matter, "he knows more about spirits than I do, I'll get him to send the information to the Tower."

"Can you stop her?" Sylvie asked, "if she's haunting Flora?"

"Every spirit has a weakness," he said, "it's a matter of finding out what kind of spirit and how it's destroyed. So yes, Fox, I think you're right, that Flora is haunted and right now that spirit isn't dangerous but it will be."

I looked at my hands, wrapped in wool, "Did she bring me to the riverside?" I had no real answers but I had broken fingers and missing nails and the knowledge I had been trying to carve a baby from the ice where it had been discarded like trash amongst the reeds, wrapped in an old piece of broadcloth like a swaddling blanket.

"It's an option," Beausant said, "but I don't know. Now, my dear *Berushka*," he lifted my hand and kissed the back of my hand through the wool glove, "I have to go before the sun gets too high, I'll send you what I know, Major, be assured, I like our little Flower, I'll help to keep her safe, not because I believe in your goals." He seemed to vanish in a wisp of darkness, his appearance only marked by the guinea he left on the table.

"Fucking vampires," the Major said and drank his cup down, and then, noticing I had no interest in mine, he drank it too. "Come on, ladies, I'll walk you back."

Chapter Eighteen

I slept most of the next day away, between the long night and the draughts given to me for the pain I collapsed into my bed and only climbed out to relieve myself. Sylvie stayed with me as much as possible, only leaving to get me trays of cold meats and bread that I could eat between periods of sleep where drops of laudanum were slipped into my tea. I needed the sleep and my hands had begun to hurt fiercely, the sharp pain of the missing nails and the dull ache of the breaks, but my aunt, when she called on me to put kisses on my brow and listen to me whine, agreed that that was normal.

I might have been wallowing a little more than I should have. I had liked Sophia and I was sure that they were wrong, that she wasn't a spirit and that she was fine: if wild and constantly running from her guardians. Beausant had said that she must have been new to have so much of her personality left but how did a vampire as old as he was measure the length of time? I didn't know what to do, so I attended my visit to the Astrologaster who was more interested in my bloody eye than my hands and made me keep the sachet of magical herbs against it held in place with my patch.

My aunt didn't mention my presentation again.

I supposed that she had decided to postpone it for another year. It was frustrating because it was something that I had been looking forward to since I had come to London. At school, it was something the girls talked of with wonders like the balls of the courts and the idea of dragons in Shangri-la and Shambala, or the Vodyanoi cities of the Black sea. They were things and experiences that they could only experience in books and it did not matter if they were real. They would gush over the latest fashion magazines and talk about what they would wear when they met the queen and how each of them would immediately catch the eye of a foreign prince to whisk them away to exotic climes where they were not the daughters of drapers or merchants expected to marry drapers or merchants.

Too young to be included, I had listened to them at night, gathered around a lamp, and wanted to be part of that. I'd wondered if, when I was old enough, I would be the one who would choose a scarlet wrapper or silver shoes, but then I had been taken from school by my aunt and within weeks she announced that I would be presented - just after my protestations that I could not do magic were verified by test after test after test.

Suddenly the saccharine dream of candle-lit balls and mountains of *amuse-bouche* on white linen table cloths and women in gowns dancing with gentlemen and reflected in the mirrors and the open doors to the winter gardens became a thing that I could have. I could bring my aunt a fashion plate and we could discuss which draper would have the best fabric, which modiste would be best to bring the fabric to, who would have the best options to trim it, would it need a bonnet or should I dress my hair?

It felt like being a character in a novel. I had been the schoolgirl learning her Latin declensions and practising her French conversation so that I would be prepared if I became a governess, and sneaking off into the woods every chance I got with my boots tied around my neck, my skirts tucked up into my belt and mud up my thighs with stockings tucked into my boots, to being the society girl who could have everything she wanted.

I had fruit flavoured ices in Gunters. I bought chocolate-covered dried fruit from a Russian vendor on Rotten Row between a milliner and a cobbler and ate them as I walked along, looking at the designs in the windows of the cobblers. I had beetled linen slippers in as many colours as I wanted, I had a tree of ribbons in different widths and an entire bushel of laces.

Yet because of what had happened; because my hair was short; because my hands were a ruined mess and my eye was full of blood for no reason any doctor could find and I was wearing an eyepatch, my presentation was being delayed to the next year so that I could heal and I was angry and frustrated, most of all because I understood.

A girl lived and died by her reputation and mine was already shaky because my aunt was a Witch and because I lived in the Witch House and my abigail was a fox who had spent too long in the summer court until she couldn't remember what shape she was meant to be, because I knew the members of His Majesty's Dragoons because I was on speaking terms with vampires. Had I walked through the British Court in the throne room to stand before the queen with my hands strapped and my eyepatch and short hair I would have been ruined before I stepped through the door.

It was not a refusal to have me presented but a postponement and I wanted to throw a tantrum - to wail and whine and throw things but it wouldn't change anything so I didn't. When my aunt told me that I would not be presented with the Lowells and that they would have their first season without me I reacted numbly, fumbling the cup of chocolate that I had been drinking, with careful palms and what fingers could bend cupped around it gingerly, and spilling it down the front of my day dress. I didn't even curse. The chocolate was cooler than I usually preferred but, with my hands, giving me boiling liquids was asking for trouble as I could not pick them up by the handle.

"I shall have to have a napkin tied around my neck like little Bobby," I said trying for levity.

"It is fine to be upset," my aunt said, "I understand that being presented to the queen is something that you and your friends were looking forward to," my aunt calling the Lowell twins my friends said that she was trying to appease me. "But we can spend the season somewhere warm, we could sail to Venice and travel upwards through Italy and sail around the Iberian peninsula and back to London that way. We could return in the late summer. A change of location would be good for us both."

A year ago I might have leapt from my seat with excitement at the promise of visiting

Italy, of seeing Milano and Fiorenze and Verona and all the places I had read about. I could even practise speaking Italian which I had been starting to learn when I left the school. I would be a flutter with the promise of new travel dresses, new boots and bonnets, and knowing that my aunt would spoil me throughout the entire journey. I would return for the next season in the height of Italian fashion, with new jewels made of Murano glass beads that clattered and caught the light more beautifully than even diamonds.

I would have that European polish. I would have learned how to behave in balls in a country where I didn't need to stand so carefully on my reputation as I danced with *Conte* and *doge* and *chevalier*, I would learn how to be witty, how to politely refuse when my dance card was full and how to snap my fan like the patronesses of Almacks.

Instead, I excused myself to take off the ruined dress.

I couldn't decide if I wanted to cry, throw myself face-first unto my freshly made bed, or destroy something. All I knew for sure was that I wanted out of the house. I felt like exploding like I was a munition that was on the verge of exploding but hadn't and was just waiting, a potential explosion but I was not one yet.

Everything was so out of my control that I made the decision that I would go and get those boots that I had seen when I had lost Sylvie and been accosted by Mr Ogilvy. I called for Sylvie that I might change and explained what my plan was and she agreed and was excited about the idea of chocolate-covered prunes that had been soaked in brandy which was her absolute favourite.

I insisted that Sylvie join me in the cobblers despite her protestations that I didn't need more shoes. This was incorrect as one can never have too many shoes, or boots, or slippers. It was the cobblers that were, despite doing nothing, entirely to blame for all of the things I was suffering now because it had been the one that I had stopped outside and lost Sylvie due to the altogether ridiculous poke bonnets we were wearing so she could not see that I was not beside her when she continued on. The boots in the window were as wonderful as I remembered them to be. They were oxblood red leather with an Adelaide blue nankeen upper, the buckles which tightened them about the ankle were decorated with dark red silk tassels and the whole thing was trimmed in dark red silk.

I had talked myself out of wanting the boots after everything that happened for they were a silly indulgence and it was unfair for me to have such a silly indulgence when so many others were suffering so fiercely with what was happening with the river and the children.

Then I had my presentation cancelled, my fingers were broken and my nails torn away - which hurt more than the broken fingers did- and my eye was red with blood under the patch. My hair cut as short as a page was a whimsy, something that could be explained as being a follower of the wrong sort of fashion, or covered with a wig. Short hair, hands bound with strips of bamboo and capped with fabric lined caps that looked like thimbles held taut by chains and an eye patch was not the sort of thing one could cover with just following the wrong fashion setters. I would have been welcomed more if I had the mumps and my face was swollen to look like a turnip, and infectious.

I was allowed to be hurt by it, and I was
allowed to take my anger out on my pocketbook.

       The man behind the counter took one look
at me and paled., "Sir, the boots in the window," I
said with my biggest most genuine smile, "would
it be possible to be measured for a pair?" I had
my hands tucked into my muff and as I pulled
one out I made sure my miser's purse came with
it. A miser's purse was perfect for a muff. There
was no room for much of anything in a reticule,
but a muff was like a bag carried on straps around
the neck, a square of fur and silk with the sides
fastened to keep the heat in, but it served as a
place for a lady to carry everything she wished to
in winter and keep her hands warm.

       It was not done for a lady to carry a miser's
purse with her, it was like a sock sewn shut at
both ends with an opening in the middle and two
rings that which served to keep the contents at
each end and which could be slid to gain access
to either end. My aunt had knit it in a rare period
of wanting to learn a craft and as such was poorly
made with uneven beading, but it held coins well
enough and I liked that it was something she had
made with her own hands.

       A misers purse did not usually land on a
counter with the heavy thump that mine did, I
was sure.

       The cobbler called out to his young
assistant who was responsible for the new design;
he had gone from wary to effusive as he fetched

me a stool, and asked me if I needed a hot drink
on this cold day. It would be the work of a
moment to fetch me some spiced wine, he assured
me. and I heard almost none of it as Sylvie said,
"oh my," as his assistant walked out from the
back room, sweeping his hair from his forehead
with the back of his hand.

The assistant was only perhaps a handful
of years older than I was, with black hair that was
in need of a cut, but he was tall and heavy set,
with biceps that strained the rolled-up sleeves of
his shirt, and a neck that I could not have put both
of my hands around. He looked like he belonged
in a forge in a fairytale creating mythical
weapons as he tucked a red kerchief into the
pocket of his leather apron, and when he saw us
he had a shy smile that made his black eyes
twinkle. He was handsome but not in the way that
statues or art was unless the art was by
Caravaggio, but his looks made everyone turn
and look, almost as if such people were not
supposed to exist in reality.

My mouth went dry looking at him.

"If you'll excuse me, miss," he said,
getting down to his knees before where I sat on
the stool, and Sylvie muttered something I hoped
that he did not hear about the muscles on his
back, "I'll need to be measuring your feet."

His hands were like slabs of wood and yet
they were so soft as they lifted my foot up onto
his thigh and unbuckled my boot. "Miss Peake," I
told him.

"A pleasure, miss," he said with trained
manners, "I'm Rodric Benevente, you like the
boots in the window, yes?" it was clear he was

under instruction to make small talk with the customers and he was as comfortable doing it as a cat in a boiling pan. "I designed them."

That was all the information I needed to unload about the boots and how I had hummed and hawed over buying them for weeks but, after my accident, I was determined to get them and with my eagerness he became easier to talk to, suggesting different colours not that I might buy more pairs of boots, although I am sure he would not have refused such an order, but because no one wanted to talk to him about these things.

We had a lovely conversation about shoes, about carving lasts and how the leather felt under his hands, and he was strikingly handsome, built like a barn but with careful fingers and perfectly trimmed nails, and he had a shy smile like a sun peaking out from behind a cloud. I had never met anyone like him, a shy and lovely brick of a man capable of shouldering his way through walls and with the deft touch of a Court embroiderer stitching phoenixes onto mist with happiness.

I had not considered the Major to be handsome until the idea was presented to me by the Lowells, and then I could not help but look at him with eyes that needed to understand what a husband would provide and what his hands upon me would feel like that there might be equity in the marital home.

Beausant made me laugh, he was cruel and powerful but he knew my sense of humour to the extent that he always made me laugh and his boyish face expressed wicked delight and the points of his sharp white teeth sat comfortably on his lip when he smiled.

Mr Reid had been handsome in the sort of classic image of Acteon or Endymion was, tall and lithe without being rangy like the Major, but with square shoulders and slim hips. He looked at me over the bridge of his glasses with a smile that devolved into hiccups and I liked having that power over him, that he was so nervous in my presence that he could not prevent himself from hiccuping in every statement he made and making those around him mock him in a way that should not have cut the way it had.

Penreith was earnest and determined and he had a line of freckles across his nose and bright red hair that marked him out of a crowd.

Rodrick Benevente was like none of them.

He told me about how his family had moved from Italy when his mother was just a baby and he mostly kept to the Italian areas of the city, but he gushed about how his Nona made pastries and ran a small restaurant for the locals because they could not always get the things needed for their recipes, which apparently had been bounteous in whatever parts of Italy they had left for London and when he spoke of them an accent I had not noticed stained his words, giving them an exotic flavour in his gravelly voice.

I could have listened to him talk all day, as he tried on different boots that they had in store until he found what he considered the best pair for me. Sylvie sat on what was his work stool, being bench height, and drank spiced wine as she tried not to laugh at the entire scene as it played itself out in front of her.

I was sad to leave the shop as I paid for

three pairs of boots and another to come, asking for them to be sent to my aunt's house with the address printed on a card I pulled from my muff, and I watched Rodrick's ears turn bright red as I asked for them to be delivered, reassuring me that he would be the one to call, with his arms full of the wrapped packages.

After the door had closed behind us Sylvie butted her shoulder against mine in a way that told me that she understood everything. "Where to next?" she asked, "perhaps the drapers, you'll have to get a new dress to go with those fur-lined boots, you don't have anything in that light purple, and, yes, the fur is white but if you wear white with them you'll just have randomly blue feet."

"I thought we could go to the library," I told her.

"We're nowhere near the Tower," she answered looking around for a hansom to flag down. The street was full of carriages and other people shopping, sometimes stopping in little enclaves to gossip that blocked the street. Shopping was a community act where the newest information was traded as people were measured for dresses, and shoes or purchased trimmings like lace or ribbons that could be tacked on to a dress to make it look new.

"They wouldn't let me near that library," I said with genuine disgust, "I'm not magickal, remember?, I probably would have to carry an actual lantern among the stacks and the Librarian would have conniptions at the idea of oil and fire amongst his precious books. Let's go to the British Library - , because if the magickal world thinks that ghosts and spirits aren't real they won't have books on them, but the British Library will, because it's not as close-minded. It probably has books on mythology from all manner of countries." I raised my nose to suggest that I was learned and aware of what I was doing, when really what I wanted to do was prove Sylvie wrong - that Sophia wasn't a spirit, that she wasn't dead.

I wanted to prove that whatever had taken over me that day at the Frost Fair had nothing to do with Sophia.

Chapter Nineteen

The British Library was not a lending library, but more of a repository for books that were considered important for scholars who lived in London to be able to access in some manner. Over the centuries since its inception it had grown and sprawled with a mish mash of architectural fashions and was ran by an army of librarians who brought the books to the people who needed them.

The librarian who came to Sylvie and I had an expression like he had just bitten down on a rancid lemon and was expected to keep the juice in his mouth. Tall and thin, like a knobbled willow branch, in an unassuming brown suit with glasses sliding down the hook of his Roman nose and narrow squinting eyes. "This is not the Euston lending library," he said from behind the desk. Other librarians came and deposited books in piles and crossed off requisition sheets and did not seem in any way to be surprised by the pair of us. We probably would have looked more at home in the magickal library under the Tower, being the niece of a Witch and a Fox who had forgotten that she was not a person in the Summer Court, but we were in the British library instead.

"That's good," I said with a crisp tone, "I wanted to be at the British Library," I smiled at him. I could imitate Lady Lowell's condescension to a degree that often had the twins in fits of laughter. I had never thought that I might need it in my day-to-day life. "I am hoping to do some research, and I'm told that this is the best place to do it."

"We don't carry the fashion papers," the librarian said, using a rubber stamp to mark a piece of paper with a thump that was meant to be a final dismissal. I didn't know what purpose this served other than driving away potential patrons.

"I don't want the fashion papers," I told him, "if I wanted the fashion papers I could find any newsagent in the city. I am hoping to find the answer to an academic hypothesis," I was pretty sure that that was true. If not, it sounded correct.

The librarian raised a grey eyebrow, "I doubt that you gained access to university." That was true, I was both too young for further education in the universities and a girl and they were excluded from such places unless they had a warrant from the Tower which I wasn't likely to get.

"If I had access to a university library I would not be here," I said, "and I am not the only woman present, so I am forced to conclude that another librarian granted them access to the works that they wanted to study." I took my hand from my muff and placed it on the counter, with its strange creation of brass thimbles held in place with chains and the bamboo strips glued to my broken fingers with gauze.

He recoiled as if I had put a snake on the

counter. "As you can see," I continued, "I am recovering from an accident but academia waits for no man, so I have engaged the services of an Amanuensis." I gestured with my head to Sylvie, "You might think we are only here to duck in from the cold and have no idea of the purpose of this building, but I can assure you that I am in the right building and you are going to help me," I leaned a little forward towards him. I had to look up at him a little. "I need whatever books and papers you have on spirits, specifically child spirits and those associated with rivers and waterways."

He scoffed again, "ghosts aren't real," he stamped the paper again.

"I never asked if they were real," I said as firm as my aunt when she thought she was being shorted and was not in the mood for such nonsense, "I asked for you to bring them to me that I might find the information that I need."

"Why do you need them?" he asked, and tugged at his cravatte which sat perfectly in a pedestrian knot. He was used to driving women out of the library I figured.

"Because they have the information that I need," I answered, "must I ask to speak to your supervisor for you are being singularly unhelpful and I would hate to tell The Haruspex that you have stood in the way of her research." The reference to my aunt's title caused the colour to run from his face like I had opened a faucet and let it drain. He opened the leaf of the counter, walking out through the newly made gap, and asked the two of us to accompany him to an empty work table.

When he turned to leave Sylvie snickered under her breath, "I shall never tire of watching you do that," she said, "he needed to be taken down a peg or two."

It took him some time to bring back some basic books, a collection of myths from Scandinavia, Greece, Germany, and some from North Africa. "When you have more information of what you want to look into I might be able to find more." He handed me a handwritten page with the titles that he had put down and asked me to sign it, smirking, Sylvie signed it for me, and, that done, he went back to the counter with the hope to never see us again. The slip of paper was to prove that none of the books would find their way into my muff which was large enough to hold at least two of them.

Sylvie picked up the book on the top of the small pile, "so what are we looking for?"

"If she is a spirit," I told her, "she will be freshly dead and not buried in consecrated ground, she'll be a victim of murder and restless."

We were quiet for a short while looking through the books for things that matched our rather vague description., "Here's one," I said turning the book to show it to Sylvie, the page was titled *Wiederganger* and showed a fleshy skeleton rising from its grave and surrounded by stone crosses. "It's also called an *aufhocker*," I told her, "and finds people who will avenge its murder and bury it in a churchyard. It kills those who can't help it. That seems to be a theme, most of them kill those that can't solve its problem, it's probably why Beausant said that they used the myths before they could feed openly."

From the small notepad Sylvie kept with her, with its own little silver pencil, she tore a page and stuck it in the book, "we'll bookmark it and see if we can find something more specific." She scribbled the name down on what was now the top page before going back to her own pile of books.

"This one," she said showing me the page, "is babies who died in stillbirth or immediately after, they can become protective spirits if you bury them under the threshold of the house where they were born." The image would haunt me for days but I didn't know it then. It was a horrid twist of a child, so unlike little Bobby that I wanted to gag.

"I don't think that fits," I said looking through the book of Greek myths and finding very little, "I think we can rule it out."

A few pages later she patted my arm to get my attention, "A *myling*," she read it out, "a child murdered by its parent who seeks out people to get revenge and to give it a Christian burial. A lot of these things seem to want a Christian burial. I think we should find out why so many of them need to be put in a church yard to go quiet. It makes it sound like there are a thousand women at this moment strangling their babies and burying them any old place. These ones get heavier the closer they are to the graveyard and when they can no longer be carried they strangle the carrier."

"These ones are dumped in the river," the

page was labelled *Nekker* and had a terrible woodcut of a child, a toddler really, waist deep in the water with its teeth open as it called out, but there was something wrong with its skin, as if it was a sock that was far too big for a foot.

I didn't want it to be true, I didn't want Sophia to be like that terrible creature in the water. She was small and pretty with blonde curls and a gap in her smile. She wasn't a child sized horror wearing the skin of the victims it dragged into the water to be fed on later, like an African crocodile, with it's cache of rotting food.

We took that notebook back to the house and were quiet in the carriage as we returned. My good mood from the cobblers and Sylvie's delight at the candies was gone, washed away by research I should not have done. Sophia was a Nekker, I thought, a child spirit bound to the river and endlessly bringing more people to the water's edge to try and assuage and endless wrath. It was a horrible thing to know.

I changed when I got back in and, I asked Sylvie if she could draw me a bath. I felt grimy, like I had had bog mud ground into my skin but no one could see it. I couldn't manage my buttons or the laces of my stays and I wanted to cry, more than anything. I hated the idea of Sophia being that terrible thing in the book that I had seen, the Nekker, but it answered so many questions. The Nekker lived at the river's edge and mimicked human calls, often that of a child asking for help, so it could take out its rage and pain on those kind enough to answer its call.

But Sophia had sat on the bench in Bunhill Fields with me. We had talked about the plants. She had not tried to hurt me. Then when I saw her at the Frost Fair I had lost nearly two hours before I had come to on the ice where I had tried to dig into it with my bare hands and a young vampire, crossing my path before the River Police had, frenzied to protect me.

I couldn't remember the young vampire's name.

I think I wanted to be sick. I wasn't sure, it was like the gorge wanted to rise but the body denied it.

The child in the ice, the one I had tried to excavate had been wrapped in cloth. Had Sophia done that in the last moments of her clarity before the rage and hate took over completely. I didn't know.

That was the problem. I didn't know.

All of the so-called grown ups, the Major, my aunt, the Tower, Lieutenant Jackson, all of them wanted to keep me out of the investigation but Sophia had brought me in. I didn't know why. I had been taken to Lady Davenport's to prevent the scandal of her missing child for as long as we could. I understood that. I had gone to Bunhill Fields because my aunt thought I could do with punishment and the major thought I could take notes. Beausant gave me information that the others wouldn't., I clutched the jade pendant I wore, the one that the investigation had dismissed and that Beausant had said was a protection marker from the opium dens, that they would take Lord Atwood's place with his wife making sure his debts didn't destroy his wife. They had said it was a ghost marker.

But Sophia had appeared before they had given me the marker. She sat with me on the bench as the Major talked to Cho about what the token was and it was only after it had been dismissed that Uncle Jack gave it to me. I couldn't say why I took such comfort from it but I could say that it was not the reason that Sophia had spoken to me.

I lay in the water and I tried to look at it from every angle, if I could find a chink in the story that would prove Sophia alive and wild, wild as i had been but the woods of Fell Leaf were secluded and private, where a child could be wild - the same could not be said of central London.

I didn't realise it at the time but the jade token, which I hadn't taken off as I did with most of my jewellery, my ear fobs and any other pendant that I wore, any bracelets or bangles, had found its way into my mouth where I was sucking on it thoughtlessly. I never took off the ring that the Winter Queen had given me, or the iron band on my smallest finger, and with the contraption of chain and thimbles on my hand I couldn't have removed anyway. I kept the jade token on, and I lay there in the bath with my hands clear of the water, sucking on it as I considered all of the terrible things about the children in the river and the Nekkers.

I blotted out the terrible memory of the Davenport house and the women weeping there, with the jangling bells and the broken clock. Could a Nekker do that? I didn't even think of it just in case that they could. Perhaps Bunny Davenport had nothing to do with the babies in the river. I didn't know, and everyone was doing their best to make sure that I did not become involved, not because I was incapable of such things, but because I was going to be a society girl., I was going to wear fine gowns and laugh at bad jokes to catch myself a husband and no good society wife served as an investigator for the Tower.

I was between two worlds and that meant no one knew what I should be. Least of all myself.

I had no magick, not even the simplest spells or cantrips sparked under my hands. I could stitch a protection sigil into a sheet to stop it needing darning as often but someone else would have to bring it to life. Even the least girl in London could trace a shape unto her cup to reheat her tea and I could not.

But my aunt was a Witch, I knew many of the people who served in the Tower. A Witch-hunter would destroy me as quickly as they would my aunt, and I couldn't even make a poultice that would speed healing.

I was neither the society maiden, sweet and innocent with nothing in her head other than catching a good husband, or the Witch who was protected by their magick. I was just Flora and that meant I stood between the Tower and the non-magickal world with the protections of neither.

I could not stay out of the investigation when I could help or conveniently forget what was happening in the face of pretty gewgaws.

Chapter Twenty

I knew the package on my balcony was from Beausant even before I opened it.

After my bath Sylvie had wrapped me in a sheet, enchanted to be warm, and to wick away the water before I put on a fresh shift and robe which had been warmed by the fire the traditional way. She helped me put on a pair of thick stockings and we decided to sit in the library which had a little snug surrounded by bookcases and a fireplace. At some point, someone had put a pair of armchairs there which were covered in blankets and seemed to embrace you with their softness. It was the best place to sit and just lament the winter and was one of Sylvie's favourite places to try and hibernate- even though foxes weren't animals that hibernated. She went to the Tantalus and opened it to pull out the decanter of brandy and poured two glasses.

I was ensconced in the chair, with my legs tugged up under me, my eyepatch left by the bath and the glass of brandy tucked into one hand when I opened the package.

It had to be from Beausant. No one else

would scale the river side of the house to leave a small package on the balcony where it might be overlooked and was only found by accident when Sylvie went to throw out the water she had used to wash my hair into the river. She had nearly tripped on it, which would have seen her tumble over the railing and into the river. It had nearly happened once before and so now she was much more careful which allowed her to catch the railing as the jug went flying into the water below.

I hadn't seen it, but I had heard the copious cursing and learned a few new words as she came in, thrust the parcel at me, and went "you have awful friends."

I emptied my glass of brandy before I got up to find a letter opener in one of the drawers of the library so I could open the parcel.

Beausant had said he knew someone who knew about spirits. It was likely his informant was better than what I had found in the Library but I didn't know what to do, I was all over the place mentally, almost choking on denial so that I could choose to believe that Sophia was still alive.

I didn't want her to be dead.

I didn't want her to be responsible for what was happening with the children found in the river.

There was a small box with a pair of simple bracelets, the likes of which I had never seen, covered in some sort of strange writing I could not read and a tag fixed in place with a string that said "tell your fox to put these on you,"

with a picture of a ladybird. I moved them out of
the way to lift out the book. It wasn't in English,
but it did use letters I recognised. There was a
pair of silk bookmarks in the book but I put the
book down and had Sylvie pour me more brandy.

If I didn't read the book it wouldn't be true,
I told myself.

And I knew better than to accept gifts from
vampires.

I woke up with a sour taste in my mouth
and an ache behind my eyes but other than that
my adventures with excess brandy had left me
unscathed. The first time I had done it I was sick
in bed for two days and promised never to drink
whiskey again - which I held true to for the very
smell made me nauseous. I was able to tuck into a
generous breakfast and felt well enough to notice
that my usual companion, Sylvie, seemed to be
missing and I was being served by Lizzy who
blushed as bright as her hair when I suggested
that she help me finish off the platter of coddled
eggs. She told me that it wasn't proper and I
assured her that this was not a house where
proper changed many things. If she was hungry
then she should sit down and make herself a
plate.

She still refused, saying that she had eaten
before starting her duties.

She was the sort of girl who, with proper
grooming, would have been considered pretty.
She had a thin face with a pointed chin and dark
hair that she kept neatly pinned under a cap, but
she was clean and the clothes that had been found
for her were well laundered and mended and even
her apron was a bright white. She did not have the

advantages I did but even in the short time she had served here she had gained a healthy glow to her skin and the dark shadows under her eyes were gone.

When I got up to clear away my plate she made protestations but I was not so disabled by the injuries on my hands to be unable to lift a plate and cup and bring them over to the serving hatch. It was only a few steps and I had been doing it as long as I had been in the house, and in Miss Featherby's school before.

"Lizzy," I said turning to her, "do you have any duties today that could not wait?" Without Sylvie here my plan to go shopping again was thwarted, I could send a card to the Lowells announcing that I would call in the afternoon but it gave me the morning to myself, and it was certainly something to pass the hours. Sylvie was right, the boots that I had ordered the day before with the fur trim had nothing to accompany them and I needed to visit the drapers and modiste. It would give me a more pleasant topic of conversation to share with the Lowells than any I had recently had.

"No, miss," she said with a clumsy curtsey, "Cook has taken my brother to the park, she thinks he might like to see the ducks and Mr Jenner said that he had nothing for me today, I was going to just work on my knitting," she bobbed her head. She didn't think I should know that she had liberty despite that this house had run like a well-oiled machine before she had arrived and all she had done was aid those who ran it.

"Then all is well, you can come with me, I need to go to the drapers and I have no idea where my chaperone is at the moment, so you can stand in for her. Do you have a winter coat? Or shall we add that to the list of things we need to collect when we're out?"

I admit that I dismissed any protestations that she had, bundling her into one of my winter pelisses and giving her a heavier bonnet to go over her cap and Frangipane gloves whilst she protested that this was all too fine, that she would be well with her shawl but I didn't listen to a word of it as Jenner opened the door to the bracing December day and the waiting Hansom cab. I had no idea how it was that he was always able to procure a cab for anyone who wanted to leave the house and I was far too polite to ask.

I bussed Lizzy into the cab and told the driver to take us to a well-renowned draper who I knew would have a cotton velvet that would match my boots exactly for they always had what I wanted long before I knew I wanted it.

A lot of what happened after that needed to be put together after the fact.

Lizzy had lifted the bracelets from Beausant's package when I was fumbling with my coat and, in the carriage, she exclaimed how lovely they were. They were a bronze colour in the light and the etching looked like a particularly fine form of language that I could not read. In the daylight they looked almost gold and shimmered with an inner glitter that I knew was the magic in them. "They're probably for protection," I told her dismissively, "but it's not proper for me to accept such fine gifts from a gentleman, it could be seen as a proposal."

"You can't marry a vampire, miss," Lizzy told me, "they're not allowed by law, on account of them being dead and all, he's just a friend, it's

all he can be." I don't know why that caused a
pang in me, probably that I was sorry for
Beausant having his eternal unlife without even a
wife to ease the centuries. That was why I held
out my wrists for her to put the bangles on me
with a final click and she also fixed the safety
chain. "In stories vampires always like giving
gifts, they have a lot of things and not much room
in their coffins." She was so earnest as she said it
I could not help but laugh.

We arrived at the drapers and paid the
hansom and I explained my injuries with the
same old lie about being in an accident which I
had done ice skating. We laughed about the
silliness of it and so close to my presentation,
made small conversation that Lizzy accompanied
me and not Sylvie, and the draper took me into
the back room - with the door open - to look at
the new fabrics that they had delivered just the
night before and were still in the process of
putting on the main floor.

After that there is a gap and I cannot fill it
in.

The draper remembered us clearly leaving
the store but Lizzy maintains that she stayed in
the store for nearly half an hour before she
realised that she had to raise the alarm, running
back to the house looking for a parish officer as
she did so. She told Jenner that I was missing and
then he contacted the Tower who sent two of his
Majesty's Dragoons to the house to find out the
details of the disappearance.

They were thorough and Lizzy gave them
every detail that she could, a process hampered
by Sylvie returning and learning of my
disappearance and questioning Lizzy much more
fiercely even as she scented the air looking for the

perfume I favoured. Neither Lizzy nor the werewolves found anything other than the story that the Draper was sure of - that the two of us had left hours before and that I had ordered a particularly expensive blue silk that would not flatter me. My aunt paid for it regardless.

I woke up sprawled across an old bare wooden bed with a threadbare shawl draped over me. I had been stripped down to my under things, which comprised of a long sleeved shift, my stays, and two petticoats, one of which was bodiced and buttoned up the back. I had my stockings but my garters of all things were gone which meant that when I got to my feet to figure out what was happening they pooled around my ankles. The room was chilly and I was unsure if I was being watched so I made a point of pulling the shawl around my shoulders as if I was cold but I didn't really feel the cold. It was an attic room with a small dormer window where one of the panes was cracked and let in a wicked draft. The plaster had been white washed years before and here and there were cracks large enough to put my finger in and the floor was swept but the floorboards were grey with age and lack of care, where years of scrubbing with soap and water had long since lifted any protection the wood once had. There were no rugs or furniture other than the bed and although there had been a fireplace it had been boarded up.

With nothing else to do, I made a point of trying to pinpoint my location from the window which was on the left of the room as I faced the door. The river was on the wrong side of where I expected it so I was south of the Thames, assuming that it was that river I could see peeking through the high roofs of the houses packed around this one. There was a courtyard around a central well that had a brick paving and arches led through the houses and a few trees here and there that were stark and dark against the darkening sky. If not for the lights on the river I would have not been able to see it at all.

I had left for the drapers with Lizzy in the late morning with the intent to be back in time to change to visit the Lowells, for the indigo nankeen dress that I had worn for shopping was certainly not suitable for tea, and now it was nearing dark. This late into December, that put the time at four or five - my watch had gone with my clothes so I could not be sure, although my jewellery remained intact except for my ear fobs - so I was missing perhaps six hours.

I had been undressed not because I had been robbed but because it prevented me from leaving. A girl such as I would not be seen abroad in such a state of undress, they thought, especially without shoes where her feet would be torn to shreds by the rough London streets.

I was also on the wrong side of the river as the Witch House.

I didn't know why I had been taken and why it was that I couldn't remember it. It certainly lent credence to the idea that the same thing that had bewitched me on the river at the Frost Fair had reached out to take me again.

Sylvie certainly had a point in that every time she let me out of her sight, even for a minute, bad things were happening to me and the thought, uncharitable as it was, made me laugh but even I had to acknowledge it was a manic sound. I was in the attic of a strange house on the wrong side of what I guessed was the Thames, even though there were seven rivers in London that I knew of, in my underwear with no idea who had taken me or why. Perhaps it was someone trying to use my aunt, I thought, but I knew the answer deep down. It was the same person that led me to the river bank where I had ruined my hands - or the same spirit.

I had spent days convincing myself Sylvie was wrong, that I wasn't haunted, but more and more it was looking like not only was she a spirit but she was a very dangerous one and that she was the one responsible for the children in the river. The book said that Nekker lured their victims by pretending hurt or distress in the hope someone would come to their aid where they would overwhelm them to drag them into the water.

What was such a spirit to do if the river was frozen as the Thames was?

Chapter Twenty-One

I sat on that bare bed in the attic room as the dark settled through the city. The strange clarity that had swept over me in the Frost Fair, the way I could understand things I did not want to vocalise, was upon me and I did not know what it meant, only that I pulled my knees to my chest, with my petticoats covering them, and tugged the shawl around me as I felt that I should. It struck me as important that I should be perceived to be suffering from the cold when in truth it was not even chill enough for me to wish for longer sleeves on my shift instead of those that came to mid forearm.

I found and used the chamberpot, covering it with the supplied cloth and leaving it by the door.

When I was a girl, at school, I had once gotten myself locked in the attic whilst the adults and girls shouted looking for me and unable to hear my responses as I banged on the window. I had sat there in the dark amongst the abandoned furniture and I waited. At first, I had explored the paths and twists of old chests and heaped furniture, but ultimately I sat there next to the door until someone came to open it again.

They had been more scared than I had been. I remembered that.

That unerring clarity that overwhelmed me on the Frost Fair, the one that was probably had something to do with the bewitchment that had brought me here, meant that I remembered that afternoon so clearly, sitting in the dark, listening, waiting for someone to make a move that I could respond to.

I played with the bangles that Beausant had given me, that Lizzy had clipped on my wrists that morning, turning them against the skin, clattering them against the ones used to hold the thimbles in place over my fingertips, and tracing the strange designs. I turned the ring that the Winter Queen had given me as a child and remembered being the little girl in her shift with mud all over waving at the Winter Queen's carriage with such delight that the Winter Knight had smiled at me and in gratitude I had been given a ring in a walnut shell box, one that looked just like the Winter Queen's carriage in miniature. I twisted the iron ring that was meant to keep me from Courtly magick. I was sure I still had them simply because who ever had taken me had been unable to take them off with the magic holding the thimbles in place or they would have been taken with my pearl ear fobs and gown.

Sitting under my breast, although I was unsure when it had gotten there, possibly working it's way free of its chain when it was taken from me, was the small jade pendant, and it felt natural and right to have it under my heart. My stays were keeping it both secret and in place, although the chain had never been long enough that it could have found its way there of its own accord. I chose not to consider it.

I had nothing but time and cold and even the smallest distraction helped pass a minute, a quarter hour, an evening.

I chose not to sleep, I would wait and outside I could hear the bells of a church ring out the hour, though I had not seen a church when I had checked the horizon from my small window.

It was gone ten, judging by the pealing of the church bells, when the door opened and a maid holding a lantern unlocked and opened the door.

At first I had no words for the maid, not even to describe her to myself, because the sight of her left me speechless.

There are many spells one can find in penny grimoires, useless things requiring impossible ingredients that promised grand magicks, I should have realised that the same person who had drawn the sigils upon the children before dumping them in the river would use all the magic that were written in those penny grimoires.

The maid was a woman in late middle life with her hair scraped back into a neat set of pins and she wore a dark dress that by the lamplight was black, but her fingers were covered in black marks scraped into her skin and embossed with ink and her lips were sewn together with unicorn hair. It was not a quick whipstitch that had been used but instead the more vicious ladder stitch that would allow her master to open her mouth enough for her to eat.

Unicorn hair was expensive and imported from the Courts. It was not the actual hair of unicorns but instead a type of hare, or at least that was what it resembled most, with long hair like an angora rabbit, but strong enough to be used in construction. Whoever this maid served, and she could not tell me who, had paid a fortune for even the single hair she had used to stitch her lips shut. It was not magick, just the trappings of it. The maid's eyes were hateful and I could not blame her for it. I didn't know why she stayed, no wage was worth what i could see to have been done, and I was sure that there was much more under her dress.

I knew, in that bizarre and absolute clarity, that she was not compelled to stay, at least not by magick.

I followed the maid down the tight stairs where they turned into a bare corridor, the walls had been washed with a pale blue but were too far from the rooms that someone showed publicly that there was no paper or fabric on the walls, and the thin carpet runner was moth eaten and full of mouse holes in places.

I said nothing.

I noticed the sconces on the walls and how they were empty and, when she led me into what I imagined to be a sitting room, the only light source was a thin fire under the mantle where brass vessels, polished to a bright shine, threw the light around the room and the small dining table that was there.

I could see brass candlesticks on the table

but they were empty and a large bowl was full of wax fruit, covered with dust on a much darned tablecloth. A plate had been set out for me, with a large lump of gristly meat in the centre of a pool of gravy. The silverware was well polished and caught the light like orange lines in the darkness. I turned to the maid, "I'm sorry," I said, as I sat in the chair she pulled out for me with a heavy screech against the wooden floor, "I can't eat this."

I could not have said how I knew she was displeased but I quickly corrected myself, I held up my hands with their thimbled fingertips, "my hands, I can't use a knife at the moment, is there something like soup instead." The maid, I didn't know her name and had no way of getting it from her, near snatched the plate from the table causing the silverware to clatter against the wood.

She closed the door behind her and I heard the key turn heavily in the lock. I wasn't sure where I would go, the only light in the building I had seen was her lamp and the fireplace, I had been stripped to a state of undress such that and my modesty was only covered by a thin shawl, and outside I knew that it was snowing. I had always been good at telling the weather in midwinter.

I sat there by the fire, watching the wood spit and crackle as it burned. It was a thin flame, a few faggots thrown on there almost as an afterthought to warm the room and the heat from it did not spread. The room's windows were unshuttered and each had a whitewashed sill covered in old bottles of different sizes and colours that had probably once held the sort of potions sold by the same people who sold the penny grimoires. I knew I was in the home of a witch, but not one with any real power or learning.

All I could do was keep paying attention, notice the little details and wait.

Lizzy would have returned to the house and told Sylvie and Sylvie would have gone straight to the Tower to tell them that I was missing. My aunt would insist that the Dragoons look for me and by now their search would be well underway. I wasn't sure how far werewolves could track scent but I knew that they were relentless. They would not stop searching for me.

I hadn't realised then that the multiple threads of their investigations would come to a knot where I was. There was what I knew and what I would not admit to be true.

In the thin heat of that room I felt sluggish and that eerie clarity I had had in the empty bedroom was fading, I was falling asleep, I told myself. The heat and the scant comfort of the chair, with the quiet of the winter night, but I snapped back to attention like a soldier when the door opened. Before me with a clatter of a pewter plate against wood the maid thrust bread and cheese. I thanked her as if she had given me the finest meat available in London. The bread was stale and the cheese had formed a hard rind but I was hungry so I ate every bite that I could pick up with my mangled fingers and was glad of it.

Many of the young ladies of London would have refused the meal on a matter of principle, of how it was beneath them, but I had never had those pretensions about food. I had bought food from street vendors and oysters by the plate from taverns, dropping the shells on the path as I walked; roast chestnuts sold by men next

to burning stoves and put in small paper bags
stained clear by grease. I had bought them once
when I was shopping with the Lowells and both
the twins and their mother looked at me as if I
had gone mad and started speaking in tongues as I
lashed about on the pavement holding up the
traffic.

After I had eaten and drank the cup of
water that I was offered afterwards, I followed the
maid back up the stairs and returned to the bare
bedroom. "Before you go," I said as she turned to
leave, "my shawl, could you help me?" I had been
struggling with it, normally such a shawl was
crossed across the bosoms and tied behind the
back so it stayed in place whilst leaving the hands
free. It was how common women wore it, ladies
who bothered with shawls had lengths of soft
Kashmir wool with designs of the seed of life.
They could not be tied off in the same way, they
were left with their ends at knee length and the
shawl hanging loose down their back to frame
their hips. I lifted the point of where the shawl
was folded over so that she could reach the ends
and tied them tight around my back and I thanked
her as politely as if she was the queen of England.

The maid started and left, slamming the
door behind her and fumbling the key in the lock.

Sitting on the floor of the bedroom, barely
visible in the thin moonlight that came through
the snow and the frosted windows, was a small
child with bouncing curls. She was sat with her
legs akimbo and leaning over something she was
drawing as if the room was bright as noon, and as
she did it she sang "London Bridge is falling
down".

I had not thought that I would see Sophia
again.

I knew that she had taken me. I knew that there was no other option for how I had gotten here. But there was still that small flame of hope that I was wrong, that she was not a spirit, that she was alive and well and that Sylvie's wild idea was just a wild idea.

When she saw me she dropped her coloured waxes and smiled, then without losing a beat of her song she covered her eye with her hand and grinned, "my fair lady."

Chapter Twenty-Two

It was not yet daylight when the owner of
the house returned in a clatter of doors and a
shouted command for Sarah, which had to be the
maid, and loud braying laughter and another door
slamming between me and the noise.

I had not slept that night.

I found it difficult when what was sat on
the floor was quite clearly a spirit, for no child
could sit like that, so still as not even to breathe -
a perfect counterpoint to how she had been in
Bunhill Fields when she had kicked her feet and
bobbed her head and spoke in a sing-song
fashion, asking questions and clearly animated. It
seemed all she could do now was sit, coloured
waxes in her hand and sheets of paper between
her spread legs as she repeated over and over, in a
sad ululation the song "London Bridge is falling
down."

There comes a point when, no matter how
deep your denial, no matter how deeply you want
to believe a thing to be true, you are faced with
the stark and absolute truth that you are wrong
and your hope is shattered. With that sundering,

and I use that word deliberately because it is not an easy thing to learn, comes a deluge of emotions but, right then, the one I felt the most was a fear that made even me feel the chill in the room.

Her hand remained over her eye as she sang, and it did not escape my attention that the eye she covered was the one that had been left bloody and striking to everyone who saw it no matter what medicine or magicks were applied to ease it.

My aunt's library was never closed to me, if I picked up a book it was never taken from my hands and she relied on me to regulate my own consumption of books, even if sometimes the house would have an opinion- a book left open on a table for a moment would be found back on its shelf, wedged in so as to prevent me from pulling it out again. I had read the books on spirits in the British Library. I had been alone with what I was told was the most dangerous vampire in London and I had not been afraid.

I had read about fear, about horror, and about dread and how it was important to separate them to properly assess the threat as it was presented to you. I could not disentangle the threads of fear and horror and the cold teeth of dread and I could not control what I was thinking. I was scared as I had never been afraid before.

I had stood on a hill and seen the Winter Queen and her Winter Knight, arguing so as to make the filament cover of the carriage quake and the creatures pulling it restless and I had smiled and waved as if it was Queen Charlotte in her carriage on royal parade. I had begun to wonder if I did not feel fear the way other people did and if they were exaggerating.

Sitting there on that bare bed with what was clearly a supernatural horror on the floor between me and the door made me afraid.

It looked like a child.

It did not move like one.

It did not move at all.

It just sat there, a dark wax crayon in one hand, the other stretched flat, laid over it's eye as it sang, flat and dull, "London Bridge is falling down".

Every time she came to the refrain, "here comes the candle to light you to bed," I thought I might scream but, although it welled up in my throat, no sound came out. Perhaps I might have been less afraid if I could see the details of her less in the dark room because it was like she was lined in moonlight, just her - like there was a glow inside her skin that should never see the light of day, a sort of lilac glaze that would forever taint my opinion of the colour.

With every repetition, I assumed that my horror would fade, that it would ease, that I would become accustomed to it, but every time I thought my heart would stop when she said the line "and here comes the chopper to chop off your head" followed by this hollow aching laughter that was a mockery of a child's. I thought of little Robert and his hearty chuckles when he was tickled, with Sylvie leaning over him and teasing his bare feet with the white tip of her braid, and then in comparison the noise this thing made that mimicked human laughter.

All of the protections I had known since I had come to London, my powerful Witch aunt, the Witches of the Tower, the werewolves of His Majesty's Dragoons, the pair of vampires from Bunhill Fields and my dear, sweet Sylvie, all of them were gone and right there was just this thing at the end of the bed.

It only stopped when the owner of the apartment came in, shouting and hollering and slamming doors, when she took her hand from her eye, raised a single finger and put it to her lips, and was gone.

The fear of her did not vanish with her.

And over and over in my head, I heard her singing - "London Bridge is falling down" until I could not think. I just wanted to cry because there was all this emotion welling up inside me and I did not know how to let it out or how to bring myself down from that state of sitting on that bed and damn near gibbering with fear.

For some reason when the maid came to get me she just slipped her own shawl around my shoulders like she thought that my shivering was from the cold and not the horror that had spent the night at the bottom of the bed and walked me back to the dining room where she had given me bread and cheese. I wanted to thank her. I had thought such manners ground into me until I did not have to consider or think about them but I said nothing. I just let her lead me, her shawl warm about my shoulders, into that room with the thin fire in the small fireplace and the heavy wooden table.

The crumbs from my bread and cheese were gone and the table was clean. I was fixating on small details - the worn patches in the carpet, the places where the face plates of the door were polished matte - so that I didn't have to think about what had happened and what it meant that I was being led here. I did not consider who the woman who had yelled 'Sarah' could be until I was in the room with her and felt nauseous from the stink of old gin and perfume that surrounded her like her petticoats had been soaked in it.

The gown she wore was fine Indian cotton, sheer in the pre-dawn half-light and the golden light of the fire, and her hair was neatly pinned, my ear fobs hung by her chin. When she saw me she leered, "So you're the one that my spirit likes," and she expected me to recognise her. She recognised me but I could not have placed her, she was one of a hundred such women that I had met in London since I had come here. "How brave you are without your dog," it was not the words that sparked my recognition, but instead the sneer, the way she said it was what allowed me to put a name to her face, sour and no better favoured by white than she was by a widow's weeds.

Mrs Haye stood in that dining room, with the table between us and a pewter cup in her hand that she waved back and forth.

I had felt bad that I had spoken to her so harshly in Lady Davenport's sitting room those weeks ago, I had genuinely felt contrite. The emotion had been wasted and right then I didn't have the strength to spare for such thoughts. I forced words out from between lips that felt like they were sculpted of wet clay, "You took Bunny?" I asked her, "You?"

She was his aunt and the idea of my Aunt doing something like that, or someone doing that to her, I could not fathom the very thought of it.

She didn't let me say more than that because she raged, throwing the cup at me so that it crashed against the plasterwork and door frame, the gin spreading down like paint. "She took my life," she roared, "all of it, left me with the baby and took my name and my place and I," the grin that spread across her face was cruel, it lacked humanity even compared to that of the spirit that sat vigil over me that night, "I'll take it all, everything she has. She took my face, she took my name, and left me with her brat." I was so tired and so afraid that my mind was not making the connections it should have. It did not recognise her as a threat the way it had the spirit. "So now," her smile slithered up her face like a garden slug, cold and unpleasant, "I'm going to take your face, I'm going to take your life, and I'll have it all. Your season, your money, all of it, it will all be mine."

Involuntarily I stepped back away from her. "She picked you for me, Emma's brat, clinging to my skirts and so desperate to please, not like Sarah," the maid was not in the room and I was glad for I did not think that I could prevent myself from throwing her into the way of Mrs Haye so that I did not have to face her; so that I could escape into the pre-dawn of wintery London in just my under things and two old shawls - and Sarah had been kind to me when no one else had been.

I did not want to be the person who would throw such kindness away but after the night that

I had had, with that spirit sitting there, singing and with her hand over her eye - the same eye that had turned red when she had lured me to the frozen river - I could not trust my reactions. The only thing I knew that I could trust was the cold.

"Such pretty things you have," she tilted her head to make the ear fobs bounce against her chin, I had repeated the behaviour, I particularly liked ones that made a noise, "when I'm you I won't have to live like this." She twirled around, drunk and warmed up to her audience. "I'll wear your face and have your life and your gowns and jewels and the dog will hover at my heels."

"He scolded me," I forced the words out, "for what I said." I was biding my time. The Dragoons would be coming after me. The vampires would be searching. It was not dawn, not yet, they would not be forced back into their graves and necropolii. They were coming to save me. I was not a Witch, capable of great feats of magick. I was not a werewolf capable of great feats of strength. I was not a vampire capable of flight or bewitchment. I was just Flora, a girl who was part of neither the magickal world nor the haute ton, too much of each to be part of the other and not enough to be part of the first. I had a house in the country that was let out as a school and I had wealth of my own. I liked shoes and dresses with loud patterns. I had a room in the Witch House and Sylvie and I, I had to find a way out of this. I had to. I couldn't leave Sylvie behind. Who would be there between the Lowell twins when they married if not me? Who would be there for Aunt Jemima? I wanted to struggle but what was I? - a girl who sat silently on a bed with an eldritch horror sat staring at her singing a nursery rhyme about a headsman and his axe, who had covered her eye, who had once sat with me on a bench in the twilit graveyard and spoke to me about flowers - and I had been too scared to scream.

Mrs Haye's smile had gone from simply cold to avaricious. I should have been more afraid than I was but perhaps I had simply reached my ability to be scared for one day. Or perhaps I knew something that she fervently wished that I did not. She thought of the Major in a way that I did not like, I would not say it was jealousy but he was not hers, he was a good man who deserved much better than her.

Her potions and vials on the window sill were just herbal teas in glasses of different colours, most undrinkable and seasoned with grass cuttings. Her penny grimoires had no real magick, just the appearance of it. She was dangerous, I could not forget that, but she was not a Witch with grand powers but instead someone who lucked into something real.

She had made Sophia a spirit and in finding that power serving her, bringing her whatever she wanted, she had tried to recreate it. She had had Sophia take the children, perhaps babies she saw on the street in the arms of loving mothers. She had tried to recreate what she had done and failed. She was killing the babies because she wanted more of the power that her own child had inadvertently given her in death. That was why the symbols carved into their skin with ink were always slightly different because she was trying to recreate what she had done and didn't know why it had worked.

I was on the verge of understanding her. The brilliant clarity that being cold brought me allowed me to understand this and, behind her, Sophia was there, in her tired black dress with her bouncing blonde curls and her hand over her eye and she so clearly said the words "my fair lady," and I understood then that Mrs Haye couldn't see her. She couldn't hear her. She thought that she was alone with me and she was not.

"You will understand. It will all make sense," she said, "when I take your face like she took mine, I'll take your life just like she took mine. She took my life!" That was spat out with flecks of saliva and the look in her eyes was empty, no more full of life than that of the spirit standing beside her like a vicious shadow.

She was leaning on the table and her gaze assessed me like a piece of meat, a slip of a girl fresh from the schoolroom in her perfect white under things with thimbles on her fingers to hide the torn-away nails.

I had to decide at that moment who Miss Flora Peake was and if I made the wrong decision this woman would kill me. I didn't need to be powerful. I needed to be clever.

"How is it done?" I asked, "I," I was so afraid I didn't have to create the quiver in my voice or the trembling in my knees.

"I've spent the last two years trying to find that out, pretty girl," Mrs Haye said. She was leaning on the table like a patriarch in a painting, the image of her spread hands was the same as that of Moses laying out the ten commandments or the Erl King setting an impossible task of some human stupid enough to fall into his realm. "But you're a witch," she said the word in such a way that it was like her tongue curled around it like she caressed it and held on to it until it could no longer be contained, "you will know. You'll know what she did, my bitch sister, you'll know how she did it."

I was trying my best to remember everything I had learned about Mrs Haye. The Major had said that she had been unwell with the birth of her child, that her sister had gone into the country to help her, that she had missed the end of her first season and was married by the time it started the next year. Lady Davenport had been abroad with her husband until she found herself with child when her father had bought the house for her, the one with the clanging bells and the strange Courtier proof room. But those things predated the sale. I was sure of that.

Or maybe, maybe the bells, could it be... I couldn't turn away from the possibility. Sophia had been the one ringing the bells. I had thought I saw a child that day in the doorway between the kitchen and the laundry, I had put it out of my mind thinking that it wasn't important. Servants couldn't always find someone to look after young children and being out of sight of their employer allowed them to be hidden away in quiet places.

I was sure that Sophia had rung the bells. Sophia had been tormenting the Davenport House and she had started it when she had taken Bunny from his bed. She hadn't tripped the wards or the protections because good modern magickal folk didn't believe in spirits. Certainly, there were folk remedies and ideas of how to protect your house from unwelcome spirits but no one believed they were real so they didn't bother. Why pay to protect your house from something that couldn't threaten it? So even protected houses like the Witch House where my aunt and I lived were wide open to creatures like Sophia.

"The Face-dancer," I blurted it out. My aunt had mentioned her once. I had no idea what it was that she did but her title had stuck in my head and so I spoke it now. "She could do it."

To be honest I had no idea if she could. But it sounded like she could and that was enough.

Mrs Haye seemed to ease a little, her frame softened and she turned her head just a little to appraise me, still measuring me up like I was a piece of meat that the butcher was keen to offload. She did not trust me. She didn't need to. She didn't have that capacity. This was a woman who had killed, to my knowledge, six children including her daughter. She had sewn the lips of her maid with unicorn hair and that was what I could see.

She had stolen her sister's baby and showed up to commiserate. The speed at which she had arrived at the house had sparked suspicion in the Major I had dismissed but this woman was broken in dangerous ways. She was going to kill me. All I could do was delay and hope that the Dragoons found me before it was too late.

Sophia, behind her and smiling, reached out her hand and swept the glass bottles and vials from the window to the floor with a crash and then returned her hand over her eye. I wondered if she was trying to tell me something but I didn't know what it was and I wished again that I had read the book that Beausant had left for me.

"Spirit?!" Mrs Haye asked, turning on her heel to look around the room, "are you here with me?" Her glee had a mania to it, a crazed delight that should have scared me more than it did but I was reaching an emotional numbness as the fire died in the grate, making the shadows into long fingers and the room cool.

I didn't know why I could see Sophia and no one else could. There was a truth there that I was not privy to, but Mrs Haye didn't know who the spirit was. She knew she had an invisible assistant but she didn't know it was her daughter. She knew that something supernatural served her - but she didn't realise what it was. As far as she understood, whatever she was doing with the children had worked with her daughter and none of the others - she thought, I realised with terrible honesty that she had sacrificed the child to something powerful enough to do her will because she had something that the spirit wanted.

I had read about all those spirits in the British Library and read over and over how the spirits only wanted one thing - a burial. Nekkers dragged people into the river because their bodies had been lost and they had nothing left but rage, Rusalki had been drowned by lovers and pulled the unwary into their ponds and dark hollows to drown but remained ultimately alone. They all wanted the peace that was given by a proper burial, a place where they could be remembered and honoured and where they had not been thrown out like trash.

Mrs Haye made exhortations about the spirit, praising its strength and wisdom, how its loyalty was its greatest gift and I wanted to reach across and scream at her, she's not loyal, she just remembers that she loved you and wants to please you. You can't even say her name and still, she craves your approval.

My heart broke a little as I pieced together the last of it. When she had seen me at Bunhill Fields, I had given the child the attention she had lacked in life, I had listened to her and talked to

her and answered her questions. She brought
Bunny to me not because she wanted to save him
but because I had been kind and she wanted me to
be kind to him. She had never known kindness so,
as she lost what humanity she had brought into
death, she had rewarded me with the one thing
she could - the child she had taken for her mother
to murder.

        "What happened to your daughter?" I
asked and I realised as soon as I said it that I had
made a terrible mistake.

        "She was not mine, my whore sister left
her with me when she stole my face."

        Sophia, a sweet child who was curious and
overwhelmed with the beauty of a vampire's
graveyard, had been left with this monster
because she had the misfortune to be her
daughter.

        Mrs Haye was around the table as fast as
she could and her slap made my ears ring, "I'm
sorry," I said, I hated simpering but I wasn't going
to challenge her, "everyone said she was yours, I
was wrong, I didn't know," I had my hands in
front of my face, my bangles level with my
mouth and I didn't meet her eyes, "Your sister's
daughter, what happened to her?"

        Mrs Haye didn't ease her quick suspicion -
even in her mania, she was aware that I was up to
something and she grabbed me by the stays to
pull me forward, "You'll see soon enough so it
doesn't hurt to tell you," her smile was like an axe
blow. "Little bitch wouldn't do as she was told.
She was loud and brash and Sarah couldn't keep
her quiet. I found a spell, just a little one, to make
her behave." She spread her left hand over the

table, "I tied her here and I used a phoenix quill to trace the array on her skin but she screamed and screamed, Mama, she screamed and I AM NOT HER MOTHER."

She turned back to me, her face kissing close to mine. I could smell the gin on her breath like a bar of juniper soap run under hot water, but with stale wine and the ghost of old meals. This close, and determined not to meet her gaze, I could see the rot in her teeth. She had clearly not taken care of herself for a long time, and I felt a new pang of sympathy for Sarah, bound probably by love for her employer as she went more and more insane and willing to accept everything she did because she felt complicit. After all, she loved her. No other bond would have held her so firm.

"She wailed and screamed, she sounded like a pig in the abattoir and I couldn't think," her hands were to the sides of her head again, caught in the memory, "the noise of her, I wanted her to be quiet, to be a good girl, and the spell was to do that, it was to keep her quiet so I could think, so I could study," her eyes went to the broken glass, "it cost so much to learn and I couldn't stop, but she was screaming and wriggling and I couldn't think," I wondered if this was a justification for what she had done, "so I put my hand over her mouth, I didn't mean to, I just wanted her to be quiet, and the ink was still fresh, phoenix quill and huldra bark ground with the blood of a ghoul from Nankeen. It took so long to get and it cost so much and the money was running out, I couldn't afford to try again, and she was so loud, so I put my hand over her mouth and told her to stop with her silliness or I would tan her hide."

Mrs Haye seemed to have calmed, the erratic violence had eased into a quiet reflection. I was no less aware of her and her capacity for violence, my cheek stung and I could not remember if I had ever been struck like that before and I could not think of a single instance. I harboured a fantasy of the Major taking his wolf form, his claws and teeth tearing into her like so much meat, but I could not let it show. The only advantage I had was she thought I was weak and powerless, terrified to act because I was terrified of her - which I was, but I understood something now that I hadn't before.

The first death had been an accident, a broken mind trying a fake spell to quiet a child and a hand over her mouth until she could not breathe. Had it happened in London? That was important, Sophia needed a burial, she needed the closure of the ritual even if it had no power - it had power to her, and if her body was dumped in the woods of some country estate she would never have peace and nothing would stop her.

I had been wrong, she was not a nekker who drowned in the river. I remembered the pictures that Sophia had left on the bedroom floor, the girl with a single red eye. I remembered the book in the British Library and it gave me a name for what she was. This was not a child whisked away by the current of the river, this was a child murdered by its parent and not given rest - she wasn't a nekker. She was a myling.

I didn't know where to take it from here. How could I use that information to keep myself safe from this crazy woman who had killed six children until rescue came. I had to. I wasn't going to die here. I was Miss Flora Peake and maybe I would never truly be of the magickal world and I would never be a diamond of the first water. I was Miss Flora Peake and I was going to have my season and I was not going to lament that I couldn't even heat a cup of tea with magic.

I was going to get out of this alive.

"I didn't mean to," Mrs Haye didn't sound repentant, but she was quieter. "I told everyone she was sick but Sarah knew. When it happened I screamed for her, I didn't know what to do, so I screamed for her and she started blubbering so I," she paused, "Sarah knows, she can't say, she can't ever say, and you'll not say anything either, because I'll get my revenge on her, when I take your face," with her fingertips she traced the curve of my cheek, "such a pretty face," she added.

Her mania was returning, "and then my spirit came and it did whatever I asked," she was grinning, it was an idiot grin, a jongleur's smile painted over large to make children laugh. I had always been unsettled by them.

But I was cold. I had the clarity of ice in my veins. "So I tried again, and again, and again, but it wouldn't work."

Of course, it wouldn't, I thought but didn't dare say, because to make a myling you needed to kill your own child. You needed to throw them away like trash.

"My dear spirit," she said and raised my head so I had to look her in the eye and there was nothing in her gaze, it was like staring into the dark and it damn near turned my bowels to water, and her hand on my chin hurt. I tried to back away from her but I was held fast and, seeing it, she raised her hand to slap me again. I grabbed her hand before she could. It was a reflex and there were claws on the tips of my fingers sharp enough to cut into her wrist.

Later I would process what had happened, what Beausant had left for me, but right then I didn't have a chance to consider it because instead of slapping me Mrs Haye punched me in the face with the form of a pugilist. I stepped back and my head hit the wall hard, causing me to slide down to my ass and spit blood all down my front. There were stars in my eyes and it seemed a great shadow swept forward and lunged towards Mrs Haye. It was a shadow of white and red and, as Mrs Haye started to scream, the room, already spinning with light flecks blurring my sight, went dark to me and the screaming was silenced by a dead child singing "London bridge is falling down."

Chapter Twenty-Three

I was woken up by someone waving a bottle of something sharp and foul under my nose. I could hear screaming and I was too out of my mind to wonder if it was even me. Kneeling in front of me was the maid, Sarah, holding a vinaigrette that must have belonged to her mistress. Once she saw that I was awake, she put her hand on my shoulder trying to tell me, I realised, not to get up, which I had no intention of because my head was spinning like a top. When I turned my head a little, trying to look around, a wave of nausea crashed over me and if I had eaten any breakfast I would have cast it over myself.

The person screaming was Mrs Haye.

Her hands were clutched over her face but her arms were covered in a cross-hatching of slashes. Hunks of her hair, already falling loose from its pins in her mania, had been torn loose and lay on the floor with patches of bloody skin, the pins standing out and proud at odd angles. Her gown was torn apart as if someone had taken a giant pair of shears to it and underneath I could see more of the bloody scratches. None of the wounds was deep enough to have killed her but

they were still deep enough and vicious enough
that I could see the white of fat against the edges.
She was screaming and when Sarah managed to
tug away her hands to try and dab a white cloth,
dipped in a bowl of water she had brought in with
her, I could see the wreckage of her face.

I was lucky that much of it was covered by
blood, but as Sarah tried to dab away the worst of
it, the moments when she dipped the cloth into
the bowl to wash it out, I could see that Mrs Haye
had no eyes left. They had been gouged from the
sockets. The sides of her nose had been slit open
and I did not know if it was intentional mutilation
or just something that happened among all the
other slashing. Her mouth was wide because the
muscles in her cheeks had been slashed open and
her blood drooled over the lack of lower lip.

It was like a dervish of blades had attacked
her and it was not that the whirlwind had had
intent but that those parts of her were further
forward. One of her arms hung limp from the
elbow where the fabric was torn and the other had
held it up in front of her face, desperate to cover
the devastation that had been a pedestrian pretty
face.

Now her appearance matched her mania.

Sarah had tended me first because it would
have been worse if I had died. Even in what
seemed a kindness, she was putting Mrs Haye
first. I sat there, head swimming and hurting with
a ferocity that I had not thought it capable of and
my stomach determined to rise if I did more than
blink, watching as Sarah tried to clean the
wounds and Mrs Haye made gurgling wails as the
blood from her destroyed mouth trickled down
her throat.

I could not have said how long it was as Sarah washed out the cloth, over and over, even though the water was almost black with blood, and, with a folded edge, tried to clean the wounds before the door was kicked in and there was male shouting and the thudding of booted feet in the corridor.

I wanted to be relieved but it looked like I was the one who had committed that atrocity upon Mrs Haye. Beausant had given me vampire claws and even now they were there, even if only in potential. There was blood all over my front, I knew that, I remembered spitting it up.

The Dragoons were here and it should have been a relief but the only thing I could think of was that I was going to hang for it.

They hung murderers and made a public spectacle of it and a pretty young girl always drew the largest crowds. They would pack the squares and inns trying to catch a glimpse and buy inches of the rope that they had used to hang me. I was doomed and I wouldn't get to say goodbye to Sylvie and my head hurt so badly I couldn't think past it. It was like a balloon in my head was pressing against my skull and my sinuses and the pressure brought with it the pain.

I was terrified and felt that I had very good cause to be.

Sarah tried to get Mrs Haye to hold the cloth to her face so that she could try and discover what was happening but, with hands torn and bloody, she grabbed her sleeve and would not let go. Her gown and arms were slashed. The devastation of her face and hair, which had been torn out in great hunks, had distracted me from the marks on her arms and breast.

I had not thought myself capable of that kind of violence but it looked like I had done it.

If not - had Sophia done it in my name?

Major McConnell kicked open the door to the sitting room and it swung close enough to bounce off my leg where I was sat on the floor with my head against the wall. He came in with his pistols cocked, looked at the tableau before him and swore. There were words ladies were not supposed to know and there were words that they did know that should not have - the words he used were new to me, or sounded so with the ringing of my ears. I lacked even the mind to understand if he spoke in English.

He was quickly followed by Lieutenant Jackson and a few others of the King's Dragoons. The door and his own body blocked my sight of most of them as people flowed in, taking Sarah away from Mrs Haye and there were shouts that made my head ring more. It was the Major who spotted me, hidden behind the door as I was. He shoved his flintlock into his belt. Later I would make fun of him for doing so for even I knew that was a good way to shoot yourself in the leg. He fumbled off his benjamin and was talking to me, I could hear him but I couldn't concentrate on what it was he was saying, and he wrapped his coat, still warm from his body, around me. I think I said something. I don't remember. My head hurt and I could see little white stars dancing across my gaze and if I didn't move I wouldn't cast up my accounts all over myself.

He picked me up as if I was a rag dolly and carried me out of the building. He had one arm under my knees and the other under my arm and I could feel his warmth, blistering hot against my skin. I was fortunate enough that I was halfway down the stairs and able to lean over the iron railing to vomit on the tiles below and not the wooden stairs where all of the traffic going up and down would slip. It was hard to think and it was only the fact that I was cold that gave me any cogency. My aunt was waiting by the carriage with Sylvie. When I saw them I tried to reach out, which caused the benjamin wrapped around me like a blanket to fall back showing the blood on my bodiced petticoat, and the violence of the movement meant that all I could manage was to say "I'm going to" before trying to turn my head and, not being hung over an iron railing where I had the ability to vaguely aim, I managed to cast what remained in my stomach all over myself, the Major's benjamin and the Major himself.

It was clearly not my best moment.

"We have to find her," I cried out, "we can't leave without her." We needed to find Sophia's body. We needed to give her a formal burial in a graveyard. I did not know if she had attacked Mrs Haye like that but if she remained uninterred she would have continued to do so to other people. She would be a myling like the ones in the books in the British Library. My head was spinning. It felt like a pigs bladder pushed so full of air it would pop at any moment. There were dots dancing like piskies in front of my eyes and the great bells of bow were chiming in my ears. I thought my stomach was determined to betray me in reaction to the blow I had taken where Mrs Haye had struck me and my head had bounced into the wooden strut of the wall behind me.

"She's taken a really nasty blow to the head," the Major said, settling me in one of the carriages, "She's going to want to see the Astrologaster."

"We need to find her," I said grabbing the front of his jacket, which was stiff with soutache braid. "Please," I managed, "try to find her."

"Mrs Haye?" he asked, it was clear he did not understand.

"Sophia," I said, "you need to find Sophia." Then it was clearly too much for me because the white dots were doing more than just swimming around before my eyes and I felt all over queer. I passed out again.

I rode back to the tower draped across the bench seat of a carriage with my head on my aunt's lap and my legs across Sylvie's. Every time I came to, it was to the quiet litany of threats of violence that Sylvie was promising to enact on someone and it made me feel warm and safe in a way that very little did.

Every time the carriage rocked over a cobble I had to make sure my eyes were squeezed tight as the entire world gyroscoped around me like it was the surface of a bowl of water someone was carrying and trying not to tip.

Word had been sent ahead to the Tower

because Mr Formin, the Astrologaster and physician to His Majesty the King, was waiting in the cold courtyard, stamping his feet and cursing at his assistants into a cup of something steaming hot that he was cupping his hands around. When the door to the carriage opened he passed over his cup to one of his milling pages, all of them had wool caps on their heads and fingerless gloves with their livery, and shouldered his way inside the carriage with a ball of white light in a lantern hanging from his jacket that made the inside of the carriage seem as bright as the sunlight outside.

"Don't get up," he said and, leaning over me so that I could smell the spiced wine on his breath, turned my head on my aunt's lap then sucked his breath in between his teeth and stuck his head out of the carriage window with a shout of "Oliver." Whatever page that was came scrabbling forward to offer the Witch the bag he was carrying and was now proffering open to the Astrologaster. He took the bag and dropped it at his feet, "Nausea? White spots? Ears ringing?" he asked, not really expecting an answer as he poked and prodded at the back of my head. "You've done yourself a wicked mischief," he muttered to himself, "I'm going to have to shave that bit of your head, don't want hair carrying heaven alone knows what into the wound after I stitch it. Jacob," that last was shouted at the door before he turned back to me, "You're squinting, is it the light?" he tapped the glass of the lantern twice and it became a rich red as if the glass was stained with cranberries or holly berries and it was better.

"You're going to be fine," he said patting me on the shoulder, "once I'm done with you you'll be fit to dance a set at Almacks."

"They won't let me in," I muttered, "I look like I killed someone."

He barked out a laugh, loud enough it hurt my ears. "Jacob, Jacob, come here," he said so he could go into the bag and from a waxed cloth he pulled what looked like a fresh honey plaster which he slapped on my head, "Jacob, get a few of those wolf lugs over here, I'll need her carried to my office. I can't be expected to work in this cold. Why, it's colder than a witch's tit out here," he climbed down from the carriage to take the steaming cup again, "and I'm a Witch and my tits are cold enough to prove it true."

Mother Demdike was not the oldest Witch in the Tower but she was old and she was not to be crossed so, when I was carried by a different dragoon, one whose name I didn't know, into her chambers, I was sure that I had been taken to the wrong place. "Oh, you poor duckling," she crooned as I was laid out on her chaise in front of the fire, "you're probably all at sixes and sevens, but we'll get you right as rain, we will." She was an older-looking woman - I did not understand the way Witches aged, some appeared to be in their twenties and others in their sixties. My aunt looked to be no more than a well-kept forty but Mother Demdike looked like a wise maven of society in a grey-blue open robe over a yellow printed chemise style dress, complete with flounces. She wore a high-collared and strict-looking chemisette and white linen cuffs over her sleeves. Her hands were wrinkled like parchment and her nails looked a little gnarled and yellowed as if she smoked a pipe. Her offices, for I did not think she lived here, were set up as a comfortable sitting room around a fire that burned merrily. As I waited, and certainly there were not many minutes, two of the older staff- pages who had graduated into assistants - carried in a large copper hip bath with a raised back and placed it on the empty space in front of the fire, away from the drafts from the window and shielded from the door.

Shooing them away she took a brass ewer from the fireplace and carried it to the tub, with a few muttered words she poured hot water from the ewer - on and on it went until the bath was full. "Would it be as easy to empty it, eh, duckling?" she said with a low laugh, "now you'll be wondering why that doctor sent you to me, am I right in that, duckling?" I didn't like the way she called me duckling; it felt proprietary.

"What about Mrs Haye?" As long as I remained still, my head did not swirl and I could keep a vague hold on my wits.

"What about her, duckling?" Mother Demdike asked, taking a bottle off the mantle, opening it and sniffing it before replacing it in favour of its fellow.

"She was more injured than I was," I was clutching the edges of the chaise with my thimble-covered fingertips so that I would not feel so very disconnected from the world around me as I felt. Whatever the Astrologaster had plastered over my cut, it was helping but I felt desperately untethered.

"Head wounds always get treated first, duckling," Mother Demdike, having found a bottle she liked, poured it into the bath. Like the ewer, it seemed to have no end but filled the air with the scent of lilacs, sweet and summery. I thought for a moment I would cast my accounts again as the smell made my gorge rise for a moment, "She'll be taken to Saint Thomas'," Saint Thomas' was the large public hospital in the centre of London. I didn't know why I had been taken to the Tower and she was going to the public hospital where the magistrate was in control. Later I would understand but on that couch, I understood very little, only that she had been torn apart and her eyes clawed out. I had just bumped my head. "they'll treat her well there, but, duckling, you were hurt much more than she was, horrible thing she did, she'll be glad they don't tell Saint Thomas of what she did, then it'll be Saint Mary of Bethlehem for her, now come, duckling, before the bath gets cold."

I swung my legs down and gripped the edge more firmly, waiting for the urge to vomit to pass. "Oh, you poor duckling," she said and went to the door and when the room stopped swimming Sylvie was there, with Mother Demdike calling her Vixen like it didn't matter, and she helped to undress me so I could get into the bath. Sylvie didn't bother with the buttons, "It's ruined anyway, love," she muttered, as she used a knife to just cut away the buttons of my petticoat, the lacing of my stays and the shoulders of my shift so when she helped me to my feet, muttering about how this happened every time she let me out of her sight, I was left in only my stockings which, with no garters, took very little help to remove. With my first aided step the jade token fell to the floor beneath me.

Mother Demdike had put a rolled-up sheet at the head of the bath for my neck and using her magical ewer she started to rinse my hair, over and over, into a bowl, then a second bowl, and then a third until it ran clear. With practice gained on sheep, she said with another of those villainous laughs, she cut away the hair near the cut and clucked about how it would need stitches but I would be well by the new year.

In the bath, I just lay boneless whilst Sylvie commented about how it was good that I had no other wounds but those on my head and face. There was a small scratch on my cheek from Mrs Haye's ring and my lip was split, there were some other wounds on the inside of my mouth, all of which would be tended with a hyssop syrup with willow bark, Mother Demdike muttering the medicines as she clipped away at my hair and I don't know why, as Sylvie so carefully washed my hands around the chains and bandages of my torn fingernails, I started to cry.

The length of the terrible night spent staring at the myling on the floor singing "London Bridge is falling down" and then the whole thing with Mrs Haye and how, unconscious, I had done that to her with the vampire claws I didn't know how to use, I just couldn't not, and once started, I couldn't stop.

With Sylvie there and I could hear Aunt Jemima shouting, demanding entrance, and the low voice of one of the servants of the tower and I was in this perfumed bath safe and and warm and loved and somewhere a little girl who loved her mother lay dead because her mother had, in her illness, tried to perform a spell that would make her quiet. I couldn't say these things. My head ached like it was holding a great thunderstorm and my joints like they were loosely tied together with old butcher's twine. But I was being tended by Sylvie, who loved me and whom I loved. Mother Demdike, a woman even the Prince Regent stepped softly around, was cutting away the hair near the wound on my head and singing softly as she worked, weaving spells into the healing and the growth, and they were doing everything that they could for me and they were doing it kindly and Sarah had been kind but she had had her lips sewn together with unicorn hair and Beausant had given me claws thinking I might use them to defend myself but I didn't know if Sophia had taken me over again and I had given Mrs Haye those terrible wounds and they were treating me and Mrs Haye was going to the public hospital and it was all so very much I could do nothing but cry.

I wept until there was nothing left and I felt like a rag slopped into a bucket and then wrung out by strong hands.

Once my bath was finished I was dressed in a page's clothes and an old set of jumps found somewhere and Mother Demdike made a joke about how there was no way that her stays would fit me as she was much broader in the back, why I was just a stripling and maybe she should call me that instead of duckling, but I felt more secure with the jumps laced tight across my chest to support my breasts, even if they weren't large.

With Sylvie's arm around my waist and the smell of her in my nose and the knowledge I was safe with her, I left Mother Demdike's rooms and returned to the Astrologaster where he could complete what treatment I needed, which I was told included stitches. The purpose of the bath was to check me for other injuries, even bruises, that would have been covered by my clothes without ruining my reputation by having been naked in front of a man.

He was quick as he stitched it, apologising for the pull, but whatever Mother Demdike had done to shave the area had left it numb so I didn't feel anything. He checked my eye which was still bloody, put an ointment on my lip and the scratch and told me I would be fit for dancing by the morrow. He told Sylvie to wake me hourly once I slept. He gave me a bottle of some sort of medicine and a small jar of ointments and assured me that everything was well and as soon as they found me some shoes that fit that I could go home.

"What about Mrs Haye?" I asked him.

"What about her?" he answered putting away his things in a basin to be cleaned.

"Why did I come here and she went to Saint Thomas'?" I wanted to understand. Why did i get the king's own physician and she would get the mustard and honey poultices of the public hospital. I knew she was a murderer and surely, as a murderer who had used magic, she was under the Tower's purview so, surely, she would be treated by the Astrologaster as I was.

I could not get the look of her, torn apart by nails and with her eyes clawed out from my head.

Mr Formin sat down to look me in the eye. "Mrs Haye is quite clearly mad," he said, "she did that to herself, her servant said, once we cut the thread holding her mouth shut, she said there was a red and black shadow and Mrs Haye started screaming and then scratched out her own eyes." He paused and took my hand, "Miss Peake," he said softly, "she did no magick, just the image of it, she did terrible things and the magistrate will deal with her, she will be tried for her crimes by the courts, the Tower has no jurisdiction of her. Even if we did I do not think any of the medical witches here in the Tower would do more for her than the bare minimum. At Saint Thomas' she will receive care before she is tried. She will be no more remarkable there than any other patient and that is the only kindness we will offer her."

"But Sophia," I protested.

"The ghost," he said, "I'm sorry, Miss Peake, but I don't think she was real, with such traumatic head wounds and events it is possible you thought that you saw her."

It wrapped everything in a neat bow, I thought, how perfectly neat it was that the woman who had killed the children, the news of which had turned London into a powder keg, had no magick, just the facsimile of it, and now would have her public trial before either the noose or more likely Saint Mary of Bethlehem. Of those, I thought the noose was kinder. And if ghosts weren't real then there really was nothing for the Tower to be held accountable for. Its actions were then not oversight but instead charity - using its facilities and skills to help solve a crime.

The Tower only existed to serve the Tower.

I just didn't know why they were telling that lie to me.

I had seen Sophia.

I had been taken by her twice.

Once on the river when I tried to dig the child from the ice with my fingers and then again when she took me to Mrs Haye. She had sat there at the foot of the bed and sang all night long.

He was so quiet and patient and determined I knew I could not counter him.

"When she's found," I said, "Sophia, she needs a proper burial, can you make sure that it happens."

With a placation that he thought I had made the thing from whole cloth, he agreed.

Chapter Twenty-Four

They found the body, in a box wrapped in burlap thick with quicklime, nine days later, behind the boards of a loose wall.

I had been the victim of a lot of cosseting which I was starting to rankle against. With the cuts on the inside of my mouth, I was unable to have food that was either too hot or too cold which meant that everything I was served was lukewarm, be it broth or tea. My stomach was apparently too weak for any kind of dairy so my tea, which I drank strong with milk and rose jam, was completely inappropriate. Instead, according to the Astrologaster, I should be served tea with bergamot and lemon which I did not care for. I was no longer given access to the Tantalus despite that a strong drink might have made those days easier to suffer.

It was kindness that meant I was served plain white bread with bone and cabbage broth for every meal, a meal that remained difficult to eat because of my thimble-covered fingers. It is hard to tear bread when you can't grip it with fingertips, and a slice of bread is far too large to dip into even the largest tankard.

I understood the care that they were taking of me, even if I despised it at the moment. My disappearance had scared them and then I had been taken from Mrs Haye's rented town-house covered in blood and unable to stand on my own two feet. That did not mean that I wanted my slippers warmed in front of the fire on the hour, something Sylvie was so eager to do she plucked them from my feet. A warm velvet jacket that was at least fifty years out of fashion had been discovered, possibly provided by the house in the weird way that it did these things, and was worn over my wool day dresses because the idea that I could catch a chill was heretical to my aunt. To match the red jacket was a red cap much like the Scottish bluebonnet which covered both the shaven part of my head and the nasty wound in the heart of it. It meant that, to someone who had not heard of my ordeal, I appeared more to be someone who chose a boyish and eccentric fashion - often with no slippers.

I had decided that the Tower would now resolve the entire thing without me and I would be treated to no more updates - what had happened to me was the actions of a very ill woman. As they understood it: ghosts did not exist and therefore spirits could not be responsible for the kidnapping of children - so Mrs Haye hadn't used spirits to acquire the children she needed to perform the rite she believed gave her power. In truth what had given her power was the murder of her own child.

If I tried to mention it then Aunt Jemima dismissed my concerns. We were to go to Venice, she said, and I should spend my time on healing and making decisions about the new fashions that were in the magazines that I might have an entirely new wardrobe and bring some London polish to that drab, damp place. As soon as I was well I was to go the drapers, wouldn't that be divine, and perhaps we could stop at Gunters for ices. Perhaps the new shoes that I had ordered would be ready for collection.

She was determined that the conversation was diverted every time I brought it up.

Sylvie was less subtle.

Every time I mentioned it, even to the point of asking if anything was yet to appear in the broadsheets, she looked me clearly in the eye and said "No," then after a break where she had to remember that she was not speaking to an infant and that I was old enough to understand why "We are not talking about that. It would be best to let it go, let the authorities deal with it. You were supposed to be involved for a moment and you nearly died."

Every time after that she would just match my gaze with her eyes hard and with no give in her expression and would repeat "You could have died."

Sylvie hadn't seen what I had and I understood her fear and my aunt's matter-of-fact dismissals. It had scared them and if the Major had appeared on my doorstep that day asking me to provide cover for an investigation I was quite certain that my aunt would turn him into a teapot before a word escaped him.

Even when I had sat on that bare bed, in my undress, and the myling at the end of my bed singing her nursery rhymes as she drew figures with a single red eye over and over, I had not truly felt like I might die. Mrs Haye had repeated over and over that she wanted to take my face, to take my place wearing my skin in a spell she was convinced that her sister had performed on her and, once I had given my statement to the magistrate as to what happened, and such things as spirits were waved away as childish imagination, because everyone knew that ghosts didn't exist.

I told the magistrate how Mrs Haye believed that Sophia, her daughter, was actually her sister's, that when she had been in confinement her sister had taken her life from her, and as she tried to find a way to reverse the spell to take back what she believed to be her own, she had attempted a ritual on the child which would make her more docile and obedient. Instead, it had killed her. I did not know where she had put the body but, yes, I was sure it had not had a proper burial. When I was asked how I knew that so firmly I repeated my so-called childish fantasy that Sophia had become a spirit called a myling which would not have happened if she had been interred in consecrated ground.

At that, my head wound was brought up and the magistrate was reminded that there might be aspects of my testimony that were clearly affected by it and, as to my adventure on the ice, that was almost certainly because I was witchborn and frost-kissed and, with so much of the magickal world attending the Frost Fair, I had clearly entered a trance and my association with the vampire Beausant was the reason for all of the folderol of the vampire protecting me and scratching Mr Ogilvy's face. Mr Ogilvy had been very understanding and had elected not to pursue damages against the Limehouse Coterie. I had not known the vampire had scratched him.

The entire affair was considered closed with the King's Dragoons searching Mrs Haye's apartment in the town-house for any truly magickal items or texts which could be considered dangerous to the public at large but would just vanish into the Tower Library and so I was cosseted, followed around, and could not sit without someone offering to plump my pillows and bring me a cup of lukewarm tea or bone and green cabbage broth.

I was, as could be best imagined, in a foul mood - which Sylvie and Aunt Jemima both attributed to lingering pain - when Thorne called on the house with the book that Beausant had given me on spirits. He took off his cap and held it in both hands before Lizzy, like he was going to propose, and asked to see me to make sure that I knew that she had been found.

"Wrapped in burlap and old papers," he said, "soaked in quicklime and stuffed between the walls like a piece of oakum," he said. Werewolves loved children, they treated them like precious gifts and could not, for that reason, prosecute cases with people who hurt children. I would not have been surprised if the Dragoons had offered to help investigate the case of the murdered children because of how they felt about them.

Thorne looked wrecked.

He looked like he had not slept in weeks and Lizzy, uncomfortable around the man, who was short and stocky with a bald head and a face that looked something like a bat, in the common livery of the Dragoons, ran to fetch him some tea.

"Bedlam is too good for a person like that."

I suspected that Thorne was working against orders coming to tell me, but he understood that I was twisted up in the horror of it and I needed to know that it was done, that I had to see her buried myself. My eye was still bloodshot looking like it was made of cranberry Murano glass. The drawings Sophia had done told me that it was associated with her - even if I didn't know why.

"Where is she?" I asked. I didn't care about Mrs Haye any more. She had taken too much from me for me to have any care left. These things, I had discovered, were finite.

"The child," Thorne said, I could see him struggle, he nearly called her something else. I didn't know if it was a pet name, like cub, or a description like corpse. "She's at the Tower, she's with the Speaker." I nodded solemnly.

"Is your cab still outside?" I asked him. He nodded and I pulled off my housecoat. I was not dressed for travel and I assured him I would be as fast as I could, running up the stairs in a way that made my aunt call after me.

I pulled an apron-fronted dress on because I could close it myself with the laces at the shoulder, normally such dresses were closed with pins but I specifically asked for one that laced months before and I pulled it on even though it was probably too light for the weather, and a pelisse, determined to go out even if it was in my house slippers.

"Flora," my aunt said, with her hands on her hips. She looked like a prison guard right then, with her dark-coloured dress and her black hair braided around her head, "what do you think you're doing?"

I raised my head to her, eyepatch on and lip split, yellow with bruising and matched her gaze, trying to feel like a queen in my badly tied dress and velvet cap, my house slippers peeking out from the lilac fabric of my skirts. "I'm doing what no one else will," I said, "I'm putting that child to rest."

I saw something change in my aunt. She was a square-faced woman which made her seem harsher than she was, and with her favouring of dark colours - which suited her olive skin much better than the brighter colours in fashion - she looked stentorian and cruel when the opposite was true.

"Not dressed like that you're not," she said firmly. "Sylvie, Lizzy, Flora is going to the Tower, let's help her get ready."

I had expected this to be a sabotage, a way to prevent me going to the Tower so they could return me to the state of nursing that had been my life for the past nine days. I thought it would take a long time, that there was no way that Thorne could hold the cab or some other excuse for it to be postponed till the next day, and then the next and the next.

My aunt surprised me for she fixed the laces of my gown herself. Tying things with thimbles on your fingers is not as easy as you'd imagine and I thought I had done a good job - I was probably showing my stays to all and sundry but it looked fine from above. As I sat Lizzy buttoned my boots and Sylvie, having pulled on her own pelisse had taken a brush to mine to make sure the red velvet was free of dust. I was vain enough to hope that it matched my cap.

It was not an invalid who left the Tower that day with Sylvie beside me, determined never to let me out of her sight ever again, but a society daughter in the appropriate finery. I was representing both myself and my aunt in that moment and I knew it, so I held my head high and kept all the emotions that swirled around inside me like kites buried.

"What are we doing?" Sylvie asked. Thorne had chosen to sit with the driver so we could talk freely, even though I did not think there was anything to be said that Thorne could not hear.

"We are going to take that child," I would not use the words body or corpse, "and we are going to bury her in consecrated ground and to hell with the consequences."

Sylvie's expression was often foxish which made it hard for strangers to understand that she was not mocking them or some other insult, but right then she just looked young. Her golden eyes, which were so clearly those of an animal, wide and her mouth pursed in thought. "She haunts you, yes?" she asked, she wanted to pull on her braid which she sometimes did when she was thinking over important things, but she had it pinned up under her bonnet.

I told her that yes, she was the little girl that haunted me. I did not tell her of the night I had spent with her sat at the foot of the bed singing because the fear would well up in me again and I could not be afraid. I had to be

resolute, I was storming the Tower and taking
from them important evidence in a magickal
crime. I could not, even for a moment, waver.

"We should have sent a note to Mr
Ogilvy," she said, "he is a vicar, he can do the
ceremony."

I had not thought of it, but there were
things needed for a burial. There had to be a vicar
and a church yard because otherwise it would be
Sylvie and Thorne with shovels under the cover
of night like a pair of resurrectionists. I had not
considered these things. I was not, at that time, in
my right mind. The stresses of the previous days
in combination with the blow to my head and
then my frustration at being an invalid and being
treated as one, frustrated at my own body's
inability to do what I wanted and those around me
trying to consider what I would not.

The books had said that a myling could be
stopped by burying them in consecrated ground. I
knew that. I had intended it to happen. I had not
considered the actions that that would mean. It
had been a thing for other people to fuss over. I
would send a note to Mr Ogilvy, the Tower
would have the address of his lodgings here in
London. He had said that he intended to stay over
the new year and I hoped his adventure on the
frozen river, where he had tried to save me from a
vampire who was frenzying trying to protect me,
had not caused him to return to his living at Fell
Leaf.

"I shall ask Beausant as well," I told her,
having made the resolution. "I first met her at
Bunhill Fields and she thought it was beautiful. I
do not know if people are still buried there in
Islington or if other provisions have been made,
but I," I frowned, "I am sure that he will agree, it

is such a little thing to ask. He was the one to realise she was a myling, and he gave me these," I looked at the bracelets I wore which had the capacity to form the beautiful filigree claws that the vampires used to feed.

"Look at me," Sylvie said breaking me from my reverie before it could take hold. "You did not do that to her," even without naming her I understood who Sylvie was talking about, "she did that to herself. The doctors at Saint Thomas all said it, she did it to herself." My jade token had fallen from me when I had been bathing in the Tower and I had not, then, noticed its lack but now I did. I didn't know why it brought me such comfort.

Sylvie was not the first to tell me I was not responsible for Mrs Haye gouging her own eyes out and pulling away her hair, she had told the doctors she was trying to find her true face, the face that she had before her sister stole her own, that she had seen the spirit and it was so beautiful she had to rip out her eyes and it had whispered. But the descriptions that the doctors had gotten from her did not sound like Sophia, who was small and blonde and wore a black dress. The spirit that Mrs Haye described was tall with black hair and wore a red robe and she whispered and Mrs Haye's mental state, already broken, shattered.

I did not know what had happened in that room. I knew that when she punched me and I reeled back I had struck my head on the edge of a shelf which was what had caused so much damage. I had hit it hard enough I had cracked the plaster around the bracket. At the time I had thought that I just hit the wall. It was a morning when my memory was fragmented and I was told that it was normal, that I had sustained a terrible injury and what I had endured had been traumatic so my mind was walling it away so that I could heal. It was possible the memories might come back but no one was hopeful and it was probably for the best if I never did.

But it meant that I did not know if I was the one who had caused the terrible injuries to Mrs Haye.

No matter how many times I was told, that doubt festered there because I could have done them, I suppose at that time I had even wanted to, but I didn't know if I did. If. It was a terrible word.

"When we get to the Tower," Sylvie said, refusing to let me wallow in my thoughts, "we'll send a note to Mr Ogilvy, we'll get the Dragoons to send word to the vampires and then we'll march down the stairs to see the Speaker and we'll tell him he best be done with her because we are taking her for a proper burial."

It was exactly what I needed to hear.

Chapter Twenty-Five

Arriving at the Tower at night, even though it was barely six of the clock, was a different experience. There were guards at the gate leading to the courtyard with the mews, which was where I usually alighted, but Thorne directed the driver around to another entrance, the one I expected was for visiting guests as it involved a very imposing set of stairs and what had been the formal gardens.

The Tower of London had a reputation as a prison but it had been built as a palace and it was as a palace that royalty was imprisoned there. They had been tortured but very few people had been imprisoned in the famous cells because, until the Royal Society of Alchemists had taken it over as their headquarters, the very nature of England's monarchy was migratory. The court was wherever the Queen was and so political prisoners were often held where they had been taken prisoner. If they suspected that the prisoner would foment rebellion they were held on the Isle of Wight so that they could control the information that was taken from the prison. If you were imprisoned in the Tower it was not so much being locked in a tower to languish as being locked in an exquisite hotel suite until the decision was made about what to do with you.

The building of Buckingham Palace had given the monarchy a defined seat but they held many other properties and things as terrible as what the Tower was infamous for had happened in those places too.

Arriving at the main entrance by night I couldn't help but shiver. The place felt cool and damp despite the frost like the very stones were weeping and the black paint on the cast iron of the pintles and portcullis was fresh and gleaming wet in the lamplight.

I was met at the gate by the Major, "Miss Peake," he said, putting his hand on my arm, "you shouldn't be here." Then he turned his attention to his batman who had brought me here, "You shouldn't have brought her here." He leaned in and his breath was hot on my cheek as he said, "You should go home, you don't have to see this."

Even in this, he was trying to protect me.

I touched my gloved fingertip to my eyepatch. I had demanded the removal of my thimbles, citing my Frangipane gloves as protection enough for the tape, and I was glad of it. "I have to see this through." I told him.

"Let her in," Beausant purred from behind me. I had not heard him approach and I knew, intellectually, that as a vampire that was something I should have been very afraid of but, for some reason, I was not. "She can not be *une petite fille* forever." I did not know how much of his French was an affectation or how much was him actually being French. I knew he was old. Everyone kept telling me how very old he was.

He was said to be the oldest vampire in London, which meant he was the oldest of the vampires in the five coteries. He was dangerous. He moved silently through the protections of the Tower so that he didn't even bother the horses that drew the carriage that we had arrived in.

He was standing as my champion but I had to remember that he was dangerous and that if they gathered to bar my entry he would cut through them like grass to get me to where I wanted to go. I didn't know how much of it was because he had pledged to protect me, the way he had at Bunhill Fields that first time we met after he touched me, or how much was that it offered relief to his ennui. I amused him. I knew so little about vampires that I thought that it meant more than it did.

I did not realise then that vampires were as prone to throw away their pretty gewgaws as anyone else.

With Beausant behind me and Thorne and Sylvie beside me I felt invincible.

The Major offered me his hand as if he was escorting me to a ball and I took the offer, relinquishing none of my dignity or the feeling of my majesty. I must have looked like a silly girl with the eyepatch to hold in place the medicinal herbs over my red eye, the yellow and brown ghosts of bruises left by Mrs Haye and quickly dressed so that we would not lose the hansom that Thorne had brought to my aunt's house to bring the news, but I walked towards the staircases, the one that led down to the quiet old cells that were the domain of the Speaker, with my held high like I was Louise of Prussia, daring those who scurried out of my path to question me.

They were pages and servants and not one
of them raised their gaze to even do more than
notice my presence so that they didn't collide with
me.

Mr Reid was not in the vaulted room with
the tables that stood in for his office. I had no
idea what the room had been when the Tower had
been a residence of the royal family, centuries
before, for it was underground but it had good
access to natural light through a series of
windows, currently almost completely occluded
by snow, and unlike a kitchen did not have a huge
fireplace, just a small stand-alone stove with a
pipe that was fixed to a gap cut in one of the
windows where a slight fire burned with a kettle
of hot water bubbling merrily on top.

The gentleman that met us was the very
definition of the word unctuous.

He was about the same height and build as
Thorne, standing taller than Sylvie but not as tall
as I was, but with a girth that I could not have put
both arms around, but he seemed used to make
himself seem smaller, curling himself around his
chest so it looked like he had no neck, instead just
a head that grew out just above his breastbone.
He wore a heavy leather apron and coat over a
shirt and matching leather gauntlets that looked
better suited to falconry than any laboratory
work.

His head was balding with the sides of his
hair grown long, like that of Mr Ogilvy, but
instead of being swept over the top, it was

gathered at the back of his head in a small queue - which looked equally ridiculous - and the pate of his head was red and shiny although marked with large brown liver spots. He had a long nose that came down over his lips which would have been, in his youth, referred to as lush but were now a saggy soft plum colour that contrasted with the leathery brown skin of his face.

"Milton," the Major said, "is The Speaker present?" His voice was no louder than it normally was but it was accompanied by putting his hand on the man's shoulder.

The man, Milton, jumped and then, from his large ears with hanging lobes that were easily the size of the pad of my thumb, he pulled two little pegs of soft wax which he put down on one of the tables. They were large and imposing and five of them dominated the room. All but one of them were empty, "Oh my goodness," he said with one hand to his cravatte, "I did not hear you come in, come, come, we get so few visitors down here, and a pair of ladies, let me get you some tea."

"Thank you, but no," Thorne said for all of us in a way that suggested that this was not an offer to accept. I did not know if it was because of where we were, which was an option, or if he made a truly awful cup of tea - the sort of thing that Thorne took personally.

I did not know where to look but I knew not to look at the tables, especially the one that had a small wrapped bundle, dwarfed by the size of the table, upon it. When the Major stepped forward towards it, Milton turned quicker than I had thought such a man could move to grab his wrist, "Don't touch her," he said and then he seemed to remember himself and patted down the sides of his head with his heavy suede gloves.

"We're here," I started.

"Yes, yes," Milton said, "but she's covered in quicklime and other things besides, supposed magical potions and old creams and face powders," as he spoke he started to undo the twine knots that held the bundle closed, "The men that found her, they had to be treated, it burned straight through the burlap and into their arms. It's not 'don't touch it because the Speaker is busy and I don't want you to touch his work without him being present', but 'if you touch it, it'll burn you like acid.' We are trying to find a solvent to wash it away."

"We're here to bury her," I told him, "is there a place where I can get pen and paper? I need to write a note to someone."

"A note, *Berushka*," Beausant said, "as soon as word reached me I negotiated with my dear Lady Below," he spoke the title like it echoed, that it should be labelled with King or Pope, "the child can be buried in Islington."

It was a weight off my shoulders. I had not thought about how I would arrange that burial. Sophia had found the cemetery beautiful and I wanted her to be surrounded by beauty. I wanted her to have all the pretty, lovely things that her short life had denied her. I wanted her to be at peace in a place where the flowers bloomed and the trees were always green.

I had not even considered asking the vampires, and a brief image of Sylvie and myself digging the grave surreptitiously bubbled through me with a little chirrup of laughter that I swallowed down knowing that if I did not I would start to weep. "Thank you," I said and I truly meant it. "The note is for a vicar of my acquaintance," I said, "Mr Ogilvy."

"The man on the ice?" Beausant asked me, "the one with the," he made a gesture at his waist which I didn't understand and then he mopped at his face with a mock kerchief in a way that at any other time might have made me laugh.

"Yes," I told him, "that is him, he is a vicar, a man of the church, he can give her a funeral, I would not know where to begin and I would not have her simply placed in a hole like the victim of some cutpurse." I stopped, "The other children," I turned to Milton, "were they given proper burials, do you know?"

"They were returned to their families, Miss," he said, "with a small amount for the church warden that they might be buried, one wasn't claimed and he was interred here in the Tower," he gestured with his head in a direction which is where I assumed the small graveyard in the Tower was located. There was a chapel in the Tower and it was possible he had been buried there, in the same ground as kings and queens. "But I'm sure their families would be reassured to know of your care," there was something in the way that he spoke, something that made me uncomfortable but I could not have said what it was about Milton that so disturbed me. He had an oiliness to his nature and speech that I could not quite reconcile. "I'll be getting you some paper and a pen." He said walking across to a table and pulling out a drawer that made a terrible screech. "You'll be more comfortable over here," he said, picking up the sheets of paper, the pen, the ink pot and a lantern and taking it to a flat surface near the stove.

I followed him over, Beausant gliding behind me like an ominous shadow, and as soon as I had scribbled out the note, clumsy with my padded fingertips and leather frangipane gloves, he took it, dusted it with sand, tipped the excess into the tray there, and folded it over, sealing it with the Speaker's fob, left on his table, with a practised speed that I did not have, and went, "Where's the address, *Berushka*? I shall guarantee our churchman's presence."

"You don't need to bully him," the Major said. "Are there pages who work in this part of the Tower?" I did not know if it was some strange shared battle between them but the two of them bickered like an old married couple where years of harmless teasing sounded cruel to outsiders. I would not have been surprised to have found them as characters in one of the novels from the lending libraries.

Milton, without losing a moment of his oily slithering across the floor opened a box set into the wall and pulled a cord. "A page will be along shortly, but perhaps Monsieur Beausant will be able to achieve it quicker, if time is of the essence."

"I am worried that Mr Ogilvy," the Major stated, scratching at his chin, "might feel that he is being held accountable for the scene on the river if London's most notorious vampire appears at his house to drag him, with a letter he can not prove the veracity of, to Islington. He might not consider himself dinner but one never knows and even if he is not to be consumed he might wonder that he might just be murdered and dumped into an empty grave."

Beausant's smile showed just enough fang

but his expression was one of mischief. He looked like he might be dangerous, but only because it was so very much fun. He was enjoying the to and fro with the Major and it meant that he might have killed Mr Ogilvy just for the fun of it, but he would stay his hand because it proved the Major wrong.

The Major had a point, I had to concede. How was Mr Ogilvy to know that the request was mine and that Beausant was just my messenger and not there to kill him for unrelated things? Taking the page was a good idea and I said so. I wanted, no, I needed, this to go well so that I could put Sophia to rest.

As the two were arguing I became aware of a strange noise, a sort of sloshing accompanied by the ticking of clockwork, and it was not loud, certainly no one else seemed to react to it, but I felt it, like each tick was struck through my veins. Through one of the other doors to the wide laboratory, with a hiccup, and accompanied by what I at first mistook for a dog, was The Speaker.

"Oh," there was a hyuck sound in the middle of the statement, "my." He was wearing a massively oversized fisherman's sweater under a leather apron with the gloves stuck into the front pocket and a pair of brightly patterned fabric house slippers. He had clearly not been expecting guests and beside him was something that I could not, for a whole moment, begin to comprehend. It had the shape and idea of a dog but a good deal of it was made of clockwork and there was some magick involved that kept the dog alive, or at least gave it an odd facsimile thereof. In life it had been a small terrier with a long shaggy coat that made it look not entirely unlike rags tied to a broom handle to mop the floor, with wet eyes and a hanging tongue under its nose, but entire parts of it's side and musculature was clockwork under curved glass.

The Speaker and his curious inability to speak around women paled in comparison to the automaton dog that ambled along beside him on two flesh feet and two clockwork ones.

Sylvie let out a great sigh. She had been so quiet amidst all of the folderol I had almost forgotten that she was there. She was as quiet as a vampire when she wanted to be. She walked over to the Speaker and looked him clear in the eye, "My temper is very short right now, sir, and if you hiccup again I am going to strike you, and I will continue to strike you for each noise you make. I am told that it is involuntary. I do not care." She separated out each word to give it emphasis. "And I must admit I am looking forward to it, so go ahead, hiccup, I dare you."

The colour ran from the Speaker's face. He was a comely young man with a snub nose and a soft mouth, an oval face and was complected fairly. He had dark brown hair and eyes that caught the light in different ways between whiskey gold and black that would have been a crowning feature in a young lady.

He turned the colour of his poorly tied cravatte.

Strangely, looking at him with his beaker of hot liquid, his house slippers, and poorly tied neck tie, I did not think that I might have to remove Sylvie bodily to prevent her slapping one of the Seven Magnificent Witches of London into the next room but that he needed a better valet. That led to the second realisation that he might be one of the suitors that attended the London season. Witches, unlike vampires, could, and often did marry only to outlive their spouses, watching them grow old whilst they themselves remained young and vital, and - being a young appearing widow or widower at their graveside - often mistaken for their child or grandchild and never for the one who was commemorated on the stone as beloved of.

For a moment I saw myself in that role, the girl who danced with him three times in one evening and whom all of London were talking about as if engaged, then the moment when he asked my aunt who would, in the fantasy, of course agree, and then the quiet service, perhaps in the Tower chapel, and then a town-house, perhaps overlooking the river like my aunt's, and then a life of children, of growing older whilst he remained young and fresh, and then the inevitable resentment. I was not and would never be considered a great beauty, my face was apparently made for mischief but I would resent a husband who did not age as I did.

Those witch-spouses must have been so full of hate for them when they died. It was inevitable. How could it not be?

It was a tragedy on both ends - and I wondered how they could bear it? Why did some Witches marry again and again, haunting a series of graves of people that they had loved enough to marry them.

But on the table was a small child, wrapped in burlap and twine because the melange of solvents and lotions on her skin dried her out like one of the mummies found in distant Egypt, and I was daydreaming of a marriage.

It was not the Speaker that Sylvie needed to strike - but me.

"I," the Speaker started.

"My apologies," I said stepping forward to put myself between him and Sylvie, "we have invaded your office," the common politesse was easy. I had been trained to be the perfect hostess, the perfect guest, so it was a role that I could step into like pulling on an old pair of shoes. "We met previously, I'm Miss Peake," I said but I did not offer him my hand, "of course you know Major McConnell and Mr Thorne," I gestured with a small incline of my head to the werewolves beside me, "and Monsieur Beausant?" I phrased it like a question so that I could give him the dignity of accepting or denying that he knew the vampire. Beausant, true to form, who was sat upon one of the work surfaces around the room with his legs crossed under him, winked at him.

"We're here to take Miss Haye," I said and looked at the small bundle on the huge table.

"You can't," he started.

"She's caustic, we know," I said. I was surprising myself how easy it was to just roll over his arguments without losing an inch of the polite facade that I was using, "It means we shall have to trouble you further," I said, "for something to wrap her in. We have an appointment in Bunhill Fields where we can lay the poor thing to rest."

"I," the Speaker started but I smiled at him, daring him to hiccup as much as Sylvie had. I knew how I looked and I knew that there was only one thing I could do for the child and that was to take her to Islington.

"I must apologise for the inconvenience," I continued, "but."

Whatever he was going to say in response was cut off by the arrival of a page and Beausant hopped down, "Just what I was waiting for," he winked at the boy who went white under his brown livery, "my chaperone. Tell me, lad," he said, "have you ever danced across the winter night with a vampire?"

"Beausant," the Major snapped, and I wanted to add "don't play with your food," but before I could join in the game two things happened, the Major continued with his scolding of Beausant's teasing of the boy and the Speaker hiccuped.

"You hit me," the Speaker said to Sylvie with his hand cupped around his reddened cheek.

"I said that I would," she said, "and I will again if you continue to make that awful noise."

"But you hit me," he repeated. His strange dog, bothered by Sylvie, started to jump around, her, barking. It sounded like the roar of a paper tiger, made with a quill and utterly unlike the tigers in the zoo.

Milton did not look like such carnival chaos bothered him at all as he lifted several stiff pieces of fabric and laid them down on the table next to where Sophia lay, "Oakum, miss," he said, "it's the best we can do." Oakum was a fabric painted over on both sides with hot tar so that it impregnated the fibres. It was used primarily as waterproofing on boats. "The lime drew out the corpse wax which mixed with all of the other things, beauty creams we think, and it formed this paste," he was explaining it as he laid out the oakum, "lime doesn't break down bodies," I was surprised by how clinical he was being and how interested I was. Perhaps it was to drown out the bickering going on around me, with the Major scolding Beausant for being himself and Sylvie threatening one of the Seven Magnificent Witches of London with repeated violence. "It draws out the moisture and prevents the liquefaction of the corpse," having laid out the oakum sheets, each of which was perhaps two-foot square, Milton turned his attention to the wrapped bundle that he had undone the twine on but had not further revealed. "Miss, it is not a pleasant thing to see, perhaps you would prefer to look away."

I told him that I would not. I felt like I should bear witness to even this, after all of this.

"Lime is used in mass graves to prevent the contagion spreading through corpse wax," I didn't know what that was, "and often it reaches a saturation point where it can take no more liquid. The body is, for a very short time, mummified until the liquids and corpse wax, drawn from the corpse by the lime, leathering the skin which causes it to tear pulling out more of the wax. This is consumed by the insects in the ground and the body will then break down normally. All things return to the earth in their time." As he said this, he opened the final layer of fabric wrapped around the body.

When I was a girl in Fell Leaf House, one of the girls there had tried to play a prank on another girl by placing a frog into her private things - in specific, a little wooden box where she kept candies that she did not want to share. A frog had been found and put in the box, and before the trick was revealed the girl had to rush home for her brother had taken very ill. The frog was forgotten, the box put away in the little cubby beside the stove, until the girl returned months later and the box was opened revealing the poor frog. It had been dried with its skin turned to leather and all of the bulk of it gone so it was like a strip of leather. That was what I thought of when I saw Sophia lying there, with her knees pressed to her chest. A memory of a frog left in a box to desiccate.

And it made me angry.

I was so angry that I could spit and that would have been perfectly keeping in what else was happening. The strange clockwork dog ambled its way over the stones at me, it had been barking at Sylvie, and cocked its head with a felt tongue lolling out as it politely asked for attention.

I got down to the dog's level and scratched it behind its ears like I would any other dog. "Mr Reid's talent is unique," Milton said as he moved the body, light as a bird's bone, from the saturated burlap into the oakum, wrapping it as carefully as a gift. "Gavin," he said to the dog in a firmer voice than the one he directed to me, "leave the poor girl be."

In the craziness of the room, of what I had been through, a dog reanimated through clockwork and bellows seemed almost normal, and certainly the least insane part of all of it.

I wanted to rage and tear and destroy, and I wanted to cry and wail and rail against it, but instead, I crouched down and paid attention to a reanimated clockwork corpse of a shaggy-haired and idiot terrier called, of all things, Gavin.

"I've got a basket," the page said loudly and put it on the table, "We can go now, Mr Vampire," because of course the page was as much of an idiot as the dog - it was inevitable I suppose.

Chapter Twenty-Six

Mr Reid asked the Major if he might accompany us to Bunhill Fields because he wished to speak to me, and thought it would be interesting to see a vampire funeral which he thought might be a once in a lifetime opportunity. When the carriage came around, which was the baroque monstrosity that could seat six comfortably Sylvie glared at Mr Reid and told him that she would ride up front with Betterwerth and Thorne but she would be listening.

"She's terrifying," Mr Reid said offering to take the basket from me so that I might climb into the carriage. It was so large it had a set of steps that folded down when the door was opened and a wide step to bridge the gap. It had, at some point, been the carriage of a visiting royal who had not taken it back and the family it had been left with bequeathed it to the Tower for it needed six horses to pull it and a lot of upkeep. It had been covered with cantrips and arrays to prevent decay, and similar things, and I was assured, by Betterwerth as he lifted me up, bodily, to the main step, that the enchantments that kept it comfortable had been replaced recently which meant that it probably would be a comfortable ride.

I sat the basket on the seat beside me, and unpinned my cap because the ribbons which held it in place had a rough edge that was irritating the back of my neck, and shook out my short hair.

Mr Reid was the next into the carriage, with a hiccup which caused Sylvie to slap the panel of the carriage to reassure him that there would be consequences.

"I can't help it," he protested, sticking his head out of the window. "It's a nervous habit."

"Break it," she said as she climbed up to the driver's seat. The carriage was so wide that she could sit with Thorne and Betterwerth, both of which were large men, with space to spare. There was a similar bench seat at the back which I was told was for guards so that the carriage wouldn't be waylaid by highwaymen.

It was a silly thing that was more to do with a show of wealth than any practicality. With the hansom that had brought us to the Tower's one horse, Uncle Jack's landau which needed two horses and this monstrosity the Tower's entire stable was used up. This stable, as could be expected, was very rarely pulled into service when a hackney could be easily hired.

I never learned why they used that carriage instead of a hackney or even a dog cart - which I knew they had access to - but we were put in the carriage which was easily as wide as most of the roads in the city.

The seats were wide cushioned velvet with black velvet covered buttons to pull it in place, and were slightly too tall for me so my feet hung an inch or so when I sat. I had the basket on the bench beside me forcing the Major and Mr Reid to sit facing me. Mr Reid seeing that my feet were hanging loose pulled out a metal bar that I had thought was decorative to act as a footstool. The carriage really did have every modern convenience.

Once we had set off, and a few hiccups had escaped the Doctor, he reached into the pocket of his waistcoat - he had pulled benjamin over his shirt and waistcoat not bothering with a jacket - and offered me something in his hand that I could not immediately see. I was wary but took it and it was a small paper packet that when I opened it revealed my jade token. I felt an amazing wave of relief to have it back in my hands. I had felt a lack without it, and I had lamented that I hadn't picked it up when it had fallen to the floor after my rescue from Mrs Haye thinking that it was lost.

"Do you know what it is?" he asked me. It said so much of his interest in the topic that he didn't hiccup for the entirety of our conversation about the jade.

"It's a token from the opium gangs that no harm is to come to Lady Atwood," I told him. He blinked in surprise and then agreed that it was that, but that was not the answer that he was asking me about.

"It's a corpse marker," I added the second time, "to be put in a tomb to represent a servant."

"No," he said, "well not really, it's more than that," talking about something he was interested in made his face animated and he was much more at ease in that moment than any other time I had seen him. "Every country has it's own magickal practitioners and jades like this were made for witches called *fang shi*," I had heard the term from Mr Cho in Bunhill Fields, "in Cathay people were buried with the things that they would need in the afterlife, jewellery, porcelain and human servants. In most cases they would buy corpses from a *fang shi* to fill those roles. The *fang shi* would buy corpses and string them up between poles of bamboo that made the corpses seem to jump. To prevent the corpses rotting they'd put a pearl in their belly and a jade slip like this in their mouths."

He leaned back, "but this jade slip is special. Jade this colour is called imperial jade and this one definitely came from a tomb, the magick in it is old, it crackles. It was," he took a deep breath looking across at the Major who had no idea why he was being checked.

"Just as there are *fang shi*," he said, "there are *Fang Shi*," I could hear the emphasis which was the same as the difference between witch and Witch. The same word was shared but they meant two very different things. "A *Fang Shi* would serve the emperor and his family. Instead of buying corpses they would use a magick to both preserve and bind the corpse. Instead of just being used to represent a person with a slip like that, they would use actual magick to bind the person to the slip."

"Yes," I agreed, I had known that too.

"And they would use magic to animate the corpse." He stopped again, "the body would seem to come back to life to protect the tomb. This kind of slip was put in what is called a *Jin Ji Gongzhu* - a forbidden princess. In death she was given a form of immortality and the tomb was probably raided centuries ago." He said it as if it was not a thing that was worthy of remark, "and to stop the animated corpse they took the slip and the pearl - things that were worth selling. So they did, and through that trading it came to the hands of the opium sellers here in London. It was a treasure that they could not sell for fear of attracting the attention of both the law, jade smuggling is illegal, and the East India Company, who are certainly fiercer so it lost any value it had - no one could use the magic that was still in the slip, and imperial jade would attract attention if it was for sale."

"Why are you so sure it's one of the magickal ones?" I asked him. As far as I knew it was simply a carved jade token. It was beautiful and I liked it greatly, certainly I felt undressed without around my neck, but that did not make it magickal.

"Because I can feel it, sparking like a galvanisation machine against my fingers." He looked at his fingers. "It is academic," he shrugged it off, "without the knowledge or affinity to use the magick it is just a pretty piece of stone that we can feel the magick in but nothing more. Just as it is a very valuable trinket that cannot be sold it is useless."

I thought of the feeling that I had had when I had first come around on the frozen river, looking at the young vampire who had frenzied to protect me - I had seen a flash of white, red and black that Dr Formin had been unable to explain and had shrugged off with the release of the enchantment.

I had seen the same waves of colour when Mrs Haye had struck me, and Mrs Haye had spoken of a beautiful woman in red that caused her to tear out her own eyes.

The thought was immediately dismissed. The human mind played tricks when it was endangered, I reassured myself, that was what Dr Formin had said, "you can't always trust what your eyes see when you are pushed to extremity."

"Major," I turned to him, "you have some familiarity with the Cataian customs, do you not?" He made a noise that suggested that he knew some, but could hardly be considered an expert. Before he had been appointed to the Tower he had served in Nankeen. I did not know how long he had been there but I knew that he had spent some time in Cathay.

"Do they still do such things?"

He made a gesture with his head "I lived in a barracks put beside the warehouses of the East India, I barely had anything to do with people who were not traders, when we went into the surrounding areas we were not welcome and often to reinforce the company's interests." He rarely spoke of his life before he came to London, but I knew that he had served in both Cathay and Kashmir and it said much of English politics that his Majesty's Dragoons represented the East India's interests more than the empire's.

"Perhaps," the Speaker said with what was truly a patronising smile, "you will be able to travel to such places and see for yourself."

"Perhaps," I answered, "you will not treat me like a child who must be mollified with empty promises and denied simple knowledge."

The Major tried, and failed, to hide his amusement at the way that I had responded. He enjoyed it when I was saucy, but I remembered how severe and stern that he was when I had spoken so to Mrs Haye what felt like a lifetime ago and made me return my gaze to the small basket that sat on the bench beside me. I doubted that he could understand the trail of my thoughts but he did try to change the subject, asking me if I had plans for Christmas supper as he was unsure if he was going to order several pork sides for the barracks or an entire brace of geese. There were only ten enlisted soldiers, and Thorne who served as batman for the group, so it always struck me that they could eat as much as they did. There was a joke about how if one of the Dragoons was invited for dinner then the cook must be informed that ten men were arriving instead.

The conversation between the two men continued in that manner for some time as the carriage rattled its way through the London streets, because it was a main thoroughfare lanterns were placed at regular intervals so the journey was never truly dark, and a lantern swung from the ceiling showing all of the red velvet and giving the uncomfortable impression that we were travelling in a giant beating heart.

I did not really listen for I had no firm opinion on whether a currant and apple stuffing was superior to sausage or a herbed breadcrumb. I had read in a novel that men were overly concerned with what went into their stomachs and as the statement had been made by a character who was using her meals to poison her husband and his awful brothers I had not taken much stock of it - but it seemed that she had had the right of it.

Their conversation was as animated as it was banal.

I let it continue for a while before I interjected, "Mr Reid," I addressed him directly, "what was it about the jade that caught your attention?" I felt it was a fair question. I didn't imagine he often went around fondling lady's jewels, especially those of girls before their presentation or come out.

"Mother Demdike brought it to my attention," he said. He had his hands folded in his lap and I noticed, belatedly I suppose, that he was not wearing gloves. The interior of the carriage was comfortable to someone in several layers of warm petticoats and a velvet pelisse, but his hands must have been cold the way that he was holding them between the folds of his benjamin which looked to be at least several inches too large for him.

"Jade is like glass," he said, "and both as strong and as fragile as glass, a slip of jade like that hitting the floor when you were getting ready for the bath should have shattered. Mother Demdike's affinities do not include the funerary, like my own, but even she could feel the magick in it and a simple scry she performed saw me as the best person to investigate it. I understand the Sorcerer Royal gave you it."

I told him that he was correct, Uncle Jack had given me the jade because it was clear that Lady Atwood didn't want it and the Tower had no use for it. Even they could not have sold it without attracting the ire of the East India and perhaps also questions that they did not want to answer.

"I have spent the last six days in the Tower library trying to understand the mysteries of it, and without the Librarian's help I doubt I would have discovered as much as I did, scant as it is, without his knowledge of languages I doubt there was anything I could have added to what Mr Cho already informed us of."

I could not help but resent that, because I was not welcome in the Tower library. I wondered what I would have found there when I was researching spirits, if I had have had a friendly librarian who understood what we needed instead of the one that we had and the information which was so misleading that we had mistaken the type of spirit that Sophia had become. I didn't realise that I was stroking the oakum in the basket like it was a cat until the Major brought my attention to it.

"A pity that this mystery you could solve but so much remains of the one that saw poor Sophia dead." I didn't really know why I was angry. It was like a cold burning in my belly and I wanted to rage and lash out but such things were not done so I could not. I barely knew Mr Reid so a tantrum such as I felt I was capable of was impossible.

"Did I not tell you?" The Major said, "the mystery of the bells, Jackson solved it because of something you said to me that day as we returned from Islington, I thought I had informed you, and with all the folderol that came after I apologise for I treated you as if you knew."

"Then you know why the bells rang, what

broke the clock and the origin of the gown stuffed into the wall?" These were not simple things, "or did you deny them knowing that there is no such things as ghosts?" My anger made me more terse than I otherwise would have been.

The Major never really reacted to my distemper with anything other than mild amusement. I didn't know if he was the same with his soldiers, or it was that he had known me since I had first come to London as a girl of fourteen, complete with poor skin and limbs that were too long for me. I had grown, according to my aunt, like a boy - in fits and spurts where things grew at their own pace and it was only recently that everything had reached an equilibrium.

"It was a combination of mysteries," he said, "that we assumed to be just one, and the story is rather detailed, but we are still a long way from Islington so I shall try to include everything." Had I been more suspicious I would have thought him trying to distract me from the more negative aspects of the journey, and certainly from the basket on the bench beside me.

"After his return from exile the king, Charles the second," he was clarifying the details for me and I did not know why for only one king had been in exile, "he brought with him a court, including the Duc D'Isle, it was the Duc who purchased the house from new." He paused, "the Duc was a witch of little skill, an ambition that far exceeded his talent and where he lacked charisma he had wealth. He was also obsessed with beauty and its preservation. No sooner did a new recipe for a cold cream, rouge or a powder than he had to have it.

"This obsession led to the determination to use the magickal arts to continue his research, which of course you know would be futile for only those of great affinity find their ageing stopped by the power that they have." Witches lived until they did not, it was not like how a witch would age and die, it was usually something external that killed them; like hanging or being burned alive.

"With his research proving fruitless in England, he started to tour the continent instead, hearing stories of the Bloody Countess and Koschei the Immortal in the east, and he spent years travelling, gathering knowledge and skills, terrible things. He started a collection of things," he paused, enunciating the word, "in the hope that he could manipulate them into prolonging his life, the sort of things that in London would be part of the Undercity but were common in Imperial Russia. He had the house changed to contain them. You said that the horseshoes were the wrong way around, that they were there to prevent the Courtiers from leaving, and that's what happened. The Duc captured, in his menagerie, a fine lady of the Winter Court, dressed her in the finest silks and jewels, and tortured her." He stopped, "He claimed to the king's court that she had chosen to be his wife and that she cared little for life at court and so he left her in the house. The gown we found was hers.

"The Duc was found out, the fine lady returned to the winter court - and her husband with her for punishment for what he did and the house and wealth passed to an English cousin who had no interest in London and so had the house rented. The solicitor in charge found it hard to keep lodgers, both for the terrible reputation that it had from the Duc's tenure and because it was said to be haunted."

I raised an eyebrow as he continued "And

the lodgers were told that there were no such thing as ghosts. Time passed, and the house was let, often in the short term, until perhaps ten years ago when the descendant of the Duc, the Right Honourable Mr Wantage, made a wager with one of his peers which he neglected to repay.

"The winner of the debt, wanting to recoup some of his losses, sold the debt to Mr Grosvenor, Lady Davenport's father, who accepted the town-house as payment. Mr Grosvenor is well known for this practise which made him very unpopular, taking several peers to debtor's court to force them to pay."

"How daring," I said in my most ironic tone.

"Exactly, and he was comfortable in the *ton*, but not the lofty reaches of the *Haute ton*. Enter Lord Davenport, he wanted to go to the peninsula to restore through battle his fortunes but needed up front blunt to buy colours."

"So he approached Mr Grosvenor about his daughters," Mr Reid filled in, recognising how these stories often went, "he was set to marry Mrs Haye when she was assaulted, she needed a quick marriage to Mr Haye, one of Mr Grosvenor's solicitors, and was given a small house in the country where she could have her daughter, all paid for, and when Mrs Haye suffered in the aftermath of birth she could be quietly attended to in a private institution. Davenport, desperate for the money, agreed to marry the now Lady Davenport quickly before word of what had happened reached London and saw her spoiled in her first season by the rumours."

"Rumours that lingered anyway," I said.

"Yes, Lady Davenport accompanied her new husband to Cadiz and had her son there and, when it came time for her to return, she went to the town-house her father had given her as a marriage gift, the Duc's house." He looked at the window, tugging back the curtain to try and work out how close we were to the cemetery before he continued, "All was well, until Mrs Haye returned to London and the myling started to appear in the house." It was strange to have the Major accommodate the word myling as if it wasn't a ghost that he had dismissed out of hand as not existing and that it was instead the sort of thing that lived in the Undercity. "The harmless creatures that the Duc had brought back, shy creatures that are commonplace in Russia but unheard of here, wanting to warn the inhabitants with no other way to do it but to ring the bells."

"What kind of creatures?" I asked, I could hardly imagine some cave wight sneaking around between the walls of a prestigious London town-house

"A hearth spirit and a bathhouse spirit," he answered. He paused, trying to find a way to explain it, "You grew up in the country, was a plate of milk left out for the brownies?" I told him that it was cream and it was best practice to prevent any brownies in the area from wreaking mischief in the house, like smashing plates, souring fresh milk, and pinching babies."

"Well, in places like St Petersburg they take the crust from the bread and put it back into the fire for the *domovoi*, the hearth spirit that stops food burning, keeps the house warm, and other similar tasks, the bath-house spirit helps with the laundry, prevents hot water scalding the maids or people taking a bath. They keep the house's secrets, and almost every house in the east has at least one, but often them and others. We are less accommodating to sharing our houses than the Russians." I shrugged. "They broke the clock, they rang the bells no matter what we did to stop them, and they stopped once Bunny was returned and the myling left the house alone. Lady Davenport was reassured to find out the cause and not just the crust of fresh bread is left for the spirits but also cream, brandy, and simples. They might be the only such in England but they are certainly the best regarded."

"So all the reports of hauntings were people encountering these things?" I asked.

"*Duende*," Mr Reid said suddenly. Then realising what he had said, and how no one seemed to understand he added, "That's what they call them on the peninsula, they are well treated and respected even if no one sees them."

"Hardly anyone," I corrected. "People must have seen them to report the hauntings."

"I imagine so," he said. I got the impression that they still believed that spirits and ghosts did not exist and that there was some placation to me when they spoke of them. It was strange, indeed, how they could maintain a denial, even in the face of contradiction, rather than admit that they were wrong.

Chapter Twenty-Seven

The approach to Bunhill Fields was hard to describe.

There are certain things that exist and you do not question, and certain truths you accept without demur. These things fall from your mind almost as if you never knew them, and so it was with the approach to the cemetery.

I knew that there were female vampires. I knew that they were rare because the transition was not as easy for them, and sometimes they were undone, which was a term I had never really researched. Like everyone I knew that the vampires were led by their mysterious "Lady Below" for each coterie and that those Ladies formed a council of shared knowledge and rule.

When I had asked my aunt, younger and more prone to questioning the magickal world of London, she had explained, doing something else and not truly paying attention but wanting to spend time with me even as she worked, that the coteries were not entirely unlike insect hives. That the men went out and fed, working in the hospitals- this was used to feed the female vampires who in turn fed the Lady Below. It was explained to me but I had not truly understood.

It was almost unheard of to see them, and if they were spotted it was amongst the foliage of their cemetery between the trees and gone before one could truly understand what they had seen.

That was the first thing that made the funeral almost surreal.

The other was their song.

Like everyone, I had heard the story of sailors at sea driven to extremity by an unearthly song. The Odyssey featured the sailors plugging their ears with wax but the song still moved them to try and dive into the sea so that the carnivorous sirens could feast on their bodies. One of the spirits I had read about in the British Library, the Rusalki, used a song to bring people to their lakes, spinning a fantasy of a beautiful lover who then pulled them under the water and drank up their breath before it consumed them, bones and all.

That was what I thought of when I heard the song. When I reached the graveside I learned it was the four female vampires of the Islington coterie, excluding their Lady Below, singing a eulogy for a lost child and it was unearthly, like the air was a great crystal bowl and some giant being was circling it with a wet finger.

There was language in the song, but I could not say which, but it was more like all of them.

It was indescribable but yet it falls upon

me to try.

I understood Odysseus tied to the mast of his ship, I understood those sailors who jumped to their deaths in the water for if the song had asked anything of me but that crushing grief I would have done it and done it gladly.

It was like a great tree made of ice and from it hung a thousand glass bells, each playing a different note and all of them chiming in a slight breeze so that it felt like the rapture of a saint in a hagiography.

When I was a child I was a voracious reader and Miss Featherby, being aware of the mischief that a series of girls could wreak upon an unattended library, had put what she considered dangerous texts in chests in the attic. The decision to plunder my father's library had left shelves with books on botany, a few books that they had clearly been gifted, and a shelf of the sort of books that people seemed to collect even if they had no intent to. Girls would also leave books behind, possibly in exchange for ones that they took - assuming they had interests in botany and garden husbandry - and being the youngest girl I was sent to bed first, with a lantern and a book, whilst I waited for Miss Featherby to join me.

There was an illustrated book of hagiography which I had read my way through and it showed saints almost insane with joy with the knowledge of god and I could not understand it until I heard the vampires sing because the sound of it created that sense of such overwhelming delight that I could have done something like set myself on fire, to be like Jeanne, or plucked out my eyes to resemble Saint Lucy - an ecstasy.

It is odd how a song you could not understand or could say that you had ever heard could put you back in the lamplight of your childhood bed waiting for your guardian to join you because you could not sleep alone.

I was not alone in that response.

The Major's face was wet as if he was weeping silently and his head was cocked slightly to the left as if he was listening to some counterpoint that was beyond my ultimately human ears.

Mr Reid's eyes were closed but his mouth was open, his tongue flickering as if he chased some taste and his fingertips, folded in his lap amongst the billows of his oversized benjamin, sought out the imaginary keys of some great pianoforte.

Even the percussion of the horse's hooves slotted into the music of it and I still lacked the words to describe it.

When the carriage stopped I wiped at my face with my gloves, sure that I was weeping as openly as the Major but I was not. I took hold of the basket, gripping it like it was a new baby, and very nearly fell to my face when I tried to climb down from the carriage. I was saved from ending up in the dirt by Thorne who picked me up with a "careful, ducky" as he brushed down the velvet of my pelisse.

At the bench where I had first met Sophia, Beausant had arranged for them to dig the grave.

A table had been set up with several items on it and beside it was a large pot of steaming hot water. The vampires stood at it, wearing aprons and with their hair in caps. They looked like they might be nurses in a fine hospital.

Pamphlets and cheap novels would have said that four female vampires stood at night waiting would have been beautiful, sleek dark haired ladies in sheer gowns with dark eyes and skin translucent like porcelain.

They were not.

The foremost of them was tall and plump with brown curls at her temples and her dress was almost Russian in its style - it had been a popular style championed by the late princess. She looked almost as young as I was, with rouged lips and cheeks and bright black eyes with a distinctly hooked Roman nose. To her left was an Amazon, taller than me by more than a head and as broad as Thorne, but her height meant that instead of square she was statuesque, and I wondered what it would feel like to be crushed against the shelf of her breasts simply because it was like a statue of Athena come to life, with a rope of golden hair in a braid down her back. The third was a Kashmir girl, younger than I by perhaps as many as five years, shoulder height to the plump woman, and eerie in her yellow muslin, she was a slip of a thing who was almost dwarfed by the others. The fourth was a woman who could easily have been the wife of any publican in England, unremarkable and worn down by years of life but she had a nasty scar that snaked down her cheek like the branches of a tree.

When they saw me they smiled, clearly at me, ignoring those around me, and their song swelled into the cold and the night making it feel darker even though there were many torches and braziers so it was almost as bright as a winter's day.

Their song was one of grief, it almost ached physically like needles on my skin where it pulled the hair to standing and it swirled around them and led us up the hill.

With my discomfort and the eerie rapture of the music, I left my cap on the bench and did not even notice. Walking up the hill to the grave step by step with the basket seeming to grow exponentially in weight with each footfall.

The Major saw me struggle, "Let me help, Miss Peake," he said. "There is no weakness in accepting help, you have been unwell, I can carry your burden."

But he couldn't. I could no more let him than he could understand why I had to do this. He hadn't seen Sophia on that bench, bouncing with life and vitality and desperate for adult attention, even though by then she was already dead. He had not seen her at the frost fair or that terrible night in Mrs Haye's lodgings where she had sat at the foot of the bed drawing and singing London Bridge is Falling Down over and over.

He had never seen her.

How could he lay her to rest when to him she was another victim of murder and he couldn't even understand what she had become because of her murder?

Desperate to please what remained of her mother after the illness had taken hold, she had taken babies from houses all over London where Mrs Haye had tried to recreate the magick that she had performed with Sophia, unable to understand that the very aspect that she lacked was the one that she denounced.

Mrs Haye maintained that Sophia was not her child, that her sister had stolen her place leaving her with the baby - but if she was not the mother, Sophia could not have become a myling. The very thing that empowered her was the truth she rejected, and Sophia continued to do things that she thought might gain her mother's approval even though she never could.

I could give Sophia attention. It was too late to give her love but I could give her dignity and I could give her a burial and the Major could not do that in my place - no matter how heavy the basket became.

And the basket kept getting heavier.

With every step I took it was like more and more rocks were placed into the basket so I kept stumbling on the path.

"*Berushka*," Beausant said and he sounded so disappointed. I had not noticed his arrival. "You still have not read the book I gave you," I did not know where he he had come from, or even where he stood, I was so determined to carry the basket, "and if you will not let the Major help, you will not accept my help either." He gave a deep and disappointed breath. I was used to the sound- the Major had been making it for some time by then. "If you will not let us help you carry Miss Haye, then we shall carry you."

When the Major had carried me from Mrs

Haye's lodging it had been a princess carry, this was not the same, although the two of them swept my legs out from under me, each turned to face the other and not me, they managed to make a sort of bench for my legs and back with their arms and used their supernatural strength to carry both of us up the few steps to the bench.

It was only then I realised what Beausant meant when he scolded me for not reading the book that he had left - the one that had the information on the mylingar, because the British Library had had information too. It had said how mylings lingered and asked kindly strangers to carry them to their graves, and when people had tried they had gotten heavier until the person could go no further at which point the myling killed them.

I did not know how I had forgotten that.

As I reached the female vampires, the plump one stopped singing and came forward to take the basket, "Let me," she said and took it clear out of my arms in a way that I could not have refused if I had wanted to and placed it beside the table, lifting out its most precious bundle and laying it on the flat surface.

This close I could see the tools and things that were laid out and they looked like they belonged to a lady's vanity with combs and brushes, squares of freshly boiled linen, bowls of oils and unguents, even scissors for the cutting of hair.

She did not hesitate, with baby fat arms crammed with bracelets, one of which had claws chained to it but the claws were inserted into spaces in the metal so the chains hung around her hands, clinking together as she moved. "Stop!" I said, it was more violent than I intended and I found myself adding "She's covered in something caustic."

The plump vampire smiled at me. She was not pretty, she had a mannish face with a strong Roman nose and slight chin, her eyes, which were brown, were a little piggish and she was wearing too much kohl, which just made them look smaller, but her smile was infectious and genuinely warming. "She won't hurt me," she said, "we don't feel pain, not any more."

I thought that this missed the point but by then she had stripped Sophia bare of the oakum cloths that Milton in the Tower had wrapped her in.

"Oh, you poor *kleine Entlein*," the vampire said, taking one of the linen cloths, dipping it into one of the bowls and wiping at her face, "what they did to you," she spoke to her in the same tone, I thought, that she might have addressed a matted kitten.

It was then, standing in front of the four vampires, as her sisters moved to the table, still singing that eerie and unearthly song of grief, that I realised what they were doing. They did not push me away, but let me stand there among them, as they prepared her body for burial. With those squares of linen, dumped into an old copper pot when they were done with them, they wiped away the congealed caustic slime that covered her. It was a mix of rancid human fat, spermaceti, quicklime, the astringent that had disappointed Mrs Haye that gave a sharp vinegary smell to the stink of her, roses and astringent and rancid grease.

I could see where the corpse wax - as Milton had called it - was burning away their fingers, the meat of it sizzling as if engulfed in acid, but they neither stopped with their ministrations or their song.

They were as careful of her as if they were preparing the queen herself. Using the unguent to wipe away the mess as if they were using a cold cream with soft, long, slow strokes. The youngest looking of the four, the Kashmir girl, lifted a silver brush, almost exactly like the one sat on my vanity table in my aunt's house, and began to brush out the blonde curls, pulling them up over the end of the table, and dislodging both tangles, with short stiff strokes, and debris - debris which included some insect carcasses, their empty carapaces glimmering like gemstones in the firelight from the braziers.

They were still singing but from a heartbreaking eulogy it had become a household work song, with the same eerie grace but it was no longer overwhelming. It was a song of belonging that they sang to the child in their care as they washed her and prepared her for her burial with the same care as if they were dressing the queen for an engagement.

There was a shift, bleached so white it seemed to glow, and warm silk stockings, tied in place with embroidered garters. There were shining black boots with new laces. There was a blue velvet dress with shining buttons and a bonnet with ruched silk and a wide ribbon. There was a grey pelisse trimmed in squirrel fur. Someone had raised the very best shops in London for the things that they dressed her in - knowing that they would be buried with her - and I couldn't help the sob that escaped me.

Vampires were supposed to be monsters but they showed this child more care than the human world had, and I was overwhelmed. To my side, Mr Reid offered me his handkerchief without a word.

I had not, could not have, imagined this when I insisted that Sophia be buried. I don't suppose I knew what I was to expect. Yet, when the Indian girl had called out a word in the midst of the song, I was undone.

From the dark of the graveyard, from the shadows of the tombs, statuary and mausoleums, the vampires came, each holding a single white candle and an arm full of flowers, and in their heart was Mr Ogilvy.

He looked harried. It was not in the way that a gentleman might be if he found himself at night in a cemetery surrounded by vampires who were marching him to his destination - which would have been understandable - but the sort of harried that comes of not quite being ready despite time having run out and people expecting more than they thought that you were capable of.

I heard him tell someone, I could not really tell who, but it might have been the Tower page that was rushing behind him carrying a leather bag in his arms and making facial gestures that suggested he really needed to wipe his nose and couldn't, "I haven't got my cassock."

With the performance and pomp I half expected the vampires to provide him with one, or at least a facsimile, but they didn't. He just clutched his topper and followed them, surrounded by the vampires at vigil and the flowers.

He reached the table and the child laid out at rest whilst another vampire, a burly fellow whose coat did not quite fit, brought out a coffer, the sort that held treasures like the house's silverware. It was as fine a coffin as any could expect. The vampire walked with a severe limp that had him standing almost at right angles to where he walked.

When the matron opened it, I could see that it had been lined in velvet with a silk pillow and, with the same care that they had prepared her, they lay her in the box and then stepped back. The plump vampire seemed to forget herself until the Indian girl hissed "Lottie," then, as if struck, she stepped away.

The bulky vampire, I did not know his name but his shoulders were crooked like there was a twist in his spine - I did not know such things were possible for vampires - lifted Sophia from the table, as careful as if she was a sleeping baby, humming tunelessly under his breath before he laid her into the brass bound coffer with a kiss upon her forehead before a length of voile was laid over her, tucked tight at the place where the velvet met the walls of the coffer.

After that, one by one, the vampires approached and put one of their flowers into the chest, around the body, until there was nothing showing except her face, then with a return to the sad song they closed the coffer, and the vampire called Lottie picked up the coffer as if it was made of paper and handed it to the twisted vampire who had climbed down into the grave. He set the box down and jumped up, as nimble as a jongleur, as the vampires continued to bury the child in flowers. It was more beauty than I had expected.

It was at this sight that Mr Ogilvy started to read the funeral service, the Tower page beside him holding his bible, and I had thought him a figure of ridicule. He was an eminently silly man with enough power to be a complication in an otherwise easy life, but I watched him perform that funeral for a murdered child surrounded by the greater undead of Islington, dozens of them, and he held them silent as he read.

I wonder if greater men would not have quavered in that position but he did not waver.

I could not help the tears as they streamed down my face, but without the hitches of breath that came from weeping. I could claim, I suppose, it was the flowers - the Major quipped they probably came from Kew and tomorrow there would be a headline about how every bloom had been plucked by mystery figures.

It was a mishmash of ceremonies, some as old as London - I suppose the burial of the maiden among the flowers, the strange and lovely song, and Mr Ogilvy's Anglican ceremony, but we all stood there as the soil was shovelled into place.

A small, vicious part of myself thought - this is it, it is over, the myling has been stopped, I am free of her. I felt no different. The largest part of myself was heartbroken at the loss of her potential.

I wondered how many of the vampires had had children in their lives that they gathered to mourn one, there were more vampires, certainly than in Islington, bringing their floral offerings to the grave. I wondered if they were laying the

blooms not just for Sophia but the children that
they had outlived, the ones that they had lost, and
that was when I started to sob and Sylvie pulled
me into her arms and let me weep against her
breast.

I returned home to the Witch House
disconsolate and tired, ignoring the entreaties of
both Mr Reid and the Major to attract my
attention. Sylvie sat in the carriage with me and
glared at the two men, Mr Reid especially for I
believed she had less patience than usual for his
nervous tic. Eventually, both men went quiet and
I sat with my head on Sylvie's shoulder as she
murmured that my ears were cold and I should
have kept on my bonnet.

I was returned to my aunt's house before
the two men continued on to the Tower and
Sylvie didn't let go of my gloved hand until we
were in the sitting room with Jenner following
behind to collect our pelisses, bonnets, and
gloves. My aunt, seeing my expression, pulled
my favourite couch directly in front of the fire
and asked Lizzy to fetch us chocolate with brandy
and cream and sweet things from the kitchens.

Aunt Jemima always reacted to my upset
with that chocolate recipe and I did not begrudge
her it; the chocolate was made with milk and the
brandy sweetened it and the cream made it a meal
for kings. She had once told me she got the recipe
in France before the war.

I spent the night on that couch with my
feet pulled up under my skirts and a heavy rug

draped over the two of us - as if I felt the cold at all - and listened to Sylvie read from a volume of Byron's poetry that she found on one of the sitting room tables. I would not have been surprised to discover that the house had supplied it. Lizzy, with her brother, Bobby, drowsing in her arms joined us to listen to Sylvie read.

I do not remember going to bed but I must have for I woke there the next morning.

I made it clear that I would not be available to callers, even the Lowell twins, and only pulled a housecoat over my shift, not even bothering with stays and petticoats and refused to leave my room where I took my meals on a tray.

That was when I finally read the book that Beausant had left for me the night before I had been taken by Mrs Haye. It had a whole chapter on the mylingar and the more I read the angrier I got. "*The myling is mostly known for the death of those who offer it kindness, as I have discussed,*" the book had spoken of how the body would get heavier, just as the book in the British Library had, and unable to continue the myling would then kill the person carrying them.

I thought of the Major and Beausant picking me up between them when I had refused to let them carry my burden. I wondered if they had read the books that I had not and knew the outcome to take such presumption with my body.

"*However a lesser-known effect of the mylingar curse is the bloodied eye. The mylingar choose a person, as much as they retain such human conceits, and mark them with a bloody eye. This is a curse mark. The myling's victim finds themself caught in a terrible dilemma, if they do not enact the myling's will the myling will kill them, often in much more violent manners than it is responsible for when crushing the victim who attempts to carry them to a formal burial. To prevent the myling killing the marked victim they must in turn kill another."*

I put the book down and thought about what it said, with my fingers against the eyepatch I wore to hold the magickal sachet against my bloodied eye. Leaving the book against the covers of my bed I went to my mirror. I had the shutters closed so the room was poorly lit. I had been using a lantern next to the bed where I had been reading but I did not immediately think to lift it when I checked the mirror and had to double back to get it.

I had a glass mirror that I was told had come from Venice not long after the discovery of Alfhame and as such, it showed its age but the reflection was much clearer than the others in the house. Such mirrors, I was told, were kept curtained to prevent the magick leaking out or the mirror version of people stealing them away to replace them. I remembered those childhood tales when I looked at the strange fruit that framed the glass.

I sat on the stool and lengthened the wick of the lamp to get more light, removing the shade to use it to light the small candelabrum that sat on my vanity. I was avoiding removing the patch for fear of what I might find.

I kept thinking of Sophia sitting at the foot of the bed in Mrs Haye's lodging drawing figures with a single red eye over and over.

I removed the patch at the sachet,

scratching at my scalp before I looked and when I
did was not surprised at the lack of the blood that
had flooded my eye before.

      I blew out the candles, reduced the wick
back on my lantern, returned to my bed, and
threw the book towards the window.

Chapter Twenty-Eight

December continued apace, as it must, and I threw myself into the preparations for the Christmas feast. I accepted every chore that either my aunt or Lady Lowell was prepared to let me do in their place.

I did my best to not think about what had happened.

I was often abroad, calling into stores to arrange things like the hamper for both my aunt and Lady Lowell, which saw me in Fortnum and Mason on no less than four different occasions as things were changed depending on mood and how it had been a poor year for plums making it hard to get the plum preserve that both insisted that they had. It was an excellent choice to go with a sharp white cheese and port but I did suspect that the request had more to do with keeping me busy than it did the specifics.

I had appointments for tea.

I interviewed an abigail to accompany us to Italy.

That week was exceedingly busy.

Lady Davenport invited me and, hearing of the Donner's arrival in the house since our meeting, insisted that both accompany me for it would do Bunny good to have someone his own age to play with.

This was something that seemed an excellent idea on paper but the two babies, who were genuinely easy to please, seemed to only accept the rules of sharing when it pertained to adults - who would pretend to share their food or toys - and not to actually sharing which caused twin wailings and complaints as the two of them decided to clash over a piece of cloth that had been used to polish the woodwork of the wall.

We had all been sitting on the floor, even Lady Davenport, with the babies quiescent between us, when the piece of cloth was discovered under a table cloth and chaos ensued. Lady Davenport, instead of just mollifying her son, made the cloth disappear and insisted on trying to explain to him that he had to share.

When the cat came in both immediately reached and grabbed for it and the cat dashed out again starting the wailing over again.

When a tray of mince pies was brought in the two of them reached for it faster than they had the cat and Bobby, Lizzy's young brother, tried to smash one into his mouth, immediately discovered that he didn't like them, and spat it back out all over himself. Lizzy was apologetic but Lady Davenport just passed her a square of muslin with a knowing gaze.

I kept an eye out for the *Duende* but I saw nothing, but Lady Davenport did agree to leave a simple out beside the hearth as thanks for their attempts to warn them about the myling.

I was careful always to call it a myling because I didn't know if she knew its identity.

She assured me that she did make the offerings and more than once had left it a glass of sherry.

It was strange, I thought in retrospect, sitting on the floor with a diamond of the first water with a pair of unhappy babies grousing, and talking about supernatural creatures that were rare in England to the extent no one really knew about them.

Young Mr Donner was so exhausted by his afternoon that he slept the whole night through without even waking for his dinner of fresh rice pudding, something Sylvie, Lizzy, and I could not bear to see go to waste.

I ordered hampers for the River Police and insisted that I accompany their delivery with an extra, smaller one for Mr Schaeffernacker and his wife as a thank you for his help on the ice - included in it was a note of credit for my favourite bootmakers that he might replace the ones he was wearing.

He assured me that such gifts were not necessary and I told him that I understood that but nevertheless I was grateful and I had the means to share and celebrate the season. I graciously ignored the others behind me in their headquarters loudly going through the large group hamper for the best bits whilst they could and their commander taking out the bottles of mead - I was unsure which liquor or wine to include and the helpful young man in the store recommended mead - with the words that they weren't to be trusted with the good stuff.

A similar hamper had been delivered to His Majesty's Dragoons with a bottle of the particular brandy wine for Thorne that I knew that he preferred.

I returned home, arriving just as it started to darken with a sky that promised more snow, and expected that I would spend my night in front of the fire with Sylvie continuing her recitation of "Childe Harold's Pilgrimage". Byron was so verbose we would probably still be listening to it in January.

My aunt was waiting for me in the vestibule which surprised Sylvie as much as it did me. "Oh, you are finally home, quick, quick, you must get dressed." She even attempted to push me up the stairs.

"I did not think we had an appointment this evening." I said. I was diligent in checking my calendar and was sure that I had no appointments until the twenty-third when Sylvie and I were attending a small Christmas party at the Lowells, the sort that were considered suitable for girls yet to have their presentation or have come out.

"Circumstances have changed," she said,

"now quickly, dress, the white satin, my love, with the blue velvet overgown and matching cap." The cap had been made up before I had cut my hair and was meant to be worn for a fine summer afternoon's engagement but it was the same velvet as the gown so the two would match.

It was then that I noticed what my aunt was wearing.

Aunt Jemima was always well presented, she always wore black, but one of the gifts of her affinity, which she considered an impediment, was that when she ordered new clothes they were always at least a few years shy of fashion. She would wear something and in as little as five and as many as ten years later everyone was wearing them and she was wearing something else.

She was wearing black silk satin with a wide neckline that sat on the curve of her shoulder, the waist of her gown was a thick sash just under the bust - a few full inches beneath the fashionable empire waist, a bell shaped skirt with a decorative stripe of the same fabric a few inches above the ankle length hem, and a pair of sleeves with uppers that were easily as large as a mutton leg although they were gathered in at the elbow to wrist. It was not a fashion that I was looking forward to because, to avoid making her look like a child's toy where a bell shape was balanced on an inner ball so that it seemed to bob and dance, it required quite tall hair and the current Roman style, where it was piled at the back of the head to fit under a neat bonnet, had waxed loops and braids that made her look somewhat like a straw doll.

She was even wearing neat black satin slippers that laced up her ankles when she was hardly ever seen without her stout walking boots.

It said something to the standard to which she expected me to dress.

Lizzy was all of a tizzy when I got to my room, "Oh miss," she managed to say, "we need to get you dressed."

The clothes that my aunt had suggested were laid out on the bed but so were fresh under things and a different set of petticoats, the fine new ones that had been ordered for my journey to Europe. She had even laid out the brand new silk stockings. I had no idea what it meant but I was to be dressed to my best. I had a momentary thought that she might intend to introduce me to a suitor but I dismissed it as the sort of silly fancy that didn't happen outside of novels.

Normally to dress for such an event it took about an hour, with the layers, the brushing out of the fabric between layers so it sat right and wasn't covered in dust or pet hair - we didn't have any animals in the house but still the odd dog or cat hair could be found on the velvet. We managed it that evening in about a quarter of an hour and were still fixing my hair with pins to hold the cap in place when we got into the carriage with Lizzy still trying to brush out the fabric with a boar bristle brush from my vanity and exclaiming that I needed a wrapper.

The carriage had departed before I was able to ask my aunt our destination for her to answer that I had an invitation to Hampton Court.

It took a long moment for me to do the mental calculations that allowed me to realise the magnitude of where we were going. Although the King resided at Buckingham Palace, Hampton Court was the seat of the royal family and had been the location of the court throughout the early years of the new England after the discovery of Alfhame. Centuries of noblemen and women had lived in its walls, walked its gardens, and caroused in its halls.

Now it was the place where Her Majesty kept her household and I had been invited.

This was in itself a curiosity for I had no idea why I, of all people, would be summoned in the last days before the Christmas feast to Hampton Court, and it seemed that my aunt was also unsure.

She made sure that I knew those behaviours that were designed to lessen offence to the haute ton, when to bow and when to curtsey, that I was to watch my sharp tongue for Her Majesty would certainly not have the fondness for it that she did.

She took my hands in hers, and it felt strange with all the layers of gloves between us, "Your two strongest features, my dove, are your tenacity and your forthright manner or speech, and in a man they would be praised and see you lifted amongst the highest ranks of what is possible, but you are not a man and what is forthright tenacity in a man is shrewish stubbornness in a woman. I trust you, and I love you, and I know that sometimes those aspects of you overwhelm, but I ask that you be careful around Her Majesty. She is fragile in ways that are often hard to comprehend."

I had mistakenly thought that with my place in society I had seen the best of what was available. I was so very wrong. The walls were clad in toffee coloured oak and tapestries large enough to dwarf my large bedroom. There was furniture enough to seat every person who worked in the Tower with room left for more, all of it perfectly maintained. There was gleaming white cloths on side tables with silver candelabrum with full wax candles illuminating the shadows. Large chandeliers of glass and mirror shards hung in the hallways which were lined with windows and thick, deep rich red carpets underfoot. Each window was as tall as a man with fine shutters overlooking a gravel path punctuated with statuary, maintained topiary, and fountains. I was overwhelmed and didn't know where to look. Liveried servants in wigs and gloves rushed past us at a walking speed that was almost a run.

The footman who led us through the halls had no patience for my gawking, hurrying us as he walked ahead with a candelabrum giving me the whimsical thought of having us follow the light.

Queen Charlotte was an old woman, propped up on a mountain of pillows in a bed large enough for six people. She had thin white hair and a ruddy complexion, years of heavy cosmetics and smoky rooms had left her skin sagging and loose and she didn't seem to have all of her teeth. She wore a white linen gown tied at her neck under a splendid velvet bed jacket and there was a tray with tea things amidst the other detritus that was spread out on the bed in her easy reach.

I curtseyed as I was introduced and the queen, a stickler for propriety, acknowledged me with a nod of the head, "Sit," she said finally, "and let me look at you."

From the gathered things on the bedspread

she fumbled around to find a pair of eyeglasses and squinted at me, "More light," she said waving her hand at the servants who hovered around her like flies. "I thought you'd be prettier, not quite so foxish," she had a strange accent that I could not quite place and I did not dare ask. She was like a horror in one of the *Contes de fee*, and I was sure if she tried to pinch my cheek it was to test the quality of the meat.

"Caroline will be holding the presentation this year," she said, "my health is no longer what it was." I was glad that my aunt made the usual polite deference, I had to bite my lip to prevent myself from saying anything, "but you caught my attention, girl," she said, "I heard you were injured."

"She was very unwell," Aunt Jemima said, "she had a terrible blow to the head, both the Astrologaster and the Bonesetter tended to her as a kindness to me, and the bruises are still fading."

"Is that why her hair is so short?" The old woman missed nothing.

"Yes, Majesty," my aunt lied. She did not want to portray me as a silly girl talked into such things by others.

The old woman reached to her tea tray and lifted a boiled sweet, slipping it into her mouth and rolling it around her mouth loudly, "My granddaughter had nothing but kind words to say of you," she said, "enough that I had to see for myself."

"Majesty?" I asked, for I had no knowledge of having had anything to do with royalty of any kind.

"My Carlotta," she said, clacking the hard candy against her teeth, "we can't see each other, it isn't done," there was a vicious hatred in her tone that would have seen me punished, and for a moment I still didn't know, but then I remembered the plump vampiress and the barked command, "Lottie". The woman who had stood first among the vampires in Islington had been the granddaughter of the queen. The queen watched me realise that, "It is not done," she said, "as if the court isn't already lousy with bloodsuckers. But she writes to me, and she wrote to me about you. She said you had caught the eye of Vincent Beausant," the name sounded more melodic in her strange accent, "have you, girl?"

"He says that I amuse him, Majesty," I answered, for it was true.

"Others will have told you about the interest of men like Beausant, but Carlotta told me what you did." The queen's hand looked like a chicken foot on the velvet bedspread. I watched it because I could not meet her eyes, I couldn't watch her face to know what she was thinking because she was the queen, and it was not done.

"I was cursed, Majesty, and I had to bury her to be free of her bewitchment." It was true but I had not known that at the time.

The queen laughed, "You did it because London hasn't made you hard and selfish yet," she said, "You did it because it was the right thing to do, you did it because it needed to be done. I suppose," she continued, "that this will serve as your presentation."

www.ingramcontent.com/pod-product-compliance
Lightning Source LLC
Chambersburg PA
CBHW061055210726
48294CB00001B/154